A Time to Kill

John Grisham is the author of thirty-five best-selling novels, the international number one non-fiction debut *The Innocent Man* and a series of short stories entitled *Ford County*. He lives with his family in Virginia and Mississippi.

Praise for John Grisham

'John Grisham is the biggest-selling author of legal thrillers. He comes up with exciting and enthralling plots, his writing is utterly compelling' *Guardian*

'Riveting' *Sunday Times*

'The best thriller writer alive' *Evening Standard*

'Grisham is a superb, instinctive storyteller' *The Times*

'Compelling ... Grisham is more adept at getting the reader to turn the page than almost any writer working today' *Daily Mail*

'No-one does it better than Grisham' *Daily Telegraph*

'Grisham reigns supreme' *Sunday Express*

John Grisham

A Time to Kill

arrow books

17 19 20 18 16

Arrow Books
20 Vauxhall Bridge Road
London SW1V 2SA

Arrow Books is part of the Penguin Random House group of companies
whose addresses can be found at global.penguinrandomhouse.com

Penguin
Random House
UK

First published in Great Britain by Century in 1989
First published in paperback by Arrow Books in 1992
Reissued by Arrow Books in 2013

www.penguin.co.uk

A CIP catalogue record for this book is available from the British Library.

ISBN 9780099590750

Typeset by Palimpsest Book Production Limited, Falkirk, Stirlingshire
Printed and bound in Great Britain by Clays Ltd, St Ives plc

Penguin Random House is committed to a sustainable future
for our business, our readers and our planet. This book is made
from Forest Stewardship Council® certified paper.

To Renée,

A woman of uncommon beauty,
A fiercely loyal friend,
A compassionate critic,
A doting mother,

A perfect wife.

Author's Note

Since I am prone to start projects that never quite get finished, my goal when I began writing this book was simply to complete it. I could envision a neat pile of typed pages over in the corner of my office, and one day I would be able to point to it with some measure of pride and explain to clients and friends that it was a novel I had written. Surely, somewhere in the deep recesses of my mind, I dreamed of getting it published, but I honestly can't remember such thoughts, at least not when I started writing. It would become my first prolonged effort at fiction.

I began in the fall of 1984, just three years out of law school and still very wet behind the ears. In those early days of my legal career I spent many hours in courtrooms, watching good lawyers try their cases. I have always been fascinated by courtrooms – still am. People discuss things in open court that they wouldn't dare mention outside their homes. The greatest dramas occur not on screens or stages, but in countless courtrooms across this country.

One day I stumbled upon a horrible trial in which a young girl testified against the man who brutally raped her. It was a gut-wrenching experience for me, and I was only a spectator. One moment she was courageous, the next pitifully frail. I was mesmerized. I could not imagine the nightmare she and her family had been through. I wondered what I would do if she were my daughter. As I watched her suffer before the jury, I wanted personally to shoot the rapist. For one brief yet interminable moment, I wanted to be her father. I wanted justice. There was a story there.

I became obsessed with the idea of a father's retribution. What would a jury of average and ordinary people do to such a father? Naturally there would be a great deal of sympathy, but would there be enough for an acquittal? The idea for this novel emerged over a three-month period in which I thought of little else.

I wrote the first chapter in longhand on a legal pad, and asked Renée, my wife, to read it. She was impressed, and said she would like to read the second chapter. A month later I gave her chapters two and three, and she said she was hooked. Renée reads five or six novels a week – mysteries, suspense, thrillers, espionage, all sorts of fiction – and she has little patience with a story that doesn't work.

I approached the writing of this book much like a hobby, an hour here and an hour there, with a somewhat disciplined effort to write at least a page a day. I never abandoned it. I remember a four-week period in which nothing was written. I occasionally skipped a day, but for the most part I plowed ahead with blind diligence. I thought the story was wonderful, but I wasn't sure about the writing. Renée liked it, so I kept going.

After a year, I was amazed at how quickly the pages had piled up, and I realized that the book was half finished. My original goal was forgotten, and I caught myself thinking of publishing contracts and royalty statements and fancy lunches with agents and editors – the dreams of every unpublished novelist.

Three years after I started, Renée read the last chapter and we shipped it off to New York. The working title was *Deathknell*, a bad idea that was scrapped as soon as the manuscript landed in the office of my new agent, Jay Garon. Jay had seen the first three chapters, and immediately sent me a contract of representation. Sixteen other agents had passed, as well as a dozen publishers. Jay took the manuscript, and told me to start writing another book. I followed his advice.

A year passed and nothing happened. I was deep into the writing of *The Firm* when Jay called in April 1988 with the wonderful news that this book would indeed be published. Bill Thompson at Wynwood Press had read the manuscript and immediately bought it. Under his guidance, I worked through countless revisions and found a new title, *A Time to Kill*. I think it was the sixth or seventh one I decided on. I'm not good with titles.

Wynwood printed 5,000 copies and published the book in June 1989. It sold well within a hundred miles of home, but was neglected by the rest of the world. There was no paperback deal, no foreign rights. But it was a first novel, and most of them are ignored. Better things were just around the corner.

I finished *The Firm* in 1989, and sent it to Jay. Doubleday/Dell bought it, and when it was published in hardcover in March 1991, my writing career took a dramatic turn. The success of *The Firm* has aroused new interest in *A Time to Kill*.

There's a lot of autobiography in this book. I no longer practice law, but for ten years I did so in a manner very similar to Jake Brigance. I represented people, never banks or insurance companies or big corporations. I was a street lawyer. Jake and I are the same age. I played quarterback in high school, though not very well. Much of what he says and does is what I think I would say and do under the circumstances. We both drive Saabs. We've both felt the unbearable pressure of murder trials, which is something I tried to capture in the story. We've both lost sleep over clients and vomited in courthouse rest rooms.

This one came from the heart. It's a first novel, and at times it rambles, but I wouldn't change a word if given the chance.

Oxford, Mississippi
January 30, 1992

Chapter 1

Billy Ray Cobb was the younger and smaller of the two rednecks. At twenty-three he was already a three-year veteran of the state penitentiary at Parchman. Possession, with intent to sell. He was a lean, tough little punk who had survived prison by somehow maintaining a ready supply of drugs that he sold and sometimes gave to the blacks and the guards for protection. In the year since his release he had continued to prosper, and his small-time narcotics business had elevated him to the position of one of the more affluent rednecks in Ford County. He was a businessman, with employees, obligations, deals, everything but taxes. Down at the Ford place in Clanton he was known as the last man in recent history to pay cash for a new pickup truck. Sixteen thousand cash, for a custom-built, four-wheel drive, canary yellow, luxury Ford pickup. The fancy chrome wheels and mudgrip racing tires had been received in a business deal. The rebel flag hanging across the rear window had been stolen by Cobb from a drunken fraternity boy at an Ole Miss football game. The pickup was Billy Ray's most prized possession. He sat on the tailgate drinking a beer, smoking a joint, watching his friend Willard take his turn with the black girl.

Willard was four years older and a dozen years slower. He was generally a harmless sort who had never been in serious trouble and had never been seriously employed. Maybe an occasional fight with a night in jail, but nothing that would distinguish him. He called himself a pulpwood cutter, but a bad back customarily kept him out of the woods. He had hurt his back working on an offshore rig somewhere in the Gulf, and the oil company paid him a nice settlement, which he lost when his ex-wife cleaned him out. His primary vocation was that of a part-time employee of Billy Ray Cobb, who didn't pay much but was liberal with his dope. For the first time in years Willard could always get his hands on something. And he always needed something. He'd been that way since he hurt his back.

She was ten, and small for her age. She lay on her elbows, which were stuck and bound together with yellow nylon rope. Her legs were spread grotesquely with the right foot tied tight to an oak sapling and the left to a rotting, leaning post of a long-neglected fence. The ski rope had cut into her ankles and the blood ran down her legs. Her face was bloody and swollen, with one eye bulging and closed and the other eye half open so she could see the other white man sitting on the truck.

She did not look at the man on top of her. He was breathing hard and sweating and cursing. He was hurting her.

When he finished, he slapped her and laughed, and the other man laughed in return, then they laughed harder and rolled around the grass by the truck like two crazy men, screaming and laughing. She turned away from them and cried softly, careful to keep herself quiet. She had been slapped earlier for crying and screaming. They promised to kill her if she didn't keep quiet.

They grew tired of laughing and pulled themselves onto the tailgate, where Willard cleaned himself with the little nigger's shirt, which by now was soaked with blood and sweat. Cobb handed him a cold beer from the cooler and commented on the humidity. They watched her as she sobbed and made strange, quiet sounds, then became still. Cobb's beer was half empty, and it was not cold anymore. He threw it at the girl. It hit her in the stomach, splashing white foam, and it rolled off in the dirt near some other cans, all of which had originated from the same cooler. For two six-packs now they had thrown their half-empty cans at her and laughed. Willard had trouble with the target, but Cobb was fairly accurate. They were not ones to waste beer, but the heavier cans could be felt better and it was great fun to watch the foam shoot everywhere.

The warm beer mixed with the dark blood and ran down her face and neck into a puddle behind her head. She did not move.

Willard asked Cobb if he thought she was dead. Cobb opened another beer and explained that she was not dead because niggers generally could not be killed by kicking and beating and raping. It took much more, something like a knife or a gun or a rope to dispose of a nigger. Although he had never taken part in such a killing, he had lived with a bunch of niggers in prison and knew all about them. They were always killing each other, and they always used a weapon of some sort. Those who were just beaten and raped never died. Some of the whites were beaten and raped, and some of them died. But none of the niggers. Their heads were harder. Willard seemed satisfied.

Willard asked what he planned to do now that they were through with her. Cobb sucked on his joint, chased it with beer, and said he wasn't through. He bounced from the tailgate and staggered across the small clearing to where she was tied. He cursed her and screamed at her to wake up, then he poured cold beer in her face, laughing like a crazy man.

She watched him as he walked around the tree on her right side, and she stared at him as he stared between her legs. When he lowered his pants she turned to the left and closed her eyes. He was hurting her again.

She looked out through the woods and saw something – a man running wildly through the vines and underbrush. It was her daddy, yelling and pointing at her and coming desperately to save her. She cried out for him, and he disappeared. She fell asleep.

When she awoke one of the men was lying under the tailgate, the other under a tree. They were asleep. Her arms and legs were numb. The blood and beer and urine had mixed with the dirt underneath her to form a sticky paste that glued her small body to the ground and crackled when she moved and wiggled. Escape, she thought, but her mightiest efforts moved her only a few inches to the right. Her feet were tied so high her buttocks barely touched the ground. Her legs and arms were so deadened they refused to move.

She searched the woods for her daddy and quietly called his name. She waited, then slept again.

When she awoke the second time they were up and moving around. The tall one staggered to her with a small knife. He grabbed her left ankle and sawed furiously on the rope until it gave way. Then he freed the right leg, and she curled into a fetal position with her back to them.

Cobb strung a length of quarter-inch ski rope over a limb and tied a loop in one end with a slip knot. He grabbed her and put the noose around her head, then walked across the clearing with the other end of the rope and sat on the tailgate, where Willard was smoking a fresh joint and grinning at Cobb for what he was about to do. Cobb pulled the rope tight, then gave a vicious yank, bouncing the little nude body along the ground and stopping it directly under the limb. She gagged and coughed, so he kindly loosened the rope to spare her a few more minutes. He tied the rope to the bumper and opened another beer.

They sat on the tailgate drinking, smoking, and staring at her. They had been at the lake most of the day, where Cobb had a friend with a boat and some extra girls who were supposed to be easy but turned out to be untouchable. Cobb had been generous with his drugs and beer, but the girls did not reciprocate. Frustrated, they left the lake and were driving to no place in particular when they happened across the girl. She was walking along a gravel road with a sack of groceries when Willard nailed her in the back of the head with a beer can.

'You gonna do it?' asked Willard, his eyes red and glazed.

Cobb hesitated. 'Naw, I'll let you do it. It was your idea.'

Willard took a drag on his joint, then spit and said, 'Wasn't my idea. You're the expert on killin' niggers. Do it.'

Cobb untied the rope from the bumper and pulled it tight. It peeled bark from the limb and sprinkled fine bits of elm around the girl, who was watching them carefully now. She coughed.

Suddenly, she heard something – like a car with loud pipes. The two men turned quickly and looked down the dirt road to the highway in the distance. They cursed and scrambled around, one slamming the tailgate and the other running toward her. He tripped and landed near her. They cursed each other while they grabbed her, removed the rope from her neck, dragged her to the pickup and threw her over the tailgate into the bed of the truck. Cobb slapped her and threatened to kill her if she did not lie still and keep quiet. He said he would take her home if she stayed down and did as told; otherwise, they would kill her. They slammed the doors and sped onto the dirt road. She was going home. She passed out.

Cobb and Willard waved at the Firebird with the loud pipes as it passed them on the narrow dirt road. Willard checked the back to make sure the little nigger was lying down. Cobb turned onto the highway and raced away.

'What now?' Willard asked nervously.

'Don't know,' Cobb answered nervously. 'But we gotta do something fast before she gets blood all over my truck. Look at her back there, she's bleedin' all over the place.'

Willard thought for a minute while he finished a beer. 'Let's throw her off a bridge,' he said proudly.

'Good idea. Damned good idea.' Cobb slammed on the brakes. 'Gimme a beer,' he ordered Willard, who stumbled out of the truck and fetched two beers from the back.

'She's even got blood on the cooler,' he reported as they raced off again.

Gwen Hailey sensed something horrible. Normally she would have sent one of the three boys to the

7

store, but they were being punished by their father and had been sentenced to weed-pulling in the garden. Tonya had been to the store before by herself – it was only a mile away – and had proven reliable. But after two hours Gwen sent the boys to look for their little sister. They figured she was down at the Pounders' house playing with the many Pounders kids, or maybe she had ventured past the store to visit her best friend, Bessie Pierson.

Mr Bates at the store said she had come and gone an hour earlier. Jarvis, the middle boy, found a sack of groceries beside the road.

Gwen called her husband at the paper mill, then loaded Carl Lee, Jr, into the car and began driving the gravel roads around the store. They drove to a settlement of ancient shot-gun houses on Graham Plantation to check with an aunt. They stopped at Broadway's store a mile from Bates Grocery and were told by a group of old black men that she had not been seen. They crisscrossed the gravel roads and dusty field roads for three square miles around their house.

Cobb could not find a bridge unoccupied by niggers with fishing poles. Every bridge they approached had four or five niggers hanging off the sides with large straw hats and cane poles, and under every bridge on the banks there would be another group sitting on buckets with the same straw hats and cane poles, motionless except for an occasional swat at a fly or a slap at a mosquito.

He was scared now. Willard had passed out and was of no help, and he was left alone to dispose of the girl in such a way that she could never tell. Willard snored as he frantically drove the gravel roads and county roads in search of a bridge or ramp on some river where he could stop and toss her without being seen by half a dozen niggers with straw hats. He looked in the mirror and saw her trying to stand. He slammed his brakes, and she crashed into the front of the bed, just under the window. Willard ricocheted off the dash into the floorboard, where he continued to snore. Cobb cursed them both equally.

Lake Chatulla was nothing more than a huge, shallow, man-made mudhole with a grass-covered dam running exactly one mile along one end. It sat in the far southwest corner of Ford County, with a few acres in Van Buren County. In the spring it would hold the distinction of being the largest body of water in Mississippi. But by late summer the rains were long gone, and the sun would cook the shallow water until the lake would dehydrate. Its once ambitious shorelines would retreat and move much closer together, creating a depthless basin of reddish brown water. It was fed from all directions by innumerable streams, creeks, sloughs, and a couple of currents large enough to be named rivers. The existence of all these tributaries necessarily gave rise to a good number of bridges near the lake.

It was over these bridges the yellow pickup flew in an all-out effort to find a suitable place to unload

9

an unwanted passenger. Cobb was desperate. He knew of one other bridge, a narrow wooden one over Foggy Creek. As he approached, he saw niggers with cane poles, so he turned off a side road and stopped the truck. He lowered the tailgate, dragged her out, and threw her in a small ravine lined with kudzu.

Carl Lee Hailey did not hurry home. Gwen was easily excited, and she had called the mill numerous times when she thought the children had been kidnapped. He punched out at quitting time, and made the thirty-minute drive home in thirty minutes. Anxiety hit him when he turned onto his gravel drive and saw the patrol car parked next to the front porch. Other cars belonging to Gwen's family were scattered along the long drive and in the yard, and there was one car he didn't recognize. It had cane poles sticking out the side windows, and there were at least seven straw hats sitting in it.

Where were Tonya and the boys?

As he opened the front door he heard Gwen crying. To his right in the small living room he found a crowd huddled above a small figure lying on the couch. The child was covered with wet towels and surrounded by crying relatives. As he moved to the couch the crying stopped and the crowd backed away. Only Gwen stayed by the girl. She softly stroked her hair. He knelt beside the couch and touched the girl's shoulder. He spoke to his daughter, and she tried to smile. Her face was bloody pulp covered with knots and lacerations. Both eyes were swollen shut and bleeding. His eyes watered as he looked at her tiny body, completely wrapped in towels and bleeding from ankles to forehead.

Carl Lee asked Gwen what happened. She began shaking and wailing, and was led to the kitchen by her brother. Carl Lee stood and turned to the crowd and demanded to know what happened.

Silence.

He asked for the third time. The deputy, Willie Hastings, one of Gwen's cousins, stepped forward and told Carl Lee that some people were fishing down by Foggy Creek when they saw Tonya lying in the middle of the road. She told them her daddy's name, and they brought her home.

Hastings shut up and stared at his feet.

Carl Lee stared at him and waited. Everyone else stopped breathing and watched the floor.

'What happened, Willie?' Carl Lee yelled as he stared at the deputy.

Hastings spoke slowly, and while staring out the window repeated what Tonya had told her mother about the white men and their pickup, and the rope and the trees, and being hurt when they got on her. Hastings stopped when he heard the siren from the ambulance.

The crowd filed solemnly through the front door and waited on the porch, where they watched the crew unload a stretcher and head for the house.

The paramedics stopped in the yard when the

11

front door opened and Carl Lee walked out with his daughter in his arms. He whispered gently to her as huge tears dripped from his chin. He walked to the rear of the ambulance and stepped inside. The paramedics closed the door and carefully removed her from his embrace.

Chapter 2

Ozzie Walls was the only black sheriff in Mississippi. There had been a few others in recent history, but for the moment he was the only one. He took great pride in that fact, since Ford County was seventy-four percent white and the other black sheriffs had been from much blacker counties. Not since Reconstruction had a black sheriff been elected in a white county in Mississippi.

He was raised in Ford County, and he was kin to most of the blacks and a few of the whites. After desegregation in the late sixties, he was a member of the first mixed graduating class at Clanton High School. He wanted to play football nearby at Ole Miss, but there were already two blacks on the team. He starred instead at Alcorn State, and was a defensive tackle for the Rams when a knee injury sent him back to Clanton. He missed football, but enjoyed being the high sheriff, especially at election time when he received more white votes than his white opponents. The white kids loved him because he was a hero, a football star who had played on TV and had his picture in magazines. Their parents respected him and voted for him because he was a tough cop who did not discriminate between black punks and white punks. The white politicians supported him because, since he became the sheriff, the Justice Department stayed out of Ford County. The blacks adored him because he was Ozzie, one of their own.

He skipped supper and waited in his office at the jail for Hastings to report from the Hailey house. He had a suspect. Billy Ray Cobb was no stranger to the sheriff's office. Ozzie knew he sold drugs – he just couldn't catch him. He also knew Cobb had a mean streak.

The dispatcher called in the deputies, and as they reported to the jail Ozzie gave them instructions to locate, but not arrest, Billy Ray Cobb. There were twelve deputies in all – nine white and three black. They fanned out across the county in search of a fancy yellow Ford pickup with a rebel flag in the rear window.

When Hastings arrived he and the sheriff left for the Ford County hospital. As usual, Hastings drove and Ozzie gave orders on the radio. In the waiting room on the second floor they found the Hailey clan. Aunts, uncles, grandparents, friends, and strangers crowded into the small room and some waited in the narrow hallway. There were whispers and quiet tears. Tonya was in surgery.

Carl Lee sat on a cheap plastic couch in a dark

corner with Gwen next to him and the boys next to her. He stared at the floor and did not notice the crowd. Gwen laid her head on his shoulder and cried softly. The boys sat rigidly with their hands on knees, occasionally glancing at their father as if waiting on words of reassurance.

Ozzie worked his way through the crowd, quietly shaking hands and patting backs and whispering that he would catch them. He knelt before Carl Lee and Gwen. 'How is she?' he asked. Carl Lee did not see him. Gwen cried louder and the boys sniffed and wiped tears. He patted Gwen on the knee and stood. One of her brothers led Ozzie and Hastings out of the room into the hall, away from the family. He shook Ozzie's hand and thanked him for coming.

'How is she?' Ozzie asked.

'Not too good. She's in surgery and most likely will be there for a while. She's got broken bones and a bad concussion. She's beat up real bad. There's rope burns on her neck like they tried to hang her.'

'Was she raped?' he asked, certain of the answer.

'Yeah. She told her momma they took turns on her and hurt her real bad. Doctors confirmed it.'

'How's Carl Lee and Gwen?'

'They're tore up pretty bad. I think they're in shock. Carl Lee ain't said a word since he got here.'

Ozzie assured him they would find the two men, and it wouldn't take long, and when they found them they would be locked up someplace safe.

The brother suggested he should hide them in another jail, for their own safety.

Three miles out of Clanton, Ozzie pointed to a gravel driveway. 'Pull in there,' he told Hastings, who turned off the highway and drove into the front yard of a dilapidated house trailer. It was almost dark.

Ozzie took his night stick and banged violently on the front door. 'Open up, Bumpous!'

The trailer shook and Bumpous scrambled to the bathroom to flush a fresh joint.

'Open up, Bumpous!' Ozzie banged. 'I know you're in there. Open up or I'll kick in the door.'

Bumpous yanked the door open and Ozzie walked in. 'You know, Bumpous, evertime I visit you I smell somethin' funny and the commode's flushin'. Get some clothes on. I gotta job for you.'

'W-what?'

'I'll explain it outside where I can breathe. Just get some clothes on and hurry.'

'What if I don't want to?'

'Fine. I'll see your parole officer tomorrow.'

'I'll be out in a minute.'

Ozzie smiled and walked to his car. Bobby Bumpous was one of his favorites. Since his parole two years earlier, he had led a reasonably clean life, occasionally succumbing to the lure of an easy drug sale for a quick buck. Ozzie watched him like a hawk and knew of such transactions, and Bumpous knew Ozzie knew; therefore, Bumpous was usually most eager to help his friend, Sheriff

16

Walls. The plan was to eventually use Bumpous to nail Billy Ray Cobb for dealing, but that would be postponed for now.

After a few minutes he marched outside, still tucking his shirttail and zipping his pants. 'Who you looking' for?' he demanded.

'Billy Ray Cobb.'

'That's no problem. You can find him without me.'

'Shut up and listen. We think Cobb was involved in a rape this afternoon. A black girl was raped by two white men, and I think Cobb was there.'

'Cobb ain't into rape, Sheriff. He's into drugs, remember?'

'Shut up and listen. You find Cobb and spend some time with him. Five minutes ago his truck was spotted at Huey's. Buy him a beer. Shoot some pool, roll dice, whatever. Find out what he did today. Who was he with? Where'd he go? You know how he likes to talk, right?'

'Right.'

'Call the dispatcher when you find him. They'll call me. I'll be somewhere close. You understand?'

'Sure, Sheriff. No problem.'

'Any questions?'

'Yeah. I'm broke. Who's gonna pay for this?'

Ozzie handed him a twenty and left. Hastings drove in the direction of Huey's, down by the lake.

'You sure you can trust him?' Hastings asked.

'Who?'

'That Bumpous kid.'

'Sure I trust him. He's proved very reliable since

17

he was paroled. He's a good kid tryin' to go straight, for the most part. He supports his local sheriff and would do anything I ask.'

'Why?'

'Because I caught him with ten ounces of pot a year ago. He'd been outta jail about a year when I caught his brother with an ounce, and I told him he was lookin' at thirty years. He started cryin' and carryin' on, cried all night in his cell. By mornin' he was ready to talk. Told me his supplier was his brother, Bobby. So I let him go and went to see Bobby. I knocked on his door and I could hear the commode flushin'. He wouldn't come to the door, so I kicked it in. I found him in his underwear in the bathroom tryin' to unstop the commode. There was dope all over the place. Don't know how much he flushed, but most of it was comin' back out in the overflow. Scared him so bad he wet his drawers.'

'You kiddin'?'

'Nope. The kid pissed all over himself. He was a sight standin' there with wet drawers, a plunger in one hand, dope in the other, and the room fillin' up with commode water.'

'What'd you do?'

'Threatened to kill him.'

'What'd he do?'

'Started cryin'. Cried like a baby. Cried 'bout his momma and prison and all this and that. Promised he'd never screw up again.'

'You arrest him?'

'Naw, I just couldn't. I talked real ugly to him

and threatened him some more. I put him on probation right there in his bathroom. He's been fun to work with ever since.'

They drove by Huey's and saw Cobb's truck in the gravel parking lot with a dozen other pickups and four-wheel drives. They parked behind a black church on a hill up the highway from Huey's, where they had a good view of the honky tonk, or tonk, as it was affectionately called by the patrons. Another patrol car hid behind some trees at the other end of the highway. Moments later Bumpous flew by and wheeled into the parking lot. He locked his brakes, spraying gravel and dust, then backed next to Cobb's truck. He looked around and casually entered Huey's. Thirty minutes later the dispatcher advised Ozzie that the informant had found the subject, a male white, at Huey's, an establishment on Highway 305 near the lake. Within minutes two more patrol cars were hidden close by. They waited.

'What makes you so sure it's Cobb?' Hastings asked.

'I ain't sure. I just got a hunch. The little girl said it was a truck with shiny wheels and big tires.'

'That narrows it down to two thousand.'

'She also said it was yellow, looked new, and had a big flag hangin' in the rear window.'

'That brings it down to two hundred.'

'Maybe less than that. How many of those are as mean as Billy Ray Cobb?'

'What if it ain't him?'

'It is.'

19

'If it ain't?'

'We'll know shortly. He's got a big mouth, 'specially when he's drinkin'.'

For two hours they waited and watched pickups come and go. Truck drivers, pulpwood cutters, factory workers, and farmhands parked their pickups and jeeps in the gravel and strutted inside to drink, shoot pool, listen to the band, but mainly to look for stray women. Some would leave and walk next door to Ann's Lounge, where they would stay for a few minutes and return to Huey's. Ann's Lounge was darker both inside and out, and it lacked the colorful beer signs and live music that made Huey's such a hit with the locals. Ann's was known for its drug traffic, whereas Huey's had it all – music, women, happy hours, poker machines, dice, dancing, and plenty of fights. One brawl spilled through the door into the parking lot, where a group of wild rednecks kicked and clawed each other at random until they grew winded and returned to the dice table.

'Hope that wasn't Bumpous,' observed the sheriff.

The restrooms inside were small and nasty, and most of the patrons found it necessary to relieve themselves between the pickups in the parking lot. This was especially true on Mondays when ten-cent beer night drew rednecks from four counties and every truck in the parking lot received at least three sprayings. About once a week an innocent passing motorist would get shocked by something he or she saw in the parking lot, and Ozzie would be forced to make an arrest. Otherwise, he left the places alone.

Both tonks were in violation of numerous laws. There was gambling, drugs, illegal whiskey, minors, they refused to close on time, etc. Shortly after he was elected the first time Ozzie made the mistake, due in part to a hasty campaign promise, of closing all the honky tonks in the county. It was a horrible mistake. The crime rate soared. The jail was packed. The court dockets multiplied. The rednecks united and drove in caravans to Clanton, where they parked around the courthouse on the square. Hundreds of them. Every night they invaded the square, drinking, fighting, playing loud music, and shouting obscenities at the horrified town folk. Each morning the square resembled a landfill with cans and bottles thrown everywhere. He closed the black tonks too, and break-ins, burglaries, and stabbings tripled in one month. There were two murders in one week.

Finally, with the city under siege, a group of local ministers met secretly with Ozzie and begged him to ease up on the tonks. He politely reminded them that during the campaign they had insisted on the closings. They admitted they were wrong and pleaded for relief. Yes, they would support him in the next election. Ozzie relented, and life returned to normal in Ford County.

Ozzie was not pleased that the establishments thrived in his county, but he was convinced beyond any doubt that his law-abiding constituents were much safer when the tonks were open.

At ten-thirty the dispatcher radioed that the informant was on the phone and wanted to see the sheriff. Ozzie gave his location, and a minute later they watched Bumpous emerge and stagger to his truck. He spun tires, slung gravel, and raced toward the church.

'He's drunk,' said Hastings.

He wheeled through the church parking lot and came to a screeching stop a few feet from the patrol car. 'Howdy, Sheriff!' he yelled.

Ozzie walked to the pickup. 'What took so long?'

'You told me to take all night.'

'You found him two hours ago.'

'That's true, Sheriff, but have you ever tried to spend twenty dollars on beer when it's fifty cents a can?'

'You drunk?'

'Naw, just havin' a good time. Could I have another twenty?'

'What'd you find out?'

''Bout what?'

'Cobb!'

'Oh, he's in there all right.'

'I know he's in there! What else?'

Bumpous quit smiling and looked at the tonk in the distance. 'He's laughin' about it, Sheriff. It's a big joke. Said he finally found a nigger who was a virgin. Somebody asked how old she was, and Cobb said eight or nine. Everybody laughed.'

Hastings closed his eyes and dropped his head. Ozzie gritted his teeth and looked away. 'What else did he say?'

22

'He's bad drunk. He won't remember any of it in the mornin'. Said she was a cute little nigger.'

'Who was with him?'

'Pete Willard.'

'Is he in there?'

'Yep, they're both laughin' about it.'

'Where are they?'

'Left-hand side, next to the pinball machines.'

Ozzie smiled. 'Okay, Bumpous. You did good. Get lost.'

Hastings called the dispatcher with the two names. The dispatcher relayed the message to Deputy Looney, who was parked in the street in front of the home of County Judge Percy Bullard. Looney rang the doorbell and handed the judge two affidavits and two arrest warrants. Bullard scribbled on the warrants and returned them to Looney, who thanked His Honor and left. Twenty minutes later Looney handed the warrants to Ozzie behind the church.

At exactly eleven, the band quit in mid-song, the dice disappeared, the dancers froze, the cue balls stopped rolling, and someone turned on the lights. All eyes followed the big sheriff as he and his men swaggered slowly across the dance floor to a table by the pinball machines. Cobb, Willard, and two others sat in a booth, the table littered with empty beer cans. Ozzie walked to the table and grinned at Cobb.

'I'm sorry, sir, but we don't allow niggers in here,' Cobb blurted out, and the four burst into laughter. Ozzie kept grinning.

When the laughing stopped, Ozzie said, 'You boys havin' a good time, Billy Ray?'

'We was.'

'Looks like it. I hate to break things up, but you and Mr Willard need to come with me.'

'Where we goin'?' Willard asked.

'For a ride.'

'I ain't movin',' Cobb vowed. With that, the other two scooted from the booth and joined the spectators.

'I'm placin' you both under arrest,' Ozzie said.

'You got warrants?' Cobb asked.

Hastings produced the warrants, and Ozzie threw them among the beer cans. 'Yeah, we got warrants. Now get up.'

Willard stared desperately at Cobb, who sipped a beer and said, 'I ain't goin' to jail.'

Looney handed Ozzie the longest, blackest nightstick ever used in Ford County. Willard was panic-stricken. Ozzie cocked it and struck the center of the table, sending beer and cans and foam in all directions. Willard bolted upright, slapped his wrists together and thrust them at Looney, who was waiting with the handcuffs. He was dragged outside and thrown into a patrol car.

Ozzie tapped his left palm with the stick and grinned at Cobb. 'You have the right to remain silent. Anything you say will be used against you in court. You have the right to a lawyer. If you can't afford one, the state'll furnish one. Any questions?'

'Yeah, what time is it?'

'Time to go to jail, big man.'

'Go to hell, nigger.'

Ozzie grabbed his hair and lifted him from the booth, then drove his face into the floor. He jammed a knee into his spine and slid his night-stick under his throat, and pulled upward while driving the knee deeper into his back. Cobb squealed until the stick began crushing his larynx.

The handcuffs were slapped into place, and Ozzie dragged him by his hair across the dance floor, out the door, across the gravel and threw him into the back seat with Willard.

News of the rape spread quickly. More friends and relatives crowded into the waiting room and the halls around it. Tonya was out of surgery and listed as critical. Ozzie talked to Gwen's brother in the hall and told of the arrests. Yes, they were the ones, he was sure.

Chapter 3

Jake Brigance rolled across his wife and staggered to the small bathroom a few feet from his bed, where he searched and groped in the dark for the screaming alarm clock. He found it where he had left it, and killed it with a quick and violent slap. It was 5:30 A.M., Wednesday, May 15.

He stood in the dark for a moment, breathless, terrified, his heart pounding rapidly, staring at the fluorescent numbers glowing at him from the face of the clock, a clock he hated. Its piercing scream could be heard down the street. He flirted with cardiac arrest every morning at this time when the thing erupted. On occasion, about twice a year, he was successful in shoving Carla onto the floor, and she would maybe turn it off before returning to bed. Most of the time, however, she was not sympathetic. She thought he was crazy for getting up at such an hour.

The clock sat on the windowsill so that Jake was required to move around a bit before it was silenced. Once up, Jake would not permit himself to crawl back under the covers. It was one of his rules. At one time the alarm was on the nightstand, and the volume was reduced. Carla would reach and turn it off before Jake heard anything. Then he would sleep until seven or eight and ruin his entire day. He would miss being in the office by seven, which was another rule. The alarm stayed in the bathroom and served its purpose.

Jake stepped to the sink and splashed cold water on his face and hair. He switched on the light and gasped in horror at the sight in the mirror. His straight brown hair shot in all directions, and the hairline had receded at least two inches during the night. Either that or his forehead had grown. His eyes were matted and swollen with the white stuff packed in the corners. A seam in a blanket left a bright red scar along the left side of his face. He touched, then rubbed it and wondered if it would go away. With his right hand he pushed his hair back and inspected the hairline. At thirty-two, he had no gray hair. Gray hair was not the problem. The problem was pattern baldness, which Jake had richly inherited from both sides of his family. He longed for a full, thick hairline beginning an inch above his eyebrows. He still had plenty of hair, Carla told him. But it wouldn't last long at the rate it was disappearing. She also assured him he was as handsome as ever, and he believed her. She had explained that a receding hairline gave him a look of maturity that was essential for a young attorney. He believed that too.

But what about old, bald attorneys, or even

mature, middle-aged bald attorneys? Why couldn't the hair return after he grew wrinkles and gray sideburns and looked very mature?

Jake pondered these things in the shower. He took quick showers, and he shaved and dressed quickly. He had to be at the Coffee Shop at 6:00 A.M. – another rule. He turned on lights and slammed and banged drawers and closet doors in an effort to arouse Carla. This was the morning ritual during the summer when she was not teaching school. He had explained to her numerous times that she had all day to catch up on any lost sleep, and that these early moments should be spent together. She moaned and tunneled deeper under the covers. Once dressed, Jake jumped on the bed with all fours and kissed her in the ear, down the neck, and all over the face until she finally swung at him. Then he yanked the covers off the bed and laughed as she curled up and shivered and begged for the blankets. He held them and admired her dark, tanned, thin, almost perfect legs. The bulky nightshirt covered nothing below the waist, and a hundred lewd thoughts danced before him.

About once a month this ritual would get out of hand. She would not protest, and the blankets would be jointly removed. On those mornings Jake undressed even quicker and broke at least three of his rules. That's how Hanna was conceived.

But not this morning. He covered his wife, kissed her gently, and turned out the lights. She breathed easier, and fell asleep.

Down the hall he quietly opened Hanna's door and knelt beside her. She was four, the only child, and there would be no others. She lay in her bed surrounded by dolls and stuffed animals. He kissed her lightly on the cheek. She was as beautiful as her mother, and the two were identical in looks and manners. They had large bluish-gray eyes that could cry instantly, if necessary. They wore their dark hair the same way – had it cut by the same person at the same time. They even dressed alike.

Jake adored the two women in his life. He kissed the second one goodbye and went to the kitchen to make coffee for Carla. On his way out he released Max, the mutt, into the backyard, where she simultaneously relieved herself and barked at Mrs Pickle's cat next door.

Few people attacked the morning like Jake Brigance. He walked briskly to the end of the driveway and got the morning papers for Carla. It was dark, clear, and cool with the promise of summer rapidly approaching.

He studied the darkness up and down Adams Street, then turned and admired his house. Two homes in Ford County were on the National Register of Historic Places, and Jake Brigance owned one of them. Although it was heavily mortgaged, he was proud of it nonetheless. It was a nineteenth-century Victorian built by a retired railroad man who died on the first Christmas Eve he spent in his new home. The facade was a huge, centered gable with hipped roof over a wide, inset front porch. Under the gable a small portico covered with bargeboard hung gently over the porch. The five supporting pillars were round and painted white and slate blue. Each column bore a handmade floral carving, each with a different flower – daffodils, irises, and sunflowers. The railing between the pillars was filled with lavish lacework. Upstairs, three bay windows opened onto a small balcony, and to the left of the balcony an octagonal tower with stained-glass windows protruded and rose above the gable until it peaked with an iron-crested finial. Below the tower and to the left of the porch, a wide, graceful veranda with ornamental railing extended from the house and served as a carport. The front panels were a collage of gingerbread, cedar shingles, scallops, fish scales, tiny intricate gables, and miniature spindles.

Carla had located a paint consultant in New Orleans, and the fairy chose six original colors – mostly shades of blue, teal, peach, and white. The paint job took two months and cost Jake five thousand dollars, and that did not include the countless hours he and Carla had spent dangling from ladders and scraping cornices. And although he was not wild about some of the colors, he had never dared suggest repainting.

As with every Victorian, the house was gloriously unique. It had a piquant, provocative, engaging quality derived from an ingenuous, joyous, almost childlike bearing. Carla had wanted it since before they married, and when the owner in Memphis finally died and the estate was closed, they bought it for a song because no one else would have it. It had been abandoned for twenty years. They borrowed heavily from two of the three banks in Clanton, and spent the next three years sweating and doting over their landmark. Now people drove by and took pictures of it.

The third local bank held the mortgage on Jake's car, the only Saab in Ford County. And a red Saab at that. He wiped the dew from the windshield and unlocked the door. Max was still barking and had awakened the army of bluejays that lived in Mrs Pickle's maple tree. They sang to him and called farewell as he smiled and whistled in return. He backed into Adams Street. Two blocks east he turned south on Jefferson, which two blocks later ran dead end into Washington Street. Jake had often wondered why every small Southern town had an Adams, a Jefferson, and a Washington, but no Lincoln or Grant. Washington Street ran east and west on the north side of the Clanton square.

Because Clanton was the county seat it had a square, and the square quite naturally had a court-house in the center of it. General Clanton had laid out the town with much thought, and the square was long and wide and the courthouse lawn was covered with massive oak trees, all lined neatly and spaced equally apart. The Ford County court-house was well into its second century, built after the Yankees burned the first one. It defiantly faced south, as if telling those from the North to politely and eternally kiss its ass. It was old and stately, with white columns along the front and black shutters around the dozens of windows. The original red brick had long since been painted white, and every four years the Boy Scouts added a thick layer of shiny enamel for their traditional summer project. Several bond issues over the years had allowed additions and renovations. The lawn around it was clean and neatly trimmed. A crew from the jail manicured it twice a week.

Clanton had three coffee shops – two for the whites and one for the blacks, and all three were on the square. It was not illegal or uncommon for whites to eat at Claude's, the black cafe on the west side. And it was safe for the blacks to eat at the Tea Shoppe, on the south side, or the Coffee Shop on Washington Street. They didn't, however, since they were told they could back in the seventies. Jake ate barbecue every Friday at Claude's, as did most of the white liberals in Clanton. But six mornings a week he was a regular at the Coffee Shop.

He parked the Saab in front of his office on Washington Street and walked three doors to the Coffee Shop. It had opened an hour earlier and by now was bustling with action. Waitresses scurried about serving coffee and breakfast and chatting incessantly with the farmers and mechanics and deputies who were the regulars. This was no white-collar cafe. The white collars gathered across the square at the Tea Shoppe later in the morning and discussed national politics, tennis, golf, and the stock market. At the Coffee Shop they talked about local politics, football, and bass fishing. Jake was one of the few white collars allowed to frequent the Coffee Shop. He was well liked and accepted by the blue collars, most of whom at one time or another had found their way to his office for a will, a deed, a divorce, a defense, or any one of a thousand other problems. They picked at him and told crooked lawyer jokes, but he had a thick skin. They asked him to explain Supreme Court rulings and other legal oddities during breakfast, and he gave a lot of free legal advice at the Coffee Shop. Jake had a way of cutting through the excess and discussing the meat of any issue. They appreciated that. They didn't always agree with him, but they always got honest answers. They argued at times, but there were never hard feelings.

He made his entrance at six, and it took five minutes to greet everyone, shake hands, slap backs, and say smart things to the waitresses. By the time he sat at his table his favorite girl, Dell, had his coffee and regular breakfast of toast, jelly, and grits. She patted him on the hand and called him honey and sweetheart and generally made a fuss over him. She griped and snapped at the others, but had a different routine for Jake.

He ate with Tim Nunley, a mechanic down at the Chevrolet place, and two brothers, Bill and Bert West, who worked at the shoe factory north of town. He splashed three drops of Tabasco on his grits and stirred them artfully with a slice of butter. He covered the toast with a half inch of homemade strawberry jelly. Once his food was properly prepared, he tasted the coffee and started eating. They ate quietly and discussed how the crappie were biting.

In a booth by the window a few feet from Jake's table, three deputies talked among themselves. The big one, Marshall Prather, turned to Jake and asked loudly, 'Say, Jake, didn't you defend Billy Ray Cobb a few years ago?'

The cafe was instantly silent as everyone looked at the lawyer. Startled not by the question but by its response, Jake swallowed his grits and searched for the name.

'Billy Ray Cobb,' he repeated aloud. 'What kind of case was it?'

'Dope,' Prather said. 'Caught him sellin' dope about four years ago. Spent time in Parchman and got out last year.'

Jake remembered. 'Naw, I didn't represent him. I think he had a Memphis lawyer.'

Prather seemed satisfied and returned to his pancakes. Jake waited.

Finally he asked, 'Why? What's he done now?'

'We picked him up last night for rape.'

'Rape!'

'Yeah, him and Pete Willard.'

'Who'd they rape?'

'You remember that Hailey nigger you got off in that murder trial a few years ago?'

'Lester Hailey. Of course I remember.'

'You know his brother Carl Lee?'

'Sure. Know him well. I know all the Haileys. Represented most of them.'

'Well, it was his little girl.'

'You're kidding?'

'Nope.'

'How old is she?'

'Ten.'

Jake's appetite disappeared as the cafe returned to normal. He played with his coffee and listened to the conversation change from fishing to Japanese cars and back to fishing. When the West brothers left, he slid into the booth with the deputies.

'How is she?' he asked.

'Who?'

'The Hailey girl.'

'Pretty bad,' said Prather. 'She's in the hospital.'

'What happened?'

'We don't know everything. She ain't been able to talk much. Her momma sent her to the store. They live on Craft Road behind Bates Grocery.'

'I know where they live.'

'Somehow they got her in Cobb's pickup and took her out in the woods somewhere and raped her.'

'Both of them?'

'Yeah, several times. And they kicked her and beat her real bad. Some of her kinfolks didn't know her, she was beat so bad.'

Jake shook his head. 'That's sick.'

'Sure is. Worst I've ever seen. They tried to kill her. Left her for dead.'

'Who found her?'

'Buncha niggers fishin' down by Foggy Creek. Saw her floppin' out in the middle of the road. Had her hands tied behind her. She was talkin' a little – told them who her daddy was and they took her home.'

'How'd you know it was Billy Ray Cobb?'

'She told her momma it was a yellow pickup truck with a rebel flag hangin' in the rear window. That's about all Ozzie needed. He had it figured out by the time she got to the hospital.'

Prather was careful not to say too much. He liked Jake, but he was a lawyer and he handled a lot of criminal cases.

'Who is Pete Willard?'

'Some friend of Cobb's.'

'Where'd y'all find them?'

'Huey's.'

'That figures.' Jake drank his coffee and thought of Hanna.

'Sick, sick, sick,' Looney mumbled.

'How's Carl Lee?'

Prather wiped syrup from his mustache. 'Personally, I don't know him, but I ain't ever heard anything bad about him. They're still at the hospital. I think Ozzie was with them all night. He knows them real well, of course, he knows all those folks real well. Hastings is kin to the girl somehow.'

'When's the preliminary hearing?'

'Bullard set it for one P.M. today. Ain't that right, Looney?'

Looney nodded.

'Any bond?'

'Ain't been set yet. Bullard's gonna wait till the hearing. If she dies, they'll be lookin' at capital murder, won't they?'

36

Jake nodded.

'They can't have a bond for capital murder, can they, Jake?' Looney asked.

'They can but I've never seen one. I know Bullard won't set a bond for capital murder, and if he did, they couldn't make it.'

'If she don't die, how much time can they get?' asked Nesbit, the third deputy.

Others listened as Jake explained. 'They can get life sentences for the rape. I assume they will also be charged with kidnapping and aggravated assault.'

'They already have.'

'Then they can get twenty years for the kidnapping and twenty years for the aggravated assault.'

'Yeah, but how much time will they serve?' asked Looney.

Jake thought a second. 'They could conceivably be paroled in thirteen years. Seven for the rape, three for the kidnapping, and three for the aggravated assault. That's assuming they're convicted on all charges and sentenced to the maximum.'

'What about Cobb? He's got a record.'

'Yeah, but he's not habitual unless he's got two prior convictions.'

'Thirteen years,' Looney repeated, shaking his head.

Jake stared through the window. The square was coming to life as pickups full of fruits and vegetables parked next to the sidewalk around the courthouse lawn, and the old farmers in faded overalls neatly arranged the small baskets of

37

tomatoes and cucumbers and squash on the tail-gates and hoods. Watermelons from Florida were placed next to the dusty slick tires, and the farmers left for an early-morning meeting under the Vietnam monument, where they sat on benches and chewed Red Man and whittled while they caught up on the gossip. They're probably talking about the rape, Jake thought. It was daylight now, and time for the office. The deputies were finished with their food, and Jake excused himself. He hugged Dell, paid his check, and for a second thought of driving home to check on Hanna.

At three minutes before seven, he unlocked his office and turned on the lights.

Carl Lee had difficulty sleeping on the couch in the waiting room. Tonya was serious but stable. They had seen her at midnight, after the doctor warned that she looked bad. She did. Gwen had kissed the little bandaged face while Carl Lee stood at the foot of the bed, subdued, motionless, unable to do anything but stare blankly at the small figure surrounded by machines, tubes, and nurses. Gwen was later sedated and taken to her mother's house in Clanton. The boys went home with Gwen's brother.

The crowd had dispersed around one, leaving Carl Lee alone on the couch. Ozzie brought coffee and doughnuts at two, and told Carl Lee all he knew about Cobb and Willard.

★　　★　　★

38

Jake's office was a two-story building in a row of two-story buildings overlooking the courthouse on the north side of the square, just down from the Coffee Shop. The building was built by the Wilbanks family back in the 1890s, back when they owned Ford County. And there had been a Wilbanks practicing law in the building from the day it was built until 1979, the year of the disbarment. Next door to the east was an insurance agent Jake had sued for botching a claim for Tim Nunley, the mechanic down at the Chevrolet place. To the west was the bank with the mortgage on the Saab. All the buildings around the square were two-story brick except the banks. The one next door had also been built by the Wilbankses and had just two floors, but the one on the southeast corner of the square had three floors, and the newest one, on the southwest corner, had four floors.

Jake practiced alone, and had since 1979, the year of the disbarment. He liked it that way, especially since there was no other lawyer in Clanton competent enough to practice with him. There were several good lawyers in town, but most were with the Sullivan firm over in the bank building with four floors. Jake detested the Sullivan firm. Every lawyer detested the Sullivan firm except those in it. There were eight in all, eight of the most pompous and arrogant jerks Jake had ever met. Two had Harvard degrees. They had the big farmers, the banks, the insurance companies, the railroads, everybody with money. The other fourteen lawyers in the county picked up the scraps and represented people – living, breathing human souls, most of whom had very little money. These were the 'street lawyers' – those in the trenches helping people in trouble. Jake was proud to be a street lawyer.

His offices were huge. He used only five of the ten rooms in the building. Downstairs there was a reception room, a large conference room, a kitchen, and a smaller storage and junk room. Upstairs, Jake had his vast office and another smaller office he referred to as the war room. It had no windows, no telephones, no distractions. Three offices sat empty upstairs and two downstairs. In years past these had been occupied by the prestigious Wilbanks firm, long before the disbarment. Jake's office upstairs, *the* office, was immense; thirty by thirty with a ten-foot hardwood ceiling, hardwood floors, huge fireplace, and three desks – his work desk, a small conference desk in one corner, and a rolltop desk in another corner under the portrait of William Faulkner. The antique oak furniture had been there for almost a century, as had the books and shelves that covered one wall. The view of the square and courthouse was impressive, and could be enhanced by opening the French doors and walking onto a small balcony overhanging the sidewalk next to Washington Street. Jake had, without a doubt, the finest office in Clanton. Even his bitter enemies in the Sullivan firm would concede that much.

For all the opulence and square footage, Jake paid the sum of four hundred dollars a month to his landlord and former boss, Lucien Wilbanks, who had been disbarred in 1979.

For decades the Wilbanks family ruled Ford County. They were proud, wealthy people, prominent in farming, banking, politics, and especially law. All the Wilbanks men were lawyers, and were educated at Ivy League schools. They founded banks, churches, schools, and several served in public office. The firm of Wilbanks & Wilbanks had been the most powerful and prestigious in north Mississippi for many years.

Then came Lucien. He was the only male Wilbanks of his generation. There was a sister and some nieces, but they were expected only to marry well. Great things were expected of Lucien as a child, but by the third grade it was evident he would be a different Wilbanks. He inherited the law firm in 1965 when his father and uncle were killed in a plane crash. Although he was forty, he had just recently, several months prior to their deaths, completed his study of the law by correspondence courses. Somehow he passed the bar exam. He took control of the firm and clients began disappearing. Big clients, like insurance companies, banks, and farmers, all left and went to the newly established Sullivan firm. Sullivan had been a junior partner in the Wilbanks firm until Lucien fired him and evicted him, after which he left with the other junior partners and most of the clients. Then Lucien fired everyone else – associates, secretaries, clerks – everyone but Ethel Twitty, his late father's favorite secretary.

Ethel and John Wilbanks had been very close through the years. In fact she had a younger son who greatly resembled Lucien. The poor fellow spent most of his time in and out of various nut houses. Lucien jokingly referred to him as his retarded brother. After the plane crash, the retarded brother appeared in Clanton and started telling folks he was the illegitimate son of John Wilbanks. Ethel was humiliated, but couldn't control him. Clanton seethed with scandal. A lawsuit was filed by the Sullivan firm as counsel for the retarded brother seeking a portion of the estate. Lucien was furious. A trial ensued, and Lucien vigorously defended his honor and pride and family name. He also vigorously defended his father's estate, all of which had been left to Lucien and his sister. At trial the jury noted the striking resemblance between Lucien and Ethel's son, who was several years younger. The retarded brother was strategically seated as close as possible to Lucien. The Sullivan lawyers instructed him to walk, talk, sit, and do everything just like Lucien. They even dressed him like Lucien. Ethel and her husband denied the boy was any kin to the Wilbanks, but the jury felt otherwise. He was found to be an heir of John Wilbanks, and was awarded one third of the estate. Lucien cursed the jury, slapped the poor boy, and was carried screaming from the courtroom and taken to jail. The jury's decision was reversed and dismissed on appeal, but Lucien feared more litigation if Ethel ever changed her story. Thus, Ethel Twitty remained with the Wilbanks firm.

Lucien was satisfied when the firm disintegrated. He never intended to practice law like his ancestors. He wanted to be a criminal lawyer, and the old firm's clientele had become strictly corporate. He wanted the rapes, the murders, the child abuses, the ugly cases no one else wanted. He wanted to be a civil rights lawyer and litigate civil liberties. But most of all, Lucien wanted to be a radical, a flaming radical of a lawyer with unpopular cases and causes, and lots of attention.

He grew a beard, divorced his wife, renounced his church, sold his share of the country club, joined the NAACP and ACLU, resigned from the bank board, and in general became the scourge of Clanton. He sued the schools because of segregation, the governor because of the prison, the city because it refused to pave streets in the black section, the bank because there were no black tellers, the state because of capital punishment, and the factories because they would not recognize organized labor. He fought and won many criminal cases, and not just in Ford County. His reputation spread, and a large following developed among blacks, poor whites, and the few unions in north Mississippi. He stumbled into some lucrative personal injury and wrongful death cases. There were some nice settlements. The firm, he and Ethel, was more profitable than ever. Lucien did not need the money. He had been born with it and never thought about it. Ethel did the counting.

The law became his life. With no family, he

became a workaholic. Fifteen hours a day, seven days a week, Lucien practiced law with a passion. He had no other interests, except alcohol. In the late sixties he noticed an affinity for Jack Daniel's. By the early seventies he was a drunk, and when he hired Jake in 1978 he was a full-fledged alcoholic. But he never let booze interfere with his work; he learned to drink and work at the same time. Lucien was always half drunk, and he was a dangerous lawyer in that condition. Bold and abrasive by nature, he was downright frightening when he was drinking. At trial he would embarrass the opposing attorneys, insult the judge, abuse the witnesses, then apologize to the jury. He respected no one and could not be intimidated. He was feared because he would say and do anything. People walked lightly around Lucien. He knew it and loved it. He became more and more eccentric. The more he drank, the crazier he acted, then people talked about him even more, so he drank even more.

Between 1966 and 1978 Lucien hired and disposed of eleven associates. He hired blacks, Jews, Hispanics, women, and not one kept the pace he demanded. He was a tyrant around the office, constantly cursing and berating the young lawyers. Some quit the first month. One lasted two years. It was difficult to accept Lucien's craziness. He had the money to be eccentric – his associates did not.

He hired Jake in 1978 fresh from law school. Jake was from Karaway, a small town of twenty-five hundred, eighteen miles west of Clanton. He was clean-cut, conservative, a devout Presbyterian with a pretty wife who wanted babies. Lucien hired him to see if he could corrupt him. Jake took the job with strong reservations because he had no other offers close to home.

A year later Lucien was disbarred. It was a tragedy for those very few who liked him. The small union at the shoe factory north of town had called a strike. It was a union Lucien had organized and represented. The factory began hiring new workers to replace the strikers, and violence followed. Lucien appeared on the picket line to rally his people. He was drunker than normal. A group of scabs attempted to cross the line and a brawl erupted. Lucien led the charge, was arrested and jailed. He was convicted in city court of assault and battery and disorderly conduct. He appealed and lost, appealed and lost.

The State Bar Association had grown weary of Lucien over the years. No other attorney in the state had received as many complaints as had Lucien Wilbanks. Private reprimands, public reprimands, and suspensions had all been used, all to no avail. The Complaints Tribunal and Disciplinary Committee moved swiftly. He was disbarred for outrageous conduct unbecoming a member of the bar. He appealed and lost, appealed and lost.

He was devastated. Jake was in Lucien's office, the big office upstairs, when word came from Jackson that the Supreme Court had upheld the disbarment. Lucien hung up the phone and walked to the doors overlooking the square. Jake watched him closely, waiting for the tirade. But Lucien said nothing. He walked slowly down the stairs, stopped and stared at Ethel, who was crying, and then looked at Jake. He opened the door and said, 'Take care of this place. I'll see you later.'

They ran to the front window and watched him speed away from the square in his ragged old Porsche. For several months there was no word from him. Jake labored diligently on Lucien's cases while Ethel kept the office from chaos. Some of the cases were settled, some left for other lawyers, some went to trial.

Six months later Jake returned to his office after a long day in court and found Lucien asleep on the Persian rug in the big office. 'Lucien! Are you all right?' he asked.

Lucien jumped up and sat in the big leather chair behind the desk. He was sober, tanned, relaxed.

'Jake, my boy, how are you?' he asked warmly.

'Fine, just fine. Where have you been?'

'Cayman Islands.'

'Doing what?'

'Drinking rum, lying on the beach, chasing little native girls.'

'Sounds like fun. Why did you leave?'

'It got boring.'

Jake sat across the desk. 'It's good to see you, Lucien.'

'Good to see you, Jake. How are things around here?'

'Hectic. But okay, I guess.'

'Did you settle Medley?'

'Yeah. They paid eighty thousand.'

'That's very good. Was he happy?'

'Yes, seemed to be.'

'Did Cruger go to trial?'

Jake looked at the floor. 'No, he hired Fredrix. I think it's set for trial next month.'

'I should've talked to him before I left.'

'He's guilty, isn't he?'

'Yes, very. It doesn't matter who represents him. Most defendants are guilty. Remember that.' Lucien walked to the French doors and gazed at the courthouse. 'What are your plans, Jake?'

'I'd like to stay here. What are your plans?'

'You're a good man, Jake, and I want you to stay. Me, I don't know. I thought about moving to the Caribbean, but I won't. It's a nice place to visit, but it gets old. I have no plans really. I may travel. Spend some money. I'm worth a ton, you know.'

Jake agreed. Lucien turned and waved his arms around the room. 'I want you to have all this, Jake. I want you to stay here and keep some semblance of a firm going. Move into this office; use this desk that my grandfather brought from Virginia after the Civil War. Keep the files, cases, clients, books, everything.'

'That's very generous, Lucien.'

'Most of the clients will disappear. No reflection

on you – you'll be a great lawyer someday. But most of my clients have followed me for years.'

Jake didn't want most of his clients. 'How about rent?'

'Pay me what you can afford. Money will be tight at first, but you'll make it. I don't need money, but you do.'

'You're being very kind.'

'I'm really a nice guy.' They both laughed awkwardly.

Jake quit smiling. 'What about Ethel?'

'It's up to you. She's a good secretary who's forgotten more law than you'll ever know. I know you don't like her, but she would be hard to replace. Fire her if you want to. I don't care.'

Lucien headed for the door. 'Call me if you need me. I'll be around. I want you to move into this office. It was my father's and grandfather's. Put my junk in some boxes, and I'll pick it up later.'

Cobb and Willard awoke with throbbing heads and red, swollen eyes. Ozzie was yelling at them. They were in a small cell by themselves. Through the bars to the right was a cell where the state prisoners were held awaiting the trip to Parchman. A dozen blacks leaned through the bars and glared at the two white boys as they struggled to clear their eyes. To the left was a smaller cell, also full of blacks. Wake up, Ozzie yelled, and stay quiet, or he would integrate his jail.

* * *

Jake's quiet time was from seven until Ethel arrived at eight-thirty. He was jealous with this time. He locked the front door, ignored the phone, and refused to make appointments. He meticulously planned his day. By eight-thirty he would have enough work dictated to keep Ethel busy and quiet until noon. By nine he was either in court or seeing clients. He would not take calls until eleven, when he methodically returned the morning's messages – all of them. He never delayed returning a phone call – another rule. Jake worked systematically and efficiently with little wasted time. These habits he had not learned from Lucien.

At eight-thirty Ethel made her usual noisy entrance downstairs. She made fresh coffee and opened the mail as she had every day for the past forty-one years. She was sixty-four and looked fifty. She was plump, but not fat, well kept, but not attractive. She chomped on a greasy sausage and biscuit brought from home and read Jake's mail.

Jake heard voices. Ethel was talking to another woman. He checked his appointment book – none until ten.

'Good morning, Mr Brigance,' Ethel announced through the intercom.

'Morning, Ethel.' She preferred to be called Mrs Twitty. Lucien and everyone else called her that. But Jake had called her Ethel since he had fired her shortly after the disbarment.

'There's a lady here to see you.'

'She doesn't have an appointment.'

'Yes, sir, I know.'

'Make one for tomorrow morning after ten-thirty. I'm busy now.'

'Yes, sir. But she says it's urgent.'

'Who is it?' he snapped. It was always urgent when they dropped in unannounced, like dropping by a funeral home or a Laundromat. Probably some urgent question about Uncle Luke's will or the case set for trial in three months.

'A Mrs Willard,' Ethel replied.

'First name?'

'Earnestine Willard. You don't know her, but her son's in jail.'

Jake saw his appointments on time, but drop-ins were another matter. Ethel either ran them off or made appointments for the next day or so. Mr Brigance was very busy, she would explain, but he could work you in day after tomorrow. This impressed people.

'Tell her I'm not interested.'

'But she says she must find a lawyer. Her son has to be in court at one this afternoon.'

'Tell her to see Drew Jack Tyndale, the public defender. He's good and he's free.'

Ethel relayed the message. 'But, Mr Brigance, she wants to hire you. Someone told her you're the best criminal lawyer in the county.' The amusement was obvious in Ethel's voice.

'Tell her that's true, but I'm not interested.'

Ozzie handcuffed Willard and led him down the hall to his office in the front section of the Ford

County jail. He removed the handcuffs and seated him in a wooden chair in the center of the cramped room. Ozzle sat in the big chair across the desk and looked down at the defendant.

'Mr Willard, this here is Lieutenant Griffin with the Mississippi Highway Patrol. Over here is Investigator Rady with my office, and this here is Deputy Looney and Deputy Prather, whom you met last night but I doubt if you remember it. I'm Sheriff Walls.'

Willard jerked his head fearfully to look at each one. He was surrounded. The door was shut. Two tape recorders sat side by side near the edge of the sheriff's desk.

'We'd like to ask you some questions, okay?'

'I don't know.'

'Before I start, I wanna make sure you understand your rights. First of all, you have the right to remain silent. Understand?'

'Uh huh.'

'You don't have to talk if you don't want to, but if you do, anything you say can and will be used against you in court. Understand?'

'Uh huh.'

'Can you read and write?'

'Yeah.'

'Good, then read this and sign it. It says you've been advised of your rights.'

Willard signed. Ozzie pushed the red button on one of the tape recorders.

'You understand this tape recorder is on?'

'Uh huh.'

'And it's Wednesday, May 15, at eight forty-three in the mornin'.'

'If you say so.'

'What's your full name?'

'James Louis Willard.'

'Nickname?'

'Pete. Pete Willard.'

'Address?'

'Route 6, Box 14, Lake Village, Mississippi.'

'What road?'

'Bethel Road.'

'Who do you live with?'

'My momma, Earnestine Willard. I'm divorced.'

'You know Billy Ray Cobb?'

Willard hesitated and noticed his feet. His boots were back in the cell. His white socks were dirty and did not hide his two big toes. Safe question, he thought.

'Yeah, I know him.'

'Was you with him yesterday?'

'Uh huh.'

'Where were y'all?'

'Down at the lake.'

'What time did you leave?'

''Bout three.'

'What were you drivin'?'

'I wasn't.'

'What were you ridin' in?'

Hesitation. He studied his toes. 'I don't think I wanna talk no more.'

Ozzie pushed another button and the recorder

52

stopped. He breathed deeply at Willard. 'You ever been to Parchman?'

Willard shook his head.

'You know how many niggers at Parchman?'

Willard shook his head.

''Bout five thousand. You know how many white boys are there?'

'No.'

''Bout a thousand.'

Willard dropped his chin to his chest. Ozzie let him think for a minute, then winked at Lieutenant Griffin.

'You got any idea what those niggers will do to a white boy who raped a little black girl?'

No response.

'Lieutenant Griffin, tell Mr Willard how white boys are treated at Parchman.'

Griffin walked to Ozzie's desk and sat on the edge. He looked down at Willard. 'About five years ago a young white man in Helena County, over in the delta, raped a black girl. She was twelve. They were waiting on him when he got to Parchman. Knew he was coming. First night about thirty blacks tied him over a fifty-five-gallon drum and climbed on. The guards watched and laughed. There's no sympathy for rapists. They got him every night for three months, and then killed him. They found him castrated, stuffed in the drum.'

Willard cringed, then threw his head back and breathed heavily toward the ceiling.

'Look, Pete,' Ozzie said, 'we're not after you. We want Cobb. I've been after that boy since he left Parchman. I want him real bad. You help us get Cobb and I'll help you as much as I can. I ain't promisin' nothin', but me and the D.A. work close together. You help me get Cobb, and I'll help you with the D.A. Just tell us what happened.'

'I wanna lawyer,' Willard said.

Ozzie dropped his head and groaned. 'What's a lawyer gonna do, Pete? Get the niggers off of you? I'm tryin' to help you and you're bein' a wiseass.'

'You need to listen to the sheriff, son. He's trying to save your life,' Griffin said helpfully.

'There's a good chance you could get off with just a few years here in this jail,' Rady said.

'It's much safer than Parchman,' Prather said.

'Choice is yours, Pete,' Ozzie said. 'You can die at Parchman or stay here. I'll even consider makin' you a trusty if you behave.'

Willard dropped his head and rubbed his temples. 'Okay, okay.'

Ozzie punched the red button.

'Where'd you find the girl?'

'Some gravel road.'

'Which road?'

'I don't know. I's drunk.'

'Where'd you take her?'

'I don't know.'

'Just you and Cobb?'

'Yeah.'

'Who raped her?'

'We both did. Billy Ray went first.'

'How many times?'

'I don't remember. I's smokin' weed and drinkin'.'

'Both of you raped her?'

'Yeah.'

'Where'd you dump her?'

'Don't remember. I swear I don't remember.'

Ozzie pushed another button. 'We'll type this up and get you to sign it.'

Willard shook his head. 'Just don't tell Billy Ray.'

'We won't,' promised the sheriff.

Chapter 4

Percy Bullard fidgeted nervously in the leather chair behind the huge, battered oak desk in the judge's chambers behind the courtroom, where a crowd had gathered to see about the rape. In the small room next door the lawyers gathered around the coffee machine and gossiped about the rape.

Bullard's small black robe hung in a corner by the window that looked north over Washington Street. His size-six feet were wearing jogging shoes that barely touched the floor. He was a small, nervous type who worried about preliminary hearings and every other routine hearing. After thirteen years on the bench he had never learned to relax. Fortunately, he was not required to hear big cases; those were for the Circuit Court judge. Bullard was just a County Court judge, and he had reached his pinnacle.

Mr Pate, the ancient courtroom deputy, knocked on the door.

'Come in!' Bullard demanded.

'Afternoon, Judge.'

'How many blacks out there?' Bullard asked abruptly.

'Half the courtroom.'

'That's a hundred people! They don't draw that much for a good murder trial. Whatta they want?'

Mr Pate shook his head.

'They must think we're trying these boys today.'

'I guess they're just concerned,' Mr Pate said softly.

'Concerned about what? I'm not turning them loose. It's just a preliminary hearing.' He quieted and stared at the window. 'Is the family out there?'

'I think so. I recognize a few of them, but I don't know her parents.'

'How about security?'

'Sheriff's got ever deputy and ever reserve close to the courtroom. We checked everybody at the door.'

'Find anything?'

'No, sir.'

'Where are the boys?'

'Sheriff's got them. They'll be here in a minute.'

The judge seemed satisfied. Mr Pate laid a hand-written note on the desk.

'What is it?'

Mr Pate inhaled deeply. 'It's a request from a TV crew from Memphis to film the hearing.'

'What!' Bullard's face turned red and he rocked furiously in the swivel chair. 'Cameras,' he yelled. 'In my courtroom!' He ripped the note and threw the pieces in the direction of the trash can. 'Where are they?'

'In the rotunda.'

'Order them out of the courthouse.'

Mr Pate left quickly.

Carl Lee Hailey sat on the row next to the back. Dozens of relatives and friends surrounded him in the rows of padded benches on the right side of the courtroom. The benches on the left side were empty. Deputies milled about, armed, apprehensive, keeping a nervous watch on the group of blacks, and especially on Carl Lee, who sat bent over, elbows on knees, staring blankly at the floor.

Jake looked out his window across the square to the rear of the courthouse, which faced south. It was 1:00 P.M. He had skipped lunch, as usual, and had no business across the street, but he did need some fresh air. He hadn't left the building all day, and although he had no desire to hear the details of the rape, he hated to miss the hearing. There had to be a crowd in the courtroom because there were no empty parking spaces around the square. A handful of reporters and photographers waited anxiously near the rear of the courthouse by the wooden doors where Cobb and Willard would enter.

The jail was two blocks off the square on the south side, down the highway. Ozzie drove the car with Cobb and Willard in the back seat. With a squad car in front and one behind, the procession turned off Washington Street into the short driveway leading under the veranda of the courthouse. Six deputies escorted the defendants past the reporters, through the doors, and up the back stairs to the small room just outside the court-room.

Jake grabbed his coat, ignored Ethel, and raced across the street. He ran up the back stairs, through a small hall outside the jury room, and entered the courtroom from a side door just as Mr Pate led His Honor to the bench.

'All rise for the court,' Mr Pate shouted. Everyone stood. Bullard stepped to the bench and sat down.

'Be seated,' he yelled. 'Where are the defendants? Where? Bring them in then.'

Cobb and Willard were led, handcuffed, into the courtroom from the small holding room. They were unshaven, wrinkled, dirty, and looked confused. Willard stared at the large group of blacks while Cobb turned his back. Looney removed the handcuffs and seated them next to Drew Jack Tyndale, the public defender, at the long table where the defense sat. Next to it was a long table where the county prosecutor, Rocky Childers, sat taking notes and looking important.

Willard glanced over his shoulder and again checked on the blacks. On the front row just behind him sat his mother and Cobb's mother, each with a deputy for protection. Willard felt safe with all the deputies. Cobb refused to turn around.

From the back row, eighty feet away, Carl Lee raised his head and looked at the backs of the two men who raped his daughter. They were mangy, bearded, dirty-looking strangers. He covered his face and bent over. The deputies stood behind him, backs against the wall, watching every move.

'Now listen,' Bullard began loudly, 'This is just a preliminary hearing, not a trial. The purpose of a preliminary hearing is to determine if there is enough evidence that a crime has been committed to bind these defendants over to the grand jury. The defendants can even waive this hearing if they want to.'

Tyndale stood. 'No sir, Your Honor, we wish to proceed with the hearing.'

'Very well. I have copies of affidavits sworn to by Sheriff Walls charging both defendants with rape of a female under the age of twelve, kidnapping, and aggravated assault. Mr Childers, you may call your first witness.'

'Your Honor, the State calls Sheriff Ozzie Walls.'

Jake sat in the jury box, along with several other attorneys, all of whom pretended to be busy reading important materials. Ozzie was sworn and sat in the witness chair to the left of Bullard, a few feet from the jury box.

'Would you state your name?'

'Sheriff Ozzie Walls.'

'You're the sheriff of Ford County?'

'Yes.'

'I know who he is,' Bullard mumbled as he flipped through the file.

'Sheriff, yesterday afternoon, did your office receive a call about a missing child?'

'Yes, around four-thirty.'

'What did your office do?'

'Deputy Willie Hastings was dispatched to the residence of Gwen and Carl Lee Hailey, the parents of the girl.'

'Where was that?'

'Down on Craft Road, back behind Bates Grocery.'

'What did he find?'

'He found the girl's mother, who made the call. Then drove around searchin' for the girl.'

'Did he find her?'

'No. When he returned to the house, the girl was there. She'd been found by some folks fishin', and they took her home.'

'What shape was the girl in?'

'She'd been raped and beaten.'

'Was she conscious?'

'Yeah. She could talk, or mumble, a little.'

'What did she say?'

Tyndale jumped to his feet. 'Your Honor, please, I know hearsay is admissible in a hearing like this, but this is triple hearsay.'

'Overruled. Shut up. Sit down. Continue, Mr Childers.'

'What did she say?'

'Told her momma it was two white men in a yellow pickup truck with a rebel flag in the window. That's about all. She couldn't say much. Had both jaws broken and her face kicked in.'

'What happened then?'

'The deputy called an ambulance and she was taken to the hospital.'

'How is she?'

61

'They say she's critical.'

'What happened then?'

'Based on what I knew at the time I had a suspect in mind.'

'So what'd you do?'

'I located an informant, a reliable informant, and placed him in a beer joint down by the lake.'

Childers was not one to dwell on details, especially in front of Bullard. Jake knew it, as did Tyndale. Bullard sent every case to the grand jury, so every preliminary was a formality. Regardless of the case, the facts, the proof, regardless of anything, Bullard would bind the defendant over to the grand jury. If there was insufficient proof, let the grand jury turn them loose, not Bullard. He had to be reelected, the grand jury did not. Voters got upset when criminals were cut loose. Most defense lawyers in the county waived the preliminary hearings before Bullard. Not Jake. He viewed such hearings as the best and quickest way to look at the prosecution's case. Tyndale seldom waived a preliminary hearing.

'Which beer joint?'

'Huey's.'

'What'd he find out?'

'Said he heard Cobb and Willard, the two defendants over there, braggin' 'bout rapin' a little black girl.'

Cobb and Willard exchanged stares. Who was the informant? They remembered little from Huey's.

'What'd you find at Huey's?'

'We arrested Cobb and Willard, then we searched a pickup titled in the name of Billy Ray Cobb.'

'What'd you find?'

'We towed it in and examined it this mornin'. Lot of blood stains.'

'What else?'

'We found a small T-shirt covered with blood.'

'Whose T-shirt?'

'It belonged to Tonya Hailey, the little girl who was raped. Her daddy, Carl Lee Hailey, identified it this mornin'.'

Carl Lee heard his name and sat upright. Ozzie stared straight at him. Jake turned and saw Carl Lee for the first time.

'Describe the truck.'

'New yellow Ford half-ton pickup. Big chrome wheels and mud tires. Rebel flag in the rear window.'

'Owned by who?'

Ozzie pointed at the defendants. 'Billy Ray Cobb.'

'Does it match the description given by the girl?'

'Yes.'

Childers paused and reviewed his notes. 'Now, Sheriff, what other evidence do you have against these defendants?'

'We talked to Pete Willard this mornin' at the jail. He signed a confession.'

'You did what!' Cobb blurted. Willard cowered and looked for help.

'Order! Order!' shouted Bullard as he banged his gavel. Tyndale separated his clients.

'Did you advise Mr Willard of his rights?'

'Yes.'

'Did he understand them?'

'Yes.'

'Did he sign a statement to that effect?'

'Yes.'

'Who was present when Mr Willard made his statement?'

'Me, two deputies, my investigator, Rady, and Lieutenant Griffin with the Highway Patrol.'

'Do you have the confession?'

'Yes.'

'Please read it.'

The courtroom was still and silent as Ozzie read the short statement. Carl Lee stared blankly at the two defendants. Cobb glared at Willard, who picked dirt off his boots.

'Thank you, Sheriff,' Childers said when Ozzie finished. 'Did Mr Willard sign the confession?'

'Yes, in front of three witnesses.'

'The State has nothing further, Your Honor.'

Bullard shouted, 'You may cross-examine, Mr Tyndale.'

'I have nothing at this time, Your Honor.'

Good move, thought Jake. Strategically, for the defense, it was best to stay quiet at preliminary hearings. Just listen, take notes, let the court reporter record the testimony, and stay quiet. The grand jury would see the case anyway, so why bother? And never allow the defendants to testify. Their testimony would serve no purpose and haunt them at trial. Jake knew they would not testify because he knew Tyndale.

64

'Call your next witness,' demanded the Judge.

'We have nothing further, Your Honor.'

'Good. Sit down. Mr Tyndale, do you have any witnesses?'

'No, Your Honor.'

'Good. The court finds there is sufficient evidence that numerous crimes have been committed by these defendants, and the court orders Mr Cobb and Mr Willard to be held to await action by the Ford County grand jury, which is scheduled to meet on Monday, May 27. Any questions?'

Tyndale rose slowly. 'Yes, Your Honor, we would request the court to set a reasonable bond for these de—'

'Forget it,' snapped Bullard. 'Bail will be denied as of now. It's my understanding that the girl is in critical condition. If she dies, there will of course be other charges.'

'Well, Your Honor, in that case, I would like to request a bail hearing a few days from now, in the hopes that her condition improves.'

Bullard studied Tyndale carefully. Good idea, he thought. 'Granted. A bail hearing is set for next Monday, May 20, in this courtroom. Until then the defendants will remain in the custody of the Ford County sheriff. Court's adjourned.'

Bullard rapped the gavel and disappeared. The deputies swarmed around the defendants, hand-cuffed them, and they too disappeared from the courtroom, into the holding room, down the back stairs, past the reporters, and into the squad car.

The hearing was typical for Bullard – less than twenty minutes. Justice could be very swift in his courtroom.

Jake talked to the other lawyers and watched the crowd file silently through the enormous wooden doors at the rear of the courtroom. Carl Lee was in no hurry to leave, and motioned for Jake to follow him. They met in the rotunda. Carl Lee wanted to talk, and he excused himself from the crowd and promised to meet them at the hospital. He and Jake walked down the winding staircase to the first floor.

'I'm truly sorry, Carl Lee,' Jake said.

'Yeah, me too.'

'How is she?'

'She'll make it.'

'How's Gwen?'

'Okay, I guess.'

'How about you?'

They walked slowly down the hall toward the rear of the courthouse. 'It ain't sunk in yet. I mean, twenty-four hours ago everything was fine. Now look at us. My little girl's layin' up in the hospital with tubes all over her body. My wife's crazy and my boys are scared to death, and all I think about is gettin' my hands on those bastards.'

'I wish I could do something, Carl Lee.'

'All you can do is pray for her, pray for us.'

'I know it hurts.'

'You gotta little girl, don't you, Jake?'

'Yeah.'

Carl Lee said nothing as they walked in silence. Jake changed the subject. 'Where's Lester?'

'Chicago.'

'What's he doing?'

'Workin' for a steel company. Good job. Got married.'

'You're kidding? Lester, married?'

'Yeah, married a white girl.'

'White girl! What's he want with a white girl?'

'Aw, you know Lester. Always an uppity nigger. He's on his way home now. Be in late tonight.'

'What for?'

They stopped at the rear door. Jake asked again: 'What's Lester coming in for?'

'Family business.'

'Y'all planning something?'

'Nope. He just wants to see his niece.'

'Y'all don't get excited.'

'That's easy for you to say, Jake.'

'I know.'

'What would you plan, Jake?'

'What do you mean?'

'You gotta little girl. Suppose she's layin up in the hospital, beat and raped. What would you do?'

Jake looked through the window of the door and could not answer. Carl Lee waited.

'Don't do anything stupid, Carl Lee.'

'Answer my question. What would you do?'

'I don't know. I don't know what I'd do.'

'Lemme ask you this. If it was your little girl, and if it was two niggers, and you could get your hands on them, what would you do?'

'Kill them.'

Carl Lee smiled, then laughed. 'Sure you would, Jake, sure you would. Then you'd hire some big-shot lawyer to say you's crazy, just like you did in Lester's trial.'

'We didn't say Lester was crazy. We just said Bowie needed killing.'

'You got him off, didn't you?'

'Sure.'

Carl Lee walked to the stairs and looked up. 'This how they get to the courtroom?' he asked without looking at Jake.

'Who?'

'Those boys.'

'Yeah. Most of the time they take them up those stairs. It's quicker and safer. They can park right outside the door here, and run them up the stairs.'

Carl Lee walked to the rear door and looked through the window at the veranda. 'How many murder trials you had, Jake?'

'Three. Lester's and two more.'

'How many were black?'

'All three.'

'How many you win?'

'All three.'

'You pretty good on nigger shootin's, ain't you?'

'I guess.'

'You ready for another one?'

'Don't do it, Carl Lee. It's not worth it. What if you're convicted and get the gas chamber? What about the kids? Who'll raise them? Those punks aren't worth it.'

'You just told me you'd do it.'

Jake walked to the door next to Carl Lee. 'It's different with me. I could probably get off.'

'How?'

'I'm white, and this is a white county. With a little luck I could get an all-white jury, which will naturally be sympathetic. This is not New York or California. A man's supposed to protect his family. A jury would eat it up.'

'And me?'

'Like I said, this ain't New York or California. Some whites would admire you, but most would want to see you hang. It would be much harder to win an acquittal.'

'But you could do it, couldn't you, Jake?'

'Don't do it, Carl Lee.'

'I have no choice, Jake. I'll never sleep till those bastards are dead. I owe it to my little girl, I owe it to myself, and I owe it to my people. It'll be done.'

They opened the doors, walked under the veranda and down the driveway to Washington Street, across from Jake's office. They shook hands. Jake promised to stop by the hospital tomorrow to see Gwen and the family.

'One more thing, Jake. Will you meet me at the jail when they arrest me?'

Jake nodded before he thought. Carl Lee smiled and walked down the sidewalk to his truck.

Chapter 5

Lester Hailey married a Swedish girl from Wisconsin, and although she still professed love for him, Lester suspected the novelty of his skin was beginning to fade. She was terrified of Mississippi, and flatly refused to travel south with Lester even though he assured her she would be safe. She had never met his family. Not that his people were anxious to meet her – they were not. It was not uncommon for Southern blacks to move north and marry white girls, but no Hailey had ever mixed. There were many Haileys in Chicago; most were kin, and all married black. The family was not impressed with Lester's blonde wife. He drove to Clanton in his new Cadillac, by himself.

It was late Wednesday night when he arrived at the hospital and found some cousins reading magazines in the second-floor waiting room. He embraced Carl Lee. They had not seen each other since the Christmas holidays, when half the blacks in Chicago trooped home to Mississippi and Alabama.

They stepped into the hall, away from the relatives. 'How is she?' Lester asked.

'Better. Much better. Might go home this weekend.'

Lester was relieved. When he left Chicago eleven hours earlier she had been near death, according to the cousin who had called and scared him from bed. He lit a Kool under the NO SMOKING sign and stared at his big brother. 'You okay?'

Carl Lee nodded and glanced down the hall.

'How's Gwen?'

'Crazier than normal. She's at her momma's. You come by yourself?'

'Yeah,' Lester answered defensively.

'Good.'

'Don't get smart. I didn't drive all day to hear crap about my wife.'

'Okay, okay. You still got gas?'

Lester smiled and chuckled. He had been plagued by stomach gas since the day he married the Swede. She prepared dishes he couldn't pronounce, and his system behaved violently. He longed for collards, peas, okra, fried chicken, barbecue pork, and fatback.

They found a small waiting room on the third floor with folding chairs and a card table. Lester bought two cups of stale, thick coffee from a machine and stirred the powdered cream with his finger. He listened intently as Carl Lee detailed the rape, the arrests, and the hearing. Lester found some napkins and diagrammed the courthouse and the jail. It had been four years since his murder trial, and he had trouble with the drawings. He had spent only a week in jail, prior to posting bond, and had not visited the place since his acquittal. In fact, he had left for Chicago shortly after his trial. The victim had relatives.

They made plans and discarded them, plotting well past midnight.

At noon Thursday Tonya was removed from intensive care and placed in a private room. She was listed as stable. The doctors relaxed, and her family brought candy, toys, and flowers. With two broken jaws and a mouthful of wire, she could only stare at the candy. Her brothers ate most of it. They clung to her bed and held her hand, as if to protect and reassure. The room stayed full of friends and strangers, all patting her gently and saying how sweet she was, all treating her as someone special, someone who had been through this horrible thing. The crowd moved in shifts, from the hall into her room, and back into the hall, where the nurses watched carefully.

The wounds hurt, and at times she cried. Every hour the nurses cleared a path through the visitors and found the patient for a dose of painkiller.

That night in her room, the crowd hushed as the Memphis station talked about the rape. The television showed pictures of the two white men, but she couldn't see very well.

The Ford County Courthouse opened at 8:00 A.M. and closed at 5:00 P.M. every day except Friday, when it closed at four-thirty. At four-thirty on Friday Carl Lee was hiding in a first-floor restroom when they locked the courthouse. He sat on a toilet and listened quietly for an hour. No janitors. No one. Silence. He walked through the wide, semidark hall to the rear doors, and peeked through the window. No one in sight. He listened for a while. The courthouse was deserted. He turned and looked down the long hall, through the rotunda and through the front doors, two hundred feet away.

He studied the building. The two sets of rear doors opened to the inside into a large, rectangular entrance area. To the far right was a set of stairs, and to the left was an identical stairway. The open area narrowed and led into the hall. Carl Lee pretended to be on trial. He grabbed his hands behind him, and touched his back to the rear door. He walked to his right thirty feet to the stairs; up the stairs, ten steps, then a small landing, then a ninety-degree turn to the left, just like Lester said; then, ten more steps to the holding room. It was a small room, fifteen by fifteen, with nothing but a window and two doors. One door he opened, and walked into the huge courtroom in front of the rows of padded pews. He walked to the aisle and sat in the front row. Surveying the room, he noticed in front of him the railing, or bar, as Lester called it, which separated the general public from the area where the judge, jury, witnesses, lawyers, defendants, and clerks sat and worked.

He walked down the aisle to the rear doors and examined the courtroom in detail. It looked much different from Wednesday. Back down the aisle, he returned to the holding room and tried the other door, which led to the area behind the bar where the trial took place. He sat at the long table where Lester and Cobb and Willard had sat. To the right was another long table where the prosecutors sat. Behind the tables was a row of wooden chairs, then the bar with swinging gates on both ends. The judge sat high and lordly behind the elevated bench, his back to the wall under the faded portrait of Jefferson Davis, frowning down on everyone in the room. The jury box was against the wall to Carl Lee's right, to the judge's left, under the yellow portraits of other forgotten Confederate heroes. The witness stand was next to the bench, but lower, of course, and in front of the jury. To Carl Lee's left, opposite the jury box, was a long, enclosed workbench covered with large red docket books. Clerks and lawyers usually milled around behind it during a trial. Behind the workbench, through the wall, was the holding room.

Carl Lee stood, still as though handcuffed, and walked slowly through the small swinging gate in the bar, and was led through the first door into the holding room; then down the steps, ten of them, through the narrow, shadowy stairway; then he stopped. From the landing halfway down the steps, he could see the rear doors of the courthouse and most of the entrance area between the doors and the hall. At the foot of the stairs, to the right, was a door that he opened and found a crowded, junky janitor's closet. He closed the door and explored the small room. It turned and ran under the stairway. It was dark, dusty, crowded with brooms and buckets and seldom used. He opened the door slightly and looked up the stairs.

For another hour he roamed the courthouse. The other rear stairway led to another holding room just behind the jury box. One door went to the courtroom, the other to the jury room. The stairs continued to the third floor, where he found the county law library and two witness rooms, just as Lester said.

Up and down, up and down, he traced and retraced the movements to be made by the men who raped his daughter.

He sat in the judge's chair and surveyed his domain. He sat in the jury box and rocked in one of the comfortable chairs. He sat in the witness chair and blew into the microphone. It was finally dark at seven when Carl Lee raised a window in the restroom next to the janitor's closet, and slid quietly through the bushes and into the darkness.

'Who would you report it to?' Carla asked as she closed the fourteen-inch pizza box and poured some more lemonade.

Jake rocked slightly in the wicker swing on the front porch and watched Hanna skip rope on the sidewalk next to the street.

'Are you there?' she asked.

'No.'

'Who would you report it to?'

'I don't plan to report it,' he said.

'I think you should.'

'I think I shouldn't.'

'Why not?'

His rocking gained speed and he sipped the lemonade. He spoke slowly. 'First of all, I don't know for sure that a crime is being planned. He said some things any father would say, and I'm sure he's having thoughts any father would have. But as far as actually planning a crime, I don't think so. Secondly, what he said to me was said in confidence, just as if he was a client. In fact, he probably thinks of me as his lawyer.'

'But even if you're his lawyer, and you know he's planning a crime, you have to report it, don't you?'

'Yes. If I'm certain of his plans. But I'm not.'

She was not satisfied. 'I think you should report it.'

Jake did not respond. It wouldn't matter. He ate his last bite of crust and tried to ignore her.

'You want Carl Lee to do it, don't you?'

'Do what?'

'Kill those boys.'

'No, I don't.' He was not convincing. 'But if he did, I wouldn't blame him because I'd do the same thing.'

'Don't start that again.'

'I'm serious and you know it. I'd do it.'

'Jake, you couldn't kill a man.'

'Okay. Whatever. I'm not going to argue. We've been through it before.'

Carla yelled at Hanna to move away from the street. She sat next to him in the swing and rattled her ice cubes. 'Would you represent him?'

'I hope so.'

'Would the jury convict him?'

'Would you?'

'I don't know.'

'Well, think of Hanna. Just look at that sweet little innocent child out there skipping rope. You're a mother. Now think of the little Hailey girl, lying there, beaten, bloody, begging for her momma and daddy—'

'Shut up, Jake!'

He smiled. 'Answer the question. You're on the jury. Would you vote to convict the father?'

She placed her glass on the windowsill and suddenly became interested in her cuticles. Jake smelled victory.

'Come on. You're on the jury. Conviction or acquittal?'

'I'm always on the jury around here. Either that or I'm being cross-examined.'

'Convict or acquit?'

She glared at him. 'It would be hard to convict.'

He grinned and rested his case.

'But I don't see how he could kill them if they're in jail.'

'Easy. They're not always in jail. They go to court and they're transported to and from.

Remember Oswald and Jack Ruby. Plus, they get out if they can make bail.'

'When can they do that?'

'Bonds will be set Monday. If they bond out, they're loose.'

'And if they can't?'

'They remain in jail until trial.'

'When is the trial?'

'Probably late summer.'

'I think you should report it.'

Jake bolted from the swing and went to play with Hanna.

Chapter 6

K. T. Bruster, or Cat Bruster, as he was known, was, to his knowledge, the only one-eyed black millionaire in Memphis. He owned a string of black topless joints in town, all of which he operated legally. He owned blocks of rental property, which he operated legally, and he owned two churches in south Memphis, which were also operated legally. He was a benefactor for numerous black causes, a friend of the politicians, and a hero to his people.

It was important for Cat to be popular in the community because he would be indicted again and tried again, and in all likelihood acquitted again by his peers, half of whom were black. The authorities had found it impossible to convict Cat of killing people and of selling such things as women, cocaine, stolen goods, credit cards, food stamps, untaxed liquor, guns, and light artillery.

He had one eye with him. The other one was somewhere in a rice paddy in Vietnam. He lost it the same day in 1971 that his buddy Carl Lee

Hailey was hit in the leg. Carl Lee carried him for two hours before they found help. After the war he returned to Memphis and brought with him two pounds of hashish. The proceeds went to buy a small saloon on South Main, and he almost starved before he won a whore in a poker game with a pimp. He promised her she could quit whoring if she would take off her clothes and dance on his tables. Overnight he had more business than he could seat, so he bought another bar, and brought in more dancers. He found his niche in the market, and within two years he was a very wealthy man.

His office was above one of his clubs just off South Main between Vance and Beale, in the roughest part of Memphis. The sign above the sidewalk advertised Bud and breasts, but much more was for sale behind the black windows.

Carl Lee and Lester found the lounge – Brown Sugar – around noon, Saturday. They sat at the bar, ordered Bud, and watched the breasts.

'Is Cat in?' Carl Lee asked the bartender when he walked behind them. He grunted and returned to the sink, where he continued his beer mug washing. Carl Lee glanced at him between sips and dance routines.

'Another beer!' Lester said loudly without taking his eyes off the dancers.

'Cat Bruster here?' Carl Lee asked firmly when the bartender brought the beer.

'Who wants to know?'

'I do.'

'So.'

'So me and Cat are good friends. Fought together in 'Nam.'

'Name?'

'Hailey. Carl Lee Hailey. From Mississippi.'

The bartender disappeared, and a minute later emerged from between two mirrors behind the liquor. He motioned for the Haileys, who followed him through a small door, past the restrooms and through a locked door up the stairs. The office was dark and gaudy. The carpet on the floor was gold, on the walls, red, on the ceiling, green. A green shag ceiling. Thin steel bars covered the two blackened windows, and for good measure a set of heavy, dusty, burgundy drapes hung from ceiling to floor to catch and smother any sunlight robust enough to penetrate the painted glass. A small, ineffective chrome chandelier with mirror panes rotated slowly in the center of the room, barely above their heads.

Two mammoth bodyguards in matching three-piece black suits dismissed the bartender and seated Lester and Carl Lee, and stood behind them.

The brothers admired the furnishings. 'Nice, ain't it?' Lester said. B.B. King mourned softly on a hidden stereo.

Suddenly, Cat entered from a hidden door behind the marble and glass desk. He lunged at Carl Lee. 'My man! My man! Carl Lee Hailey!' He shouted and grabbed Carl Lee. 'So good to see you, Carl Lee! So good to see you!'

Carl Lee stood and they bearhugged. 'How are you, my man?' Cat demanded.

'Doin' fine, Cat, just fine. And you?'

'Great! Great! Who's this?' He turned to Lester and threw a hand in his chest. Lester shook it violently.

'This here's my brother, Lester,' Carl Lee said. 'He's from Chicago.'

'Glad to know you, Lester. Me and the big man here are mighty tight. Mighty tight.'

'He's told me all about you,' Lester said. Cat admired Carl Lee. 'My, my, Carl Lee. You lookin' good. How's the leg?'

'It's fine, Cat. Tightens up sometimes when it rains, but it's fine.'

'We mighty tight, ain't we?'

Carl Lee nodded and smiled. Cat released him. 'You fellas want a drink?'

'No thanks,' said Carl Lee.

'I'll take a beer,' said Lester. Cat snapped his fingers and a bodyguard disappeared. Carl Lee fell into his chair and Cat sat on the edge of his desk, his feet dangling and swinging like a kid on a pier. He grinned at Carl Lee, who squirmed under all the admiration.

'Why don't you move to Memphis and go to work for me?' Cat said. Carl Lee knew it was coming. Cat had been offering him jobs for ten years.

'No thanks, Cat. I'm happy.'

'And I'm happy for you. What's on your mind?'

Carl Lee opened his mouth, hesitated, crossed

his legs and frowned. He nodded, and said, 'Need a favor, Cat. Just a small favor.'

Cat spread his arms. 'Anything, big man, anything you want.'

'You remember them M-16's we used in 'Nam? I need one of them. As quick as possible.'

Cat recoiled his arms and folded them across his chest. He studied his friend. 'That's a bad gun. What kinda squirrels you huntin' down there?'

'It ain't for squirrels.'

Cat analyzed them both. He knew better than to ask why. It was serious, or Carl Lee wouldn't be there. 'Semi?'

'Nope. The real thing.'

'You talkin' some cash.'

'How much?'

'It's illegal as hell, you know?'

'If I could buy it at Scars I wouldn't be here.'

Cat grinned again. 'When do you need it?'

'Today.'

The beer arrived and was served to Lester. Cat moved behind his desk, to his orange vinyl captain's chair. 'Thousand bucks.'

'I got it.'

Cat was mildly surprised, but didn't show it. Where did this simple small-town Mississippi nigger find a thousand dollars? Must have borrowed it from his brother.

'Thousand for anyone else, but not for you, big man.'

'How much?'

83

'Nothin', Carl Lee, nothin'. I owe you some-thin' worth much more than money.'

'I'll be glad to pay for it.'

'Nope. I won't hear it. The gun's yours.'

'That's mighty kind, Cat.'

'I'd give you fifty of them.'

'Just need one. When can I get it?'

'Lemme check.' Cat phoned someone and mumbled a few sentences into the receiver. The orders given, he hung up and explained it would take about an hour.

'We can wait,' Carl Lee said.

Cat removed the patch from his left eye and wiped the empty socket with a handkerchief. 'I gotta better idea.' He snapped at the bodyguards. 'Get my car. We'll drive over and pick it up.'

They followed Cat through a secret door and down a hall. 'I live here, you know.' He pointed. 'Through that door is my pad. Usually keep some naked women around.'

'I'd like to see it.' Lester volunteered.

'That's okay,' said Carl Lee.

Farther down the hall Cat pointed to a thick, black, shiny iron door at the end of a short hallway. He stopped as if to admire it. 'That's where I keep my cash. Post a guard in there around the clock.'

'How much?' Lester asked with a sip of beer.

Cat glared at him and continued down the hall. Carl Lee frowned at his brother and shook his head. Where the hall ended they climbed a narrow stairway to the fourth floor. It was darker, and somewhere in the darkness Cat found a button on a wall. They waited silently for a few seconds until the wall opened and revealed a bright elevator with red carpet and a NO SMOKING sign. Cat pushed another button.

'You gotta walk up to catch the elevator goin' down,' he said with amusement. 'Security reasons.' They nodded approval and admiration.

It opened in the basement. One of the bodyguards waited by the open door of a clean white stretch limo, and Cat invited his guests in for a ride. They moved slowly past a row of Fleetwoods, several more limos, a Rolls, and an assortment of European luxury cars. 'They're all mine,' he said proudly.

The driver honked and a heavy door rolled up to reveal a one-way side street. 'Drive slow,' Cat yelled to the chauffeur and the bodyguard way up front. 'I wanna show you fellas around some.'

Carl Lee had received the tour a few years earlier during his last visit to Cat. There were rows of beaten and paintless shacks that the great man referred to as rental properties. There were ancient red-bricked warehouses with blackened or boarded windows and no clue as to what was stored inside. There was a church, a prosperous church, and a few blocks away, another one. He owned the preachers too, he said. There were dozens of corner taverns with open doors and groups of young blacks sitting on benches outside drinking quart bottles of Stag beer. He pointed proudly to a burned-out building near Beale and told with great zeal the story of a competitor who had attempted to gain a foothold in the topless business. He had no competitors, he said. And then there were the clubs, places with names like Angels and Cat's House and Black Paradise, places where a man could go for good drink, good food, good music, naked women, and possibly more, he said. The clubs had made him a very rich man. Eight of them in all.

They were shown all eight. Plus what seemed like most of the real estate in south Memphis. At the dead end of a nameless street near the river, the driver turned sharply between two of the red-bricked warehouses and drove through a narrow alley until a gate opened to the right. Past the gate a door opened next to a loading dock and the limo disappeared into the building. It stopped and the bodyguard got out.

'Keep your seats,' Cat said.

The trunk opened, then shut. In less than a minute the limo was again cruising the streets of Memphis.

'How 'bout lunch?' Cat asked. Before they answered he yelled at the driver, 'Black Paradise. Call and tell them I'm comin' for lunch.

'Got the best prime rib in Memphis, right here in one of my clubs. Course you won't read about it in the Sunday paper. I've been shunned by the critics. Can you imagine?'

'Sounds like discrimination,' Lester said.

'Yeah, I'm sure it is. But I don't use that until I'm indicted.'

'We ain't read about you lately, Cat,' Carl Lee said.

'It's been three years since my last trial. Tax evasion. Feds spent three weeks puttin' on proof, and the jury stayed out twenty-seven minutes and returned with the two most precious words in the Afro-English language – "Not guilty."'

'I've heard them myself,' Lester said.

A doorman waited under the canopy at the club, and a set of matching bodyguards, different bodyguards, escorted the great one and his guests to a private booth away from the dance floor. Drinks and food were served by a squad of waiters. Lester switched to Scotch and was drunk when the prime rib arrived. Carl Lee drank iced tea and swapped war stories with Cat.

When the food was gone, a bodyguard approached and whispered to Cat. He grinned and looked at Carl Lee. 'Y'all in the red Eldorado with Illinois plates?'

'Yeah. But we left it at the other place.'

'It's parked outside . . . in the trunk.'

'What?' said Lester. 'How—'

Cat roared and slapped him on the back. 'Don't ask, my man, don't ask. It's all taken care of, my man. Cat can do anything.'

As usual, Jake worked Saturday morning, after breakfast at the Coffee Shop. He enjoyed the tranquility of his office on Saturday – no phones, no Ethel. He locked the office, ignored the phone, and avoided clients. He organized files, read recent decisions from the Supreme Court and planned strategy if a trial was approaching. His best thoughts and ideas came during quiet Saturday mornings.

At eleven he phoned the jail. 'Sheriff in?' he asked the dispatcher.

'Lemme check,' came the reply.

Moments passed before the sheriff answered. 'Sheriff Walls,' he announced.

'Ozzie, Jake Brigance. How are you?'

'Fine, Jake. You?'

'Fine. Will you be there for a while?'

'Coupla hours. What's up?'

'Not much. Just need to talk for a minute. I'll be there in thirty minutes.'

'I'll be waitin'.'

Jake and the sheriff had a mutual like and respect for each other. Jake had roughed him up a few times during cross-examinations, but Ozzie considered it business and nothing personal. Jake campaigned for Ozzie, and Lucien financed the campaigns, so Ozzie didn't mind a few sarcastic and pointed questions during trial. He liked to watch Jake at trial. And he liked to kid him about *the game*. In 1969, when Jake was a sophomore quarterback at Karaway, Ozzie was a senior all-conference, all-state tackle at Clanton. The two rivals, both undefeated, met in the final game at Clanton for the conference championship. For four long quarters Ozzie terrorized the Karaway offense, which was much smaller and led by a gutsy but battered sophomore quarterback. Late in the fourth quarter, leading 44–0, Ozzie broke Jake's leg on a blitz.

For years now he had threatened to break the other one. He always accused Jake of limping and asked about the leg.

'What's on your mind, buddy?' Ozzie asked as they sat in his small office.

'Carl Lee. I'm a little worried about him.'

'What way?'

'Look, Ozzie, whatever we say here is said in confidence. I don't want anyone to know about this conversation.'

'You sound serious, Jake.'

'I am serious. I talked to Carl Lee Wednesday after the hearing. He's out of his mind, and I understand that. I would be too. He was talking about killing the boys, and he sounded serious. I just think you ought to know.'

'They're safe, Jake. He couldn't get to them if he wanted to. We've had some phone calls, anonymous of course, with all kinds of threats. Black folks are bad upset. But the boys're safe. They're in a cell by themselves, and we're real careful.'

'That's good. I haven't been hired by Carl Lee, but I've represented all the Haileys at one time or another and I'm sure he considers me to be his lawyer, for whatever reason. I feel a responsibility to let you know.'

'I'm not worried, Jake.'

'Good. Let me ask you something. I've got a daughter, and you've got a daughter, right?'

'Got two of them.'

'What's Carl Lee thinking? I mean, as a black father?'

'Same thing you'd be thinkin'.'

'And what's that?'

Ozzie reared back in his chair and crossed his arms. He thought for a moment. 'He's wonderin' if she's okay, physically, I mean. Is she gonna live, and if she does, how bad is she hurt. Can she ever have kids? Then he's wonderin' if she's okay mentally and emotionally, and how will this affect her for the rest of her life. Thirdly, he wants to kill the bastards.'

'Would you?'

'It's easy to say I would, but a man don't know what he'd do. I think my kids need me at home a whole lot more than Parchman needs me. What would you be thinkin', Jake?'

'About the same, I guess. I don't know what I'd do. Probably go crazy.' He paused and stared at the desk. 'But I might seriously plan to kill whoever did it. It'd be mighty hard to lie down at night knowing he was still alive.'

'What would a jury do?'

'Depends on who's on the jury. You pick the right jury and you walk. If the D.A. picks the right jury you get the gas. It depends strictly on the jury, and in this county you can pick the right folks. People are tired of raping and robbing and killing. I know white folks are.'

'Everybody is.'

'My point is that there'd be a lot of sympathy for a father who took matters into his own hands. People don't trust our judicial system. I think I could at least hang a jury. Just convince one or two that the bastard needed to die.'

'Like Monroe Bowie.'

'Exactly. Just like Monroe Bowie. He was a sorry nigger who needed killing and Lester took a walk. By the way, Ozzie, why do you suppose Lester drove from Chicago?'

'He's pretty close to his brother. We're watchin' him too.'

The conversation changed and Ozzie finally asked about the leg. They shook hands and Jake left. He drove straight home, where Carla was waiting with her list. She didn't mind the Saturdays at the office as long as he was home by noon and pretty much followed orders thereafter.

On Sunday afternoon a crowd gathered at the hospital and followed the little Hailey girl's wheel-chair as it was pushed by her father down the hall, through the doors, and into the parking lot, where he gently raised her and sat her in the front seat. As she sat between her parents, with her three brothers in the back seat, he drove away, followed by a procession of friends and relatives and strangers. The caravan moved slowly, deliberately out of town and into the country.

She sat up in the front seat like a big girl. Her father was silent, her mother tearful, and her brothers mute and rigid.

Another throng waited at the house and rushed to the porch as the cars moved up the driveway and parked on the grass on the long front yard. The crowd hushed as he carried her up the steps, through the door, and laid her on the couch. She was glad to be home, but tired of the spectators. Her mother held her feet as cousins, uncles, aunts, neighbors, and everybody walked to her and touched her and smiled, some through tears, and said nothing. Her daddy went outside and talked to Uncle Lester and the men. Her brothers were in the kitchen with the crowd devouring the pile of food.

Chapter 7

Rocky Childers had been the prosecutor for Ford County for more years than he cared to remember. The job paid fifteen thousand a year and required most of his time. It also destroyed any practice he hoped to build. At forty-two he was washed up as a lawyer, stuck in a dead-end part-time, full-time job, elected permanently every four years. Thankfully, he had a wife with a good job so they could drive new Buicks and afford the country club dues and in general put on the necessary airs of educated white people in Ford County. At a younger age he had political ambitions, but the voters dissuaded him, and he was malcontent to exhaust his career prosecuting drunks, shoplifters, and juvenile delinquents, and being abused by Judge Bullard, whom he despised. Excitement crept up occasionally when people like Cobb and Willard screwed up, and Rocky, by statutory authority, handled the preliminary and other hearings before the cases were sent to the grand jury and then to Circuit Court, and then to the real prosecutor, the big prosecutor, the district attorney, Mr Rufus Buckley, from Polk County. It was Buckley who had disposed of Rocky's political career.

Normally, a bail hearing was no big affair for Childers, but this was a bit different. Since Wednesday he had received dozens of phone calls from blacks, all registered voters or claiming to be, who were very concerned about Cobb and Willard being released from jail. They wanted the boys locked up, just like the black ones who got in trouble and could not make bail before trial. Childers promised his best, but explained the bonds would be set by County Judge Percy Bullard, whose number was also in the phone book. On Benington Street. They promised to be in court Monday to watch him and Bullard.

At twelve-thirty Monday, Childers was summoned to the judge's chambers, where the sheriff and Bullard were waiting. The judge was so nervous he could not sit.

'How much bond do you want?' he snapped at Childers.

'I dunno, Judge. I haven't thought much about it.'

'Don't you think it's about time you thought about it?' He paced rapidly back and forth behind his desk, then to the window, then back to his desk. Ozzie was amused and silent.

'Not really,' Childers answered softly. 'It's your decision. You're the judge.'

'Thanks! Thanks! Thanks! How much will you ask for?'

'I always ask for more than I expect,' replied Childers coolly, thoroughly enjoying the judge's neurosis.

'How much is that?'

'I dunno. I hadn't thought much about it.'

Bullard's neck turned dark red and he glared at Ozzie. 'Whatta you think, Sheriff?'

'Well,' Ozzie drawled, 'I would suggest pretty stiff bonds. These boys need to be in jail for their own safety. Black folk are restless out there. They might get hurt if they bond out. Better go high.'

'How much money they got?'

'Willard's broke. Can't tell about Cobb. Drug money's hard to trace. He might find twenty, thirty thousand. I hear he's hired some big-shot Memphis lawyer.Supposed to be here today. He must have some money.'

'Damn, why don't I know these things. Who'd he hire?'

'Bernard. Peter K. Bernard,' answered Childers. 'He called me this morning.'

'Never heard of him,' retorted Bullard with an air of superiority, as though he memorized some kind of judicial rap sheet on all lawyers.

Bullard studied the trees outside the window as the sheriff and prosecutor exchanged winks. The bonds would be exorbitant, as always. The bail bondsmen loved Bullard for his outrageous bonds. They watched with delight as desperate families scraped and mortgaged to collect the ten percent premiums they charged to write the bonds. Bullard would be high, and he didn't care. It was politically safe to set them high and keep the criminals in jail. The blacks would appreciate it and that was important even if the county was seventy-four percent white. He owed the blacks a few favors.

'Let's go a hundred thousand on Willard and two hundred on Cobb. That oughtta satisfy them.'

'Satisfy who?' asked Ozzie.

'Er, uh, the people, the people out there. Sound okay to you?'

'Fine with me,' said Childers. 'But what about the hearing?' he asked with a grin.

'We'll give them a hearing, a fair hearing, then I'll set the bonds at a hundred and two hundred.'

'And I suppose you want me to ask for three hundred apiece so you can look fair?' asked Childers.

'I don't care what you ask for!' yelled the judge.

'Sounds fair to me,' said Ozzie as he headed for the door. 'Will you call me to testify?' he asked Childers.

'Naw, we don't need you. I don't guess the State will call anybody since we're having such a fair hearing.'

They left the chambers and Bullard stewed. He locked the door behind them and pulled a half pint of vodka from his briefcase, and gulped it furiously. Mr Pate waited outside the door. Five minutes later Bullard barged into the packed courtroom.

'All rise for the court!' Mr Pate shouted.

'Be seated!' screamed the judge before anyone could stand. 'Where are the defendants? Where?'

96

Cobb and Willard were escorted from the holding room and seated at the defense table. Cobb's new lawyer smiled at his client as the handcuffs were removed. Willard's lawyer, Tyndale, the public defender, ignored him.

The same crowd of blacks had returned from last Wednesday, and had brought some friends. They closely followed the movements of the two white boys. Lester saw them for the first time. Carl Lee was not in the courtroom.

From the bench Bullard counted deputies – nine in all. That had to be a record. Then he counted blacks – hundreds of them all bunched together, all glaring at the two rapists, who sat at the same table between their lawyers. The vodka felt good. He took a sip of what appeared to be ice water from a Styrofoam cup and managed a slight grin. It burned slowly downward and his cheeks flushed. What he ought to do was order the deputies out of the courtroom and throw Cobb and Willard to the niggers. That would be fun to watch, and justice would be served. He could just see the fat nigger women stomping up and down while their men carved on the boys with switchblades and machetes. Then, when they were finished, they would collect themselves and all march quietly from the courtroom. He smiled to himself.

He motioned for Mr Pate, who approached the bench. 'I've got a half pint of ice water in my desk drawer,' he whispered. 'Pour me some in a Styrofoam cup.'

Mr Pate nodded and disappeared.

'This is a bail hearing,' he declared loudly, 'and I don't intend for it to last long. Are the defendants ready?'

'Yes, sir,' said Tyndale.

'Yes, Your Honor,' said Mr Bernard.

'The State ready?'

'Yes, sir,' answered Childers without standing.

'Good. Call your first witness.'

Childers addressed the judge. 'Your Honor, the State will call no witnesses. His Honor is well aware of the charges against these two defendants, since His Honor held the preliminary hearing last Wednesday. It is my understanding the victim is now home, so we do not anticipate further charges. The grand jury will be asked next Monday to indict the two defendants for rape, kidnapping, and aggravated assault. Because of the violent nature of these crimes, because of the age of the victim, and because Mr Cobb is a convicted felon, the State would ask for the maximum bonds, and not a penny less.'

Bullard almost choked on his ice water. What maximum? There's no such thing as a maximum bond.

'What do you suggest, Mr Childers?'

'Half a million apiece!' Childers announced proudly and sat down.

Half a million! Out of the question, thought Bullard. He sipped furiously and glared at the prosecutor. Half a million! Double-crossed in open court. He sent Mr Pate after more ice water.

'The defense may proceed.'

Cobb's new lawyer stood purposefully. He cleared his throat and removed his horn-rimmed, academic, go-to-hell reading glasses. 'May it please the court, Your Honor, my name is Peter K. Bernard. I am from Memphis, and I have been retained by Mr Cobb to represent him—'

'Do you have a license to practice in Mississippi?' interrupted Bullard.

Bernard was caught off-guard. 'Well, uh, not exactly, Your Honor.'

'I see. When you say "not exactly," do you mean something other than no?'

Several lawyers in the jury box snickered. Bullard was famous for this. He hated Memphis lawyers, and required them to associate local counsel before appearing in his court. Years before when he was practicing, a Memphis judge had kicked him out of court because he was not licensed in Tennessee. He had enjoyed revenge since the day he was elected.

'Your Honor, I am not licensed in Mississippi, but I am licensed in Tennessee.'

'I would hope so,' came the retort from the bench. More suppressed laughter from the jury box. 'Are you familiar with our local rules here in Ford County?' His Honor asked.

'Er, uh, yes, sir.'

'Do you have a copy of these rules?'

'Yes, sir.'

'And you read them carefully before you ventured into my courtroom?'

'Uh, yes, sir, most of them.'

'Did you understand Rule 14 when you read it?'

Cobb glanced up suspiciously at his new lawyer.

'Uh, I don't recall that one,' Bernard admitted.

'I didn't think so. Rule 14 requires out-of-state unlicensed attorneys to associate local counsel when appearing in my courtroom.'

'Yes, sir.'

From his looks and mannerisms, Bernard was a polished attorney, at least he was known as such in Memphis. He was, however, in the process of being totally degraded and humbled before a small-town, redneck judge with a quick tongue.

'Yes, sir, what?' snapped Bullard.

'Yes, sir, I think I've heard of that rule.'

'Then where's the local counsel?'

'There is none, but I planned—'

'Then you drove down here from Memphis, carefully read my rules, and deliberately ignored them. Right?'

Bernard lowered his head and stared at a blank yellow legal pad on the table.

Tyndale rose slowly. 'Your Honor, for the record, I show myself as associated counsel for Mr Bernard for purposes of this hearing and for no other purpose.'

Bullard smiled. Slick move, Tyndale, slick move. The ice water warmed him and he relaxed. 'Very well. Call your first witness.'

Bernard stood straight again. He cocked his head. 'Your Honor, on behalf of Mr Cobb, I would like to call his brother, Mr Fred Cobb, to the stand.'

'Make it brief,' Bullard mumbled.

Cobb's brother was sworn and seated in the witness chair. Bernard assumed the podium and began a long, detailed direct examination. He was well prepared. He elicited proof that Billy Ray Cobb was gainfully employed, owned real estate in Ford County, grew up there, had most of his family there, and friends, and had no reason to leave. A solid citizen with deep roots with much to lose if he fled. A man who could be trusted to show up for court. A man worthy of a low bond.

Bullard sipped, tapped his pen, and searched the black faces in the audience.

Childers had no questions. Bernard called Cobb's mother, Cora, who repeated what her son Fred said about her son Billy Ray. She managed a couple of tears at an awkward moment, and Bullard shook his head.

Tyndale was next. He went through the same motions with Willard's family.

Half a million dollars bond! Anything less would be too little, and the blacks wouldn't like it. The judge had new reason to hate Childers. But he liked the blacks because they elected him last time. He received fifty-one percent of the vote county-wide, but he got all the nigger vote.

'Anything else?' he asked when Tyndale finished.

The three lawyers looked blankly at each other, then at the judge. Bernard stood. 'Your Honor, I would like to summarize my client's position in regard to a reasonable bond—'

'Forget it, pal. I've heard enough from you and your client. Sit down.'

Bullard hesitated, then rapidly announced: 'Bond is hereby set at one hundred thousand for Pete Willard, and two hundred thousand for Billy Ray Cobb. Defendants will remain in the custody of the sheriff until they are able to make bail. Court's adjourned.' He rapped the gavel and disappeared into his chambers, where he finished the half pint and opened another one.

Lester was pleased with the bonds. His had been fifty thousand for the murder of Monroe Bowie. Of course, Bowie was black, and bonds were generally lower for those cases.

The crowd inched toward the rear door, but Lester did not move. He watched closely as the two white boys were handcuffed and taken through the door into the holding room. When they were out of sight, he placed his head in his hands and said a short prayer. Then he listened.

At least ten times a day Jake walked through the French doors and onto the balcony to inspect downtown Clanton. He sometimes puffed a cheap cigar and blew smoke over Washington Street. Even in the summer he left the windows open in the big office. The sounds of the busy small town made good company as he worked quietly. At times he was amazed at the volume of noise generated on the streets around the courthouse, and at other times he walked to the balcony to see why things were so quiet.

Just before 2:00 P.M., Monday, May 20, he walked to the balcony and lit a cigar. A heavy silence engulfed downtown Clanton, Mississippi.

Cobb went first down the stairs, cautiously, with his hands cuffed behind him, then Willard, then Deputy Looney. Ten steps down, then the landing, turn right, then ten steps to the first floor. Three other deputies waited outside by the patrol cars smoking cigarettes and watching reporters.

When Cobb reached the second step from the floor, and Willard was three steps behind, and Looney was one step off the landing, the small, dirty, neglected, unnoticed door to the janitor's closet burst open and Mr Carl Lee Hailey sprung from the darkness with an M-16. At point-blank range he opened fire. The loud, rapid, clapping, popping gunfire shook the courthouse and exploded the silence. The rapists froze, then screamed as they were hit – Cobb first, in the stomach and chest, then Willard in the face, neck, and throat. They twisted vainly up the stairs, hand-cuffed and helpless, stumbling over each other as their skin and blood splashed together.

Looney was hit in the leg but managed to scramble up the stairs into the holding room, where he crouched and listened as Cobb and Willard screamed and moaned and the crazy nigger laughed. Bullets ricocheted between the walls of the narrow stairway, and Looney could see, looking down toward the landing, blood and flesh splashing on the walls and dripping down.

In short, sudden bursts of seven or eight rounds each, the enormous booming sound of the M-16 echoed through the courthouse for an eternity. Through the gunfire and the sounds of the bullets rattling around the walls of the stairway, the high-pitched, shrill, laughing voice of Carl Lee could be plainly heard.

When he stopped, he threw the rifle at the two corpses and ran. Into the restroom, he jammed the door with a chair, crawled out a window into the bushes, then onto the sidewalk. Nonchalantly, he walked to his pickup and drove home.

Lester froze when the shooting started. The gunfire was heard loudly in the courtroom. Willard's mother screamed and Cobb's mother screamed, and the deputies raced into the holding room, but did not venture down the stairs. Lester listened intently for the sounds of handguns, and hearing none, he left the courtroom.

With the first shot, Bullard grabbed the half pint and crawled under his desk while Mr Pate locked the door.

Cobb, or what was left of him, came to rest on Willard. Their blood mixed and puddled on each step, then it overflowed and dripped to the next step, where it puddled before overflowing and dripping to the next. Soon the foot of the stairway was flooded with the mixture.

* * *

Jake sprinted across the street to the rear door of the courthouse. Deputy Prather crouched in front of the door, gun drawn, and cursed the reporters who pressed forward. The other deputies knelt fearfully on the doorsteps next to the patrol cars. Jake ran to the front of the courthouse, where more deputies were guarding the door and evacuating the county employees and courtroom spectators. A mass of bodies poured onto the front steps. Jake fought through the stampede and into the rotunda and found Ozzie directing people and yelling in all directions. He motioned for Jake, and they walked down the hall to the rear doors, where a half dozen deputies stood, guns in hand, gazing silently at the stairway. Jake felt nauseated. Willard had almost made it to the landing. The front of his head was missing, and his brains rolled out like jelly covering his face. Cobb had been able to twist over and absorb the bullets with his back. His face was buried in Willard's stomach, and his feet touched the fourth step from the floor. The blood continued from the lifeless bodies, and it covered completely the bottom six steps. The crimson pool on the floor inched quickly toward the deputies, who slowly backed away. The weapon was between Cobb's legs on the fifth step, and it too was covered with blood.

The group stood silently, mesmerized by the two bodies, which, though dead, continued to spew blood. The thick smell of gunfire hung over the stairway and drifted toward the hall into the rotunda, where the deputies continued to move people toward the front door.

'Jake, you'd better leave,' Ozzie said without looking from the bodies.

'Why?'

'Just leave.'

'Why?'

''Cause we gotta take pictures and collect evidence and stuff, and you don't need to be here.'

'Okay. But you don't interrogate him out of my presence. Understand?'

Ozzie nodded.

The photographs were taken, the mess cleaned, the evidence gathered, the bodies removed, and two hours later Ozzie left town followed by five patrol cars. Hastings drove and led the convoy into the country, toward the lake, past Bates Grocery, onto Craft Road. The Hailey driveway was empty except for Gwen's car, Carl Lee's pickup, and the red Cadillac from Illinois.

Ozzie expected no trouble as the patrol cars parked in a row across the front yard, and the deputies crouched behind the open doors, watching as the sheriff walked alone to the house. He stopped. The front door opened slowly and the Hailey family emerged. Carl Lee walked to the edge of the porch with Tonya in his arms. He looked down at his friend the sheriff, and behind him at the row of cars and deputies. To his right was Gwen, and to his left were his three sons, the smallest one crying softly but the older ones brave and proud. Behind them stood Lester.

The two groups watched each other, each

waiting for the other to say or do something, each wanting to avoid what was about to happen. The only sounds were the soft sniffles of the little girl, her mother, and the youngest boy.

The children had tried to understand. Their daddy had explained to them what he had just done, and why. They understood that, but they could not comprehend why he had to be arrested and taken to jail.

Ozzie kicked at a clod of dirt, occasionally glancing at the family, then at his men.

Finally, he said, 'You better come with me.'

Carl Lee nodded slightly, but did not move. Gwen and the boy cried louder as Lester took the girl from her daddy. Then Carl Lee knelt before the three boys and whispered to them again that he must leave but wouldn't be gone long. He hugged them, and they all cried and clutched him. He turned and kissed his wife, then walked down the steps to the sheriff.

'You wanna handcuff me, Ozzie?'

'Naw, Carl Lee, just get in the car.'

Chapter 8

Moss Junior Tatum, the chief deputy, and Jake talked quietly in Ozzie's office while deputies, reserves, trusties, and other jailhouse regulars gathered in the large, cluttered workroom next to the office and waited anxiously for the arrival of the new prisoner. Two of the deputies peered through the blinds at the reporters and cameramen waiting in the parking lot between the jail and the highway. The television vans were from Memphis, Jackson, and Tupelo, and they were parked in various directions throughout the crowded lot. Moss did not like this, so he walked slowly down the sidewalk and ordered the press to regroup in a certain area, and to move the vans.

'Will you make a statement?' yelled a reporter.

'Yeah, move the vans.'

'Can you say anything about the murders?'

'Yeah, two people got killed.'

'How about the details?'

'Nope. I wasn't there.'

'Do you have a suspect?'

'Yep.'

'Who is it?'

'I'll tell you when the vans are moved.'

The vans were immediately moved and the cameras and microphones were bunched together near the sidewalk. Moss pointed and directed until he was satisfied, then stepped to the crowd. He calmly chewed on a toothpick and stuck both thumbs in the front belt loops, just under the overlapping belly.

'Who did it?'

'Is he under arrest?'

'Was the girl's family involved?'

'Are both dead?'

Moss smiled and shook his head. 'One at a time. Yes we have a suspect. He's under arrest and will be here in a minute. Keep the vans outta the way. That's all I have.' Moss walked back to the jail as they continued to call at him. He ignored them and entered the crowded workroom.

'How's Looney?' he asked.

'Prather's with him at the hospital. He's fine – slight wound to the leg.'

'Yeah, that and a slight heart attack,' Moss said with a smile. The others laughed.

'Here they come!' a trusty shouted, and everyone inside moved to the windows as the line of blue lights rolled slowly into the parking lot. Ozzie drove the first car with Carl Lee seated, unhandcuffed, in the front. Hastings reclined in the back and waved at the cameras as the car passed them and continued through the crowd, past the vans and around to the rear of the jail, where Ozzie parked and the three walked casually inside. Carl Lee was given to the jailer, and Ozzie walked down the hall to his office where Jake was waiting.

'You can see him in a minute, Jake,' he said.

'Thanks. You sure he did it?'

'Yeah, I'm sure.'

'He didn't confess, did he?'

'No, he didn't say much of nothin'. I guess Lester coached him.'

Moss walked in. 'Ozzie, them reporters wanna talk to you. I said you'd be out in a minute.'

'Thanks, Moss,' Ozzie sighed.

'Anybody see it?' Jake asked.

Ozzie wiped his forehead with a red handkerchief. 'Yeah, Looney can I.D. him. You know Murphy, the little crippled man who sweeps floors in the courthouse?'

'Sure. Stutters real bad.'

'He saw the whole thing. He was sittin' on the east stairs, directly across from where it happened. Eatin' his lunch. Scared him so bad he couldn't talk for an hour.' Ozzie paused and eyed Jake. 'Why am I tellin' you all this?'

'What difference does it make? I'll find out sooner or later. Where's my man?'

'Down the hall in the jail. They gotta take his picture and all that. Be 'bout thirty minutes.'

Ozzie left and Jake used his phone to call Carla and remind her to watch the news and record it.

Ozzie faced the microphones and cameras. 'I

ain't answerin' no questions. We have a suspect in custody. Name of Carl Lee Hailey from Ford County. Arrested for two counts of murder.'

'Is he the girl's father?'

'Yes, he is.'

'How do you know he did it?'

'We're very smart.'

'Any eyewitnesses?'

'None that we know of.'

'Has he confessed?'

'No.'

'Where'd you find him?'

'At his house.'

'Was a deputy shot?'

'Yes.'

'How is he?'

'He's fine. He's in the hospital, but he's okay.'

'What's his name?'

'Looney. DeWayne Looney.'

'When's the preliminary hearing?'

'I'm not the judge.'

'Any idea?'

'Maybe tomorrow, maybe Wednesday. No more questions, please. I have no further information to release at this time.'

The jailer took Carl Lee's wallet, money, watch, keys, ring, and pocketknife and listed the items on an inventory form that Carl Lee signed and dated. In a small room next to the jailer's station, he was photographed and fingerprinted, just as Lester said. Ozzie waited outside the door and led him down the hall to a small room where the drunks were taken to blow into the Intoxilyzer. Jake sat at a small table next to the machine. Ozzie excused himself.

The lawyer and client sat across the table and analyzed each other carefully. They grinned admiringly but neither spoke. They had last talked five days before, on Wednesday after the preliminary hearing, the day after the rape.

Carl Lee was not as troubled now. His face was relaxed and his eyes were clear. Finally he said: 'You didn't think I'd do it, Jake.'

'Not really. You did do it?'

'You know I did.'

Jake smiled, nodded, and crossed his arms. 'How do you feel?'

Carl Lee relaxed and sat back in the folding chair. 'Well, I feel better. I don't feel good 'bout the whole thing. I wish it didn't happen. But I wish my girl was okay too, you know. I didn't have nothin' against them boys till they messed with her. Now they got what they started. I feel sorry for their mommas and daddies, if they got daddies, which I doubt.'

'Are you scared?'

'Of what?'

'How about the gas chamber?'

'Naw, Jake, that's why I got you. I don't plan to go to no gas chamber. I saw you get Lester off, now just get me off. You can do it, Jake.'

'It's not quite that easy, Carl Lee.'

'Say what?'

'You just don't shoot a person, or persons, in

cold blood, and then tell the jury they needed killing, and expect to walk out of the courtroom.'

'You did with Lester.'

'But every case is different. And the big difference here is that you killed two white boys and Lester killed a nigger. Big difference.'

'You scared, Jake?'

'Why should I be scared? I'm not facing the gas chamber.'

'You don't sound too confident.'

You big stupid idiot, thought Jake. How could he be confident at a time like this. The bodies were still warm. Sure, he was confident before the killings, but now it was different. His client was facing the gas for a crime which he admits he committed.

'Where'd you get the gun?'

'A friend in Memphis.'

'Okay. Did Lester help?'

'Nope. He knew 'bout what I's gonna do, and he wanted to help, but I wouldn't let him.'

'How's Gwen?'

'She's pretty crazy right now, but Lester's with her. She didn't know a thing about it.'

'The kids?'

'You know how kids are. They don't want their daddy in jail. They upset, but they'll make it. Lester'll take care of them.'

'Is he going back to Chicago?'

'Not for a while. Jake, when do we go to court?'

'The preliminary should be tomorrow or Wednesday, depends on Bullard.'

'Is he the judge?'

'He will be for the preliminary hearing. But he won't hear the trial. That'll be in Circuit Court.'

'Who's the judge there?'

'Omar Noose from Van Buren County; same judge who tried Lester.'

'Good. He's okay, ain't he?'

'Yeah, he's a good judge.'

'When will the trial be?'

'Late summer or early fall. Buckley will push for a quick trial.'

'Who's Buckley?'

'Rufus Buckley. District attorney. Same D.A. who prosecuted Lester. You remember him. Big, loud guy—'

'Yeah, yeah, I remember. Big bad Rufus Buckley. I'd forgot all about him. He's pretty mean, ain't he?'

'He's good, very good. He's corrupt and ambitious, and he'll eat this up because of the publicity.'

'You've beat him, ain't you?'

'Yeah, and he's beat me.'

Jake opened his briefcase and removed a file. Inside was a contract for legal services, which he studied although he had it memorized. His fees were based on the ability to pay, and the blacks generally could pay little unless there was a close and generous relative in St Louis or Chicago with a good-paying job. Those were rare. In Lester's trial there had been a brother in California who worked for the post office but he'd been unwilling or unable to help. There were some sisters scattered around but they had their own problems and had offered only moral support for Lester. Gwen had a big family, and they stayed out of trouble, but they were not prosperous. Carl Lee owned a few acres around his house and had mortgaged it to help Lester pay Jake before.

He had charged Lester five thousand for his murder trial; half was paid before trial and the rest in installments over three years.

Jake hated to discuss fees. It was the most difficult part of practicing law. Clients wanted to know up front, immediately, how much he would cost, and they all reacted differently. Some were shocked, some just swallowed hard, a few had stormed out of his office. Some negotiated, but most paid or promised to pay.

He studied the file and the contract and thought desperately of a fair fee. There were other lawyers out there who would take such a case for almost nothing. Nothing but publicity. He thought about the acreage, and the job at the paper mill, and the family, and finally said, 'My fee is ten thousand.'

Carl Lee was not moved. 'You charged Lester five thousand.'

Jake anticipated this. 'You have three counts; Lester had one.'

'How many times can I go to the gas chamber?'

'Good point. How much can you pay?'

'I can pay a thousand now,' he said proudly. 'And I'll borrow as much as I can on my land and give it all to you.'

Jake thought a minute. 'I've got a better idea. Let's agree on a fee. You pay a thousand now and sign a note for the rest. Borrow on your land and pay against the note.'

'How much you want?' asked Carl Lee.

'Ten thousand.'

'I'll pay five.'

'You can pay more than that.'

'And you can do it for less than ten.'

'Okay, I can do it for nine.'

'Then I can pay six.'

'Eight?'

'Seven.'

'Can we agree on seventy-five hundred?'

'Yeah, I think I can pay that much. Depends on how much they'll loan me on my land. You want me to pay a thousand now and sign a note for sixty-five hundred?'

'That's right.'

'Okay, you got a deal.'

Jake filled in the blanks in the contract and promissory note, and Carl Lee signed both.

'Jake, how much would you charge a man with plenty of money?'

'Fifty thousand.'

'Fifty thousand! You serious?'

'Yep.'

'Man, that's a lotta money. You ever get that much?'

'No, but I haven't seen too many people on trial for murder with that kind of money.'

Carl Lee wanted to know about his bond, the

116

grand jury, the trial, the witnesses, who would be on the jury, when could he get out of jail, could Jake speed up the trial, when could he tell his version, and a thousand other questions. Jake said they would have plenty of time to talk. He promised to call Gwen and his boss at the paper mill.

He left and Carl Lee was placed in his cell, the one next to the cell for state prisoners.

The Saab was blocked by a television van. Jake inquired as to who owned it. Most of the reporters had left but a few loitered about, expecting something. It was almost dark.

'Are you with the sheriff's department?' asked a reporter.

'No, I'm a lawyer,' Jake answered nonchalantly, attempting to seem disinterested.

'Are you Mr Hailey's attorney?'

Jake turned and stared at the reporter as the others listened. 'Matter of fact, I am.'

'Will you answer some questions?'

'You can ask some. I won't promise any answers.'

'Will you step over here?'

Jake walked to the microphones and cameras and tried to act annoyed by the inconvenience. Ozzie and the deputies watched from inside. 'Jake loves cameras,' he said.

'All lawyers do,' added Moss.

'What is your name, sir?'

'Jake Brigance.'

'You're Mr Hailey's attorney.'

'Correct,' Jake answered coolly.

'Mr Hailey is the father of the young girl raped by the two men who were killed today?'

'Correct.'

'Who killed the two men?'

'I don't know.'

'Was it Mr Hailey?'

'I said I don't know.'

'What's your client been charged with?'

'He's been arrested for the murders of Billy Ray Cobb and Pete Willard. He hasn't formally been charged with anything.'

'Do you expect Mr Hailey to be indicted for the two murders?'

'No comment.'

'Why no comment?'

'Have you talked with Mr Hailey?' asked another reporter.

'Yes, just a moment ago.'

'How is he?'

'What do you mean?'

'Well, uh, how is he?'

'You mean, how does he like jail?' Jake asked with a slight grin.

'Uh, yeah.'

'No comment.'

'When will he be in court?'

'Probably tomorrow or Wednesday.'

'Will he plead guilty?'

Jake smiled and replied, 'Of course not.'

After a cold supper, they sat in the swing on the front porch and watched the lawn sprinkler and talked about the case. The killings were big news across the country, and Carla recorded as many television reports as possible. Two of the networks covered the story live through their Memphis affiliates, and the Memphis, Jackson, and Tupelo stations replayed footage of Cobb and Willard being led into the courthouse surrounded by deputies, and seconds later, being carried from the courthouse under white sheets. One of the stations played the actual audio of the gunfire over film of the deputies scrambling for cover.

Jake's interview was too late for the evening news, so he and Carla waited, with the recorder, for the ten o'clock, and there he was, briefcase in hand, looking trim, fit, handsome, and arrogant, and very disgusted with the reporters for the inconvenience. Jake thought he looked great on TV, and he was excited to be there. There had been one other brief appearance, after Lester's acquittal, and the regulars at the Coffee Shop had kidded him for months.

He felt good. He relished the publicity and anticipated much more. He could not think of another case, another set of facts, another setting which could generate as much publicity as the trial of Carl Lee Hailey. And the acquittal of Carl Lee Hailey, for the murder of the two white men who raped his daughter, before an all-white jury in rural Mississippi—

'What're you smiling about?' Carla interrupted.

'Nothing.'

'Sure. You're thinking about the trial, and the

cameras, the reporters, the acquittal, and walking out of the courthouse, arm around Carl Lee, reporters chasing you with the cameras rolling, people slapping you on the back, congratulations everywhere. I know exactly what you're thinking about.'

'Then why'd you ask?'

'To see if you'd admit it.'

'Okay, I admit it. This case could make me famous and make us a million bucks, in the long run.'

'If you win.'

'Yes, if I win.'

'And if you lose?'

'I'll win.'

'But if you don't?'

'Think positive.'

The phone rang and Jake spent ten minutes with the editor, owner, and only reporter of *The Clanton Chronicle*. It rang again, and Jake talked with a reporter with the Memphis morning paper. He hung up and called Lester and Gwen, then the foreman at the paper mill.

At eleven-fifteen it rang again, and Jake received his first death threat, anonymous of course. He was called a nigger-loving son of a bitch, one who would not live if the nigger walked.

Chapter 9

Dell Perkins served more coffee and grits than usual Tuesday morning after the killings. All the regulars and some extras had gathered early to read the papers and talk about the killings, which had taken place less than three hundred feet from the front door of the Coffee Shop. Claude's and the Tea Shoppe were also crowded earlier than usual. Jake's picture made the front page of the Tupelo paper, and the Memphis and Jackson papers had front-page photos of Cobb and Willard, both before the shootings and afterward as the bodies were loaded into the ambulance. There were no pictures of Carl Lee. All three papers ran detailed accounts of the past six days in Clanton.

It was widely accepted around town that Carl Lee had done the killing, but rumors of additional gunmen surfaced and flourished until one table at the Tea Shoppe had a whole band of wild niggers in on the attack. However, the deputies in the Coffee Shop, though not talkative, throttled the gossip and kept it pretty much under control.

Deputy Looney was a regular, and there was concern for his wounds, which appeared to be more serious than originally reported. He remained in the hospital, and he had identified the gunman as Lester Hailey's brother.

Jake entered at six and sat near the front with some farmers. He nodded at Prather and the other deputy, but they pretended not to see him. They'll be okay once Looney is released, he thought. There were some remarks about the front-page picture, but no one questioned Jake about his new client or the killings. He detected a certain coolness among some of the regulars. He ate quickly and left.

At nine Ethel called Jake. Bullard was holding.

'Hello, Judge. How are you?'

'Terrible. You represent Carl Lee Hailey?'

'Yes, sir.'

'When do you want the preliminary?'

'Why are you asking me, Judge?'

'Good question. Look, the funerals are tomorrow morning sometime, and I think it would be best to wait till they bury those bastards, don't you?'

'Yeah, Judge, good idea.'

'How 'bout tomorrow afternoon at two?'

'Fine.'

Bullard hesitated. 'Jake, would you consider waiving the preliminary and letting me send the case straight to the grand jury?'

'Judge, I never waive a preliminary, you know that.'

'Yeah, I know. Just thought I'd ask a favor. I won't hear this trial, and I have no desire to get near it. See you tomorrow.'

An hour later Ethel squawked through the intercom again: 'Mr Brigance, there are some reporters here to see you.'

Jake was ecstatic. 'From where?'

'Memphis and Jackson, I believe.'

'Seat them in the conference room. I'll be down in a minute.'

He straightened his tie and brushed his hair, and checked the street below for television vans. He decided to make them wait, and after a couple of meaningless phone calls he walked down the stairs, ignored Ethel, and entered the conference room. They asked him to sit at one end of the long table, because of the lighting. He declined, told himself he would control things, and sat at one side with his back to the rows of thick, expensive law books.

The microphones were placed before him and the camera lights adjusted, and finally an attractive lady from Memphis with streaks of bright orange across her forehead and under her eyes cleared her throat and asserted herself. 'Mr Brigance, you represent Carl Lee Hailey?'

'Yes, I do.'

'And he's been charged with the murders of Billy Ray Cobb and Pete Willard?'

'That's correct.'

'And Cobb and Willard were charged with raping Mr Hailey's daughter?'

'Yes, that's correct.'

'Does Mr Hailey deny killing Cobb and Willard?'

'He will plead not guilty to the charges.'

'Will he be charged for the shooting of the deputy, Mr Looney?'

'Yes. We anticipate a third charge of aggravated assault against the officer.'

'Do you anticipate a defense of insanity?'

'I'm not willing to discuss the defense at this time because he has not been indicted.'

'Are you saying there's a chance he may not be indicted?'

A fat pitch, one Jake was hoping for. The grand jury would either indict him or not, and the grand jurors would not be selected until Circuit Court convened on Monday, May 27. So the future members of the grand jury were walking the streets of Clanton, tending their shops, working in the factories, cleaning house, reading newspapers, watching TV, and discussing whether or not he should be indicted.

'Yes, I think there's a chance he may not be indicted. It's up to the grand jury, or will be after the preliminary hearing.'

'When's the preliminary hearing?'

'Tomorrow. Two P.M.'

'You're assuming Judge Bullard will bind him over to the grand jury?'

'That's a pretty safe assumption,' replied Jake, knowing Bullard would be thrilled with the answer.

'When will the grand jury meet?'

'A new grand jury will be sworn in Monday morning. It could look at the case by Monday afternoon.'

'When do you anticipate a trial?'

'Assuming he's indicted, the case could be tried in late summer or early fall.'

'Which court?'

'Circuit Court of Ford County.'

'Who would be the judge?'

'Honorable Omar Noose.'

'Where's he from?'

'Chester, Mississippi. Van Buren County.'

'You mean the case will be tried here in Clanton?'

'Yes, unless venue is changed.'

'Will you request a change of venue?'

'Very good question, and one I'm not prepared to answer at this time. It's a bit premature to talk defense strategy.'

'Why would you want a change of venue?'

To find a blacker county, Jake thought. He answered thoughtfully, 'The usual reasons. Pretrial publicity, etc.'

'Who makes the decision to change venue?'

'Judge Noose. The decision is within his sole discretion.'

'Has bond been set?'

'No, and it probably won't be until after the indictments come down. He's entitled to a reasonable bond now, but as a matter of practice in this county bonds are not set in capital murder cases until after the indictment and arraignment in

125

Circuit Court. At that point the bond will be set by Judge Noose.'

'What can you tell us about Mr Hailey?'

Jake relaxed and reflected a minute while the cameras continued. Another fat pitch, with a golden chance to plant some seeds. 'He's thirty-seven years old. Married to the same woman for twenty years. Four kids – three boys and a girl. Nice guy with a clean record. Never been in trouble before. Decorated in Vietnam. Works fifty hours a week at the paper mill in Coleman. Pays his bills and owns a little land. Goes to church every Sunday with his family. Minds his own business and expects to be left alone.'

'Will you allow us to talk to him?'

'Of course not.'

'Wasn't his brother tried for murder several years ago?'

'He was, and he was acquitted.'

'You were his attorney?'

'Yes, I was.'

'You've handled several murder trials in Ford County, haven't you?'

'Three.'

'How many acquittals?'

'All of them,' he answered slowly.

'Doesn't the jury have several options in Mississippi?' asked the lady from Memphis.

'That's right. With a capital murder indictment, the jury at trial can find the defendant guilty of manslaughter, which carries twenty years, or capital murder, which carries life or death as determined by the jury. And the jury can find the defendant not guilty.' Jake smiled at the cameras. 'Again, you're assuming he'll be indicted.'

'How's the Hailey girl?'

'She's at home. Went home Sunday. She's expected to be fine.'

The reporters looked at each other and searched for other questions. Jake knew this was the dangerous part, when they ran out of things to ask and began serving up screwball questions.

He stood and buttoned his coat. 'Look, I appreciate you folks stopping by. I'm usually available, just give a little more notice and I'll be glad to talk to you anytime.'

They thanked him and left.

At ten Wednesday morning, in a no-frills double service at the funeral home, the rednecks buried their dead. The minister, a freshly ordained Pentecostal, struggled desperately for comforting and reassuring thoughts to lay upon the small crowd and over the two closed caskets. The service was brief with few tears.

The pickups and dirty Chevrolets moved slowly behind the single hearse as the procession left town and crawled into the country. They parked behind a small red brick church. The bodies were laid to rest one at a time at opposite ends of the tiny, overgrown cemetery. After a few additional words of inspiration, the crowd dispersed.

Cobb's parents had divorced when he was small, and his father drove from Birmingham for the funeral. After the burial he disappeared. Mrs Cobb lived in a small, clean white frame house near the settlement of Lake Village, ten miles south of Clanton. Her other two sons and their cousins and friends gathered under an oak tree in the backyard while the women made a fuss over Mrs Cobb. The men talked about niggers in general, and chewed Red Man and sipped whiskey, and reminisced about the other days when niggers knew their place. Now they were just pampered and protected by the government and courts. And there was nothing white people could do. One cousin knew a friend or someone who used to be active in the Klan, and he might give him a call. Cobb's grandfather had been in the Klan long before his death, the cousin explained, and when he and Billy Ray were kids the old man would tell stories about hanging niggers in Ford and Tyler counties. What they should do was the same thing the nigger had done, but there were no volunteers. Maybe the Klan would be interested. There was a chapter farther down south near Jackson, near Nettles County, and the cousin was authorized to contact them.

The women prepared lunch. The men ate quietly, then returned to the whiskey under the shade tree. The nigger's hearing at 2:00 P.M. was mentioned, and they loaded up and drove to Clanton.

There was a Clanton before the killings, and there was a Clanton after the killings, and it would be months before the two resembled each other. One tragic, bloody event, the duration of which was less than fifteen seconds, transformed the quiet Southern town of eight thousand into a mecca for journalists, reporters, camera crews, photographers, some from neighboring towns, others from the national news organizations. Cameramen and TV reporters bumped into one another on the sidewalks around the square as they asked the man in the street for the hundredth time how he or she felt about the Hailey event and how he or she would vote if he or she was on the jury. There was no clear verdict from the man on the street. Television vans followed small, marked, imported television cars around the square and down the streets chasing leads, stories, and interviews. Ozzie was a favorite at first. He was interviewed a half dozen times the day after the shooting, then found other business and delegated the interviewing to Moss Junior, who enjoyed bantering with the press. He could answer twenty questions and not divulge one new detail. He also lied a lot, and the ignorant foreigners could not tell his lies from his truth.

'Sir, is there any evidence of additional gunmen?'

'Yes.'

'Really! Who?'

'We have evidence that the shootin's were authorized and financed by an offshoot of the Black Panthers,' Moss Junior replied with a straight face.

Half the reporters would either stutter or stare

blankly while the other half repeated what he said and scribbled furiously.

Bullard refused to leave his office or take calls. He called Jake again and begged him to waive the preliminary. Jake refused. Reporters waited in the lobby of Bullard's office on the first floor of the courthouse, but he was safe with his vodka behind the locked door.

There was a request to film the funeral. The Cobb boys said yes, for a fee, but Mrs Willard vetoed the proposal. The reporters waited outside the funeral home and filmed what they could. Then they followed the procession to the grave sites, and filmed the burials, and followed the mourners to Mrs Cobb's, where Freddie, the oldest, cursed them and made them leave.

The Coffee Shop on Wednesday was silent. The regulars, including Jake, eyed the strangers who had invaded their sanctuary. Most of them had beards, spoke with unusual accents, and did not order grits.

'Aren't you Mr Hailey's attorney?' shouted one from across the room.

Jake worked on his toast and said nothing.

'Aren't you? Sir?'

'What if I am?' shot Jake.

'Will he plead guilty?'

'I'm eating breakfast.'

'Will he?'

'No comment.'

'Why no comment?'

'No comment.'

'But why?'

'I don't comment during breakfast. No comment.'

'May I talk to you later?'

'Yeah, make an appointment. I talk at sixty bucks an hour.'

The regulars hooted, but the strangers were undaunted.

Jake consented to an interview, without charge, with a Memphis paper Wednesday, then barricaded himself in the war room and prepared for the preliminary hearing. At noon he visited his famous client at the jail. Carl Lee was rested and relaxed. From his cell he could see the coming and going of the reporters in the parking lot.

'How's jail?' Jake asked.

'Not that bad. Food's good. I eat with Ozzie in his office.'

'You what!'

'Yep. Play cards too.'

'You're kidding, Carl Lee.'

'Nope. Watch TV too. Saw you on the news last night. You looked real good. I'm gonna make you famous, Jake, ain't I?'

Jake said nothing.

'When do I get on TV? I mean, I did the killin' and you and Ozzie gettin' famous for it.' The client was grinning – the lawyer was not.

'Today, in about an hour.'

'Yeah, I heard we's goin' to court. What for?'

'Preliminary hearing. It's no big deal, at least it's not supposed to be. This one will be different because of the cameras.'

'What do I say?'

'Nothing! You don't say a word to anyone. Not to the judge, the prosecutor, the reporters, anyone. We just listen. We listen to the prosecutor and see what kind of case he's got. They're supposed to have an eyewitness, and he might testify. Ozzie will testify and tell the judge about the gun, the fingerprints, and Looney—'

'How's Looney?'

'Don't know. Worse than they thought.'

'Man, I feel bad 'bout shootin' Looney. I didn't even see the man.'

'Well, they're going to charge you with aggravated assault for shooting Looney. Anyway, the preliminary is just a formality. Its purpose is to allow the judge to determine if there's enough evidence to bind you over to the grand jury. Bullard always does that, so it's just a formality.'

'Then why do it?'

'We could waive it,' replied Jake, thinking of all the cameras he would miss. 'But I don't like to. It's a good chance to see what kind of case the State has.'

'Well, Jake, I'd say they gotta pretty good case, wouldn't you?'

'I would think so. But let's just listen. That's the strategy of a preliminary hearing. Okay?'

'Sounds good to me. You talked to Gwen or Lester today?'

'No, I called them Monday night.'

'They were here yesterday in Ozzie's office. Said they'd be in court today.'

'I think everyone will be in court today.'

Jake left. In the parking lot he brushed by some of the reporters who were awaiting Carl Lee's departure from jail. He had no comments for them and no comments for the reporters waiting outside his office. He was too busy at the moment for questions, but he was very aware of the cameras. At one-thirty he went to the courthouse and hid in the law library on the third floor.

Ozzie and Moss Junior and the deputies watched the parking lot and quietly cursed the mob of reporters and cameramen. It was one forty-five, time to transport the prisoner to court.

'Kinda reminds me of a buncha vultures waitin' for a dead dog beside the highway,' Moss Junior observed as he gazed through the blinds.

'Rudest buncha folks I ever saw,' added Prather. 'Won't take no for an answer. They expect the whole town to cater to them.'

'And that's only half of them – other half's waitin' at the courthouse.'

Ozzie hadn't said much. One newspaper had criticized him for the shooting, implying the security around the courthouse was intentionally relaxed. He was tired of the press. Twice Wednesday he had ordered reporters out of the jail.

'I got an idea,' he said.

'What?' asked Moss Junior.

'Is Curtis Todd still in jail?'

'Yep. Gets out next week.'

'He sorta favors Carl Lee, don't he?'

'Whatta you mean?'

'Well, I mean, he's 'bout as black as Carl Lee, roughly the same height and weight, ain't he?'

'Yeah, well, so what?' asked Prather.

Moss Junior grinned and looked at Ozzie, whose eyes never left the window. 'Ozzie, you wouldn't.'

'What?' asked Prather.

'Let's go. Get Carl Lee and Curtis Todd,' Ozzie ordered. 'Drive my car around back. Bring Todd here for some instructions.'

Ten minutes later the front door of the jail opened and a squad of deputies escorted the prisoner down the sidewalk. Two deputies walked in front, two behind, and one on each side of the man with the thick sunglasses and handcuffs, which were not fastened. As they approached the reporters, the cameras clicked and rolled. The questions flew:

'Sir, will you plead guilty?'

'Sir, will you plead not guilty?'

'Sir, how will you plead?'

'Mr Hailey, will you plead insanity?'

The prisoner smiled and continued the slow walk to the waiting patrol cars. The deputies smiled grimly and ignored the mob. The photographers scrambled about trying to get the perfect shot of the most famous vigilante in the country.

Suddenly, with the nation watching, with deputies all around him, with dozens of reporters recording his every move, the prisoner broke and ran. He jolted, jumped, twisted, and squirmed, running wildly across the parking lot, over a ditch,

134

across the highway, into some trees and out of sight. The reporters shouted and broke ranks and several even chased him for a moment. Curiously, the deputies ran back to the jail and slammed the door, leaving the vultures roaming in circles of disarray. In the woods, the prisoner removed the handcuffs and walked home. Curtis Todd had just been paroled one week early.

Ozzie, Moss Junior, and Carl Lee quickly left through the rear of the jail and drove down a back street to the courthouse, where more deputies waited to escort him into the courthouse. 'How many niggers out there?' Bullard screamed at Mr Pate.

'A ton.'

'Wonderful! A ton of niggers. I guess there's a ton of rednecks too?'

'Quite a few.'

'Is the courtroom full?'

'Packed.'

'My God – it's only a preliminary!' Bullard screamed. He finished a half pint of vodka as Mr Pate handed him another one.

'Take it easy, Judge.'

'Brigance. It's all his fault. He could waive this if he wanted to. I asked him to. Asked him twice. He knows I'll send it to the grand jury. He knows that. All lawyers know that. But now I gotta make all the niggers mad because I won't turn him loose, and I'll make all the rednecks mad because I won't execute him today in the courtroom. I'll get Brigance for this. He's playing for the cameras. I have to get reelected, but he doesn't, does he?'

'No, Judge.'

'How many officers out there?'

'Plenty. Sheriff's called in the reserves. You're safe.'

'How about the press?'

'They're lined up on the front rows.'

'No cameras!'

'No cameras.'

'Is Hailey here?'

'Yes, sir. He's in the courtroom with Brigance. Everbody's ready, just waitin' on you.'

His Honor filled a Styrofoam cup with straight vodka. 'Okay, let's go.'

Just like in the old days before the sixties, the courtroom was neatly segregated with the blacks and whites separated by the center aisle. The officers stood solemnly in the aisle and around the walls of the courtroom. Of particular concern was an assemblage of slightly intoxicated whites sitting together in two rows near the front. A couple were recognized as brothers or cousins of the late Billy Ray Cobb. They were watched closely. The two front rows, the one on the right in front of the blacks and the one on the left in front of the whites, were occupied by two dozen journalists of various sorts. Some took notes while some sketched the defendant, his lawyer, and now finally, the judge.

'They gonna make this nigger a hero,' mumbled one of the rednecks, loud enough for the reporters.

When Bullard assumed the bench, the deputies locked the rear door.

'Call your first witness,' he ordered in the direction of Rocky Childers.

'The State calls Sheriff Ozzie Walls.'

The sheriff was sworn and took the stand. He relaxed and began a long narrative describing the scene of the shooting, the bodies, the wounds, the gun, the fingerprints on the gun and the fingerprints of the defendant. Childers produced an affidavit signed by Officer Looney and witnessed by the sheriff and Moss Junior. It identified the gunman as Carl Lee. Ozzie verified Looney's signature and read the affidavit into the record.

'Sheriff, do you know of any other eyewitness?' asked Childers with no enthusiasm.

'Yes, Murphy, the janitor.'

'What's his first name?'

'Nobody knows. He's just Murphy.'

'Okay. Have you talked to him?'

'No, but my investigator did.'

'Who is your investigator?'

'Officer Rady.'

Rady was sworn and seated in the witness chair. Mr Pate fetched the judge another cup of ice water from chambers. Jake took pages of notes. He would call no witnesses, and he chose not to cross-examine the sheriff. Occasionally, the State's witnesses would get their lies confused in a preliminary, and Jake would ask a few questions on cross-examination to nail down, for the record, the discrepancies. Later at trial when the lying started again, Jake would produce the testimony from the preliminary to further confuse the liars. But not today.

'Sir, have you had an occasion to talk with Murphy?' Childers asked.

'Murphy who?'

'I don't know – just Murphy, the janitor.'

'Oh him. Yes, sir.'

'Good. What did he say?'

'About what?'

Childers hung his head. Rady was new, and had not testified much. Ozzie thought this would be good practice.

'About the shooting! Tell us what he told you about the shooting.'

Jake stood. 'Your Honor. I object. I know hearsay is admissible in a preliminary, but this Murphy fella is available. He works here in the courthouse. Why not let him testify?'

'Because he stutters,' replied Bullard.

'What!'

'He stutters. And I don't want to hear him stutter for the next thirty minutes. Objection overruled. Continue, Mr Childers.'

Jake sat in disbelief. Bullard snickered at Mr Pate, who left for more ice water.

'Now, Mr Rady, what did Murphy tell you about the shooting?'

'Well, he's hard to understand because he was so excited, and when he gets excited he stutters real bad. I mean he stutters anyway, but—'

'Just tell us what he said!' Bullard shouted.

138

'Okay. He said he saw a male black shoot the two white boys and the deputy.'

'Thank you,' said Childers. 'Now where was he when this took place?'

'Who?'

'Murphy!'

'He was sittin' on the stairs directly opposite the stairs where they got shot.'

'And he saw it all?'

'Said he did.'

'Has he identified the gunman?'

'Yes, we showed him photos of ten male blacks, and he identified the defendant, sittin' over there.'

'Good. Thank you. Your Honor, we have nothing further.'

'Any questions, Mr Brigance?' asked the judge.

'No, sir,' Jake said as he stood.

'Any witnesses?'

'No, sir.'

'Any requests, motions, anything?'

'No, sir.'

Jake knew better than to request bail. First, it would do no good. Bullard would not set bail for capital murder. Second, it would make the judge look bad.

'Thank you, Mr Brigance. The court finds sufficient evidence exists to hold this defendant for action by the Ford County grand jury. Mr Hailey shall remain in the custody of the sheriff, without bond. Court's adjourned.'

Carl Lee was quickly handcuffed and escorted from the courtroom. The area around the rear door downstairs was sealed and guarded. The cameras outside caught a glimpse of the defendant between the door and the waiting patrol car. He was in jail before the spectators cleared the courtroom.

The deputies directed the whites on one side to leave first, followed by the blacks.

The reporters requested some of Jake's time, and they were instructed to meet him in the rotunda in a few minutes. He made them wait by first going to chambers and giving his regards to the judge. Then he walked to the third floor to check on a book. When the courtroom was empty and they had waited long enough, he walked through the rear door, into the rotunda and faced the cameras.

A microphone with red letters on it was thrust into his face. 'Why didn't you request bond?' a reporter demanded.

'That comes later.'

'Will Mr Hailey plead an insanity defense?'

'As I've stated, it's too early to answer that question. We must now wait for the grand jury – he may not be indicted. If he is, we'll start planning his defense.'

'Mr Buckley, the D.A., has stated he expects easy convictions. Any comment?'

'I'm afraid Mr Buckley often speaks when he shouldn't. It's asinine for him to make any comment on this case until it is considered by the grand jury.'

'He also said he would vigorously oppose any request for a change of venue.'

'That request hasn't been made yet. He really doesn't care where the trial is held. He'd try it in the desert as long as the press showed up.'

'Can we assume there are hard feelings between you and the D.A.?'

'If you want to. He's a good prosecutor and a worthy adversary. He just talks when he shouldn't.'

He answered a few other assorted questions and excused himself.

Late Wednesday night the doctors cut below Looney's knee and removed the lower third of his leg. They called Ozzie at the jail, and he told Carl Lee.

Chapter 10

Rufus Buckley scanned the Thursday morning papers and read with great interest the accounts of the preliminary hearing in Ford County. He was delighted to see his name mentioned by the reporters and by Mr Brigance. The disparaging remarks were greatly outweighed by the fact that his name was in print. He didn't like Brigance, but he was glad Jake mentioned his name before the cameras and reporters. For two days the spotlight had been on Brigance and the defendant; it was about time the D.A. was mentioned. Brigance should not criticize anyone for seeking publicity. Lucien Wilbanks wrote the book on manipulating the press both before and during a trial, and he had taught Jake well. But Buckley held no grudge. He was pleased. He relished the thought of a long, nasty trial with his first opportunity at real, meaningful exposure. He looked forward to Monday, the first day of the May term of court in Ford County.

He was forty-one, and when he was first elected

nine years earlier he had been the youngest D.A. in Mississippi. Now he was one year into his third term and his ambitions were calling. It was time to move on to another public office, say, attorney general, or possibly governor. And then to Congress. He had it all planned, but he was not well known outside the Twenty-second Judicial District (Ford, Tyler, Polk, Van Buren, and Milburn counties). He needed to be seen, and heard. He needed publicity. What Rufus needed more than anything else was a big, nasty, controversial, well-publicized conviction in a murder trial.

Ford County was directly north of Smithfield, the county seat of Polk County, where Rufus lived. He had grown up in Tyler County, near the Tennessee line, north of Ford County. He had a good base, politically. He was a good prosecutor. During elections he boasted of a ninety percent conviction rate, and of sending more men to death row than any prosecutor in the state. He was loud, abrasive, sanctimonious. His client was the people of the State of Mississippi, by God, and he took that obligation seriously. The people hated crime, and he hated crime, and together they could eliminate it.

He could talk to a jury; oh, how he could talk to a jury. He could preach, pray, sway, plead, beg. He could inflame a jury to the point it couldn't wait to get back to that jury room and have a prayer meeting, then vote and return with a rope to hang the defendant. He could talk like the blacks and he could talk like the rednecks, and that was enough to satisfy most of the jurors in the Twenty-second. And the juries were good to him in Ford County. He liked Clanton.

When he arrived at his office in the Polk County Courthouse, Rufus was delighted to see a camera crew waiting in his reception room. He was very busy, he explained, looking at his watch, but he might have a minute for a few questions.

He arranged them in his office and sat splendidly in his leather swivel behind the desk. The reporter was from Jackson.

'Mr Buckley, do you have any sympathy for Mr Hailey?'

He smiled seriously, obviously in deep thought. 'Yes, I do. I have sympathy for any parent whose child is raped. I certainly do. But what I cannot condone, and what our system cannot tolerate, is this type of vigilante justice.'

'Are you a parent?'

'I am. I have one small son and two daughters, one the age of the Hailey girl, and I'd be outraged if one of my daughters were raped. But I would hope our judicial system would deal effectively with the rapist. I have that much confidence in the system.'

'So you anticipate a conviction?'

'Certainly. I normally get a conviction when I go after one, and I intend to get a conviction in this case.'

'Will you ask for the death penalty?'

'Yes, it looks like a clear case of premeditated murder. I think the gas chamber would be appropriate.'

'Do you predict a death penalty verdict?'

'Of course. Ford County jurors have always been willing to apply the death penalty when I ask for it and it's appropriate. I get very good juries up there.'

'Mr Brigance, the defendant's attorney, has stated the grand jury may not indict his client.'

Buckley chuckled at this. 'Well, Mr Brigance should not be so foolish. The case will be presented to the grand jury Monday, and we'll have our indictments Monday afternoon. I promise you that. Really, he knows better.'

'You think the case will be tried in Ford County?'

'I don't care where it's tried. I'll get a conviction.'

'Do you anticipate the insanity defense?'

'I anticipate everything. Mr Brigance is a most capable criminal defense attorney. I don't know what ploy he will use, but the State of Mississippi will be ready.'

'What about a plea bargain?'

'I don't much believe in plea negotiating. Neither does Brigance. I wouldn't expect that.'

'He said he's never lost a murder case to you.'

The smile disappeared instantly. He leaned forward on the desk and looked harshly at the reporter. 'True, but I bet he didn't mention a number of armed robberies and grand larcenies, did he? I've won my share. Ninety percent to be exact.'

The camera was turned off and the reporter

thanked him for his time. No problem, said Buckley. Anytime.

Ethel waddled up the stairs and stood before the big desk. 'Mr Brigance, my husband and I received an obscene phone call last night, and I've just taken the second one here at the office. I don't like this.'

He motioned to a chair. 'Sit down, Ethel. What did these people say?'

'They weren't really obscene. They were threatening. They threatened me because I work for you. Said I'd be sorry because I worked for a nigger lover. The ones here threaten to harm you and your family. I'm just scared.'

Jake was worried too, but shrugged it off for Ethel. He had called Ozzie on Wednesday and reported the calls to his house.

'Change your number, Ethel. I'll pay for it.'

'I don't want to change my number. I've had it for seventeen years.'

'Good, then don't. I've had my home number changed, and it's no big deal.'

'Well, I'll not do it.'

'Fine. What else do you want?'

'Well, I don't think you should have taken that case. I—'

'And I don't care what you think! You're not paid to think about my cases. If I want to know what you think, I'll ask. Until I do, keep quiet.'

She huffed and left. Jake called Ozzie again.

An hour later Ethel announced through the

intercom: 'Lucien called this morning. He asked me to copy some recent cases, and he wants you to deliver them this afternoon. Said it had been five weeks since your last visit.'

'Four weeks. Copy the cases, and I'll take them this afternoon.'

Lucien stopped by the office or called once a month. He read cases and kept abreast of current developments in the law. He had little else to do except drink Jack Daniel's and play the stock market, both of which he did recklessly. He was a drunk, and he spent most of his time on the front porch of his big white house on the hill, eight blocks off the square, overlooking Clanton, sipping Jack in the Black and reading cases.

He had deteriorated since the disbarment. A full-time maid doubled as a nurse who served drinks on the porch from noon until midnight. He seldom ate or slept, preferring instead to rock away the hours.

Jake was expected to visit at least once a month. The visits were made out of some sense of duty. Lucien was a bitter, sick old man who cursed lawyers, judges, and especially the State Bar Association. Jake was his only friend, the only audience he could find and keep captive long enough to hear his sermons. Along with the preaching he also freely dispensed unsolicited advice on Jake's cases, a most annoying habit. He knew about the cases, although Jake never knew how Lucien knew so much. He was seldom seen downtown or anywhere in Clanton except at the package store in the black section.

The Saab parked behind the dirty, dented Porsche, and Jake handed the cases to Lucien. There were no hellos or other greetings, just the handing of the copies to Lucien, who said nothing. They sat in the wicker rockers on the long porch and looked out over Clanton. The top floor of the courthouse stood above the buildings and houses and trees around the square.

Finally he offered whiskey, then wine, then beer. Jake declined. Carla frowned on drinking, and Lucien knew it.

'Congratulations.'

'For what?' Jake asked.

'For the Halley case.'

'Why am I to be congratulated?'

'I never had a case that big, and I had some big ones.'

'Big in terms of what?'

'Publicity. Exposure. That's the name of the game for lawyers, Jake. If you're unknown, you starve. When people get in trouble they call a lawyer, and they call someone they've heard of. You must sell yourself to the public, if you're a street lawyer. Of course it's different if you're in a big corporate or insurance firm where you sit on your ass and bill a hundred bucks an hour, ten hours a day, ripping off little people and—'

'Lucien,' Jake interrupted quietly, 'we've talked about this many times. Let's talk about the Hailey case.'

'All right, all right. I'll bet Noose refuses to change venue.'

'Who said I would request it?'

'You're stupid if you don't.'

'Why?'

'Simple statistics! This county is twenty-six percent black. Every other county in the Twenty-second is at least thirty percent black. Van Buren County is forty percent. That means more black jurors, potential jurors. If you get it moved, you have a better chance for blacks in the jury box. If it's tried here, you run the risk of an all-white jury, and believe me, I've seen enough all-white juries in this county. All you need is one black to hang it and get a mistrial.'

'But then it'll be retried.'

'Then hang it again. They'll give up after three trials. A hung jury is the same as a loss on Buckley's scorecard. He'll quit after the third trial.'

'So I simply tell Noose I want the trial moved to a blacker county so I can get a blacker jury.'

'You can if you want to, but I wouldn't. I'd go through the usual crap about pretrial publicity, a biased community, and on and on.'

'And you don't think Noose'll buy it.'

'Naw. This case is too big, and it'll get bigger. The press has intervened and already started the trial. Everyone's heard of it, and not just in Ford County. You couldn't find a person in this state without a preconceived notion of guilt or innocence. So why move it to another county?'

'Then why should I request it?'

'Because when that poor man is convicted, you'll need something to argue on appeal. You can claim he was denied a fair trial because venue was not changed.'

'Thanks for the encouragement. What're the chances of getting it moved to another district, say somewhere in the delta?'

'Forget it. You can request a change of venue, but you cannot request a certain location.'

Jake didn't know that. He usually learned something during these visits. He nodded confidently and studied the old man with the long, dirty gray beard. There had never been a time when he stumped Lucien on a point of criminal law.

'Sallie!' Lucien screamed, throwing his ice cubes into the shrubs.

'Who's Sallie?'

'My maid,' he replied as a tall, attractive black lady opened the screen door and smiled at Jake.

'Yeah, Lucien?' she answered.

'My glass is empty.'

She walked elegantly across the porch and took his glass. She was under thirty, shapely, pretty, and very dark. Jake ordered iced tea.

'Where'd you find her?' he asked.

Lucien stared at the courthouse.

'Where'd you find her?'

'I dunno.'

'How old is she?'

Lucien was silent.

'She live here?'

No response.

'How much do you pay her?'

'Why is it any of your business? More than you pay Ethel. She's a nurse too, you know.'

Sure, Jake thought with a grin. 'I'll bet she does a lot of things.'

'Don't worry about it.'

'I take it you're not thrilled with my chances for an acquittal.'

Lucien reflected a moment. The maid/nurse returned with the whiskey and tea.

'Not really. It will be difficult.'

'Why?'

'Looks like it was premeditated. From what I gather it was well planned. Right?'

'Yes.'

'I'm sure you'll plead insanity.'

'I don't know.'

'You must plead insanity,' Lucien lectured sternly. 'There is no other possible defense. You can't claim it was an accident. You can't say he shot those two boys, handcuffed and unarmed, with a machine gun in self-defense, can you?'

'No.'

'You won't create an alibi and tell the jury he was at home with his family?'

'Of course not.'

'Then what other defense do you have? You must say he was crazy!'

'But, Lucien, he was not insane, and there's no way I can find some bogus psychiatrist to say he was. He planned it meticulously, every detail.'

Lucien smiled and took a drink. 'That's why you're in trouble, my boy.'

Jake sat his tea on the table and rocked slowly. Lucien savored the moment. 'That's why you're in trouble,' he repeated.

'What about the jury? You know they'll be sympathetic.'

'That's exactly why you must plead insanity. You must give the jury a way out. You must show them a way to find him not guilty, if they are so inclined. If they're sympathetic, if they want to acquit, you must provide them with a defense they can use to do it. It makes no difference if they believe the insanity crap. That's not important in the jury room. What's important is that the jury have a legal basis for an acquittal, assuming they want to acquit.'

'Will they want to acquit?'

'Some will, but Buckley will make an awfully strong case of premeditated murder. He's good. He'll take away their sympathy. Hailey'll be just another black on trial for killing a white man when Buckley gets through with him.'

Lucien rattled his ice cubes and stared at the brown liquid. 'And what about the deputy? Assault with intent to kill a peace officer carries life, no parole. Talk your way out of that one.'

'There was no intent.'

'Great. That'll be real convincing when the poor guy hobbles to the witness stand and shows the jury his nub.'

'Nub?'

'Yes. Nub. They cut his leg off last night.'

'Looney!'

'Yes, the one Mr Hailey shot.'

'I thought he was okay.'

'Oh he's fine. Just minus a leg.'

'How'd you find out?'

'I've got sources.'

Jake walked to the edge of the porch and leaned on a column. He felt weak. The confidence was gone, taken away again by Lucien. He was an expert at poking holes in every case Jake tried. It was sport to him, and he was usually right.

'Look, Jake, I don't mean to sound so hopeless. The case can be won – it's a long shot, but it can be won. You can walk him out of there, and you need to believe you can. Just don't get too cocky. You've said enough to the press for a while. Back off, and go to work.'

Lucien walked to the edge of the porch and spat in the shrubs. 'Always keep in mind that Mr Hailey is guilty, guilty as hell. Most criminal defendants are, but especially this one. He took the law into his own hands, and he murdered two people. Planned it all, very carefully. Our legal system does not permit vigilante justice. Now, you can win the case, and if you do, justice will prevail. But if you lose it, justice will also prevail. Kind of a strange case, I guess. I just wish I had it.'

'You serious?'

'Sure I'm serious. It's a trial lawyer's dream. Win it and you're famous. The biggest gun in these parts. It could make you rich.'

'I'll need your help.'

'You've got it. I need something to do.'

★   ★   ★

After dinner, and after Hanna was asleep, Jake told Carla about the calls at the office. They had received a strange call before during one of the other murder trials, but no threats were made, just some groaning and breathing. But these were different. They mentioned Jake's name and his family, and promised revenge if Carl Lee was acquitted.

'Are you worried?' she asked.

'Not really. It's probably just some kids, or some of Cobb's friends. Does it scare you?'

'I would prefer they didn't call.'

'Everybody's getting calls. Ozzie's had hundreds. Bullard, Childers, everybody. I'm not worried about it.'

'What if it becomes more serious?'

'Carla, I would never endanger my family. It's not worth it. I'll withdraw from the case if I think the threats are legitimate. I promise.'

She was not impressed.

Lester peeled off nine one-hundred-dollar bills and laid them majestically on Jake's desk.

'That's only nine hundred,' Jake said. 'Our agreement was a thousand.'

'Gwen needed groceries.'

'You sure Lester didn't need some whiskey?'

'Come on, Jake, you know I wouldn't steal from my own brother.'

'Okay, okay. When's Gwen going to the bank to borrow the rest?'

'I'm goin' right now to see the banker. Atcavage?'

'Yeah, Stan Atcavage, next door at Security Bank. Good friend of mine. He loaned it before on your trial. You got the deed?'

'In my pocket. How much you reckon he'll give us?'

'No idea. Why don't you go find out.'

Lester left, and ten minutes later Atcavage was on the phone.

'Jake, I can't loan the money to these people. What if he's convicted – no offense, I know you're a good lawyer – my divorce, remember – but how's he gonna pay me sitting on death row?'

'Thanks. Look Stan, if he defaults you own ten acres, right?'

'Right, with a shack on it. Ten acres of trees and kudzu plus an old house. Just what my new wife wants. Come on, Jake.'

'It's a nice house, and it's almost paid for.'

'It's a shack, a clean shack. But it's not worth anything, Jake.'

'It's gotta be worth something.'

'Jake, I don't want it. The bank does not want it.'

'You loaned it before.'

'And he wasn't in jail before; his brother was, remember. He was working at the paper mill. Good job, too. Now he's headed for Parchman.'

'Thanks, Stan, for the vote of confidence.'

'Come on, Jake, I've got confidence in your ability, but I can't loan money on it. If anybody can get him off, you can. And I hope you do. But I can't make this loan. The auditors would scream.'

155

Lester tried the Peoples Bank and Ford National, with the same results. They hoped his brother was acquitted, but what if he wasn't.

Wonderful, thought Jake. Nine hundred dollars for a capital murder case.

Chapter 11

Claude had never seen the need for printed menus in his cafe. Years before when he first opened he couldn't afford menus, and now that he could he didn't need them because most folks knew what he served. For breakfast he cooked everything but rice and toast, and the prices varied. For Friday lunch he barbecued pork shoulder and spare ribs, and everybody knew it. He had few white customers during the week, but at noon Friday, every Friday, his small cafe was half white. Claude had known for some time that whites enjoyed barbecue as much as blacks; they just didn't know how to prepare it.

Jake and Atcavage found a small table near the kitchen. Claude himself delivered two plates of ribs and slaw. He leaned toward Jake and said softly, 'Good luck to you. Hope you get him off.'

'Thanks, Claude. I hope you're on the jury.'

Claude laughed and said louder, 'Can I volunteer?'

Jake attacked the ribs and chewed on Atcavage

for not making the loan. The banker was stead-fast, but did offer to lend five thousand if Jake would cosign. That would be unethical, Jake explained.

On the sidewalk a line formed and faces squinted through the painted letters on the front windows. Claude was everywhere, taking orders, giving orders, cooking, counting money, shouting, swearing, greeting customers, and asking them to leave. On Friday, the customers were allotted twenty minutes after the food was served, then Claude asked and sometimes demanded that they pay and leave so he could sell more barbecue.

'Quit talkin' and eat!' he would yell.

'I've got ten more minutes, Claude.'

'You got seven.'

On Wednesday he fried catfish, and allowed thirty minutes because of the bones. The white folks avoided Claude's on Wednesday, and he knew why. It was the grease, a secret recipe grease handed down by his grandmother, he said. It was heavy and sticky and wreaked havoc with the lower intestines of white people. It didn't faze the blacks, who piled in by the carloads every Wednesday.

Two foreigners sat near the cash register and watched Claude fearfully as he directed lunch. Probably reporters, thought Jake. Each time Claude drew nigh and glared, they obediently picked up and gnawed a rib. They had not experienced ribs before, and it was obvious to everyone they were from the North. They had wanted chef salads, but Claude cursed them, and told them to eat barbecue or leave. Then he announced to the crowd these silly fools wanted chef salads.

'Here's your food. Hurry up and eat it,' he had demanded when he served them.

'No steak knives?' one had asked crisply.

Claude rolled his eyes and staggered away mumbling.

One noticed Jake, and, after staring for a few minutes, finally walked over and knelt by the table. 'Aren't you Jake Brigance, Mr Hailey's attorney?'

'Yes, I am. Who are you?'

'I'm Roger McKittrick, with *The New York Times*.'

'Nice to meet you,' Jake said with a smile and a new attitude.

'I'm covering the Hailey case, and I'd like to talk with you sometime. As soon as possible, really.'

'Sure. I'm not too busy this afternoon. It's Friday.'

'I could do it late.'

'How about four?'

'Fine,' said McKittrick, who noticed Claude approaching from the kitchen. 'I'll see you then.'

'Okay, buddy,' Claude yelled at McKittrick. 'Time's up. Get your check and leave.'

Jake and Atcavage finished in fifteen minutes, and waited for the verbal assault from Claude. They licked their fingers and mopped their faces and commented on the tenderness of the ribs.

'This case'll make you famous, won't it?' asked Atcavage.

'I hope. Evidently it won't make any money.'

'Seriously, Jake, won't it help your practice?'

'If I win, I'll have more clients than I can handle. Sure it'll help. I can pick and choose my cases, pick and choose my clients.'

'Financially, what'll it mean?'

'I have no idea. There's no way to predict who or what it might attract. I'll have more cases to choose from, so that means more money. I could quit worrying about the overhead.'

'Surely you don't worry about the overhead.'

'Look, Stan, we're not all filthy rich. A law degree is not worth what it once was – too many of us. Fourteen in this little town. Competition is tough, even in Clanton – not enough good cases and too many lawyers. It's worse in the big towns, and the law schools graduate more and more, many of whom can't find jobs. I get ten kids a year knocking on my door looking for work. A big firm in Memphis laid off some lawyers a few months ago. Can you imagine? Just like a factory, they laid them off. I suppose they went down to the unemployment office and stood in line with the 'dozer operators. Lawyers now, not secretaries or truck drivers, but lawyers.'

'Sorry I asked.'

'Sure I worry about the overhead. It runs me four thousand a month, and I practice alone. That's fifty thousand a year before I clear a dime. Some months are good, others slow. They're all unpredictable. I wouldn't dare estimate what I'll gross next month. That's why this case is so important. There will never be another one like it. It's the biggest. I'll practice the rest of my life and never have another reporter from *The New York Times* stop me in a cafe and ask for an interview. If I win, I'll be the top dog in this part of the state. I can forget about the overhead.'

'And if you lose?'

Jake paused and glanced around for Claude. 'The publicity will be abundant regardless of the outcome. Win or lose, the case will help my practice. But a loss will really hurt. Every lawyer in the county is secretly hoping I blow it. They want him convicted. They're jealous, afraid I might get too big and take away their clients. Lawyers are extremely jealous.'

'You too?'

'Sure. Take the Sullivan firm. I despise every lawyer in that firm, but I'm jealous to an extent. I wish I had some of their clients, some of their retainers, some of their security. They know that every month they'll get a nice check, it's guaranteed almost, and every Christmas they'll get a big bonus. They represent old money, steady money. That would be enjoyable for a change. Me, I represent drunks, thugs, wife beaters, husband beaters, injured people, most of whom have little or no money. And I never know from one month to the next how many of these people will show up at my office.'

'Look, Jake,' Atcavage interrupted. 'I would really like to finish this discussion, but Claude just looked at his watch and then looked at us. I think our twenty minutes are up.'

Jake's check was seventy-one cents more than

Atcavage's, and since both orders were identical, Claude was interrogated. No problem, he explained, Jake got an extra rib.

McKittrick was personable and precise, thorough and pushy. He had arrived in Clanton on Wednesday to investigate and write about what was billed as the most famous murder in the country, at the moment. He talked to Ozzie and Moss Junior, and they suggested he talk to Jake. He talked to Bullard, through the door, and the judge suggested he talk to Jake. He interviewed Gwen and Lester, but was not permitted to meet the girl. He visited with the regulars at the Coffee Shop and the Tea Shoppe, and he visited with the regulars at Huey's and Ann's Lounge. He talked to Willard's ex-wife and mother, but Mrs Cobb was through with reporters. One of Cobb's brothers offered to talk for a fee. McKittrick declined. He drove to the paper mill and talked to the co-workers, and he drove to Smithfield to interview the D.A. He would be in town for a few more days, then return for the trial.

He was from Texas, and retained, when convenient, a slight drawl, which impressed the locals and opened them up. He even said 'you all' and 'y'all' occasionally, and this distinguished him from most of the other reporters who clung to their crisp, precise, modern American pronunciation.

'What's that?' McKittrick pointed to the center of Jake's desk.

'That's a tape recorder,' Jake answered.

McKittrick sat his own recorder on the desk and looked at Jake's. 'May I ask why?'

'You may. It's my office, my interview, and if I want to record it, I will.'

'Are you expecting trouble?'

'I'm trying to prevent it. I hate to be misquoted.'

'I'm not known for misquoting.'

'Good. Then you won't mind if both of us record everything.'

'You don't trust me, do you, Mr Brigance?'

'Hell no. And my name is Jake.'

'Why don't you trust me?'

'Because you're a reporter, you're from a New York paper, you're looking for a sensational story, and if you're true to form, you'll write some well-informed, moralistic piece of trash depicting us all as racist, ignorant rednecks.'

'You're wrong. First of all, I'm from Texas.'

'Your paper is from New York.'

'But I consider myself a Southerner.'

'How long have you been gone?'

'About twenty years.'

Jake smiled and shook his head, as if to say: That's too long.

'And I don't work for a sensational newspaper.'

'We'll see. The trial is several months away. We'll have time to read your stories.'

'Fair enough.'

Jake punched the play button on his tape recorder, and McKittrick did likewise.

'Can Carl Lee Hailey receive a fair trial in Ford County?'

'Why couldn't he?' Jake asked.

'Well, he's black. He killed two white men, and he will be tried by a white jury.'

'You mean he will be tried by a bunch of white racists.'

'No, that's not what I said, nor what I implied. Why do you automatically assume I think you are all a bunch of racists?'

'Because you do. We're stereotyped, and you know it.'

McKittrick shrugged and wrote something on his steno pad. 'Will you answer the question?'

'Yes. He can receive a fair trial in Ford County, if he's tried here.'

'Do you want it tried here?'

'I'm sure we'll try to move it.'

'To where?'

'We won't suggest a place. That's up to the judge.'

'Where did he get the M-16?'

Jake chuckled and stared at the tape recorder. 'I do not know.'

'Would he be indicted if he were white?'

'He's black, and he has not been indicted.'

'But if he were white, would there be an indictment?'

'Yes, in my opinion.'

'Would he be convicted?'

'Would you like a cigar?' Jake opened a desk drawer and found a Roi-Tan. He unwrapped it, then lit it with a butane lighter.

'No thanks.'

'No, he would not be convicted if he were white. In my opinion. Not in Mississippi, not in Texas, not in Wyoming. I'm not sure about New York.'

'Why not?'

'Do you have a daughter?'

'No.'

'Then you wouldn't understand.'

'I think I do. Will Mr Hailey be convicted?'

'Probably.'

'So the system does not work as fairly for blacks?'

'Have you talked with Raymond Hughes?'

'No. Who is he?'

'He ran for sheriff last time, and had the misfortune of making the runoff against Ozzie Walls. He's white. Ozzie, of course, is not. If I'm not mistaken, he got thirty-one percent of the vote. In a county that's seventy-four percent white. Why don't you ask Mr Hughes if the system treats blacks fairly?'

'I was referring to the judicial system.'

'It's the same system. Who do you think sits in the jury box? The same registered voters who elected Ozzie Walls.'

'Well, if a white man would not be convicted, and Mr Hailey will probably be convicted, explain to me how the system treats both fairly.'

'It doesn't.'

'I'm not sure I'm following you.'

'The system reflects society. It's not always fair, but it's as fair as the system in New York, or Massachusetts, or California. It's as fair as biased, emotional humans can make it.'

'And you think Mr Hailey will be treated as fairly here as he would be in New York?'

'I'm saying there's as much racism in New York as in Mississippi. Look at our public schools – they're as desegregated as any.'

'By court order.'

'Sure, but what about the courts in New York? For years you pious bastards pointed your fingers and noses at us down here and demanded that we desegregate. It happened, and it has not been the end of the world. But you've conveniently ignored your own schools and neighborhoods, your own voting irregularities, your own all-white juries and city councils. We were wrong, and we've paid dearly for it. But we learned, and although the change has been slow and painful, at least we're trying. Y'all are still pointing fingers.'

'I didn't intend to refight Gettysburg.'

'I'm sorry. What defense will we use? I do not know at this point. Honestly, it's just too early. He hasn't even been indicted.'

'Of course he will?'

'Of course we don't know yet. More than likely. When will this be printed?'

'Maybe Sunday.'

'Makes no difference. No one here takes your paper. Yes, he will be indicted.'

McKittrick glanced at his watch, and Jake turned off his recorder.

'Look, I'm not a bad guy,' McKittrick said. 'Let's drink a beer sometime and finish this.'

'Off the record, I don't drink. But I accept your invitation.'

The First Presbyterian Church of Clanton was directly across the street from the First United Methodist Church of Clanton, and both churches were within sight of the much larger First Baptist Church. The Baptists had more members and money, but the Presbyterians and Methodists adjourned earlier on Sunday and outraced the Baptists to the restaurants for Sunday dinner. The Baptists would arrive at twelve-thirty and stand in line while the Presbyterians and Methodists ate slowly and waved at them.

Jake was content not to be a Baptist. They were a bit too narrow and strict, and they were forever preaching about Sunday night church, a ritual Jake had always struggled with. Carla was raised as a Baptist, Jake a Methodist, and during the courtship a compromise was negotiated, and they became Presbyterians. They were happy with their church and its activities, and seldom missed.

On Sunday, they sat in their usual pew, with Hanna asleep between them, and ignored the sermon. Jake ignored it by watching the preacher and picturing his confronting Buckley, in court, before twelve good and lawful citizens, as the nation watched and waited, and Carla ignored it by watching the preacher and mentally redecorating the dining room. Jake caught a few inquisitive stares during the worship service, and he figured his fellow church members were somewhat awed to have a

167

celebrity among them. There were some strange faces in the congregation, and they were either long-lost repentant members or reporters. Jake was unsure until one persisted in staring at him – then he knew they were all reporters.

'Enjoyed your sermon, Reverend,' Jake lied as he shook hands with the minister on the steps outside the sanctuary.

'Good to see you, Jake,' replied the reverend. 'We've watched you all week on TV. My kids get excited every time they see you.'

'Thanks. Just pray for us.'

They drove to Karaway for Sunday lunch with Jake's parents. Gene and Eva Brigance lived in the old family house, a sprawling country home on five acres of wooded land in downtown Karaway, three blocks from Main Street and two blocks from the school where Jake and his sister put in twelve years. Both were retired, but young enough to travel the continent in a mobile home each summer. They would leave Monday for Canada and return after Labor Day. Jake was their only son. An older daughter lived in New Orleans.

Sunday lunch on Eva's table was a typical Southern feast of fried meats, fresh garden vegetables – boiled, battered, baked, and raw, homemade rolls and biscuits, two gravies, watermelon, cantaloupe, peach cobbler, lemon pie, and strawberry shortcake. Little of it would be eaten, and the leftovers would be neatly packaged by Eva and Carla and sent to Clanton, where it would last for a week.

'How are your parents, Carla?' Mr Brigance asked as he passed the rolls.

'They're fine. I talked to Mother yesterday.'

'Are they in Knoxville?'

'No, sir. They're already in Wilmington for the summer.'

'Will y'all be going to visit them?' asked Eva as she poured the tea from a one-gallon ceramic pitcher.

Carla glanced at Jake, who was dipping butterbeans onto Hanna's plate. He did not want to discuss Carl Lee Hailey. Every meal since Monday night had centered around the case, and Jake was in no mood to answer the same questions.

'Yes, ma'am. We plan to. It depends on Jake's schedule. It could be a busy summer.'

'So we've heard,' Eva said flatly, slowly as if to remind her son he had not called since the killings.

'Is something wrong with your phone, son?' asked Mr Brigance.

'Yes. We've had the number changed.'

The four adults ate slowly, apprehensively, while Hanna looked at the shortcake.

'Yes, I know. That's what the operator told us. To an unlisted number.'

'Sorry. I've been very busy. It's been hectic.'

'So we've read,' said his father.

Eva stopped eating and cleared her throat. 'Jake, do you really think you can get him off?'

'I'm worried about your family,' said his father. 'It could be a very dangerous case.'

'He shot them in cold blood,' Eva said.

'They raped his daughter, Mother. What would you do if someone raped Hanna?'

'What's rape?' asked Hanna.

'Never mind, dear,' Carla said. 'Could we please change the subject.' She looked firmly at the three Brigances, and they started eating again. The daughter-in-law had spoken, with wisdom, as usual.

Jake smiled at his mother without looking at Mr Brigance. 'I just don't want to talk about the case, Mother. I'm tired of it.'

'I guess we'll have to read about it,' said Mr Brigance.

They talked about Canada.

At about the time the Brigances finished lunch, the sanctuary of the Mt Zion Chapel CME rocked and swayed as the Right Reverend Ollie Agee whipped the devotees into a glorifled frenzy. Deacons danced. Elders chanted. Women fainted. Grown men screamed and raised their arms toward the heavens as the small children looked upward in holy terror. Choir members lurched and lunged and jerked, then broke down and shrieked different stanzas of the same song. The organist played one song, the pianist another, and the choir sang whatever came over it. The reverend hopped around the pulpit in his long white robe with purple trim, yelling, praying, screaming at God, and perspiring.

The bedlam rose and fell, rising it seemed with each new fainting, and falling with fatigue. Through years of experience Agee knew precisely when the fury reached its peak, when the delirium gave way to weariness, and when the flock needed a break. At that precise moment, he jigged to the pulpit and slapped it with the power of God Almighty. Instantly the music died, the convulsions ceased, the fainters awoke, the children stopped crying, and the multitude settled submissively into the pews. It was time for the sermon.

As the reverend was about to preach, the rear doors opened and the Haileys entered the sanctuary. Little Tonya walked by herself, limping, holding her mother's hand. Her brothers marched behind, and Uncle Lester followed. They moved slowly down the aisle and found a seat near the front. The reverend nodded at the organist, who began to play softly, then the choir began to hum and sway. The deacons stood and swayed with the choir. Not to be outdone, the elders stood and began to chant. Then, of all things, Sister Crystal fainted violently. Her fainting was contagious, and the other sisters began dropping like flies. The elders chanted louder than the choir, so the choir got excited. The organist could not be heard, so she increased the volume. The pianist joined in with a clanging rendition of a hymn unlike the hymn being played by the organist. The organist thundered back. Reverend Agee fluttered down from the podium and danced his way toward the Haileys. Everyone followed – the choir, the deacons, the elders, the women, the crying children – everyone followed the reverend to greet the little Hailey girl.

★   ★   ★

171

Jail did not bother Carl Lee. Home was more pleasant, but under the circumstances, he found jail life tolerable. It was a new jail, built with federal money under the mandate of a prisoners' rights lawsuit. The food was cooked by two huge black women who knew how to cook and write bad checks. They were eligible for early release, but Ozzie had not bothered to tell them. The food was served to forty prisoners, give or take a few, by the trusties. Thirteen of the prisoners belonged at Parchman, but it was full. So they waited, never knowing if the next day would be their day for the dreaded trip to the sprawling, enclosed delta farm where the food was not as good, the beds were not as soft, the air conditioning was non-existent, the mosquitoes immense, plentiful, and vicious, and where toilets were scarce and clogged.

Carl Lee's cell was next to Cell Two, where the state prisoners waited. With two exceptions, they were black, and with no exceptions, they were violent. But they were all afraid of Carl Lee. He shared Cell One with two shoplifters who were not just scared, but downright terrified of their famous cellmate. Each evening he was escorted to Ozzie's office, where he and the sheriff ate dinner and watched the news. He was a celebrity, and he liked that almost as much as did his lawyer and the D.A. He wanted to explain things to the reporters, tell them about his daughter and why he should not be in jail, but his lawyer said no.

After Gwen and Lester left late Sunday afternoon, Ozzie, Moss Junior, and Carl Lee sneaked out the rear of the jail and went to the hospital. It was Carl Lee's idea, and Ozzie saw no harm. Looney was alone in a private room when the three entered. Carl Lee took one look at the leg, then stared at Looney. They shook hands. With watery eyes and a breaking voice Carl Lee said he was sorry, that he had no intention of hurting anyone but the two boys, that he wished and prayed he could undo what he had done to Looney. Without hesitation, Looney accepted the apology.

Jake was waiting in Ozzie's office when they sneaked back into the jail. Ozzie and Moss Junior excused themselves, leaving the defendant with his lawyer.

'Where have y'all been?' Jake asked suspiciously.

'Went to the hospital to see Looney.'

'You what!'

'Nothin' wrong, is it?'

'I wish you would check with me before you make any more visits.'

'What's wrong with seein' Looney?'

'Looney will be the star witness for the State when they attempt to send you to the gas chamber. That's all. He ain't on our side, Carl Lee, and any talking you do with Looney should be with your attorney present. Understand?'

'Not really.'

'I can't believe Ozzie would do that,' Jake mumbled.

'It was my idea,' Carl Lee admitted.

'Well, if you get any more ideas, please let me know about them. Okay?'

'Okay.'

'You talked to Lester lately?'

'Yeah, him and Gwen came by today. Brought me goodies. Told me 'bout the banks.'

Jake planned to play hardball about his fee; no way he could represent Carl Lee for nine hundred dollars. The case would consume his practice for the next three months at least, and nine hundred would be less than minimum wage. It would not be fair to him or his family to work for nothing. Carl Lee would simply have to raise the money. There were plenty of relatives. Gwen had a big family. They would just have to sacrifice, maybe sell a few automobiles, maybe some land, but Jake would get his fee. If not, Carl Lee could find another lawyer.

'I'll give you the deed to my place,' Carl Lee offered.

Jake melted. 'I don't want your place, Carl Lee. I want cash. Sixty-five hundred dollars.'

'Show me how, and I'll do it. You the lawyer, you figure out a way. I'm with you.'

Jake was beat and he knew it. 'I can't do it for nine hundred dollars, Carl Lee. I can't let this case bankrupt me. I'm a lawyer. I'm supposed to make money.'

'Jake, I'll pay you the money. I promise. It may take a long time, but I'll pay you. Trust me.'

Not if you're on death row, thought Jake. He changed the subject. 'You know the grand jury meets tomorrow, and it'll take up your case.'

'So I go to court?'

'Naw, it means you'll be indicted tomorrow. The courthouse will be full of people and reporters. Judge Noose will be here to open the May term of court. Buckley'll be running around chasing cameras and blowing smoke. It's a big day. Noose starts an armed robbery trial in the afternoon. If you're indicted tomorrow, we'll be in court Wednesday or Thursday for the arraignment.'

'The what?'

'The arraignment. In a capital murder case, the judge is required by law to read the indictment to you in open court in front of God and everybody. They'll make a big deal out of it. We'll enter a plea of not guilty, and Noose sets the trial date. We ask for a reasonable bond, and he says no. When I mention bond Buckley'll scream and turn cartwheels. The more I think of him the more I hate him. He'll be a large pain in the ass.'

'Why don't I get a bond?'

'For capital murder, the judge does not have to set a bond. He can if he wants to, but most don't. Even if Noose set a bond, you couldn't pay it, so don't worry about it. You'll be in jail until trial.'

'I lost my job, you know.'

'When?'

'Gwen drove over Friday and got my paycheck. They told her. Nice, ain't it. Work there eleven years, miss five days, and they fire me. Guess they think I ain't comin' back.'

'I'm sorry to hear that, Carl Lee. Real sorry.'

Chapter 12

The Honorable Omar Noose had not always been so honorable. Before he became the circuit judge for the Twenty-second Judicial District, he was a lawyer with meager talent and few clients, but he was a politician of formidable skills. Five terms in the Mississippi Legislature had corrupted him and taught him the art of political swindling and manipulation. Senator Noose prospered handsomely as chairman of the Senate Finance Committee, and few people in Van Buren County questioned how he and his family lived so affluently on his legislative salary of seven thousand dollars a year.

Like most members of the Mississippi Legislature, he ran for reelection one time too many, and in the summer of 1971 he was humiliated by an unknown opponent. A year later, Judge Loopus, his predecessor on the bench, died, and Noose persuaded his friends in the Legislature to persuade the governor to appoint him to serve the unexpired term. That's how ex-State Senator

Noose became Circuit Judge Noose. He was elected in 1975, and reelected in 1979 and 1983.

Repentant, reformed, and very humbled by his rapid descent from power, Judge Noose applied himself to the study of the law, and after a shaky start, grew to the job. It paid sixty thousand a year, so he could afford to be honest. Now, at sixty-three, he was a wise old judge, well respected by most lawyers and by the state Supreme Court, which seldom reversed his rulings. He was quiet but charming, patient but strict, and he had a huge monument of a nose that was very long and very pointed and served as a throne for his black-rimmed, octagon-shaped reading glasses, which he wore constantly but never used. His nose, plus his tall, gawky frame, plus his wild, untamed, dense gray hair, plus his squeaky voice, had given rise to his secret nickname, whispered among lawyers, of Ichabod. Ichabod Noose. The Honorable Ichabod Noose.

He assumed the bench, and the crowded court-room stood as Ozzie mumbled incoherently a statutorily required paragraph to officially open the May term of the Ford County Circuit Court. A long, flowery prayer was offered by a local minister, and the congregation sat down. Prospective jurors filled one side of the courtroom. Criminals and other litigants, their families and friends, the press, and the curious filled the other side. Noose required every lawyer in the county to attend the opening of the term, and the members of the bar sat in the jury box, all decked out in full regalia, all looking important. Buckley and his assistant, D. R. Musgrove, sat at the prosecution's table, splendidly representing the State. Jake sat by himself in a wooden chair in front of the railing. The clerks and court reporters stood behind the large red docket books on the workbench, and with everyone else watched intently as Ichabod situated himself in his chair upon the bench, straightened his robe, adjusted his hideous reading glasses, and peered over them at the assemblage.

'Good morning,' he squeaked loudly. He pulled the microphone closer and cleared his throat. 'It's always nice to be in Ford County for the May term of court. I see most members of the bar found time to appear for the opening of court, and as usual, I will request Madam Clerk to note those absent attorneys so that I may personally contact them. I see a large number of potential jurors present, and I thank each of you for being here. I realize you had no choice, but your presence is vital to our judicial process. We will empanel a grand jury momentarily, and then we will select several trial juries to serve this week and next. I trust each member of the bar has a copy of the docket, and you will note it looks somewhat crowded. My calendar reveals at least two cases set for trial each day this week and next, but it's my understanding most of the criminal cases set for trial will go off on negotiated plea bargains. Nonetheless, we have many cases to move, and I request the diligent cooperation of the bar. Once the new grand jury is empaneled and goes to work, and once the indictments start coming down, I will schedule arraignments and first appearances. Let's quickly call the docket, criminal first, then civil; then the attorneys may be excused as we select a grand jury.

'State versus Warren Moke. Armed robbery, set for trial this afternoon.'

Buckley rose slowly, purposefully. 'The State of Mississippi is ready for trial, Your Honor,' he announced gloriously for the spectators.

'So's the defense,' said Tyndale, the court-appointed lawyer.

'How long do you anticipate for trial?' asked the judge.

'Day and a half,' answered Buckley. Tyndale nodded in agreement.

'Good. We'll select the trial jury this morning and start the trial at one P.M. today. State versus William Daal, forgery, six counts, set for tomorrow.'

'Your Honor,' answered D.R. Musgrove, 'there will be a plea in that case.'

'Good. State versus Roger Hornton, grand larceny, two counts, set for tomorrow.'

Noose continued through the docket. Each case drew the same response. Buckley would stand and proclaim the State ready for trial, or Musgrove would quietly inform the court that a plea had been negotiated. The defense attorneys would stand and nod. Jake had no cases in the May term, and although he tried his best to look bored, he enjoyed the call of the docket because he could learn who had the cases and what the competition was doing. It was also a chance to look good before some of the local folks. Half the members of the Sullivan firm were present, and they too looked bored as they sat arrogantly together in the front row of the jury box. The older partners of the Sullivan firm would not dare make an appearance at docket call, and they would lie and tell Noose they were in trial in Federal Court over in Oxford or perhaps before the Supreme Court in Jackson. Dignity prevented their mingling with the ordinary members of the bar, so the firm's younger lieutenants were sent to satisfy Noose and request that all the firm's civil cases be continued, postponed, delayed, stalled, or acted upon in such a way that the firm could drag them on forever and continue to bill by the hour. Their clients were insurance companies who generally preferred not to go to trial and would pay by the hour for legal maneuvering designed solely to keep the cases away from the juries. It would be cheaper and fairer to pay a reasonable settlement and avoid both litigation and the parasitic defense firms like Sullivan & O'Hare, but the insurance companies and their adjusters were too stupid and cheap, so street lawyers like Jake Brigance earned their livelihoods suing insurance companies and forcing them to pay more than what they would have paid had they dealt fairly from the beginning. Jake hated insurance companies, and he hated insurance defense attorneys, and he especially hated the

Sullivan firm's younger members, all of whom were his age, and all of whom would gladly cut his throat, their associates' throats, their partners' throats, anyone's throat to make partner and earn two hundred thousand a year and skip docket calls.

Jake particularly hated Lotterhouse, or L. Winston Lotterhouse, as the letterhead proclaimed him, a little four-eyed wimp with a Harvard degree and a bad case of haughty self-importance who was next in line to make partner and thus had been especially indiscriminate with his throat cutting during the past year. He sat smugly between two other Sullivan associates and held seven files, each of which was being charged a hundred dollars per hour while he answered the docket call.

Noose began the civil docket. 'Collins versus Royal Consolidated General Mutual Insurance Company.'

Lotterhouse stood slowly. Seconds meant minutes. Minutes meant hours. Hours meant fees, retainers, bonuses, partnerships.

'Your Honor, sir, that case is set prime for a week from Wednesday.'

'I realize that,' Noose said.

'Yes, sir, Well, sir, I'm afraid I must ask for a continuance. A conflict has developed in my trial calendar for that Wednesday, and I have a pretrial conference in Federal Court in Memphis that the judge has refused to continue. I regret this. I filed a motion this morning asking for a continuance.'

Gardner, the plaintiff's attorney, was furious.

'Your Honor, that case has been set prime for two months. It was set for trial in February, and Mr Lotterhouse had a death in his wife's family. It was set for trial last November, and an uncle died. It was set for trial last August, and there was another funeral. I guess we should be thankful that this time no one has died.'

There were pockets of light laughter in the courtroom. Lotterhouse blushed.

'Enough is enough, Your Honor,' Gardner continued. 'Mr Lotterhouse would prefer to postpone this trial forever. The case is ripe for trial, and my client is entitled to one. We strenuously oppose any motion for a continuance.'

Lotterhouse smiled at the judge and removed his glasses. 'Your Honor, if I may respond—'

'No, you may not, Mr Lotterhouse,' interrupted Noose. 'No more continuances. The case is set for trial next Wednesday. There will be no more delays.'

Hallelujah, thought Jake. Noose was generally soft on the Sullivan firm. Jake smiled at Lotterhouse.

Two of Jake's civil cases were continued to the August term. When Noose finished the civil docket, he dismissed the attorneys, and turned his attention to the pool of prospective jurors. He explained the role of the grand jury, its importance and procedure. He distinguished it from the trial juries, equally important but not as time consuming. He began asking questions, dozens of questions, most of them required by law, all dealing with ability to serve as jurors, physical and moral fitness, exemptions, and age. A few were useless, but nonetheless required by some ancient statute. 'Are any of you common gamblers or habitual drunkards?'

There were laughs but no volunteers. Those over sixty-five were automatically excused, at their option. Noose granted the usual exemptions for illnesses, emergencies, and hardships, but he excused only a few of the many who requested pardons for economic reasons. It was amusing to watch the jurors stand, one at a time, and meekly explain to the judge how a few days of jury duty would cause irreparable damage to the farm, or the body shop, or the pulpwood cutting. Noose took a hard line and delivered several lectures on civic responsibility to the flimsier excuses.

From the venire of ninety or so prospects, eighteen would be selected for the grand jury, and the rest would remain available for selection as trial jurors. When Noose completed his questioning, the clerk drew eighteen names from a box and laid them on the bench before His Honor, who began calling names. The jurors, one by one, rose and walked slowly toward the front of the courtroom, through the gate in the railing, and into the cushioned, swivel rocking seats in the jury box. There were fourteen such seats, twelve for the jurors and two for the alternates. When the box was filled, Noose called four more who joined their colleagues in wooden chairs placed in front of the jury box.

'Stand and take the oath,' instructed Noose as

the clerk stood before them holding and reading from a little black book that contained all the oaths. 'Raise your right hands,' she directed. 'Do you solemnly swear or affirm that you will faithfully discharge your duties as grand jurors; that you will fairly hear and decide all issues and matters brought before you, so help you God?'

A chorus of assorted 'I do's' followed, and the grand jury was seated. Of the five blacks, two were women. Of the thirteen whites, eight were women, and most were rural. Jake recognized seven of the eighteen.

'Ladies and gentlemen,' Noose began his usual speech, 'You have been selected and duly sworn as grand jurors for Ford County, and you will serve in that capacity until the next grand jury is empaneled in August. I want to stress that your duties will not be time consuming. You will meet every day this week, then several hours each month until September. You have the responsibility of reviewing criminal cases, listening to law enforcement officials and victims, and determining whether or not reasonable grounds exist to believe the accused has committed the crime. If so, you issue an indictment, which is a formal charge placed against the accused. There are eighteen of you, and when at least twelve believe a person should be indicted, the indictment is issued, or returned, as we say. You have considerable power. By law, you can investigate any criminal act, any citizen suspected of wrongdoing, any public official; really anybody or anything that smells bad.

184

You may convene yourself whenever you choose, but normally you meet whenever the district attorney, Mr Buckley, wants you. You have the power to subpoena witnesses to testify before you, and you may also subpoena their records. Your deliberations are extremely private, with no one being present but yourselves, the D.A. and his staff, and the witnesses. The accused is not allowed to appear before you. You are expressly forbidden to discuss anything that is said or transpires in the grand jury room.

'Mr Buckley, would you please stand. Thank you. This is Mr Rufus Buckley, the district attorney. He's from Smithfield, in Polk County. He will sort of act as your supervisor while you deliberate. Thank you, Mr Buckley. Mr Musgrove, will you stand. This is D.R. Musgrove, assistant district attorney, also from Smithfield. He will assist Mr Buckley while you are in session. Thank you, Mr Musgrove. Now, these gentlemen represent the State of Mississippi, and they will present the cases to the grand jury.

'One final matter: the last grand jury in Ford County was empaneled in February, and the foreman was a white male. Therefore, in keeping with tradition and following the wishes of the Justice Department, I will appoint a black female as foreman of this grand jury. Let's see. Laverne Gossett. Where are you, Mrs Gossett? There you are, good. I believe you are a schoolteacher, correct? Good. I'm sure you'll be able to handle your new duties. Now, it's time for you to get to

185

work. I understand there are over fifty cases waiting on you. I will ask that you follow Mr Buckley and Mr Musgrove down the hall to the small court-room that we use for a grand jury room. Thank you and good luck.'

Buckley proudly marched his new grand jury out of the courtroom and down the hall. He waved at reporters and had no comments – for the time being. In the small courtroom they seated them-selves around two long, folding tables. A secretary rolled in boxes of files. An ancient half-crippled, half-deaf, long-retired deputy in a faded uniform took his position by the door. The room was secure. Buckley had second thoughts, excused himself, and met with the reporters in the hall. Yes, he said, the Hailey case would be presented that after-noon. In fact, he was calling a press conference for 4:00 P.M. on the front steps of the courthouse, and he would have the indictments at that time.

After lunch, the chief of the Karaway Police Department sat at one end of the long table and shuffled nervously through his files. He avoided looking at the grand jurors, who anxiously awaited their first case.

'State your name!' barked the D.A.

'Chief Nolan Earnhart, Karaway City Police.'

'How many cases do you have, Chief?'

'We have five from Karaway.'

'Let's hear the first one.'

'Okay, let's see, all right,' the chief mumbled and stuttered as he flipped through his paperwork.

'Okay, the first case is Fedison Bulow, male black, age twenty-five, got caught red-handed in the rear of Griffin's Feed Store in Karaway at two o'clock in the mornin', April 12. Silent alarm went off and we caught him in the store. Cash register had been broken into, and some fertilizer was gone. We found the cash and the goods in a car registered in his name parked behind the store. He gave a three-page confession at the jail, and I've got copies here.'

Buckley walked casually around the room smiling at everyone. 'And you want this grand jury to indict Fedison Bulow on one count of breaking and entering a commercial building, and one count of grand larceny?' Buckley asked helpfully.

'Yes, sir, that's right.'

'Now, members of the grand jury, you have the right to ask any questions. This is your hearing. Any questions?'

'Yes, does he have a record?' asked Mack Loyd Crowell, an unemployed truck driver.

'No,' replied the chief. 'This is his first offense.'

'Good question, always ask that question because if they have prior records we may need to indict them as habitual criminals,' lectured Buckley. 'Any more questions? None? Good. Now at this point, someone needs to make a motion that the grand jury return a true bill of indictment against Fedison Bulow.'

Silence. The eighteen stared at the table and waited for someone else to make a motion. Buckley waited. Silence. This is great, he thought. A soft grand jury. A bunch of timid souls afraid to speak. Liberals. Why couldn't he have a bloodthirsty grand jury eager to make motions to indict everybody for everything?

'Mrs Gossett, would you like to make the first motion, since you're the foreman?'

'I so move,' she said.

'Thank you,' said Buckley. 'Now let's vote. How many vote to indict Fedison Bulow on one count of breaking and entering a commercial building and one count of grand larceny? Raise your hands.'

Eighteen hands went up, and Buckley was relieved.

The chief presented the other four cases from Karaway. Each involved defendants equally guilty as Bulow, and each received unanimous true bills. Buckley slowly taught the grand jury how to operate itself. He made them feel important, powerful, and laden with the heavy burden of justice. They became inquisitive:

'Does he have a record?'

'How much time does that carry?'

'When will he get out?'

'How many counts can we give him?'

'When will he be tried?'

'Is he out of jail now?'

With five indictments out of the way, with five true bills and no dissension, with the grand jury eager for the next case, whatever it might be, Buckley decided the mood was ripe. He opened the door and motioned for Ozzie, who was standing in the hall talking quietly with a deputy and watching the reporters.

'Present Hailey first,' Buckley whispered as the two met in the door.

'Ladies and gentlemen, this is Sheriff Walls. I'm sure most of you know him. He has several cases to present. What's first, Sheriff?'

Ozzie scrambled through his files, lost whatever he was looking for, and finally blurted, 'Carl Lee Hailey.'

The jurors became quiet again. Buckley watched them closely to gauge their reactions. Most of them stared at the table again. No one spoke while Ozzie reviewed the file, then excused himself to get another briefcase. He had not planned to present the Hailey case first.

Buckley prided himself on reading jurors, of watching their faces and knowing precisely their thoughts. He watched the jury constantly during a trial, always predicting to himself what each was thinking. He would cross-examine a witness and never take his eyes off the jury. He would sometimes stand and face the jury box and interrogate a witness and watch the faces react to the answers. After hundreds of trials he was good at reading jurors, and he knew instantly he was in trouble with Hailey. The five blacks grew tense and arrogant as if they welcomed the case and the inevitable argument. The foreman, Mrs Gossett, looked particularly pious as Ozzie mumbled to himself and flipped papers. Most of the whites looked noncommittal, but Mack Loyd Crowell, a hard-looking middle-aged rural type, appeared as arrogant as the blacks. Crowell pushed back his chair and walked to the window, which looked over the north side of the courtyard. Buckley could not read him precisely, but he knew Crowell was trouble.

'Sheriff, how many witnesses do you have for the Hailey case?' Buckley asked, somewhat nervously.

Ozzie stopped shuffling paper and said, 'Well, uh, just me. We can get another if we need one.'

'All right, all right,' replied Buckley. 'Just tell us about the case.'

Ozzie reared back, crossed his legs, and said, 'Shoot, Rufus, everybody knows about this case. Been on TV for a week.'

'Just give us the evidence.'

'The evidence. Okay, one week ago today, Carl Lee Hailey, male black, age thirty-seven, shot and killed one Billy Ray Cobb and one Pete Willard, and he shot a peace officer, one DeWayne Looney, who's still in the hospital with his leg cut off. The weapon was an M-16 machine gun, illegal, which we recovered and matched the fingerprints with those of Mr Hailey. I have an affidavit signed by Deputy Looney, and he states, under oath, that the man who did the shootin' was Carl Lee Hailey. There was an eyewitness, Murphy, the little crippled man that sweeps the courthouse and stutters real bad. I can get him here if you want.'

'Any questions?' interrupted Buckley.

The D.A. nervously watched the jurors, who

nervously watched the sheriff. Crowell stood with his back to the others, looking through the window.

'Any questions?' Buckley repeated.

'Yeah,' answered Crowell as he turned and glared at the D.A., then at Ozzie. 'Those two boys he shot, they raped his little girl, didn't they, Sheriff?'

'We're pretty sure they did,' answered Ozzie.

'Well, one confessed, didn't he?'

'Yep.'

Crowell walked slowly, boldly, arrogantly across the room, and stood at the other end of the tables. He looked down at Ozzie. 'You got kids, Sheriff?'

'Yep.'

'You got a little girl?'

'Yep.'

'Suppose she got raped and you got your hands on the man who did it. What would you do?'

Ozzie paused and looked anxiously at Buckley, whose neck had turned a deep red.

'I don't have to answer that,' Ozzie replied.

'Is that so. You came before this grand jury to testify, didn't you? You're a witness, ain't you? Answer the question.'

'I don't know what I'd do.'

'Come on, Sheriff. Give us a straight answer. Tell the truth. What would you do?'

Ozzie felt embarrassed, confused, and angry at this stranger. He would like to tell the truth, and explain in detail how he would gladly castrate and mutilate and kill any pervert who touched his little girl. But he couldn't. The grand jury might agree

191

and refuse to indict Carl Lee. Not that he wanted him indicted, but he knew the indictment was necessary. He looked sheepishly at Buckley, who was perspiring and seated now.

Crowell zeroed in on the sheriff with the zeal and fervor of a lawyer who had just caught a witness in an obvious lie.

'Come on, Sheriff,' he taunted. 'We're all listenin'. Tell the truth. What would you do to the rapist? Tell us. Come on.'

Buckley was near panic. The biggest case of his wonderful career was about to be lost, not at trial, but in the grand jury room, in the first round, at the hands of an unemployed truck driver. He stood and struggled for words. 'The witness does not have to answer.'

Crowell turned and shouted at Buckley, 'You sit down and shut up! We don't take orders from you. We can indict you if we want to, can't we?'

Buckley sat and looked blankly at Ozzie. Crowell was a ringer. He was too smart to be on a grand jury. Someone must have paid him. He knew too much. Yes, the grand jury could indict anyone.

Crowell retreated and returned to the window. They watched him until it appeared he was finished.

'Are you absolutely sure he done it, Ozzie?' asked Lemoyne Frady, an illegitimate distant cousin to Gwen Hailey.

'Yes, we're sure,' Ozzie answered slowly, with both eyes on Crowell.

'And you want us to indict him for what?' asked Mr Frady, the admiration for the sheriff obvious.

'Two counts of capital murder, and one count of assault on a peace officer.'

'How much time you talkin' about?' asked Barney Flaggs, another black.

'Capital murder carries the gas chamber. Assault on a deputy carries life with no parole.'

'And that's what you want, Ozzie?' asked Flaggs.

'Yeah, Barney, I say this grand jury should indict Mr Hailey. I sure do.'

'Any more questions?' interrupted Buckley.

'Not so fast,' replied Crowell as he turned from the window. 'I think you're tryin' to ram this case down our throats, Mr Buckley, and I resent it. I wanna talk about it some. You sit down and if we need you, we'll ask you.'

Buckley glared fiercely and pointed his finger. 'I don't have to sit, and I don't have to stay quiet!' he yelled.

'Yes. Yes, you do,' Crowell answered coolly with a caustic grin. 'Because if you don't, we can make you leave, can't we, Mr Buckley? We can ask you to leave this room, and if you refuse, we'll go ask the judge. He'll make you leave, won't he, Mr Buckley?'

Rufus stood motionless, speechless, and stunned. His stomach turned flips and his knees were spongy, but he was frozen in place.

'So, if you would like to hear the rest of our deliberations, sit down and shut up.'

Buckley sat next to the bailiff, who was now awake.

'Thank you,' said Crowell. 'I wanna ask you folks a question. How many of you would do or wanna do what Mr Hailey did if someone raped your daughter, or maybe your wife, or what about your mother? How many? Raise your hands.'

Seven or eight hands shot up, and Buckley dropped his head. Crowell smiled and continued, 'I admire him for what he did. It took guts. I'd hope I'd have the courage to do what he did, 'cause Lord knows I'd want to. Sometimes a man's just gotta do what he's gotta do. This man deserves a trophy, not an indictment.'

Crowell walked slowly around the tables, enjoying the attention. 'Before you vote, I want you to do one thing. I want you to think about that poor little girl. I think she's ten. Try to picture her layin' there, hands tied behind her, cryin', beggin' for her daddy. And think of those two outlaws, drunk, doped up, takin' turns rapin' and beatin' and kickin' her. Hell, they even tried to kill her. Think of your own daughter. Put her in the place of the little Hailey girl.

'Now, wouldn't you say they got pretty much what they deserved? We should be thankful they're dead. I feel safer just knowin' those two bastards are no longer here to rape and kill other children. Mr Hailey has done us a great service. Let's don't indict him. Let's send him home to his family, where he belongs. He's a good man who's done a good thing.'

Crowell finished and returned to the window. Buckley watched him fearfully, and when he was certain he was finished, he stood. 'Sir, are you finished?' There was no response.

'Good. Ladies and gentlemen of the grand jury. I would like to explain a few things. A grand jury is not supposed to try the case. That's what a trial jury is for. Mr Hailey will get a fair trial before twelve fair and impartial jurors, and if he's innocent, he'll be acquitted. But his guilt or innocence is not supposed to be determined by the grand jury. You're supposed to decide, after listening to the State's version of the evidence, if there is a strong possibility a crime has been committed. Now, I submit to you that a crime has been committed by Carl Lee Hailey. Three crimes actually. He killed two men, and he wounded another. We have eyewitnesses.'

Buckley was warming as he circled the tables. The confidence was back. 'The duty of this grand jury is to indict him, and if he has a valid defense, he'll have a chance to present it at trial. If he has a legal reason for doing what he did, let him prove it at trial. That's what trials are for. The State charges him with a crime, and the State must prove at trial he committed the crime. If he has a defense, and if he can convince the trial jury, he will be acquitted, I assure you. Good for him. But it's not the duty of this grand jury to decide today that Mr Hailey should go free. There'll be another day for that, right, Sheriff?'

Ozzie nodded and said, 'That's right. The grand jury is to indict if the evidence is presented. The trial jury will not convict him if the State can't prove its case, or if he puts a good defense. But the grand jury don't worry 'bout things like that.'

'Anything further from the grand jury?' Buckley asked anxiously. 'Okay, we need a motion.'

'I make a motion we don't indict him for anything,' yelled Crowell.

'Second,' mumbled Barney Flaggs.

Buckley's knees quivered. He tried to speak, but nothing came forth. Ozzie suppressed his joy.

'We have a motion and a second,' announced Mrs Gossett. 'All in favor raise your hands.'

Five black hands went up, along with Crowell's. Six votes. The motion failed.

'Whatta we do now?' asked Mrs Gossett.

Buckley spoke rapidly: 'Someone make a motion to indict Mr Hailey for two counts of capital murder and one count of assault on a peace officer.'

'So move,' said one of the whites.

'Second,' said another.

'All in favor, raise your hands,' said Mrs Gossett. 'I count twelve hands. All opposed – I count five plus mine makes six. Twelve to six. What does that mean?'

'That means he's been indicted,' Buckley replied proudly. He breathed normally again, and the color returned to his face. He whispered to a secretary, then addressed the grand jury. 'Let's take a ten-minute recess. We have about forty more cases to work on, so please don't be gone long. I would like to remind you of something Judge Noose said this morning. These deliberations are extremely

196

confidential. You are not to discuss any of your work outside this room—'

'What he's tryin' to say,' interrupted Crowell, 'is that we can't tell anybody that he came within one vote of not gettin' the indictments. Ain't that right, Buckley?'

The D.A. quickly left the room and slammed the door.

Surrounded by dozens of cameras and reporters, Buckley stood on the front steps of the courthouse and waved copies of the indictments. He preached, lectured, moralized, praised the grand jury, sermonized against crime and vigilantes, and condemned Carl Lee Hailey. Bring on the trial. Put the jury in the box. He guaranteed a conviction. He guaranteed a death penalty. He was obnoxious, offensive, arrogant, self-righteous. He was himself. Vintage Buckley. A few of the reporters left, but he labored on. He extolled himself and his trial skills and his ninety, no, ninety-five percent conviction rate. More reporters left. More cameras were turned off. He praised Judge Noose for his wisdom and fairness. He acclaimed the intelligence and good judgment of Ford County jurors.

He outlasted them. They grew weary of him and they all left.

Chapter 13

Stump Sisson was the Klan's Imperial Wizard for Mississippi, and he had called the meeting at the small cabin deep in the pine forests of Nettles County, two hundred and thirty miles south of Ford County. There were no robes, rituals, or speeches. The small group of Klansmen discussed the events in Ford County with a Mr Freddie Cobb, brother of Billy Ray Cobb, deceased. Freddie had called a friend who called Stump to arrange the meeting.

Had they indicted the nigger? Cobb was not sure, but he had heard the trial would be in late summer, or early fall. What concerned him most was all the talk about the nigger pleading insanity and getting off. It wasn't right. The nigger killed his brother in cold blood, planned the shooting. He hid in a closet and waited for his brother. It was cold-blooded murder, and now there was talk of the nigger walking free. What could the Klan do about it? The niggers have plenty of protection nowadays – the NAACP, ACLU, a thousand other civil rights groups, plus the courts and the government. Hell, white folks ain't got a chance, except for the Klan. Who else would march and stand up for white people? All the laws favor the niggers, and the liberal nigger-loving politicians keep making more laws against white people. Somebody's got to stand up for them. That's why he called the Klan.

Is the nigger in jail? Yes, and he's treated like a king. Got a nigger sheriff up there, Walls, and he likes this nigger. Gives him special privileges and extra protection. The sheriff's another story. Someone said Hailey might get out of jail this week on bond. Just a rumor. They hoped he got out.

What about your brother? Did he rape her? We're not sure, probably not. Willard, the other guy, confessed to rape, but Billy Ray never confessed. He had plenty of women. Why would he rape a little nigger girl? And if he did, what was the big deal?

Who's the nigger's lawyer? Brigance, a local boy in Clanton. Young, but pretty good. Does a lot of criminal work and has a good reputation. Won several murder trials. He told some reporters the nigger would plead insanity and get off.

Who's the judge? Don't know yet. Bullard was the county judge, but someone said he would not hear the case. There's talk of moving the case to another county, so who knows who will be the judge.

Sisson and the Kluxers listened intently to this

ignorant redneck. They liked the part about the NAACP and the government and the politicians, but they had also read the papers and watched TV and they knew his brother had received justice. But at the hands of a nigger. It was unthinkable.

The case had real potential. With the trial several months away, there was time to plan a rebellion. They could march during the day around the courthouse in their white robes and pointed, hooded masks. They could make speeches to a captive audience and parade in front of the cameras. The press would love it – hate them, but love the altercations, the disruptions. And at night they could intimidate with burning crosses and threatening phone calls. The targets would be easy and unsuspecting. Violence would be unavoidable. They knew how to provoke it. They fully appreciated what the sight of marching white robes did to crowds of angry niggers.

Ford County could be their playground for hide and seek, search and destroy, and hit and run. They had time to organize and call in comrades from other states. What Kluxer would miss this golden moment? And new recruits? Why, this case could fuel the fires of racism and bring nigger haters out of the woods and onto the streets. Membership was down. Hailey would be their new battle cry, the rallying point.

'Mr Cobb, can you get us the names and addresses of the nigger, his family, his lawyer, the judge, and the jurors?' asked Sisson.

Cobb pondered this task. 'Everybody but the jurors. They ain't been picked yet.'

'When will you know them?'

'Damned if I know. I guess at trial. What're y'all thinkin'?'

'We're not sure, but the Klan most likely will get involved. We need to flex our muscle a bit, and this could be a good opportunity.'

'Can I help?' Cobb asked eagerly.

'Sure, but you need to be a member.'

'We ain't got no Klan up there. It folded a long time ago. My granddaddy used to be a member.'

'You mean the grandfather of the victim was a Klansman?'

'Yep,' Cobb answered proudly.

'Well, then, we must get involved.' The Klansmen shook their heads in disbelief and vowed revenge. They explained to Cobb that if he could get five or six friends of similar thinking and motivation to agree to join, they would have a big, secret ceremony deep in the woods of Ford County with a huge burning cross and all sorts of rituals. They would be inducted as members, full-fledged members, of the Ku Klux Klan. Ford County Klavern. And they would all join in and make a spectacle of the trial of Carl Lee Hailey. They would raise so much hell in Ford County this summer that no juror with any common sense would consider voting to acquit the nigger. Just recruit half a dozen more, and they would make him the leader of the Ford County Klavern.

Cobb said he had enough cousins to start a

klavern. He left the meeting drunk with excitement of being a Klansman, just like his grandfather.

Buckley's timing was a little off. His 4:00 P.M. press show was ignored by the evening news. Jake flipped the channels on a small black and white in his office, and laughed out loud when the networks and then Memphis, then Jackson, then Tupelo signed off with no news of the indictments. He could see the Buckley family in their den glued to the set, turning knobs and searching desperately for their hero while he yelled at them all to be quiet. And then at seven, after the Tupelo weather, the last weather, they backed away and left him alone in his recliner. Maybe at ten, he probably said.

At ten, Jake and Carla laid cross-legged and tangled in the dark on the sofa, waiting on the news. Finally, there he was, on the front steps, waving papers and shouting like a street preacher while the Channel 4 man on the scene explained that this was Rufus Buckley, the D.A. who would prosecute Carl Lee Hailey now that he had been indicted. After an awful glimpse of Buckley, the report panned around the square for a wonderful view of downtown Clanton, and then finally back to the reporter for two sentences about a trial in late summer.

'He's offensive,' Carla said. 'Why would he call a press conference to announce the indictments?'

'He's a prosecutor. We defense lawyers hate the press.'

'I've noticed. My scrapbook is rapidly filling up.'

'Be sure and make copies for Mom.'

'Will you autograph it for her?'

'Only for a fee. Yours, I will autograph for free.'

'Fine. And if you lose, I'll send you a bill for clipping and pasting.'

'I remind you, dear, that I have never lost a murder case. Three and oh, as a matter of fact.'

Carla punched the remote control and the weatherman remained but his volume disappeared. 'You know what I dislike most about your murder trials?' She kicked the cushions from her thin, bronze, almost perfect legs.

'The blood, the carnage, the gruesomeness?'

'No.' She unfolded her shoulder-length hair and let it fall around her on the arm of the sofa.

'The loss of life, regardless of how insignificant?'

'No.' She was wearing one of his old, starched-out, sixteen-by-thirty-four, pinpoint Oxford button-downs, and she began to play with the buttons.

'The horrible specter of an innocent man facing the gas chamber?'

'No.' She was unbuttoning it. The bluish gray rays from the television flashed like a strobe in the dark room as the anchorperson smiled and mouthed good night.

'The fear of a young family as the father walks into the courtroom and faces a jury of his peers?'

'No.' It was unbuttoned, and under it a thin,

fluorescent band of white silk glittered against the brown skin.

'The latent unfairness of our judicial system?'

'No.' She slid an almost perfect bronze leg up, up, up to the back of the sofa where it gently came to rest.

'The unethical and unscrupulous tactics employed by cops and prosecutors to nail innocent defendants?'

'No.' She unsnapped the band of silk between the two almost perfect breasts.

'The fervor, the fury, the intensity, the uncontrolled emotions, the struggle of the human spirit, the unbridled passion?'

'Close enough,' she said. Shirts and shorts ricocheted off the lamps and coffee tables as the bodies meshed deep under the cushions. The old sofa, a gift from her parents, rocked and squeaked on the ancient hardwood floor. It was sturdy, and accustomed to the rocking and squeaking. Max the mixbreed instinctively ran down the hall to stand guard by Hanna's door.

Chapter 14

Harry Rex Vonner was a huge slob of a lawyer who specialized in nasty divorce cases and perpetually kept some jerk in jail for back child support. He was vile and vicious, and his services were in great demand by divorcing parties in Ford County. He could get the children, the house, the farm, the VCR, and microwave, everything. One wealthy farmer kept him on retainer just so the current wife couldn't hire him for the next divorce. Harry Rex sent his criminal cases to Jake, and Jake sent his nasty divorces to Harry Rex. They were friends and disliked the other lawyers, especially the Sullivan firm.

Tuesday morning he barged in and growled at Ethel: 'Jake in?' He lumbered toward the stairs, glaring at her and daring her to speak. She nodded, knowing better than to ask if he was expected. He had cursed her before. He had cursed everybody before.

The stairway shook as he thundered upward. He was gasping for air as he entered the big office.

'Morning, Harry Rex. You gonna make it?'

'Why don't you get an office downstairs?' he demanded between breaths.

'You need the exercise. If it weren't for those stairs your weight would be over three hundred.'

'Thanks. Say, I just came from the courtroom. Noose wants you in chambers at ten-thirty if possible. Wants to talk about Hailey with you and Buckley. Set up arraignment, trial date, all that crap. He asked me to tell you.'

'Good. I'll be there.'

'I guess you heard about the grand jury?'

'Sure. I've got a copy of the indictment right here.'

Harry Rex smiled. 'No. No, I mean the vote on the indictment.'

Jake froze and looked at him curiously. Harry Rex moved in silent and dark circles like a cloud over the county. He was an endless source of gossip and rumor, and took great pride in spreading only the truth – most of the time. He was the first to know almost everything. The legend of Harry Rex began twenty years earlier with his first jury trial. The railroad he had sued for millions refused to offer a dime, and after three days of trial the jury retired to deliberate. The railroad lawyers became concerned when the jury failed to return with a quick verdict in their favor. They offered Harry Rex twenty-five thousand to settle when the deliberations went into the second day. With nerves of steel, he told them to go to hell. His client wanted the money. He told his client to go to hell. Hours later a weary and

fatigued jury returned with a verdict for one hundred
fifty thousand. Harry Rex shot the bird at the railroad lawyers, snubbed his clients and went to the
bar at the Best Western. He bought drinks for
everyone, and during the course of the long evening
explained in detail exactly how he had wired the
jury room and knew exactly what the jury was up
to. Word spread, and Murphy found a series of wires
running through the heating ducts to the jury room.
The State Bar Association snooped around, but
found nothing. For twenty years the judges had
ordered the bailiffs to inspect the jury room when
Harry Rex was in any way connected with a case.

'How do you know the vote?' Jake asked, suspicion hanging on every syllable.

'I got sources.'

'Okay, what was the vote?'

'Twelve to six. One fewer vote and you wouldn't
be holding that indictment.'

'Twelve to six,' Jake repeated.

'Buckley near 'bout died. A guy named Crowell,
white guy, took charge and almost convinced
enough of them not to indict your man.'

'Do you know Crowell?'

'I handled his divorce two years ago. He lived
in Jackson until his first wife was raped by a nigger.
She went crazy and they got a divorce. She took
a steak knife and sliced her wrists. Then he moved
to Clanton and married some sleazebag out in the
county. Lasted about a year. He ate Buckley's
lunch. Told him to shut up and sit down. I wish
I could've seen it.'

'Sounds like you did.'

'Naw. Just got a good source.'

'Who?'

'Jake, come on.'

'You been wiring rooms again?'

'Nope. I just listen. That's a good sign, ain't it?'

'What?'

'The close vote. Six outta eighteen voted to let him walk. Five niggers and Crowell. That's a good sign. Just get a couple of niggers on the jury and hang it. Right?'

'It's not that easy. If it's tried in this county there's a good chance we'll have an all-white jury. They're common here, and as you know, they're still very constitutional. Plus this guy Crowell sounds like he came outta nowhere.'

'That's what Buckley thought. You should see that ass. He's in the courtroom strutting around ready to sign autographs over his big TV splash last night. No one wants to talk about it, so he manages to work it into every conversation. He's like a kid begging for attention.'

'Be sweet. He may be your next governor.'

'Not if he loses Hailey. And he's gonna lose Hailey, Jake. We'll pick us a good jury, twelve good and faithful citizens, then we'll buy them.'

'I didn't hear that.'

'Works every time.'

A few minutes after ten-thirty, Jake entered the judge's chamber behind the courtroom and coolly shook hands with Buckley, Musgrove, and

Ichabod. They had been waiting on him. Noose waved him toward a seat and sat behind the desk.

'Jake, this will take just a few minutes.' He peered down that nose. 'I would like to arraign Carl Lee Hailey in the morning at nine. Any problems with that?'

'No. That'll be fine,' replied Jake.

'We'll have some other arraignments in the morning, then we start a burglary case at ten. Right, Rufus?'

'Yes, sir.'

'Okay. Now let's discuss a trial date for Mr Hailey. As you know, the next term of court here is in late August – third Monday – and I'm sure the docket will be just as crowded then. Because of the nature of this case and, frankly, because of the publicity, I think it would be best if we had a trial as soon as practical.'

'The sooner the better,' inserted Buckley.

'Jake, how long will you need to prepare for trial?'

'Sixty days.'

'Sixty days!' Buckley repeated in disbelief. 'Why so long?'

Jake ignored him and watched Ichabod adjust his reading glasses and study his calendar. 'Would it be safe to anticipate a request for a change of venue?' he asked.

'Yes.'

'Won't make any difference,' Buckley said. 'We'll get a conviction anywhere.'

'Save it for the cameras, Rufus,' Jake said quietly.

'You shouldn't talk about cameras,' Buckley shot back. 'You seem to enjoy them yourself.'

'Gentlemen, please,' Noose said. 'What other pretrial motions can we expect from the defense?'

Jake thought for a moment. 'There will be others.'

'May I inquire about the others?' asked Noose with a hint of irritation.

'Judge, I really don't care to discuss my defense at this time. We just received the indictment and I haven't discussed it with my client. We obviously have some work to do.'

'How much time do you need?'

'Sixty days.'

'Are you kidding!' Buckley shouted. 'Is this a joke? The State could try it tomorrow, Judge. Sixty days is ridiculous.'

Jake began to burn but said nothing. Buckley walked to the window and mumbled to himself in disbelief.

Noose studied his calendar. 'Why sixty days?'

'It could be a complicated case.'

Buckley laughed and continued shaking his head.

'Then we can expect a defense of insanity?' asked the judge.

'Yes, sir. And it will take time to have Mr Hailey examined by a psychiatrist. Then the State will of course want him examined by its doctors.'

'I see.'

'And we may have other pretrial matters. It's a big case, and I want to make sure we have time to adequately prepare.'

'Mr Buckley?' said the judge.

'Whatever. It makes no difference to the State. We'll be ready. We could try it tomorrow.'

Noose scribbled on his calendar and adjusted his reading glasses, which were perched on the tip of that nose and held in place by a tiny wart located perfectly at the foot of the beak. Due to the size of the nose and the odd shape of the head, specially built reading glasses with extra long stems were required for His Honor, who never used them for reading or any other purpose except in a vain effort to distract from the size and shape of the nose. Jake had always suspected this, but lacked the courage to inform His Honor that the ridiculous, orange-tinted hexagonal glasses diverted attention from everything else directly to the nose.

'How long do you anticipate for trial, Jake?' Noose asked.

'Three or four days. But it could take three days to pick the jury.'

'Mr Buckley?'

'Sounds about right. But I don't understand why it takes sixty days to prepare for a three-day trial. I think it should be tried sooner.'

'Relax, Rufus,' Jake said calmly. 'The cameras will be here in sixty days, even ninety days. They won't forget about you. You can give interviews, hold press conferences, preach sermons, everything. The works. But don't worry so much. You'll get your chance.'

Buckley's eyes narrowed and his face reddened. He took three steps in Jake's direction. 'If I'm not

mistaken, Mr Brigance, you've given more interviews and seen more cameras than I have during
the past week.'

'I know, and you're jealous, aren't you?'

'No, I'm not jealous! I don't care about the
cameras—'

'Since when?'

'Gentlemen, please,' Noose interrupted. 'This
promises to be a long, emotional case. I expect
my attorneys to act like professionals. Now, my
calendar is congested. The only opening I have is
the week of July 22. Does that present a problem?'

'We can try it that week,' said Musgrove.

Jake smiled at Buckley and flipped through his
pocket calendar. 'Looks good to me.'

'Fine. All motions must be filed and pretrial
matters disposed of by Monday, July 8.
Arraignment is set for tomorrow at nine. Any questions?'

Jake stood and shook hands with Noose and
Musgrove, and left.

After lunch he visited his famous client in
Ozzie's office at the jail. A copy of the indictment
had been served on Carl Lee in his cell. He had
some questions for his lawyer.

'What's capital murder?'

'The worst kind.'

'How many kinds are there?'

'Basically three. Manslaughter, regular murder,
and capital murder.'

'What's manslaughter?'

'Twenty years.'

'What's regular murder?'

'Twenty to life.'

'What's capital murder?'

'Gas chamber.'

'What's aggravated assault on an officer?'

'Life. No parole.'

Carl Lee studied the indictment carefully. 'You mean I got two gas chambers and a life sentence.'

'Not yet. You're entitled to a trial first. Which, by the way, has been set for July 22.'

'That's two months away! Why so long?'

'We need the time. It'll take that long to find a psychiatrist who'll say you were crazy. Then Buckley gets to send you to Whitfield to be examined by the State's doctors, and they'll all say you were not crazy at the time. We file motions, Buckley files motions, we have a bunch of hearings. It takes time.'

'No way to have it sooner?'

'We don't want it sooner.'

'What if I do?' Carl Lee snapped.

Jake studied him carefully. 'What's the matter, big man?'

'I gotta get outta here, and fast.'

'I thought you said jail wasn't so bad.'

'It ain't, but I need to get home. Gwen's outta money, can't find a job. Lester's in trouble with his wife. She's callin' all the time, so he won't last much longer. I hate to ask my folk for help.'

'But they will, won't they?'

'Some. They got their own problems. You gotta get me outta here, Jake.'

'Look, you'll be arraigned in the morning at nine. The trial is July 22, and the date won't be changed, so forget about that. Have I explained the arraignment to you?'

Carl Lee shook his head.

'It won't last twenty minutes. We appear before Judge Noose in the big courtroom. He'll ask you some questions, then ask me some questions. He'll read the indictment to you in open court, and ask if you've received a copy. Then he'll ask you to plead guilty or not guilty. When you answer not guilty, he'll set the trial date. You'll sit down, and me and Buckley will get into a big fight over your bond. Noose will refuse to set a bond, then they'll bring you back to the jail, where you'll stay until the trial.'

'What about after the trial?'

Jake smiled. 'Naw, you won't be in jail after the trial.'

'You promise?'

'Nope. No promises. Any questions about tomorrow?'

'No. Say, Jake, uh, how much money did I pay you?'

Jake hesitated and smelled trouble. 'Why do you ask?'

'Just thinkin'.'

'Nine hundred, plus a note.'

Gwen had less than a hundred dollars. Bills were due and food was low. She had visited on Sunday and cried for an hour. Panic was a part of her life, her makeup, her composition. But he knew they were broke and she was scared. Her family would be of little help, maybe some vegetables from the garden and a few bucks for milk and eggs. When it came to funerals and hospital stays they were very dependable. They were generous and gave of their time freely to wail and moan and put on a show. But when real money was needed they scattered like chickens. He had little use for her family, and his wasn't much better.

He wanted to ask Jake for a hundred dollars, but decided to wait until Gwen was completely broke. It would be easier then.

Jake flipped through his legal pad and waited for Carl Lee to ask for money. Criminal clients, especially the blacks, always asked for some of the fee back after it was paid. He doubted he would ever see more than nine hundred dollars, and he was not about to return any. Besides, the blacks always took care of their own. The families would be there and the churches would get involved. No one would starve.

He waited and placed the legal pad and file in his briefcase. 'Any questions, Carl Lee?'

'Yeah. What can I say tomorrow?'

'What do you want to say?'

'I wanna tell that judge why I shot them boys. They raped my daughter. They needed shootin'.'

'And you want to explain that to the judge tomorrow?'

'Yeah.'

'And you think he'll turn you loose once you explain it all?'

Carl Lee said nothing.

'Look, Carl Lee, you hired me to be your lawyer. And you hired me because you have confidence in me, right? And if I want you to say something tomorrow, I'll tell you. If I don't, you stay quiet. When you go to trial in July you'll have the chance to tell your side. But in the meantime, I'll do the talking.'

'You got that right.'

Lester and Gwen piled the boys and Tonya in the red Cadillac and drove to the doctor's building next to the hospital. The rape was two weeks in the past. Tonya walked with a slight limp and wanted to run and climb steps with her brothers. But her mother held her hand. The soreness in her legs and buttocks was almost gone, the bandages on her wrists and ankles had been removed by the doctor last week, and the cuts were healing nicely. The gauze and cotton between her legs remained.

In a small room she undressed and sat next to her mother on a padded table. Her mother hugged her and helped her stay warm. The doctor poked in her mouth and rubbed her jaw. He held her wrists and ankles and inspected them. He laid her on the table and touched between her legs. She cried and clutched her mother, who leaned over her.

She was hurting again.

Chapter 15

At five Wednesday morning, Jake sipped coffee in his office and stared through the French doors across the dark courtyard square. He had slept fitfully, and several hours earlier had given up and left his warm bed in a desperate effort to find a nameless Georgia case that, as he thought he remembered from law school, required the judge to allow bail in a capital murder case if the defendant had no prior criminal record, owned property in the county, had a stable job, and had plenty of relatives nearby. It had not been found. He did find a battery of recent, well-reasoned, clear, and unambiguous Mississippi cases allowing the judge complete discretion in denying bail to such defendants. That was the law and Jake now knew it well, but he needed something to argue to Ichabod. He dreaded asking bail for Carl Lee. Buckley would scream and preach and cite those wonderful cases, and Noose would smile and listen, then deny bail. Jake would get his tail kicked in the first skirmish.

'You're here early this morning, sweetheart,'

217

Dell said to her favorite customer as she poured his coffee.

'At least I'm here.' He had missed a few mornings since the amputation. Looney was popular, and there was resentment at the Coffee Shop and around town for Hailey's lawyer. He was aware of it and tried to ignore it.

There was resentment among many for any lawyer who would defend a nigger for killing two white men.

'You got a minute?' Jake asked.

'Sure,' Dell said, looking around. At five-fifteen, the cafe was not yet full. She sat across from Jake in a small booth and poured coffee.

'What's the talk in here?' he asked.

'The usual. Politics, fishing, farming. It never changes. I've been here for twenty-one years, serving the same food to the same people, and they're still talking about the same things.'

'Nothing new?'

'Hailey. We get a lotta talk about that. Except when the strangers are here, then it goes back to the usual.'

'Why?'

'Because if you act like you know anything about the case, some reporter will follow you outside with a bunch of questions.'

'That bad, huh?'

'No. It's great. Business has never been better.'

Jake smiled and buttered his grits, then added Tabasco.

'How do you feel about the case?'

218

Dell scratched her nose with long, red, fake fingernails and blew into her coffee. She was famous for her bluntness, and he was hoping for a straight answer.

'He's guilty. He killed them. It's cut and dried. But he had the best damned excuse I've ever seen. There's some sympathy for him.'

'Let's say you're on the jury. Guilty or innocent?'

She watched the front door and waved at a regular. 'Well, my instinct is to forgive anyone who kills a rapist. Especially a father. But, on the other hand, we can't allow people to grab guns and hand out their own justice. Can you prove he was crazy when he did it?'

'Let's assume I can.'

'Then I would vote not guilty, even though I don't think he was crazy.'

He smeared strawberry preserves on dry toast and nodded his approval.

'But what about Looney?' she asked. 'He's a friend of mine.'

'It was an accident.'

'Is that good enough?'

'No. No, it's not. The gun did not go off by accident. Looney was accidentally shot, but I doubt if that's valid defense. Would you convict him for shooting Looney?'

'Maybe,' she answered slowly. 'He lost a leg.'

How could he be insane when he shot Cobb and Willard, and not when he shot Looney, Jake thought, but didn't ask. He changed the subject.

'What's the gossip on me?'

'About the same. Someone was asking where you were the other day, and said you don't have time for us now that you're a celebrity. I've heard some mumbling, about you and the nigger, but it's pretty quiet. They don't criticize you loudly. I won't let them.'

'You're a sweetheart.'

'I'm a mean bitch and you know it.'

'No. You just try to be.'

'Yeah, watch this.' She jumped from the booth and shouted abuse at a table of farmers who had motioned for more coffee. Jake finished alone, and returned to the office.

When Ethel arrived at eight-thirty, two reporters were loitering on the sidewalk outside the locked door. They followed Ethel inside and demanded to see Mr Brigance. She refused, and asked them to leave. They refused, and repeated their demand. Jake heard the commotion downstairs and locked his door. Let Ethel fight with them.

From his office he watched a camera crew set up by the rear door of the courthouse. He smiled and felt a wonderful surge of adrenaline. He could see himself on the evening news walking briskly, stern, businesslike, across the street followed by reporters begging for dialogue but getting no comments. And this was just the arraignment. Imagine the trial! Cameras everywhere, reporters yelling questions, front page stories, perhaps magazine covers. An Atlanta paper had called it the most sensational murder in the South in twenty years. He would have taken the case for free, almost.

Moments later he interrupted the argument downstairs, and warmly greeted the reporters. Ethel disappeared into the conference room.

'Could you answer some questions?' one of them asked.

'No,' Jake answered politely. 'I have to meet with Judge Noose.'

'Just a couple of questions?'

'No. But there will be a press conference at three P.M.' Jake opened the door, and the reporters followed him onto the sidewalk.

'Where's the press conference?'

'In my office.'

'What's the purpose?'

'To discuss the case.'

Jake walked slowly across the street and up the short driveway to the courthouse answering questions along the way.

'Will Mr Hailey be at the press conference?'

'Yes, along with his family.'

'The girl, too?'

'Yes, she will be there.'

'Will Mr Hailey answer questions?'

'Maybe. I haven't decided.'

Jake said good day, and disappeared into the courthouse, leaving the reporters to chat and gossip about the press conference.

Buckley entered the courthouse through the huge wooden front doors, amid no fanfare. He had hoped for a camera or two, but was dismayed to learn they were gathering at the rear door to catch a glimpse of the defendant. He would use the rear door in the future.

Judge Noose parked by a fire hydrant in front of the post office and loped along the east sidewalk across the courtyard square and into the courthouse. He, too, attracted no attention, except for a few curious stares.

Ozzie peered through the front windows of the jail and watched the mob waiting for Carl Lee in the parking lot. The ploy of another end run crossed his mind, but he dismissed it. His office had received two dozen death threats on Carl Lee, and Ozzie took a few seriously. They were specific, with dates and places. But most were just general, everyday death threats. And this was just the arraignment. He thought of the trial, and mumbled something to Moss Junior. They surrounded Carl Lee with uniformed bodies and marched him down the sidewalk, past the press and into a rented step van. Six deputies and a driver piled in. Escorted by Ozzie's three newest patrol cars, the van drove quickly to the courthouse.

Noose had scheduled a dozen arraignments for 9:00 A.M., and when he settled into the chair on the bench he shifted through the files until he found Hailey's. He looked to the front row in the courtroom and saw a somber group of suspicious-looking men, all newly indicted. At the far end of the front row, two deputies sat next to a hand-cuffed defendant, and Brigance was whispering to him. Must be Hailey.

Noose picked up a red court file and adjusted his reading glasses so they would not hinder his reading. 'State versus Carl Lee Hailey, case number 3889. Will Mr Hailey come forward?'

The handcuffs were removed, and Carl Lee followed his attorney to the bench, where they stood looking up to His Honor, who quietly and nervously scanned the indictment in the file. The courtroom grew silent. Buckley rose and strutted slowly to within a few feet of the defendant. The artists near the railing busily sketched the scene.

Jake glared at Buckley, who had no reason to stand before the bench during the arraignment. The D.A. was dressed in his finest black three-piece polyester suit. Every hair on his huge head had been meticulously combed and plastered in place. He had the appearance of a television evangelist.

Jake walked to Buckley and whispered, 'That's a nice suit, Rufus.'

'Thanks,' he replied, somewhat off-guard.

'Does it glow in the dark?' Jake asked, then returned to the side of his client.

'Are you Carl Lee Hailey?' asked the judge.

'Yes.'

'Mr Brigance your attorney?'

'Yes.'

'I'm holding here a copy of an indictment returned against you by the grand jury. Have you been served a copy of this?'

'Yes.'

'Have you read it?'

'Yes.'

'Have you discussed it with your attorney?'

'Yes.'

'Do you understand it?'

'Yes.'

'Good. I'm required by law to read it to you in open court.' Noose cleared his throat. '"The grand jurors of the State of Mississippi, taken from the body of good and lawful citizens of Ford County thereof, duly elected, empaneled, sworn, and charged to inquire in and for said county and state aforesaid, in the name and under the authority of the State of Mississippi, upon their oaths present that Carl Lee Hailey, late of the county and state aforesaid, within the jurisdiction of this court, did unlawfully, willfully, and feloniously and intentionally and with malice aforethought, kill and murder Billy Ray Cobb, a human being, and Pete Willard, a human being, and did shoot and attempt to kill DeWayne Looney, a peace officer, in direct violation of the Mississippi Code, and against the peace and dignity of the State of Mississippi. A true bill. Signed, Laverne Gossett, foreman of the grand jury."'

Noose caught his breath. 'Do you understand the charges against you?'

'Yes.'

'Do you understand that if convicted you could be put to death in the gas chamber at the state penitentiary at Parchman?'

'Yes.'

'Do you wish to plead guilty or not guilty?'

'Not guilty.'

Noose reviewed his calendar as the audience watched intently. The reporters took notes. The artists focused on the principals, including Buckley, who had managed to enter the picture and stand sideways, allowing for a profile shot. He was anxious to say something. He scowled contemptuously at the rear of Carl Lee's head, as if he could not wait to fry this murderer. He swaggered to the table where Musgrove was sitting and the two whispered importantly. He marched across the courtroom and engaged in hushed conversation with one of the clerks. Then he returned to the bench where the defendant stood motionless next to his attorney, who was aware of Buckley's show and was trying desperately to ignore it.

'Mr Hailey,' Noose squeaked, 'your trial is set for Monday, July 22. All pretrial motions and matters must be filed by June 24, and disposed of by July 8.'

Carl Lee and Jake nodded.

'Anything further?'

'Yes, Your Honor,' Buckley boomed loud enough for the reporters in the rotunda. 'The State opposes any request for bail by this defendant.'

Jake gripped his fists and wanted to scream. 'Your Honor, the defendant has not yet asked for bail. Mr Buckley, as usual, is confused about the procedure. He cannot oppose a request until it is made. He should've learned that in law school.'

Buckley was stung, but continued. 'Your Honor, Mr Brigance always requests bail, and I'm sure he'll request it today. The State will oppose any such request.'

'Well, why don't you wait until he makes his request?' Noose asked the D.A. with a touch of irritation.

'Very well,' Buckley said. His face had reddened and he glared at Jake.

'Do you plan to request bail?' Noose asked.

'I had planned to at the proper time, but before I got a chance Mr Buckley intervened with his theatrics—'

'Never mind Mr Buckley,' Noose interrupted.

'I know, Judge, he's just confused.'

'Bail, Mr Brigance?'

'Yes, I had planned to request it.'

'I thought so, and I've already considered whether bail should be allowed in this case. As you know, it is completely within my discretion, and I never allow bail in a capital murder case. I don't feel as though an exception is in order in this case.'

'You mean you've decided to deny bail?'

'Yes.'

Jake shrugged his shoulders and laid a file on the table. 'Good enough.'

'Anything further?' Noose asked.

'No, Your Honor,' Jake said.

Buckley shook his head in silence.

'Good. Mr Hailey, you are hereby ordered to remain in the custody of the Ford County sheriff until trial. You are dismissed.'

Carl Lee returned to the front row, where a

deputy waited with the handcuffs. Jake opened his briefcase, and was stuffing it with files and papers when Buckley grabbed his arm.

'That was a cheap shot, Brigance,' he said through clenched teeth.

'You asked for it,' Jake replied. 'Let go of my arm.'

Buckley released his arm. 'I don't appreciate it.'

'Too bad, big man. You shouldn't talk so much. Big mouths get burned.'

Buckley had three inches and fifty pounds on Jake, and his irritation was growing. The exchange had drawn attention, and a deputy moved between them. Jake winked at Buckley and left the courtroom.

At two the Hailey clan, led by Uncle Lester, entered Jake's office through the rear door. Jake met them in a small office next to the conference room downstairs. They talked about the press conference. Twenty minutes later, Ozzie and Carl Lee strolled nonchalantly through the rear door, and Jake led them to the office, where Carl Lee was reunited with his family. Ozzie and Jake left the room.

The press conference was carefully orchestrated by Jake, who marveled at his ability to manipulate the press and its willingness to be manipulated. On one side of the long conference table he sat with the three Hailey boys standing behind him. Gwen was seated to his left, Carl Lee to his right holding Tonya.

Legal etiquette forbade revealing the identity of a child rape victim, but Tonya was different. Her name, face, and age were well known because of her daddy. She had already been exposed to the world, and Jake wanted her to be seen and photographed in her best white Sunday dress sitting on her daddy's knee. The jurors, whoever they were and wherever they lived, would be watching.

Reporters crammed into the room, which overflowed and trailed down the hall to the reception area, where Ethel rudely ordered them to sit and leave her alone. A deputy guarded the front door, and two others sat on the rear steps. Sheriff Walls and Lester stood awkwardly behind the Haileys and their lawyer. Microphones were clustered on the table in front of Jake, and the cameras clicked and flashed under the warm television lights.

'I have a few prefatory remarks,' Jake began. 'First, all questions will be answered by me. No questions are to be directed to Mr Hailey or any member of his family. If he is asked a question, I will instruct him not to answer. Second, I would like to introduce his family. To my left is his wife, Gwen Hailey. Standing behind us are his sons, Carl Lee, Jr, Jarvis, and Robert. Behind the boys is Mr Hailey's brother, Lester Hailey.'

Jake paused and smiled at Tonya. 'Sitting in her daddy's lap is Tonya Hailey. Now I'll answer questions.'

'What happened in court this morning?'

'Mr Hailey was arraigned, he pled not guilty, and his trial was set for July 22.'

'Was there an altercation between you and the district attorney?'

'Yes. After the arraignment, Mr Buckley approached me, grabbed my arm, and looked as if he planned to assault me when a deputy intervened.'

'What caused it?'

'Mr Buckley has a tendency to crack under pressure.'

'Are you and Mr Buckley friends?'

'No.'

'Will the trial be in Clanton?'

'A motion to change venue will be filed by the defense. The location of the trial will be determined by Judge Noose. No predictions.'

'Could you describe what this has done to the Hailey family?'

Jake thought a minute while the cameras rolled. He glanced at Carl Lee and Tonya. 'You're looking at a very nice family. Two weeks ago life was good and simple. There was a job at the paper mill, a little money in the bank, security, stability, church every Sunday together, a loving family. Then, for reasons known only to God, two drunk, drugged punks committed a horrible, violent act against this little ten-year-old girl. They shocked us, and made us all feel sick. They ruined her life, and the lives of her parents and family. It was too much for her father. He snapped. He broke. Now he's in jail facing trial and the prospect of the gas chamber. The job is gone. The money is gone. The innocence is gone. The children face the possibility of growing up without their father. Their mother must now find a job to support them, and she'll have to beg and borrow from friends and relatives in order to survive.

'To answer your question, sir, the family has been devastated and destroyed.'

Gwen began crying quietly, and Jake handed her a handkerchief.

'Are you hinting at a defense of insanity?'

'Yes.'

'Will there in fact be a plea of insanity?'

'Yes.'

'Can you prove it?'

'That will be left for the jury. We will provide them experts in the field of psychiatry.'

'Have you already consulted with these experts?'

'Yes,' lied Jake.

'Could you give us their names?'

'No, that would be inappropriate at this point.'

'We've heard rumors of death threats against Mr Hailey. Could you confirm?'

'There continue to be threats against Mr Hailey, his family, my family, the sheriff, the judge, just about everyone involved. I don't know how serious they are.'

Carl Lee patted Tonya on the leg and looked blankly at the table. He looked scared, pitiful, and in need of sympathy. His boys looked scared too, but, according to strict orders, they stood at attention, afraid to move. Carl Lee, Jr., the oldest at fifteen, stood behind Jake. Jarvis, the middle son at thirteen, stood behind his daddy. And Robert, age eleven, stood behind his mother. They wore identical navy suits with white shirts and little red bow ties. Robert's suit was once Carl Lee, Jr.'s, then Jarvis's, and now his, and it looked a bit more worn than the other two. But it was clean, neatly pressed, and perfectly cuffed. The boys looked sharp. How could any juror vote to force these children to live without their father?

The press conference was a hit. Segments of it ran on the networks and local stations, both on the evening and late news. The Thursday papers ran front page pictures of the Haileys and their lawyer.

Chapter 16

The Swede had called several times during the two weeks her husband had been in Mississippi. She didn't trust him down there. There were old girlfriends he had confessed to. Each time she called, Lester was not around, and Gwen lied and explained that he was fishing or cutting pulpwood so they could buy groceries. Gwen was tired of lying, and Lester was tired of carousing, and they were tired of each other. When the phone rang before dawn Friday morning, Lester answered it. It was the Swede.

Two hours later the red Cadillac was parked at the jail. Moss Junior led Lester into Carl Lee's cell. The brothers whispered above the sleep of the inmates.

'Gotta go home,' Lester mumbled, somewhat ashamed, somewhat timid.

'Why?' Carl Lee asked as if he had been expecting it.

'My wife called this mornin'. I gotta be at work tomorrow or I'm fired.'

Carl Lee nodded approvingly.

'I'm sorry, bubba. I feel bad about goin', but I ain't got no choice.'

'I understand. When you comin' back?'

'When you want me back?'

'For the trial. It'll be real hard on Gwen and the kids. Can you be back then?'

'You know I'll be here. I got some vacation time and all. I'll be here.'

They sat on the edge of Carl Lee's bunk and watched each other in silence. The cell was dark and quiet. The two bunks opposite Carl Lee's were empty.

'Man, I forgot how bad this place is,' Lester said.

'I just hope I ain't here much longer.'

They stood and embraced, and Lester called for Moss Junior to open the cell. 'I'm proud of you, bubba,' he said to his older brother, then left for Chicago. Carl Lee's second visitor of the morning was his attorney, who met him in Ozzie's office. Jake was red eyed and irritable.

'Carl Lee, I talked to two psychiatrists in Memphis yesterday. Do you know what the minimum fee is to evaluate you for trial purposes? Do you?'

'Am I supposed to know?' asked Carl Lee.

'One thousand dollars,' Jake shouted. 'One thousand dollars. Where can you find a thousand dollars?'

'I gave you all the money I got. I even offered—'

'I don't want the deed to your land. Why? Because nobody wants to buy it, and if you can't sell it, it's no good. We've got to have cash, Carl Lee. Not for me, but for the psychiatrists.'

'Why?'

'Why!' Jake repeated in disbelief. 'Why? Because I'd like to keep you away from the gas chamber, and it's only a hundred miles from here. It's not that far. And to do that, we've got to convince the jury that you were insane when you shot those boys. I can't tell them you were crazy. You can't tell them you were crazy. It takes a psychiatrist. An expert. A doctor. And they don't work for free. Understand?'

Carl Lee leaned on his knees and watched a spider crawl across the dusty carpet. After twelve days in jail and two court appearances, he had had enough of the criminal justice system. He thought of the hours and minutes before the killings. What was he thinking? Sure the boys had to die. He had no regrets. But did he contemplate jail, or poverty, or lawyers, or psychiatrists? Maybe, but only in passing. Those unpleasantries were only by-products to be encountered and endured temporarily before he was set free. After the deed, the system would process him, vindicate him, and send him home to his family. It would be easy, just as Lester's episode had been virtually pain-less.

But the system was not working now. It was conspiring to keep him in jail, to break him, to make orphans of his children. It seemed determined to punish him for performing an act he considered unavoidable. And now, his only ally was making demands he could not meet. His lawyer asked the impossible. His friend Jake was angry and yelling.

'Get it,' Jake shouted as he headed for the door. 'Get it from your brothers and sisters, from Gwen's family, get it from your friends, get it from your church. But get it. And as soon as possible.'

Jake slammed the door and marched out of the jail.

Carl Lee's third visitor of the morning arrived before noon in a long black limousine with a chauffeur and Tennessee plates. It maneuvered through the small parking lot and came to rest straddling three spaces. A large black bodyguard emerged from behind the wheel and opened the door to release his boss. They strutted up the sidewalk and into the jail.

The secretary stopped typing and smiled suspiciously. 'Good mornin'.'

'Mornin',' said the smaller one, the one with the patch. 'My name is Cat Bruster, and I'd like to see Sheriff Walls.'

'May I ask what for?'

'Yes ma'am. It's regardin' a Mr Hailey, a resident of your fine facility.'

The sheriff heard his name mentioned, and appeared from his office to greet this infamous visitor. 'Mr Bruster, I'm Ozzie Walls.' They shook hands. The bodyguard did not move.

'Nice to meet you, Sheriff. I'm Cat Bruster, from Memphis.'

'Yes. I know who you are. Seen you in the news. What brings you to Ford County?'

'Well, I gotta buddy in bad trouble. Carl Lee Hailey, and I'm here to help.'

'Okay. Who's he?' Ozzie asked, looking up at the bodyguard. Ozzie was six feet four, and at least five inches shorter than the bodyguard. He weighed at least three hundred pounds, most of it in his arms.

'This here is Tiny Tom,' Cat explained. 'We just call him Tiny for short.'

'I see.'

'He's sort of like a bodyguard.'

'He's not carryin' a gun, is he?'

'Naw, Sheriff, he don't need a gun.'

'Fair enough. Why don't you and Tiny step into my office?'

In the office, Tiny closed the door and stood by it while his boss took a seat across from the sheriff.

'He can sit if he wants to,' Ozzie explained to Cat.

'Naw, Sheriff, he always stands by the door. That's the way he's been trained.'

'Sorta like a police dog?'

'Right.'

'Fine. What'd you wanna talk about?'

Cat crossed his legs and laid a diamond-clustered hand on his knee. 'Well, Sheriff, me and Carl Lee go way back. Fought together in 'Nam.

We was pinned down near Da Nang, summer of '71. I got hit in the head, and, bam!, two seconds later he got hit in the leg. Our squad disappeared, and the gooks was usin' us for target practice. Carl Lee limped to where I's layin', put me on his shoulders, and ran through the gunfire to a ditch next to a trail. I hung on his back while he crawled two miles. Saved my life. He got a medal for it. You know that?'

'No.'

'It's true. We laid next to each other in a hospital in Saigon for two months, then got our black asses outta Vietnam. Don't plan to go back.'

Ozzie was listening intently.

'And now that my man is in trouble, I'd like to help.'

'Did he get the M-16 from you?'

Tiny grunted and Cat smiled. 'Of course not.'

'Would you like to see him?'

'Why sure. It's that easy?'

'Yep. If you can move Tiny away from that door, I'll get him.'

Tiny stepped aside, and two minutes later Ozzie was back with the prisoner. Cat yelled at him, hugged him, and they patted each other like boxers. Carl Lee looked awkwardly at Ozzie, who took the hint and left. Tiny again closed the door and stood guard. Carl Lee moved two chairs together so they could face each other closely and talk.

Cat spoke first. 'I'm proud of you, big man, for what you did. Real proud. Why didn't you tell me that's why you wanted the gun?'

'Just didn't.'

'How was it?'

'Just like 'Nam, except they couldn't shoot back.'

'That's the best way.'

'Yeah, I guess. I just wish none of this had to happen.'

'You ain't sorry, are you?'

Carl Lee rocked in his chair and studied the ceiling. 'I'd do it over, so I got no regrets about that. I just wish they hadn't messed with my little girl. I wish she was the same. I wish none of it ever happened.'

'Right, right. It's gotta be tough on you here.'

'I ain't worried 'bout me. I'm real concerned with my family.'

'Right, right. How's the wife?'

'She's okay. She'll make it.'

'I saw in the paper where the trial's in July. You been in the paper more than me here lately.'

'Yeah, Cat. But you always get off. I ain't so sure 'bout me.'

'You gotta good lawyer, don't you?'

'Yeah. He's good.'

Cat stood and walked around the office, admiring Ozzie's trophies and certificates. 'That's the main reason I came to see you, my man.'

'What's that?' Carl Lee asked, unsure of what his friend had in mind, but certain his visit had a purpose.

'Carl Lee, you know how many times I been on trial?'

'Seems like all the time.'

'Five! Five times they put me on trial. The federal boys. The state boys. The city boys. Dope, gamblin', bribery, guns, racketeerin', whores. You name it, and they've tried me for it. And you know somethin', Carl Lee, I've been guilty of it all. Evertime I've gone to trial, I've been guilty as hell. You know how many times I been convicted?'

'No.'

'None! Not once have they got me. Five trials, five not guilties.'

Carl Lee smiled with admiration.

'You know why they can't convict me?'

Carl Lee had an idea, but he shook his head anyway.

'Because, Carl Lee, I got the smartest, meanest, crookedest criminal lawyer in these parts. He cheats, he plays dirty, and the cops hate him. But I'm sittin' here instead of some prison. He'll do whatever it takes to win a case.'

'Who is he?' Carl Lee asked eagerly.

'You've seen him on television walkin' in and outta court. He's in the papers all the time. Evertime some big-shot crook gets in trouble, he's there. He gets the drug dealers, the politicians, me, all the big-time thugs.'

'What's his name?'

'He handles nothin' but criminal cases, mainly dope, bribery, extortion, stuff like that. But you know what his favorite is?'

'What?'

'Murder. He loves murder cases. Ain't never

lost one. Gets all the big ones in Memphis. Remember when they caught those two niggers throwin' a dude off the bridge into the Mississippi. Caught them redhanded. 'Bout five years ago?'

'Yeah, I remember.'

'Had a big trial for two weeks, and they got off. He was the man. Walked them outta there. Not guilty.'

'I think I remember seein' him on TV.'

'Sure you did. He's a bad dude, Carl Lee. I'm tellin' you the man never loses.'

'What's his name?'

Cat landed in his chair and stared solemnly into Carl Lee's face. 'Bo Marsharfsky,' he said.

Carl Lee gazed upward as if he remembered the name. 'So what?'

Cat laid five fingers with eight carats on Carl Lee's knee. 'So he wants to help you, my man.'

'I already got one lawyer I can't pay. How I'm gonna pay another?'

'You ain't gotta pay, Carl Lee. That's where I come in. He's on my retainer all the time. I own him. Paid the guy 'bout a hundred thousand last year just to keep me outta trouble. You don't pay.'

Suddenly, Carl Lee had a keen interest in Bo Marsharfsky. 'How does he know 'bout me?'

'Because he reads the paper and watches the tube. You know how lawyers are. I was in his office yesterday and he was studyin' the paper with your picture on the front. I told him 'bout me and you. He went crazy. Said he had to have your case. I said I would help.'

'And that's why you're here?'

'Right, right. He said he knew just the folks to get you off.'

'Like who?'

'Doctors, psychiatrists, folks like that. He knows them all.'

'They cost money.'

'I'll pay for it, Carl Lee! Listen to me! I'll pay for it all. You'll have the best lawyer and doctors money can buy, and your old pal Cat will pay the tab. Don't worry 'bout money!'

'But I gotta good lawyer.'

'How old is he?'

'I guess 'bout thirty.'

Cat rolled his eyes in amazement. 'He's a child, Carl Lee. He ain't been outta school long enough. Marsharfsky's fifty, and he's handled more murder cases than your boy'll ever see. This is your life, Carl Lee. Don't trust it to no rookie.'

Suddenly, Jake was awful young. But then there was Lester's trial when Jake had been even younger.

'Look, Carl Lee, I been in many trials, and that crap is complicated and technical. One mistake and your ass is gone. If this kid misses one trick, it might be the difference between life and death. You can't afford to have no young kid in there hopin' he don't mess up. One mistake,' Cat snapped his fingers for special effect, 'and you're in the gas chamber. Marsharfsky don't make mistakes.'

Carl Lee was on the ropes. 'Would he work with my lawyer?' he asked, seeking compromise.

'No! No way. He don't work with nobody. He don't need no help. Your boy'd be in the way.'

Carl Lee placed his elbows on his knees and stared at his feet. A thousand bucks for a doctor would be impossible. He did not understand the need for one since he had not felt insane at the time, but evidently one would be necessary. Everyone seemed to think so. A thousand bucks for a cheap doctor. Cat was offering the best money could buy.

'I hate to do this to my lawyer,' he muttered quietly.

'Don't be stupid, man,' Cat scolded. 'You better be lookin' out for Carl Lee and to hell with this child. This ain't no time to worry 'bout hurtin' feelin's. He's a lawyer, forget him. He'll get over it.'

'But I already paid him—'

'How much?' Cat demanded, snapping his fingers at Tiny.

'Nine hundred bucks.'

Tiny produced a wad of cash, and Cat peeled off nine one-hundred-dollar bills and stuffed them in Carl Lee's shirt pocket. 'Here's somethin' for the kids,' he said as he unraveled a one-thousand-dollar bill and stuffed it with the rest.

Carl Lee's pulse jumped as he thought of the cash covering his heart. He felt it move in the pocket and press gently against his chest. He wanted to look at the big bill and hold it firmly in his hand. Food, he thought, food for his kids.

'We gotta deal?' Cat asked with a smile.

'You want me to fire my lawyer and hire yours?' he asked carefully.

'Right, right.'

'And you gonna pay for everthing?'

'Right, right.'

'What about this money?'

'It's yours. Lemme know if you need more.'

'Mighty nice of you, Cat.'

'I'm a very nice man. I'm helpin' two friends. One saved my life many years ago, and the other saves my ass ever two years.'

'Why does he want my case so bad?'

'Publicity. You know how lawyers are. Look at how much press this kid's already made off you. It's a lawyer's dream. We gotta deal?'

'Yeah. It's a deal.'

Cat struck him on the shoulder with an affectionate blow, and walked to the phone on Ozzie's desk. He punched the numbers. 'Collect to 901-566-9800. From Cat Bruster. Person to person to Bo Marsharfsky.'

On the twentieth floor in a downtown office building, Bo Marsharfsky hung up the phone and asked his secretary if the press release was prepared. She handed it to him, and he read it carefully.

'This looks fine,' he said. 'Get it to both newspapers immediately. Tell them to use the file photograph, the new one. See Frank Fields at the *Post*. Tell him I want it on the front page in the morning. He owes me a favor.'

243

'Yes, sir. What about the TV stations?' she asked.

'Deliver them a copy. I can't talk now, but I'll hold a news conference in Clanton next week.'

Lucien called at six-thirty Saturday morning. Carla was buried deep under the blankets and did not respond to the phone. Jake rolled toward the wall and grappled with the lamp until he found the receiver. 'Hello,' he managed weakly.

'What're you doing?' Lucien asked.

'I was sleeping until the phone rang.'

'You seen the paper?'

'What time is it?'

'Go get the paper and call me after you read it.'

The phone was dead. Jake stared at the receiver, then placed it on the table. He sat on the edge of the bed, rubbed the fog from his eyes, and tried to remember the last time Lucien called his house. It must be important.

He made the coffee, turned out the dog, and walked quickly in his gym shorts and sweatshirt to the edge of the street where the three morning papers had fallen within ten inches of each other. He rolled the rubber bands off onto the kitchen table and spread the papers next to his coffee. Nothing in the Jackson paper. Nothing from Tupelo. *The Memphis Post* carried a headline of death in the Middle East, and, then, he saw it. On the bottom half of the front page he saw himself, and under his picture was the caption: 'Jake Brigance – Out.' Next was a picture of Carl

Lee, and then a splendid picture of a face he had seen before. Under it, the words: 'Bo Marsharfsky – In.' The headline announced that the noted Memphis criminal attorney had been hired to represent the 'vigilante killer.'

He was stunned, weak, and confused. Surely it was a mistake. He had seen Carl Lee only yesterday. He read the story slowly. There were few details, just a history of Marsharfsky's greatest verdicts. He promised a news conference in Clanton. He said the case would present new challenges, etc. He had faith in the jurors of Ford County.

Jake slipped silently into starched khakis and a button-down. His wife was still lost somewhere deep in the bed. He would tell her later. He took the paper and drove to the office. The Coffee Shop would not be safe. At Ethel's desk he read the story again and stared at his picture on the front page.

Lucien had a few words of comfort. He knew Marsharfsky, or 'The Shark,' as he was known. He was a sleazy crook with polish and finesse. Lucien admired him.

Moss Junior led Carl Lee into Ozzie's office, where Jake waited with a newspaper. The deputy quickly left and closed the door. Carl Lee sat on the small black vinyl couch.

Jake threw the newspaper at him. 'Have you seen this?' he demanded.

Carl Lee glared at him and ignored the paper.

'Why, Carl Lee?'

'I don't have to explain, Jake.'

'Yes, you do. You didn't have the guts to call me like a man and tell me. You let me read it in the paper. I demand an explanation.'

'You wanted too much money, Jake. You're always gripin' over the money. Here I am sittin' in jail and you're bitchin' 'bout somethin' I can't help.'

'Money. You can't afford to pay me. How can you afford Marsharfsky?'

'I ain't gotta pay him.'

'What!'

'You heard me. I ain't payin' him.'

'I guess he works for free.'

'Nope. Somebody else is payin'.'

'Who!' Jake shouted.

'I ain't tellin'. It ain't none of your business, Jake.'

'You've hired the biggest criminal lawyer in Memphis, and someone else is payin' his bill?'

'Yep.'

The NAACP, thought Jake. No, they wouldn't hire Marsharfsky. They've got their own lawyers. Besides, he was too expensive for them. Who else?

Carl Lee took the newspaper and folded it neatly. He was ashamed, and felt bad, but the decision had been made. He had asked Ozzie to call Jake and convey the news, but the sheriff wanted no part of it. He should have called, but he was not going to apologize. He studied his picture on the front page. He liked the part about the vigilante business.

'And you're not going to tell me who?' Jake said, somewhat quieter.

'Naw, Jake. I ain't tellin'.'

'Did you discuss it with Lester?'

The glare returned to his eyes. 'Nope. He ain't on trial, and it ain't none of his business.'

'Where is he?'

'Chicago. Left yesterday. And don't you go call him. I've made up my mind, Jake.'

We'll see, Jake said to himself. Lester would find out shortly.

Jake opened the door. 'That's it. I'm fired. Just like that.'

Carl Lee stared at his picture and said nothing.

Carla was eating breakfast and waiting. A reporter from Jackson had called looking for Jake, and had told her about Marsharfsky.

There were no words, just motions. He filled a cup with coffee and went to the back porch. He sipped from the steaming cup and surveyed the unkempt hedges that lined the boundary of his long and narrow backyard. A brilliant sun baked the rich green Bermuda and dried the dew, creating a sticky haze that drifted upward and hung to his shirt. The hedges and grass were waiting on their weekly grooming. He kicked off his loafers – no socks – and walked through the soggy turf to inspect a broken birdbath near a scrawny crepe myrtle, the only tree of any significance.

She followed the wet footprints and stood

behind him. He took her hand and smiled. 'You okay?' she asked.

'Yeah, I'm fine.'

'Did you talk to him?'

'Yes.'

'What did he say?'

He shook his head and said nothing.

'I'm sorry, Jake.'

He nodded and stared at the birdbath.

'There will be other cases,' she said without confidence.

'I know.' He thought of Buckley, and could hear the laughter. He thought of the guys at the Coffee Shop, and vowed not to return. He thought of the cameras and reporters, and a dull pain moved through his stomach. He thought of Lester, his only hope of retrieving the case.

'Would you like some breakfast?' she asked.

'No. I'm not hungry. Thanks.'

'Look on the bright side,' she said. 'We won't be afraid to answer the phone.'

'I think I'll cut the grass,' he said.

Chapter 17

The Council of Ministers was a group of black preachers that had been formed to coordinate political activities in the black communities of Ford County. It met infrequently during the off years, but during election years it met weekly, on Sunday afternoons, to interview candidates and discuss issues, and, more importantly, to determine the benevolence of each office seeker. Deals were cut, strategies developed, money exchanged. The council had proven it could deliver the black vote. Gifts and offerings to black churches rose dramatically during elections.

The Reverend Ollie Agee called a special meeting of the council for Sunday afternoon at his church. He wrapped up his sermon early, and by 4:00 P.M. his flock had scattered when the Cadillacs and Lincolns began filling his parking lot. The meetings were secret, with only ministers who were council members invited. There were twenty-three black churches in Ford County, and twenty-two members were present when Reverend

Agee called the meeting to order. The meeting would be brief, since some of the ministers, especially from the Church of Christ, would begin their evening services shortly.

The purpose of the meeting, he explained, was to organize moral, political, and financial support of Carl Lee Hailey, a member in good standing of his church. A legal defense fund must be established to assure the best legal representation. Another fund must be established to provide support for his family. He, Reverend Agee, would chair the fund-raising efforts, with each minister responsible for his own congregation, as usual. A special offering would be taken during the morning and evening services, starting next Sunday. Agee would use his discretion in disbursing the money to the family. Half of the proceeds would go to the defense fund. Time was important. The trial was next month. The money had to be raised quickly while the issue was hot, and the people were in a giving mood.

The council unanimously agreed with Reverend Agee. He continued.

The NAACP must become active in the Hailey case. He would not be on trial if he was white. Not in Ford County. He was on trial only because he was black, and this must be addressed by the NAACP. The national director had been called. The Memphis and Jackson chapters had promised help. Press conferences would be held. Demonstrations and marches would be important. Maybe boycotts of white-owned businesses – that was a popular tactic at the moment, and it worked with amazing results.

This must be done immediately, while the people were willing and in a giving mood. The ministers unanimously agreed and left for their evening services.

In part due to fatigue, and in part due to embarrassment, Jake slept through church. Carla fixed pancakes, and they enjoyed a long breakfast with Hanna on the patio. He ignored the Sunday papers after he found, on the front page of the second section of *The Memphis Post*, a full-page spread on Marsharfsky and his famous new client. The story was complete with pictures and quotes from the great lawyer. The Hailey case presented his biggest challenge, he said. Serious legal and social issues would be addressed. A novel defense would be employed, he promised. He had not lost a murder case in twelve years, he boasted. It would be difficult, but he had confidence in the wisdom and fairness of Mississippi jurors.

Jake read the article without comment and laid the paper in the trash can.

Carla suggested a picnic, and although he needed to work he knew better than to mention it. They loaded the Saab with food and toys and drove to the lake. The brown, muddy waters of Lake Chatulla had crested for the year, and within days would begin their slow withdrawal to the center. The high water attracted a flotilla of skiboats, bass rigs, catamarans, and dinghies.

Carla threw two heavy quilts under an oak on the side of a hill while Jake unloaded the food and doll house. Hanna arranged her large family with pets and automobiles on one quilt and began giving orders and setting up house. Her parents listened and smiled. Her birth had been a harrowing, gut-wrenching nightmare, two and a half months premature and shrouded with conflicting symptoms and prognoses. For eleven days Jake sat by the incubator in ICU and watched the tiny, purple, scrawny, beautiful three-pound body cling to life while an army of doctors and nurses studied the monitors and adjusted tubes and needles, and shook their heads. When he was alone he touched the incubator and wiped tears from his cheeks. He prayed as he had never prayed. He slept in a rocking chair near his daughter and dreamed of a beautiful blue-eyed, dark-haired little girl playing with dolls and sleeping on his shoulder. He could hear her voice.

After a month the nurses smiled and the doctors relented. The tubes were removed one at a time each day for a week. Her weight ballooned to a hearty four and a half pounds, and the proud parents took her home. The doctors suggested no more children, unless adopted.

She was perfect now, and the sound of her voice could still bring tears to his eyes. They ate and chuckled as Hanna lectured her dolls on proper hygiene.

'This is the first time you've relaxed in two weeks.' Carla said as they lay on their quilt. Wildly colored catamarans crisscrossed the lake below dodging a hundred roaring boats pulling half-drunken skiers.

'We went to church last Sunday,' he replied.

'And all you thought about was the trial.'

'Still thinking about it.'

'It's over, isn't it?'

'I don't know.'

'Will he change his mind?'

'He might, if Lester talks to him. It's hard to say. Blacks are so unpredictable, especially when they're in trouble. He's got a good deal, really. He's got the best criminal lawyer in Memphis, and he's free.'

'Who's paying the bill?'

'An old friend of Carl Lee's from Memphis, a guy by the name of Cat Bruster.'

'Who's he?'

'A very rich pimp, dope pusher, thug, thief. Marsharfsky's his lawyer. A couple of crooks.'

'Did Carl Lee tell you this?'

'No. He wouldn't tell me, so I asked Ozzie.'

'Does Lester know?'

'Not yet.'

'What do you mean by that? You're not going to call him, are you?'

'Well, yes, I had planned to.'

'That's going a bit far, isn't it?'

'I don't think so. Lester has a right to know, and—'

'Then Carl Lee should tell him.'

'He should, but he won't. He's made a mistake, and he does not realize it.'

'But it's his problem, not yours. At least not anymore.'

'Carl Lee's too embarassed to tell Lester. He knows Lester will cuss him and tell him he's made another mistake.'

'So it's up to you to intervene in their family affairs.'

'No. But I think Lester should know.'

'I'm sure he'll see it in the papers.'

'Maybe not,' Jake said without any conviction. 'I think Hanna needs some more orange juice.'

'I think you want to change the subject.'

'The subject doesn't bother me. I want the case, and I intend to get it back. Lester's the only person who can retrieve it.'

Her eyes narrowed and he could feel them. He watched a bass rig drift into a mud bar on the near shore.

'Jake, that's unethical, and you know it.' Her voice was calm, yet controlled and firm. The words were slow and scornful.

'That's not true, Carla. I'm a very ethical attorney.'

'You've always preached ethics. But at this moment you're scheming to solicit the case. That's wrong, Jake.'

'Retrieve, not solicit.'

'What's the difference?'

'Soliciting is unethical. I've never seen a prohibition against retrieving.'

'It's not right, Jake. Carl Lee's hired another lawyer and it's time for you to forget it.'

'And I suppose you think Marsharfsky reads ethics opinions. How do you think he got the case? He's been hired by a man who's never heard of him. He chased the case, and he's got it.'

'So that makes it okay if you chase it now?'

'Retrieve, not chase.'

Hanna demanded cookies, and Carla searched through the picnic basket. Jake reclined on an elbow and ignored them both. He thought of Lucien. What would he do in this situation? Probably rent a plane, fly to Chicago, get Lester, slip him some money, bring him home, and convince him to browbeat Carl Lee. He would assure Lester that Marsharfsky could not practice in Mississippi, and since he was a foreigner, the rednecks on the jury wouldn't believe him anyway. He would call Marsharfsky and curse him for chasing cases and threaten him with an ethics complaint the minute he stepped into Mississippi. He would get his black cronies to call Gwen and Ozzie and persuade them that the only lawyer with a dog's chance in hell of winning the case was Lucien Wilbanks. Finally, Carl Lee would knuckle under and send for Lucien.

That's exactly what Lucien would do. Talk about ethics.

'Why are you smiling?' Carla interrupted.

'Just thinking about how nice it is out here with you and Hanna. We don't do this enough.'

'You're disappointed, aren't you?'

'Sure. There will never be another case like this one. Win it, and I'm the greatest lawyer in these

255

parts. We would never have to worry about money again.'

'And if you lost it?'

'It would still be a drawing card. But I can't lose what I don't have.'

'Embarrassed?'

'A little. It's hard to accept. Every lawyer in the county is laughing about it, except maybe Harry Rex. But I'll get over it.'

'What should I do with the scrapbook?'

'Save it. You might fill it up yet.'

The cross was a small one, nine feet long and four feet wide, made to fit inconspicuously in the long bed of a pickup. Much larger crosses were used for the rituals, but the small ones worked better in the nocturnal raids into residential areas. They were not used often, or often enough according to their builders. In fact, it had been many years since one had been used in Ford County. The last one was planted in the yard of a nigger accused of raping a white woman.

Several hours before dawn on Monday morning, the cross was lifted quietly and quickly from the pickup and thrust into a ten-inch, freshly dug slot in the front yard of the quaint Victorian house on Adams Street. A small torch was thrown at the foot of the cross, and in seconds it was in flames. The pickup disappeared into the night and stopped at a pay phone at the edge of town, where a call was placed to the dispatcher.

Moments later, Deputy Marshall Prather turned

down Adams and instantly saw the blazing cross in Jake's front yard. He turned into the driveway and parked behind the Saab. He punched the doorbell and stood on the porch watching the flames. It was almost three-thirty. He punched it again. Adams was dark and silent except for the glow of the cross and the snapping and crackling of the wood burning fifty feet away. Finally, Jake stumbled through the front door and froze, wild-eyed and stunned, next to the deputy. The two stood side by side on the porch, mesmerized not only by the burning cross, but by its purpose.

'Mornin', Jake,' Prather finally said without looking from the fire.

'Who did it?' Jake asked with a scratchy, dry throat.

'Don't know. They didn't leave a name. Just called and told us about it.'

'When did they call?'

'Fifteen minutes ago.'

Jake ran his fingers through his hair in an effort to keep it from blowing wild in the soft breeze. 'How long will it burn?' he asked, knowing Prather knew as little or even less than he about burning crosses.

'No tellin'. Probably soaked in kerosene. Smells like it anyway. Might burn for a couple of hours. You want me to call a fire truck?'

Jake looked up and down the street. Every house was silent and dark.

'Naw. No need to wake everybody. Let it burn. It won't hurt anything, will it?'

'It's your yard.'

Prather never moved; just stood there, hands in his pockets, his belly hanging over his belt. 'Ain't had one of these in a long time around here. Last one I remember was in Karaway, nineteen-sixty—'

'Nineteen sixty-seven.'

'You remember?'

'Yeah. I was in high school. We drove out and watched it burn.'

'What was that nigger's name?'

'Robinson, something Robinson. Said he raped Velma Thayer.'

'Did he?' asked Prather.

'The jury thought so. He's in Parchman chopping cotton for the rest of his life.'

Prather seemed satisfied.

'Let me get Carla,' Jake mumbled as he disappeared. He returned with his wife behind him.

'My God, Jake! Who did it?'

'Who knows.'

'Is it the KKK?' she asked.

'Must be,' answered the deputy. 'I don't know anybody else who burns crosses, do you, Jake?'

Jake shook his head.

'I thought they left Ford County years ago,' said Prather.

'Looks like they're back,' said Jake.

Carla stood frozen, her hand over her mouth, terrified. The glow of the fire reddened her face. 'Do something, Jake. Put it out.'

Jake watched the fire and again glanced up and down the street. The snapping and popping grew louder and the orange flames reached higher into the night. For a moment he hoped it would die quickly without being seen by anyone other than the three of them, and that it would simply go away and be forgotten and no one in Clanton would ever know. Then he smiled at his foolishness.

Prather grunted, and it was obvious he was tired of standing on the porch. 'Say, Jake, uh, I don't mean to bring this up, but accordin' to the papers they got the wrong lawyer. That true?'

'I guess they can't read,' Jake muttered.

'Probably not.'

'Tell me, Prather, do you know of any active Klan members in this county?'

'Not a one. Got some in the southern part of the state, but none around here. Not that I know of. FBI told us the Klan was a thing of the past.'

'That's not very comforting.'

'Why not?'

'Because these guys, if they're Klan members, are not from around here. Visitors from parts unknown. It means they're serious, don't you think, Prather?'

'I don't know. I'd worry more if it was local people workin' with the Klan. Could mean the Klan's comin' back.'

'What does it mean, the cross?' Carla asked the deputy.

'It's a warnin'. Means stop what you're doin', or the next time we'll do more than burn a little wood. They used these things for years to intimidate whites

259

who were sympathetic to niggers and all that civil rights crap. If the whites didn't stop their nigger lovin', then violence followed. Bombs, dynamite, beatings, even murder. But that was a long time ago, I thought. In your case, it's their way of tellin' Jake to stay away from Hailey. But since he ain't Hailey's lawyer no more, I don't know what it means.'

'Go check on Hanna,' Jake said to Carla, who went inside.

'If you got a water hose, I'll be glad to put it out,' offered Prather.

'That's a good idea,' Jake said. 'I'd hate for the neighbors to see it.'

Jake and Carla stood on the porch in their bathrobes and watched the deputy spray the burning cross. The wood fizzed and smoked as the water covered the cross and snuffed out the flames. Prather soaked it for fifteen minutes, then neatly rolled the hose and placed it behind the shrubs in the flower bed next to the front steps.

'Thanks, Marshall. Let's keep this quiet, okay?'

Prather wiped his hands on his pants and straightened his hat. 'Sure. Y'all lock up good. If you hear anything, call the dispatcher. We'll keep a close watch on it for the next few days.'

He backed from the driveway and drove slowly down Adams Street toward the square. They sat in the swing and watched the smoking cross.

'I feel like I'm looking at an old issue of *Life* magazine,' Jake said.

'Or a chapter from a Mississippi history text-book. Maybe we should tell them you got fired.'

'Thanks.'

'Thanks?'

'For being so blunt.'

'I'm sorry. Should I say discharged, or terminated, or—'

'Just say he found another lawyer. You're really scared aren't you?'

'You know I'm scared. I'm terrified. If they can burn a cross in our front yard, what's to stop them from burning the house? It's not worth it, Jake. I want you to be happy and successful and all that wonderful stuff, but not at the expense of our safety. No case is worth this.'

'You're glad I got fired?'

'I'm glad he found another lawyer. Maybe they'll leave us alone now.'

Jake put his arm around her, and pulled her into his lap. The swing rocked gently. She was beautiful, at three-thirty in the morning in her bathrobe.

'They won't be back, will they?' she asked.

'Naw. They're through with us. They'll find out I'm off the case, then they'll call and apologize.'

'It's not funny, Jake.'

'I know.'

'Do you think people will know?'

'Not for another hour. When the Coffee Shop opens at five, Dell Perkins will know every detail before she pours the first cup of coffee.'

'What're you going to do with it?' she asked,

nodding at the cross, now barely visible under the half moon.

'I've got an idea. Let's load it up, take it to Memphis, and burn it in Marsharfsky's yard.'

'I'm going to bed.'

By 9:00 A.M. Jake had finished dictating his motion to withdraw as counsel of record. Ethel was typing it with zest when she interrupted him: 'Mr Brigance, there's a Mr Marsharfsky on the phone. I told him you were in conference, and he said he would hold.'

'I'll talk to him.' Jake gripped the receiver. 'Hello.'

'Mr Brigance, Bo Marsharfsky in Memphis. How are you?'

'Terrific.'

'Good. I'm sure you saw the morning paper Saturday and Sunday. You do get the paper in Clanton?'

'Yes, and we have telephones and mail.'

'So you saw the stories on Mr Hailey?'

'Yes. You write some very nice articles.'

'I'll ignore that. I wanted to discuss the Hailey case if you have a minute.'

'I would love to.'

'As I understand Mississippi procedure, out-of-state counsel must associate local counsel for trial purposes.'

'You mean you don't have a Mississippi license?' Jake asked incredulously.

'Well, no, I don't.'

'That wasn't mentioned in your articles.'

'I'll ignore that too. Do the judges require local counsel in all cases?'

'Some do, some don't.'

'I see. What about Noose?'

'Sometimes.'

'Thanks. Well, I usually associate local counsel when I try cases out in the country. The locals feel better with one of their own sitting there at counsel table with me.'

'That's real nice.'

'I don't suppose you'd be interested in—'

'You must be kidding!' Jake yelled. 'I've just been fired and now you want me to carry your briefcase. You're crazy. I wouldn't have my name associated with yours.'

'Wait a minute, hayseed—'

'No, you wait a minute, counselor. This may come as a surprise to you, but in this state we have ethics and laws against soliciting litigation and clients. Champerty – ever hear of it? Of course not. It's a felony in Mississippi, as in most states. We have canons of ethics that prohibit ambulance chasing and solicitation. Ethics, Mr Shark, ever hear of them?'

'I don't chase cases, sonny. They come to me.'

'Like Carl Lee Hailey. I'm supposed to believe he picked your name out of the yellow pages. I'm sure you have a full-page ad, next to the abortionists.'

'He was referred to me.'

'Yeah, by your pimp. I know exactly how you

got him. Outright solicitation. I may file a complaint with the bar. Better yet, I might have your methods reviewed by the grand jury.'

'Yeah, I understand you and the D.A. are real close. Good day, counselor.'

Marsharfsky got the last word before he hung up. Jake fumed for an hour before he could concentrate on the brief he was writing. Lucien would have been proud of him.

Just before lunch Jake received a call from Walter Sullivan, of the Sullivan firm.

'Jake, my boy, how are you?'

'Wonderful.'

'Good. Listen, Jake, Bo Marsharfsky is an old friend of mine. We defended a couple of bank officials years ago on fraud charges. Got them off, too. He's quite a lawyer. He's associated me as local counsel for Carl Lee Hailey. I was just wanting to know—'

Jake dropped the receiver and walked out of his office. He spent the afternoon on Lucien's front porch.

Chapter 18

Gwen did not have Lester's number. Neither did Ozzie, nor did anyone else. The operator said there were two pages of Haileys in the Chicago phone book, at least a dozen Lester Haileys, and several L. S.'s. Jake asked for the first five Lester Haileys and called each one. They were all white. He called Tank Scales, the owner of one of the safer and finer black honky tonks in the county. Tank's Tonk, as it was known. Lester was especially fond of the place. Tank was a client and often provided Jake with valuable and confidential information on various blacks, their dealings and whereabouts.

Tank stopped by the office Tuesday morning on the way to the bank.

'Have you seen Lester Hailey in the past two weeks?' Jake asked.

'Sure. Spent several days at the place shootin' pool, drinkin' beer. Went back to Chicago last weekend, I heard. Must've, I didn't see him all weekend.'

'Who was he with?'

'Hisself mostly.'

'What about Iris?'

'Yeah, he brung her a couple of times when Henry was outta town. Makes me nervous when he brings her. Henry's a bad dude. He'd cut them both if he knew they's datin'.'

'They've been doing it for ten years, Tank.'

'Yeah, she got two kids by Lester. Everybody knows it but Henry. Poor old Henry. He'll find out one day, and you'll have another murder case.'

'Listen, Tank, can you talk to Iris?'

'She don't come in too often.'

'That's not what I asked. I need Lester's phone number in Chicago. I figure Iris knows it.'

'I'm sure she does. I think he sends her money.'

'Can you get it for me? I need to talk to Lester.'

'Sure, Jake. If she's got it, I'll get it.'

By Wednesday Jake's office had returned to normal. Clients began to reappear. Ethel was especially sweet, or as sweet as possible for a cranky old nag. He went through the motions of practicing law, but the pain showed. He skipped the Coffee Shop each morning and avoided the courthouse by making Ethel do the filing or checking or whatever business required his presence across the street. He was embarrassed, humiliated, and troubled. It was difficult to concentrate on other cases. He contemplated a long vacation, but couldn't afford it. Money was tight, and he was not motivated to work. He spent most of his time in his office doing little but

266

watching the courthouse and the town square below.

He dwelt on Carl Lee, sitting in his cell a few blocks away, and asked himself a thousand times why he had been betrayed. He had pushed too hard for money, and forgot there were other lawyers willing to take the case for free. He hated Marsharfsky. He recalled the many times he had seen Marsharfsky parade in and out of Memphis courtrooms proclaiming the innocence and mistreatment of his pitiful, oppressed clients. Dope dealers, pimps, crooked politicians, and slimy corporate thugs. All guilty, all deserving of long prison terms, or perhaps even death. He was a yankee, with an obnoxious twang from somewhere in the upper Midwest. It would irritate anybody south of Memphis. An accomplished actor, he would look directly into the cameras and whine: 'My client has been horribly abused by the Memphis police.' Jake had seen it a dozen times. 'My client is completely, totally, absolutely innocent. He should not be on trial. My client is a model citizen, a taxpayer.' What about his four prior convictions for extortion? 'He was framed by the FBI. Set up by the government. Besides, he's paid his debt. He's innocent this time.' Jake hated him, and to his recollection, he had lost as many as he had won.

By Wednesday afternoon, Marsharfsky had not been seen in Clanton. Ozzie promised to notify Jake if he showed up at the jail.

Circuit Court would be in session until Friday,

and it would be respectful to meet briefly with Judge Noose and explain the circumstances of his departure from the case. His Honor was presiding over a civil case, and there was a good chance Buckley would be absent. He had to be absent. He could not be seen or heard.

Noose usually recessed for ten minutes around three-thirty, and precisely at that time Jake entered chambers through the side door. He had not been seen. He sat patiently by the window waiting for Ichabod to descend from the bench and stagger into the room. Five minutes later the door flung open, and His Honor walked in.

'Jake, how are you?' he asked.

'Fine, Judge. Can I have a minute?' Jake asked as he closed the door.

'Sure, sit down. What's on your mind?' Noose removed his robe, threw it over a chair, and lay on top of the desk, knocking off books, files, and the telephone in the process. Once his gawky frame had ceased moving, he slowly folded his hands over his stomach, closed his eyes, and breathed deeply. 'It's my back, Jake. My doctor tells me to rest on a hard surface when possible.'

'Uh, sure, Judge. Should I leave?'

'No, no. What's on your mind?'

'The Hailey case.'

'I thought so. I saw your motion. Found a new lawyer, huh?'

'Yes, sir. I had no idea it was coming. I expected to try the case in July.'

'You owe no apologies, Jake. The motion to

withdraw will be granted. It's not your fault. Happens all the time. Who's the new guy Marsharfsky?'

'Yes, sir. From Memphis.'

'With a name like that he should be a hit in Ford County.'

'Yes, sir.' Almost as bad as Noose, thought Jake.

'He has no Mississippi license,' Jake explained, helpfully.

'That's interesting. Is he familiar with our procedure?'

'I'm not sure he's ever tried a case in Mississippi. He told me he normally associates a local boy when he's out in the country.'

'In the country?'

'That's what he said.'

'Well, he'd better associate if he comes into my court. I've had some bad experiences with out-of-state attorneys, especially from Memphis.'

'Yes, sir.'

Noose was breathing harder, and Jake decided to leave. 'Judge, I need to go. If I don't see you in July, I'll see you during the August term of court. Take care of your back.'

'Thanks, Jake. Take care.'

Jake almost made it to the rear door of the small office when the main door from the courtroom opened and the Honorable L. Winston Lotterhouse and another hatchet man from the Sullivan firm strutted into chambers.

'Well, hello, Jake,' Lotterhouse announced. 'You know K. Peter Otter, our newest associate.'

'Nice to meet you K. Peter,' replied Jake.

'Are we interrupting anything?'

'No, I was just leaving. Judge Noose is resting his back, and I was on my way out.'

'Sit down, gentlemen,' Noose said.

Lotterhouse smelled blood. 'Say, Jake, I'm sure Walter Sullivan has informed you that our firm will serve as local counsel for Carl Lee Hailey.'

'I have heard.'

'I'm sorry it happened to you.'

'Your grief is overwhelming.'

'It does present an interesting case for our firm. We don't get too many criminal cases, you know.'

'I know,' Jake said, looking for a hole to crawl in. 'I need to run. Nice chatting with you, L. Winston. Nice meeting you, K. Peter. Tell J. Walter and F. Robert and all the boys I said hello.'

Jake slid out of the rear door of the courthouse and cursed himself for showing his face where he could get it slapped. He ran to his office.

'Has Tank Scales called?' he asked Ethel as he started up the stairs.

'No. But Mr Buckley is waiting.'

Jake stopped on the first step. 'Waiting where?' he asked without moving his jaws.

'Upstairs. In your office.'

He walked slowly to her desk and leaned across to within inches of her face. She had sinned, and she knew it.

He glared at her fiercely. 'I didn't know he had an appointment.' Again, the jaws did not move.

'He didn't,' she replied, her eyes glued to the desk.

'I didn't know he owned this building.'

She didn't move, didn't answer.

'I didn't know he had a key to my office.'

Again, no movement, no answer.

He leaned closer. 'I should fire you for this.'

Her lip quivered and she looked helpless.

'I'm sick of you, Ethel. Sick of your attitude, your voice, your insubordination. Sick of the way you treat people, sick of everything about you.'

Her eyes watered. 'I'm sorry.'

'No you're not. You know, and have known for years, that no one, no one in the world, not even my wife, goes up those stairs into my office if I'm not here.'

'He insisted.'

'He's an ass. He gets paid for pushing people around. But not in this office.'

'Shhh. He can hear you.'

'I don't care. He knows he's an ass.'

He leaned even closer until their noses were six inches apart. 'Would you like to keep your job, Ethel?'

She nodded, unable to speak.

'Then do exactly as I say. Go upstairs to my office, fetch Mr Buckley, and lead him into the conference room, where I'll meet him. And don't ever do it again.'

Ethel wiped her face and ran up the stairs. Moments later the D.A. was seated in the conference room with the door closed. He waited.

Jake was next door in the small kitchen drinking orange juice and assessing Buckley. He drank slowly. After fifteen minutes he opened the door and entered the room. Buckley was seated at one end of the long conference table. Jake sat at the other end, far away.

'Hello, Rufus. What do you want?'

'Nice place you have here. Lucien's old offices, I believe.'

'That's right. What brings you here?'

'Just wanted to visit.'

'I'm very busy.'

'And I wanted to discuss the Hailey case.'

'Call Marsharfsky.'

'I was looking forward to the battle, especially with you on the other side. You're a worthy adversary, Jake.'

'I'm honored.'

'Don't get me wrong. I don't like you, and I haven't for a long time.'

'Since Lester Hailey.'

'Yeah, I guess you're right. You won, but you cheated.'

'I won, that's all that counts. And I didn't cheat. You got caught with your pants down.'

'You cheated and Noose let you by with it.'

'Whatever. I don't like you either.'

'Good. That makes me feel better. What do you know about Marsharfsky?'

'Is that the reason you're here?'

'Could be.'

'I've never met the man, but if he was my father

I wouldn't tell you anything. What else do you want?'

'Surely you've talked to him.'

'We had some words on the phone. Don't tell me you're worried about him.'

'No. Just curious. He's got a good reputation.'

'Yes, he does. You didn't come here to discuss his reputation.'

'No, not really. I wanted to talk about the case.'

'What about it?'

'Chances for an acquittal, possible defenses, was he really insane. Things like that.'

'I thought you guaranteed a conviction. In front of the cameras, remember? Just after the indictment. One of your press conferences.'

'Do you miss the cameras already, Jake?'

'Relax, Rufus. I'm out of the game. The cameras are all yours, at least yours and Marsharfsky's, and Walter Sullivan's. Go get them, tiger. If I've stolen some of your spotlight, then I'm deeply sorry. I know how it hurts you.'

'Apology accepted. Has Marsharfsky been to town?'

'I don't know.'

'He promised a press conference this week.'

'And you came here to talk about his press conference, right?'

'No, I wanted to discuss Hailey, but obviously you're too busy.'

'That's right. Plus I have nothing to discuss with you, Mr Governor.'

'I resent that.'

'Why? You know it's true. You'd prosecute your mother for a couple of headlines.'

Buckley stood and began pacing back and forth behind his chair. 'I wish you were still on this case, Brigance,' he said, the volume increasing.

'So do I.'

'I'd teach you a few things about prosecuting murderers. I really wanted to clean your plow.'

'You haven't been too successful in the past.'

'That's why I wanted you on this one, Brigance. I wanted you so bad.' His face had returned to the deep red that was so familiar.

'There'll be others, Governor.'

'Don't call me that,' he shouted.

'It's true, isn't it, Governor. That's why you chase the cameras so hard. Everybody knows it. There goes old Rufus, chasing cameras, running for governor. Sure it's true.'

'I'm doing my job. Prosecuting thugs.'

'Carl Lee Hailey's no thug.'

'Watch me burn him.'

'It won't be that easy.'

'Watch me.'

'It takes twelve out of twelve.'

'No problem.'

'Just like your grand jury?'

Buckley froze in his tracks. He squinted his eyes and frowned at Jake. Three huge wrinkles creased neatly across his mammoth forehead. 'What do you know about the grand jury?'

'As much as you do. One vote less and you'd have sucked eggs.'

'That's not true!'

'Come on, Governor. You're not talking to a reporter. I know exactly what happened. Knew it within hours.'

'I'll tell Noose.'

'And I'll tell the newspapers. That'll look good before the trial.'

'You wouldn't dare.'

'Not now. I have no reason to. I've been fired, remember? That's the reason you're here, right, Rufus? To remind me that I'm no longer on the case, but you are. To rub a little salt in the wounds. Okay, you've done it. Now I wish you'd leave. Go check on the grand jury. Or maybe there's a reporter hanging around the courthouse. Just leave.'

'Gladly. I'm sorry I bothered.'

'Me too.'

Buckley opened the door leading into the hall, then stopped. 'I lied, Jake. I'm tickled to death you're not on this case.'

'I know you lied. But don't count me out.'

'What does that mean?'

'Good day, Rufus.'

The Ford County grand jury had been busy, and by Thursday of the second week of the term Jake had been retained by two freshly indicted defendants. One was a black who cut another black at Massey's Tonk back in April. Jake enjoyed the stabbings because acquittals were possible; just get an all-white jury full of rednecks who could care less if all niggers stabbed each other. They were just having a little fun down at the tonk, things got out of hand, one got stabbed, but didn't die. No harm, no conviction. It was similar to the strategy Jake had learned with Lester Hailey. The new client promised fifteen hundred dollars, but first had to post bond.

The other new indictee was a white kid caught driving a stolen pickup. It was the third time he'd been caught in a stolen pickup, and there was no way to keep him out of Parchman for seven years.

Both were in jail, and their presence there afforded Jake the opportunity, and duty, to visit them and check with Ozzie. Late Thursday afternoon he found the sheriff in his office.

'Are you busy?' Jake asked. A hundred pounds of paper was strewn over the desk and onto the floor.

'No, just paperwork. Any more burnin' crosses?'

'No, thank God. One's enough.'

'I haven't seen your friend from Memphis.'

'That's strange,' said Jake. 'I thought he would be here by now. Have you talked to Carl Lee?'

'Every day. He's gettin' nervous. The lawyer ain't even called, Jake.'

'Good. Let him sweat. I don't feel sorry for him.'

'You think he made a mistake?'

'I know he did. I know these rednecks around here, Ozzie, and I know how they act when you put them on a jury. They won't be impressed by some slick-talking foreigner. You agree?'

'I don't know. You're the lawyer. I don't doubt what you say, Jake. I've seen you work.'

'He's not even licensed to practice in Mississippi. Judge Noose is laying for him. He hates out-of-state lawyers.'

'You're kiddin'?'

'Nope. I talked to him yesterday.'

Ozzie looked disturbed and eyed Jake carefully. 'You wanna see him?'

'Who?'

'Carl Lee.'

'No! I have no reason to see him.' Jake glanced in his briefcase. 'I need to see Leroy Glass, aggravated assault.'

'You got Leroy?'

'Yeah. His folks came in this morning.'

'Follow me.'

Jake waited in the Intoxilyzer room while a trusty went for the new client. Leroy wore the standard Ford County jail issue of glow-in-the-dark orange coveralls. Pink sponge rollers shot in all directions from his scalp, and two long greasy cornrows clung to the back of his neck. His black leathery feet were protected from the dirty linoleum by a pair of lime green terrycloth slides. No socks. A wicked, aged scar started next to his right ear lobe, made the ridge over his cheek-bone, and connected neatly with his right nostril. It proved beyond a reasonable doubt that Leroy was no stranger to stabbings and carvings. He wore it like a medal. He smoked Kools.

'Leroy, I'm Jake Brigance,' the lawyer introduced

himself and pointed to a folding chair next to the Pepsi machine. 'Your momma and brother hired me this morning.'

'Good to know you, Mr Jake.'

A trusty waited in the hall by the door as Jake asked questions. He filled three pages of notes on Leroy Glass. Of primary interest, at least at this point, was money. How much did he have, and where could he find more. They would talk about the stabbing later. Aunts, uncles, brothers, sisters, friends, anyone with a job who might be able to make a loan. Jake took phone numbers.

'Who referred you to me?' Jake asked.

'Saw you on TV, Mr Jake. You and Carl Lee Hailey.'

Jake was proud, but did not smile. Television was just part of his job. 'You know Carl Lee?'

'Yeah, know Lester too. You's Lester's lawyer, wasn't you?'

'Yes.'

'Me and Carl Lee in the same cell. Moved me last night.'

'You don't say.'

'Yeah. He don't talk much. He said you's a real good lawyer and all, but he found somebody else from Memphis.'

'That's right. What does he think of his new lawyer?'

'I don't know, Mr Jake. He was fussin' this mornin' cause the new lawyer ain't been to see him yet. He say you come to see him all the time and talk 'bout the case, but the new lawyer, some funny name, ain't even been down to meet him yet.'

Jake concealed his delight with a grim face, but it was difficult. 'I'll tell you something if you promise you won't tell Carl Lee.'

'Okay.'

'His new lawyer can't come to see him.'

'No! Why not?'

'Because he doesn't have a license to practice law in Mississippi. He's a Tennessee lawyer. He'll get thrown out of court if he comes down here by himself. I'm afraid Carl Lee's made a big mistake.'

'Why don't you tell him?'

'Because he's already fired me. I can't give him advice anymore.'

'Somebody ought to.'

'You just promised you won't, okay?'

'Okay. I won't.'

'Promise?'

'I swear.'

'Good. I gotta go. I'll meet with the bondsman in the morning, and maybe we'll have you out in a day or so. Not a word to Carl Lee, right?'

'Right.'

Tank Scales was leaning on the Saab in the parking lot when Jake left the jail. He stepped on a cigarette butt and pulled a piece of paper from his shirt pocket. 'Two numbers. Top one's for home, bottom for work. But don't call at work unless you have to.'

'Good work, Tank. Did you get them from Iris?'

'Yeah. She didn't want to. She stopped by the tonk last night and I got her drunk.'

'I owe you one.'

'I'll get it, sooner or later.'

It was dark, almost eight o'clock. Dinner was cold, but that was not unusual. That's why he had bought her a microwave. She was accustomed to the hours and the warmed-over dinners, and she did not complain. They would eat when he came home, whether it was six or ten.

Jake drove from the jail to his office. He wouldn't dare call Lester from home, not with Carla listening. He settled behind his desk and stared at the numbers Tank had located. Carl Lee had told him not to make this call. Why should he do it? Would it be solicitation? Unethical? Would it be unethical to call Lester and tell him that Carl Lee had fired him and hired another lawyer? No. And to answer Lester's questions about the new lawyer? No. And to express concern? No. And to criticize the new lawyer? Probably not. Would it be unethical to encourage Lester to talk to his brother? No. And convince him to fire Marsharfsky? Probably so. And to rehire Jake? Yes, no doubt about it. That would be very unethical. What if he just called Lester and talked about Carl Lee and allowed the conversation to follow its own course.

'Hello.'

'Is there a Lester Hailey there?'

'Yes. Who's calling?' came the accented reply from the Swede.

'Jake Brigance, from Mississippi.'

'One moment.'

Jake checked his watch. Eight-thirty. It was the same time in Chicago, wasn't it?

'Jake!'

'Lester, how are you?'

'Fine, Jake. Tired, but fine. How 'bout you?'

'Great. Listen, have you talked to Carl Lee this week?'

'No. I left Friday, and I've been workin' two shifts since Sunday. I ain't had time for nothin'.'

'You seen the newspapers?'

'No. What's happened?'

'You won't believe it, Lester.'

'What is it, Jake?'

'Carl Lee fired me and hired a big-shot lawyer from Memphis.'

'What! You're kiddin'? When?'

'Last Friday. I guess after you left. He didn't bother to tell me. I read it in the Memphis paper Saturday morning.'

'He's crazy. Why'd he do it, Jake? Who'd he hire?'

'You know a guy named Cat Bruster from Memphis?'

'Of course.'

'It's his lawyer. Cat's paying for it. He drove down from Memphis last Friday and saw Carl Lee at the jail. Next morning I saw my picture in the paper and read where I've been fired.'

'Who's the lawyer?'

'Bo Marsharfsky.'

'He any good?'

'He's a crook. He defends all the pimps and drug dealers in Memphis.'

'Sounds like a Polack.'

'He is. I think he's from Chicago.'

'Yeah, bunch of Polacks up here. Does he talk like these?'

'Like he's got a mouthful of hot grease. He'll go over big in Ford County.'

'Stupid, stupid, stupid. Carl Lee never was too bright. I always had to think for him. Stupid, stupid.'

'Yeah, he's made a mistake, Lester. You know what a murder trial is like because you've been there. You realize how important that jury is when they leave the courtroom and go to the jury room. Your life is in their hands. Twelve local people back there fighting and arguing over your case, your life. The jury's the most important part. That's why you gotta be able to talk to the jury.'

'That's right, Jake. You can do it too.'

'I'm sure Marsharfsky can do it in Memphis, but not Ford County. Not in rural Mississippi. These people won't trust him.'

'You're right, Jake. I can't believe he did it. He's screwed up again.'

'He did it, Lester, and I'm worried about him.'

'Have you talked to him?'

'Last Saturday, after I saw the newspaper, I went straight to the jail. I asked him why, and he could not answer. He felt bad about it. I haven't talked to him since then. But neither has Marsharfsky.

He hasn't found Clanton yet, and I understand Carl Lee's upset. As far as I can tell, nothing has been done on the case this week.'

'Has Ozzie talked to him?'

'Yeah, but you know Ozzie. He's not gonna say too much. He knows Bruster's a crook and Marsharfsky's a crook, but he won't lean on Carl Lee.'

'Man oh man. I can't believe it. He's stupid if he thinks those rednecks'll listen to some shyster from Memphis. Hell, Jake, they don't trust the lawyers from Tyler County and it's next door. Man oh man.'

Jake smiled at the receiver. So far, nothing unethical.

'What should I do, Jake?'

'I don't know, Lester. He needs some help, and you're the only one he'll listen to. You know how headstrong he is.'

'I guess I'd better call him.'

No, thought Jake, it would be easier for Carl Lee to say no over the phone. Confrontation was needed between the brothers. A drive from Chicago would make an impact.

'I don't think you'll get very far over the phone. His mind's made up. Only you can change it, and you can't do it over the phone.'

Lester paused a few seconds while Jake waited anxiously. 'What's today?'

'Thursday, June 6.'

'Let's see,' Lester mumbled. 'I'm ten hours away. I work the four-to-midnight shift tomorrow and again Sunday. I could leave here midnight tomorrow, and be in Clanton by ten Saturday mornin'. Then I could leave early Sunday mornin' and be back by four. That's a lot of drivin', but I can handle it.'

'It's very important, Lester. I think it's worth the trip.'

'Where will you be Saturday, Jake?'

'Here at the office.'

'Okay. I'll go to the jail, and if I need you I'll call the office.'

'Sounds good. One other thing, Lester. Carl Lee told me not to call you. Don't mention it.'

'What'll I tell him?'

'Tell him you called Iris, and she gave you the story.'

'Iris who?'

'Come on, Lester. It's been common knowledge around here for years. Everybody knows it but her husband, and he'll find out.'

'I hope not. We'll have us another murder. You'll have another client.'

'Please. I can't keep the ones I've got. Call me Saturday.'

He ate from the microwave at ten-thirty. Hanna was asleep. They talked about Leroy Glass and the white kid in the stolen pickup. About Carl Lee, but not about Lester. She felt better, safer now that Carl Lee Hailey was behind them. No more calls. No more burning crosses. No more stares at church. There would be other cases, she promised. He said little; just ate and smiled.

Chapter 19

Just before the courthouse closed on Friday, Jake called the clerk to see if a trial was in progress. No, she said, Noose was gone. Buckley, Musgrove, everybody was gone. The courtroom was deserted. Secure with that knowledge, Jake eased across the street, through the rear door of the courthouse, and down the hall to the clerk's office. He flirted with the clerks and secretaries while he located Carl Lee's file. He held his breath as he flipped through the pages. Good! Just as he had hoped. Nothing had been added to the file all week, with the exception of his motion to withdraw as counsel. Marsharfsky and his local counsel had not touched the file. Nothing had been done. He flirted some more and eased back to his office.

Leroy Glass was still in jail. His bond was ten thousand dollars, and his family couldn't raise the thousand-dollar premium to pay a bondsman. So he continued to share the cell with Carl Lee. Jake had a friend who was a bondsman and who took care of Jake's clients. If a client needed out of jail, and there was little danger of him disappearing once he was sprung, the bond would be written. Terms were available for Jake's clients. Say, five percent down and so much a month. If Jake wanted Leroy Glass out of jail, the bond could be written anytime. But Jake needed him in jail.

'Look, Leroy, I'm sorry. I'm working with the bondsman,' Jake explained to his client in the Intoxilyzer room.

'But you said I'd be out by now.'

'Your folks don't have the money, Leroy. I can't pay it myself. We'll get you out, but it'll take a few days. I want you out so you can go to work, make some money and pay me.'

Leroy seemed satisfied. 'Okay, Mr Jake, just do what you can.'

'Food's pretty good here, isn't it?' Jake asked with a smile.

'It ain't bad. Better at home.'

'We'll get you out,' Jake promised.

'How's the nigger I stabbed?'

'Not sure. Ozzie said he's still in the hospital. Moss Tatum says he's been released. Who knows. I don't think he's hurt too bad.'

'Who was the woman?' Jake asked, unable to remember the details.

'Willie's woman.'

'Willie who?'

'Willie Hoyt.'

Jake thought for a second and tried to recall the indictment. 'That's not the man you stabbed.'

'Naw, he's Curtis Sprawling.'

'You mean, y'all were fighting over another man's woman?'

'That's right.'

'Where was Willie?'

'He was fightin' too.'

'Who was he fighting?'

'Some other dude.'

'You mean the four of you were fighting over Willie's woman?'

'Yeah, you got it.'

'What caused the fight?'

'Her husband was outta town.'

'She's married?'

'That's right.'

'What's her husband's name?'

'Johnny Sands. When he's outta town, there's normally a fight.'

'Why is that?'

''Cause she ain't got no kids, can't have any, and she likes to have company. Know what I mean? When he leaves, everybody knows it. If she shows up at a tonk, look out for a fight.'

What a trial, thought Jake. 'But I thought you said she showed up with Willie Hoyt?'

'That's right. But that don't mean nothin' because everybody at the tonk starts easin' up on her, buyin' drinks, wantin' to dance. You can't help it.'

'Some woman, huh?'

'Oh, Mr Jake, she looks so good. You oughtta see her.'

'I will. On the witness stand.'

Leroy gazed at the wall, smiling, dreaming, lusting after the wife of Johnny Sands. Never mind that he stabbed a man and could get twenty years. He had proven, in hand-to-hand combat, that he was worthy.

'Listen, Leroy, you haven't talked to Carl Lee, have you?'

'Sure. I'm still in his cell. We talk all the time. Ain't much else to do.'

'You haven't told him what we discussed yesterday?'

'Oh no. I told you I wouldn't.'

'Good.'

'But I'll tell you this, Mr Jake, he's some kinda worried. He ain't heard from his new lawyer. He's bad upset. I had to bite my tongue to keep from tellin' him, but I didn't. I did tell him you were my lawyer.'

'That's okay.'

'He said you was good 'bout comin' by the jail and talkin' 'bout the case and all. He said I hired a good lawyer.'

'Not good enough for him, though.'

'I think Carl Lee's confused. He ain't sure who to trust or anything. He's a good dude.'

'Well, don't be telling him what we discussed, right? It's confidential.'

'Right. But somebody needs to.'

'He didn't consult with me or anyone else before he fired me and hired his new lawyer. He's a grown man. He made the decision. It's his baby.' Jake paused and moved closer to Leroy. He lowered

288

his voice. 'And I'll tell you something else, but you can't tell it. I checked his court file thirty minutes ago. His new lawyer hasn't touched the case all week. Not one thing has been filed. Nothing.'

Leroy frowned and shook his head. 'Man oh man.'

His lawyer continued. 'These big shots operate like that. Talk a lot, blow a lot of smoke, fly by the seat of their pants. Take more cases than they can handle, and end up losing more than they win. I know them. I watch them all the time. Most are overrated.'

'Is that why he ain't been to see Carl Lee?'

'Sure. He's too busy. Plus he's got plenty of other big cases. He don't care about Carl Lee.'

'That's bad. Carl Lee deserves better.'

'It was his choice. He'll have to live with it.'

'You think he'll be convicted, Mr Jake?'

'No doubt about it. He's looking at the gas chamber. He's hired a bogus big-shot lawyer who doesn't have time to work on his case, doesn't even have the time to talk to him in jail.'

'Are you sayin' you could get him off?'

Jake relaxed and crossed his legs. 'No, I never make that promise, and I won't make it for your trial. A lawyer is stupid if he promises an acquittal. Too many things can go wrong at trial.'

'Carl Lee said his lawyer promised a not guilty in the newspaper.'

'He's a fool.'

* * *

'Where you been?' Carl Lee asked his cellmate as the jailer locked the door.

'Talkin' to my lawyer.'

'Jake?'

'Yeah.'

Leroy sat on his bunk directly across the cell from Carl Lee, who was rereading a newspaper. He folded the paper and laid it under his bunk.

'You look worried,' Carl Lee said. 'Bad news about your case?'

'Naw. Just can't make my bail. Jake says it'll be a few days.'

'Jake talk about me?'

'Naw. Not much.'

'Not much? What'd he say?'

'Just ask how you was.'

'That all?'

'Yeah.'

'He's not mad at me?'

'Naw. He might be worried about you, but I don't think he's mad.'

'Why's he worried about me?'

'I don't know,' Leroy answered as he stretched out on his bunk, folding his hands behind his head.

'Come on, Leroy. You know somethin' you ain't tellin'. What'd Jake say about me?'

'Jake said I can't tell you what we talk about. He says it's confidential. You wouldn't want your lawyer repeatin' what y'all talk about, would you?'

'I ain't seen my lawyer.'

'You had a good lawyer till you fired him.'

'I gotta good one now.'

'How do you know? You ain't ever met him. He's too busy to come talk to you, and if he's that busy, he ain't got time to work on your case.'

'How do you know about him?'

'I asked Jake.'

'Yeah. What'd he say?'

Leroy was silent.

'I wanna know what he said,' demanded Carl Lee as he sat on the edge of Leroy's bunk. He glared at his smaller, weaker cellmate. Leroy decided he was frightened and now had a good excuse to tell Carl Lee. Either talk or get slapped.

'He's a crook,' Leroy said. 'He's a big-shot crook who'll sell you out. He don't care about you or your case. He just wants the publicity. He hasn't touched your case all week. Jake knows, he checked in the courthouse this afternoon. Not a sign of Mr Big Shot. He's too busy to leave Memphis and check on you. He's got too many other crooked clients in Memphis, includin' your friend Mr Bruster.'

'You're crazy, Leroy.'

'Okay, I'm crazy. Wait and see who pleads insaneness. Wait and see how hard he works on your case.'

'What makes you such an expert?'

'You asked me and I'm tellin' you.'

Carl Lee walked to the door and grabbed the bars, gripping them tightly with his huge hands. The cell had shrunk in three weeks, and the smaller it became the harder it was for him to think, to reason, to plan, to react. He could not concentrate in jail. He knew only what was told to him and had no one to trust. Gwen was irrational. Ozzie was noncommittal. Lester was in Chicago. There was no other person he trusted except Jake, and for some reason he had found a new lawyer. Money, that was the reason. Nineteen hundred dollars cash, paid by the biggest pimp and dope dealer in Memphis, whose lawyer specialized in defending pimps and dope dealers, and all kinds of cutthroats and hoodlums. Did Marsharfsky represent decent people? What would the jury think when they watched Carl Lee sit at the defense table next to Marsharfsky? He was guilty, of course. Why else would he hire a famous, big-city crook like Marsharfsky?

'You know what them rednecks on the jury'll say when they see Marsharfsky?' Leroy asked.

'What?'

'They're gonna think this poor nigger is guilty, and he's sold his soul to hire the biggest crook in Memphis to tell us he ain't guilty.'

Carl Lee mumbled something through the bars.

'They're gonna fry you, Carl Lee.'

Moss Junior Tatum was on duty at six-thirty Saturday morning when the phone rang in Ozzie's office. It was the sheriff.

'What're you doing awake?' asked Moss.

'I'm not sure I'm awake,' answered the sheriff. 'Listen, Moss, do you remember an old black preacher named Street, Reverend Isaiah Street?'

'Not really.'

'Yeah you do. He preached for fifty years at Springdale Church, north of town. First member of the NAACP in Ford County. He taught all the blacks around here how to march and boycott back in the sixties.'

'Yeah, now I remember. Didn't the Klan catch him once?'

'Yeah, they beat him and burned his house, but nothin' serious. Summer of '65.'

'I thought he died a few years back.'

'Naw, he's been half dead for ten years, but he still moves a little. He called me at five-thirty and talked for an hour. Reminded me of all the political favors I owe him.'

'What's he want?'

'He'll be there at seven to see Carl Lee. Why, I don't know. But treat him nice. Put them in my office and let them talk. I'll be in later.'

'Sure, Sheriff.'

In his heyday in the sixties, the Reverend Isaiah Street had been the moving force behind civil rights activity in Ford County. He walked with Martin Luther King in Memphis and Montgomery. He organized marches and protests in Clanton and Karaway and other towns in north Mississippi. In the summer of '64 he greeted students from the North and coordinated their efforts to register black voters. Some had lived in his home that memorable summer, and they still visited him from time to time. He was no radical. He was quiet, compassionate, intelligent, and had earned the respect of all blacks and most whites.

His was a calm, cool voice in the midst of hatred and controversy. He unofficially officiated the great public school desegregation in '69, and Ford County saw little trouble.

A stroke in '75 deadened the right side of his body but left his mind untouched. Now, at seventy-eight, he walked by himself, slowly and with a cane. Proud, dignified, erect as possible. He was ushered into the sheriff's office and seated. He declined coffee, and Moss Junior left to get the defendant.

'You awake, Carl Lee?' he whispered loudly, not wanting to wake the other prisoners, who would begin screaming for breakfast, medicine, lawyers, bondsmen, and girlfriends.

Carl Lee sat up immediately. 'Yeah, I didn't sleep much.'

'You have a visitor. Come on.' Moss quietly unlocked the cell.

Carl Lee had met the reverend years earlier when he addressed the last senior class at East High, the black school. Desegregation followed, and East became the junior high. He had not seen the reverend since the stroke.

'Carl Lee, do you know Reverend Isaiah Street?' Moss asked properly.

'Yes, we met years ago.'

'Good, I'll close the door and let y'all talk.'

'How are you, sir?' Carl Lee asked. They sat next to each other on the couch.

'Fine, my son, and you?'

'As good as possible.'

'I've been in jail too, you know. Years ago. It's a terrible place, but I guess it's necessary. How are they treating you?'

'Fine, just fine. Ozzie lets me do as I please.'

'Yes, Ozzie. We're very proud of him, aren't we?'

'Yes, suh. He's a good man.' Carl Lee studied the frail, feeble old man with the cane. His body was weak and tired, but his mind was sharp, his voice strong.

'We're proud of you too, Carl Lee. I don't condone violence, but at times it's necessary too, I guess. You did a good deed, my son.'

'Yes, suh,' answered Carl Lee, uncertain of the appropriate response.

'I guess you wonder why I'm here.'

Carl Lee nodded. The reverend tapped his cane on the floor.

'I'm concerned about your acquittal. The black community is concerned. If you were white, you would most likely go to trial, and most likely be acquitted. The rape of a child is a horrible crime, and who's to blame a father for rectifying the wrong? A white father, that is. A black father evokes the same sympathy among blacks, but there's one problem: the jury will be white. So a black father and a white father would not have equal chances with the jury. Do you follow me?'

'I think so.'

'The jury is all important. Guilt versus innocence. Freedom versus prison. Life versus death. All to be determined by the jury. It's a fragile system, this trusting of lives to twelve average, ordinary people who do not understand the law and are intimidated by the process.'

'Yes, suh.'

'Your acquittal by a white jury for the killings of two white men will do more for the black folk of Mississippi than any event since we integrated the schools. And it's not just Mississippi; it's black folk everywhere. Yours is a most famous case, and it's being watched carefully by many people.'

'I just did what I had to do.'

'Precisely. You did what you thought was right. It was right; although it was brutal and ugly, it was right. And most folks, black and white, believe that. But will you be treated as though you were white? That's the question.'

'And if I'm convicted?'

'Your conviction would be another slap at us; a symbol of deep-seated racism; of old prejudices, old hatreds. It would be a disaster. You must not be convicted.'

'I'm doin' all I can do.'

'Are you? Let's talk about your attorney, if we may.'

Carl Lee nodded.

'Have you met him?'

'No.' Carl Lee lowered his head and rubbed his eyes. 'Have you?'

'Yes, I have.'

'You have? When?'

'In Memphis in 1968. I was with Dr King. Marsharfsky was one of the attorneys representing the garbage workers on strike against the city. He asked Dr King to leave Memphis, claimed he was agitating the whites and inciting the blacks, and that he was impeding the contract negotiations. He was arrogant and abusive. He cursed Dr King – in private, of course. We thought he was selling out the workers and getting money under the table from the city. I think we were right.'

Carl Lee breathed deeply and rubbed his temples.

'I've followed his career,' the reverend continued. 'He's made a name for himself representing gangsters, thieves, and pimps. He gets some of them off, but they're always guilty. When you see one of his clients, you know he's guilty. That's what worries me most about you. I'm afraid you'll be considered guilty by association.'

Carl Lee sunk lower, his elbows resting on his knees. 'Who told you to come here?' he asked softly.

'I had a talk with an old friend.'

'Who?'

'Just an old friend, my son. He's concerned about you too. We're all concerned about you.'

'He's the best lawyer in Memphis.'

'This isn't Memphis, is it?'

'He's an expert on criminal law.'

'That could be because he's a criminal.'

Carl Lee stood abruptly and walked across the room, his back to the reverend.

'He's free. He's not costin' me a dime.'

'His fee won't seem important when you're on death row, my son.'

Moments passed and neither spoke. Finally, the reverend lowered his cane and struggled to his feet. 'I've said enough. I'm leaving. Good luck, Carl Lee.'

Carl Lee shook his hand. 'I do appreciate your concern and I thank you for visitin'.'

'My point is simply this, my son. Your case will be difficult enough to win. Don't make it more difficult with a crook like Marsharfsky.'

Lester left Chicago just before midnight Friday. He headed south alone, as usual. Earlier his wife went north to Green Bay for a weekend with her family. He liked Green Bay much less than she liked Mississippi, and neither cared to visit the other's family. They were nice people, the Swedes, and they would treat him like family if he allowed it. But they were different, and it wasn't just their whiteness. He grew up with whites in the South and knew them. He didn't like them all and didn't like most of their feelings toward him, but at least he knew them. But the Northern whites, especially the Swedes, were different. Their customs, speech, food, almost everything was foreign to him, and he would never feel comfortable with them.

There would be a divorce, probably within a year. He was black, and his wife's older cousin had married a black in the early seventies and received a lot of attention. Lester was a fad, and she was tired of him. Luckily, there were no kids. He suspected someone else. He had someone else too, and Iris had promised to marry him and move to Chicago once she ditched Henry.

Both sides of Interstate 57 looked the same after midnight – scattered lights from the small, neat farms strewn over the countryside, and occasionally a big town like Champaign or Effingham. The north was where he lived and worked, but it wasn't home. Home was where Momma was, in Mississippi, although he would never live there again. Too much ignorance and poverty. He didn't mind the racism; it wasn't as bad as it once was and he was accustomed to it. It would always be there, but gradually becoming less visible. The whites still owned and controlled everything, and that in itself was not unbearable. It was not about to change. What he found intolerable was the ignorance and stark poverty of many of the blacks; the dilapidated, shotgun houses, the high infant mortality rate, the hopelessly unemployed, the unwed mothers and their unfed babies. It was depressing to the point of being intolerable, and intolerable to the point he fled Mississippi like thousands of others and migrated north in search of a job, any decent-paying job which could ease the pain of poverty.

It was both pleasant and depressing to return to Mississippi. Pleasant in that he would see his family; depressing because he would see their poverty. There were bright spots. Carl Lee had a decent job, a clean house, and well-dressed kids. He was an exception, and now it was all in jeopardy because of two drunk, low-bred pieces of white trash. Blacks had an excuse for being worthless, but for whites in a white world, there were no excuses. They were dead, thank God, and he was proud of his big brother.

Six hours out of Chicago the sun appeared as he crossed the river at Cairo. Two hours later he crossed it again at Memphis. He drove southeast into Mississippi, and an hour later circled the courthouse in Clanton. He'd been awake for twenty hours.

'Carl Lee, you have a visitor,' Ozzie said through the iron bars in the door.

'I'm not surprised. Who is it?'

'Just follow me. I think you better use my office. This could take a while.'

Jake loitered at his office waiting on the phone to ring. Ten o'clock. Lester should be in town, if he's coming. Eleven. Jake riffled through some stale files and made notes for Ethel. Noon. He called Carla and lied about meeting a new client at one o'clock, so forget lunch. He would work in the yard later. One o'clock. He found an ancient case from Wyoming where a husband was acquitted after tracking down the man who raped his wife. In 1893. He copied the case, then threw it in the garbage. Two o'clock. Was Lester in town? He could go visit Leroy and snoop around the jail. No, that didn't feel right. He napped on the couch in the big office.

At two-fifteen the phone rang. Jake bolted

upright and scrambled from the couch. His heart was pounding as he grabbed the phone. 'Hello!'

'Jake, this is Ozzie.'

'Yeah, Ozzie, what's up?'

'Your presence is requested here at the jail.'

'What?' Jake asked, feigning innocence.

'You're needed down here.'

'By who?'

'Carl Lee wants to talk to you.'

'Is Lester there?'

'Yeah. He wants you too.'

'Be there in a minute.'

'They've been in there for over four hours,' Ozzie said, pointing to the office door.

'Doing what?' asked Jake.

'Talkin', cussin', shoutin'. Things got quiet about thirty minutes ago. Carl Lee came out and asked me to call you.'

'Thanks. Let's go in.'

'No way, man. I ain't goin' in there. They didn't send for me. You're on your own.'

Jake knocked on the door.

'Come in!'

He opened it slowly, walked inside and closed it. Carl Lee was sitting behind the desk. Lester was lying on the couch. He stood and shook Jake's hand. 'Good to see you, Jake.'

'Good to see you, Lester. What brings you home?'

'Family business.'

Jake looked at Carl Lee, then walked to the

301

desk and shook his hand. The defendant was clearly irritated.

'Y'all sent for me?'

'Yeah, Jake, sit down. We need to talk,' said Lester. 'Carl Lee's got somethin' to tell you.'

'You tell him,' Carl Lee said.

Lester sighed and rubbed his eyes. He was tired and frustrated. 'I ain't sayin' another word. This is between you and Jake.' Lester closed his eyes and relaxed on the couch. Jake sat in a padded, folding chair that he leaned against the wall opposite the couch. He watched Lester carefully, but did not look at Carl Lee, who rocked slowly in Ozzie's swivel chair. Carl Lee said nothing. Lester said nothing. After three minutes of silence, Jake was annoyed.

'Who sent for me?' he demanded.

'I did,' answered Carl Lee.

'Well, what do you want?'

'I wanna give you my case back.'

'You assume I want it back.'

'What!' Lester sat up and looked at Jake.

'It's not a gift you give or take away. It's an agreement between you and your attorney. Don't act as though you're doing me a great favor.' Jake's voice was rising, his anger apparent.

'Do you want the case?' asked Carl Lee.

'Are you trying to rehire me, Carl Lee?'

'That's right.'

'Why do you want to rehire me?'

''Cause Lester wants me to.'

'Fine, then I don't want your case.' Jake stood

and started for the door. 'If Lester wants me and you want Marsharfsky, then stick with Marsharfsky. If you can't think for yourself, you need Marsharfsky.'

'Wait, Jake. Be cool, man,' Lester said as he met Jake at the door. 'Sit down, sit down. I don't blame you for bein' mad at Carl Lee for firin' you. He was wrong. Right, Carl Lee?'

Carl Lee picked at his fingernails.

'Sit down, Jake, sit down and let's talk,' Lester pleaded as he led him back to the folding chair. 'Good. Now, let's discuss this situation. Carl Lee, do you want Jake to be your lawyer?'

Carl Lee nodded. 'Yeah.'

'Good. Now, Jake—'

'Explain why.' Jake asked Carl Lee.

'What?'

'Explain why you want me to handle your case. Explain why you're firing Marsharfsky.'

'I don't have to explain.'

'Yes! Yes, you do. You at least owe me an explanation. You fired me a week ago and didn't have the guts to call me. I read it in the newspaper. Then I read about your new high-priced lawyer who evidently can't find his way to Clanton. Now you call me and expect me to drop everything because you might change your mind again. Explain, please.'

'Explain, Carl Lee. Talk to Jake,' Lester said.

Carl Lee leaned forward and placed his elbows on the desk. He buried his face in his hands and spoke between his palms. 'I'm just confused. This place is drivin' me crazy. My nerves are shot. I'm worried about my little girl. I'm worried about my family. I'm worried about my own skin. Everbody's tellin' me to do somethin' different. I ain't ever been in a situation like this and I don't know what to do. All I can do is trust people. I trust Lester, and I trust you, Jake. That's all I can do.'

'You trust my advice?' asked Jake.

'I always have.'

'And you trust me to handle your case?'

'Yeah, Jake, I want you to handle it.'

'Good enough.'

Jake relaxed, and Lester eased into the couch. 'You'll need to notify Marsharfsky. Until you do, I can't work on your case.'

'We'll do that this afternoon,' Lester said.

'Good. Once you talk to him, give me a call. There's a lot of work to do, and the time will disappear.'

'What about the money?' asked Lester.

'Same fee. Same arrangements. Is that satisfactory?'

'Okay with me,' replied Carl Lee. 'I'll pay you any way I can.'

'We'll discuss that later.'

'What about the doctors?' asked Carl Lee.

'We'll make some arrangements. I don't know. It'll work out.'

The defendant smiled. Lester snored loudly and Carl Lee laughed at his brother. 'I figured you called him, but he swears you didn't.'

Jake smiled awkwardly but said nothing. Lester

was a smooth liar, a talent which had proved extremely beneficial during his murder trial.

'I'm sorry, Jake. I was wrong.'

'No apologies. There's too much work to spend time apologizing.'

Next to the parking lot outside the jail, a reporter stood under a shade tree waiting for something to happen.

'Excuse me, sir, aren't you Mr Brigance?'

'Who wants to know?'

'I'm Richard Flay, with *The Jackson Daily*. You're Jake Brigance.'

'Yes.'

'Mr Hailey's ex-lawyer.'

'No. Mr Hailey's lawyer.'

'I thought he had retained Bo Marsharfsky. In fact, that's why I'm here. I heard a rumor Marsharfsky would be here this afternoon.'

'If you see him, tell him he's too late.'

Lester slept hard on the couch in Ozzie's office. The dispatcher woke him at 4:00 A.M. Sunday, and after filling a tall Styrofoam cup with black coffee, he left for Chicago. Late Saturday night he and Carl Lee had called Cat in his office above the club and informed him of Carl Lee's conversion. Cat was indifferent and busy. He said he would call Marsharfsky. There was no mention of the money.

Chapter 20

Not long after Lester disappeared, Jake staggered down his driveway in his bathrobe to get the Sunday papers. Clanton was an hour southeast of Memphis, three hours north of Jackson, and forty-five minutes from Tupelo. All three cities had daily papers with fat Sunday editions that were available in Clanton. Jake had long subscribed to all three, and was now glad he did so Carla would have plenty of material for her scrapbook. He spread the papers and began the task of plowing through five inches of print.

Nothing in the Jackson paper. He hoped Richard Flay had reported something. He should have spent more time with him outside the jail. Nothing from Memphis. Nothing from Tupelo. Jake was not surprised, just hopeful that somehow the story had been discovered. But it happened too late yesterday. Maybe Monday. He was tired of hiding; tired of feeling embarrassed. Until it was in the papers and read by the boys at the Coffee Shop, and the people at church, and the other lawyers, including Buckley and Sullivan and Lotterhouse, until everybody knew it was his case again, he would stay quiet and out of view. How should he tell Sullivan? Carl Lee would call Marsharfsky, or the pimp, probably the pimp, who would then call Marsharfsky with the news. What kind of press release would Marsharfsky write for that? Then the great lawyer would call Walter Sullivan with the wonderful news. That should happen Monday morning, if not sooner. Word would spread quickly throughout the Sullivan firm, and the senior partners, junior partners, and little associates would all gather in the long, mahogany-laced conference room and curse Brigance and his low ethics and tactics. The associates would try to impress their bosses by spouting rules and code numbers of ethics Brigance probably violated. Jake hated them, every one of them. He would send Sullivan a short, curt letter with a copy to Lotterhouse.

He wouldn't call or write Buckley. He would be in shock after he saw the paper. A letter to Judge Noose with a copy to Buckley would work fine. He would not honor him with a personal letter.

Jake had a thought, then hesitated, then dialed Lucien's number. It was a few minutes after seven. The nurse/maid/bartender answered the phone.

'Sallie?'

'Yes.'

'This is Jake. Is Lucien awake?'

'Just a moment.' She rolled over and handed the phone to Lucien.

'Hello.'

'Lucien, it's Jake.'

'Yeah, whatta you want?'

'Good news. Carl Lee Hailey rehired me yesterday. The case is mine again.'

'Which case?'

'The Hailey case!'

'Oh, the vigilante. He's yours?'

'As of yesterday. We've got work to do.'

'When's the trial? July sometime?'

'Twenty-second.'

'That's pretty close. What's priority?'

'A psychiatrist. A cheap one who'll say anything.'

'I know just the man,' said Lucien.

'Good. Get busy. I'll call in a couple of days.'

Carla awoke at a decent hour and found her husband in the kitchen with newspapers strewn over and under the breakfast table. She made fresh coffee and, without a word, sat across the table. He smiled at her and continued reading.

'What time did you get up?' she asked.

'Five-thirty.'

'Why so early? It's Sunday.'

'I couldn't sleep.'

'Too excited?'

Jake lowered the paper. 'As a matter of fact, I am excited. Very excited. It's too bad the excitement will not be shared.'

'I'm sorry about last night.'

'You don't have to apologize. I know how you feel. Your problem is that you only look at the negative, never the positive. You have no idea what this case can do for us.'

'Jake, this case scares me. The phone calls, the threats, the burning cross. If the case means a million dollars, is it worth it if something happens?'

'Nothing will happen. We'll get some more threats and they'll stare at us at church and around town, but nothing serious.'

'But you can't be sure.'

'We went through this last night and I don't care to rehash it this morning. I do have an idea, though.'

'I can't wait to hear it.'

'You and Hanna fly to North Carolina and stay with your parents until after the trial. They'd love to have you, and we wouldn't worry about the Klan or whoever likes to burn crosses.'

'But the trial is six weeks away! You want us to stay in Wilmington for six weeks?'

'Yes.'

'I love my parents, but that's ridiculous.'

'You don't see enough of them, and they don't see enough of Hanna.'

'And we don't see enough of you. I'm not leaving for six weeks.'

'There's a ton of preparation. I'll eat and sleep this case until the trial is over. I'll work nights, weekends—'

'What else is new?'

'I'll ignore y'all and think of nothing but this case.'

'We're used to that.'

Jake smiled at her. 'You're saying you can handle it?'

'I can handle you. It's those crazies out there that scare me.'

'When the crazies get serious, I'll back off. I will run from this case if my family is in danger.'

'You promise?'

'Of course I promise. Let's send Hanna.'

'If we're not in danger, why do you want to send anybody?'

'Just for safety. She'd have a great time spending the summer with her grandparents. They'd love it.'

'She wouldn't last a week without me.'

'And you wouldn't last a week without her.'

'That's true. It's out of the question. I don't worry about her as long as I can hold her and squeeze her.'

The coffee was ready and Carla filled their cups. 'Anything in the paper?'

'No. I thought the Jackson paper might run something, but it happened too late, I guess.'

'I guess your timing is a little rusty after a week's layoff.'

'Just wait till in the morning.'

'How do you know?'

'I promise.'

She shook her head and searched for the fashion and food sections. 'Are you going to church?'

'No.'

'Why not? You've got the case. You're a star again.'

'Yeah, but no one knows it yet.'

'I see. Next Sunday.'

'Of course.'

* * *

At Mount Hebron, Mount Zion, Mount Pleasant, and at Brown's Chapel, Green's Chapel, and Norris Road, Section Line Road, Bethel Road, and at God's Temple, Christ's Temple, and Saints' Temple, the buckets and baskets and plates were passed and re-passed and left at the altars and front doors to collect the money for Carl Lee Hailey and his family. The large, family-size Kentucky Fried Chicken buckets were used in many of the churches. The bigger the bucket, or basket, the smaller the individual offerings appeared as they fell to the bottom, thus allowing the minister just cause to order another passing through the flock. It was a special offering, separate from the regular giving, and was preceded in virtually every church with a heart-wrenching account of what happened to the precious little Hailey girl, and what would happen to her daddy and family if the buckets were not filled. In many instances the sacred name of the NAACP was invoked and the effect was a loosening of the wallets and purses.

It worked. The buckets were emptied, the money counted, and the ritual repeated during the evening services. Late Sunday night the morning offerings and evening offerings were combined and counted by each minister, who would then deliver a great percentage of the total to the Reverend Agee sometime Monday. He would keep the money somewhere in his church, and a great percentage of it would be spent for the benefit of the Hailey family.

★   ★   ★

311

From two to five each Sunday afternoon, the prisoners in the Ford County jail were turned out into a large fenced yard across the small back street behind the jail. A limit of three friends and/or relatives for each prisoner was allowed inside for no more than an hour. There were a couple of shade trees, some broken picnic tables, and a well-maintained basketball hoop. Deputies and dogs watched carefully from the other side of the fence.

A routine was established. Gwen and the kids would leave church after the benediction around three, and drive to the jail. Ozzie allowed Carl Lee early entrance to the recreation area so he could assume the best picnic table, the one with four legs and a shade tree. He would sit there by himself, speaking to no one, and watch the basketball skirmish until his family arrived. It wasn't basketball, but a hybrid of rugby, wrestling, judo, and basketball. No one dared officiate. No blood, no foul. And, surprisingly, no fights. A fight meant quick admittance to solitary and no recreation for a month.

There were a few visitors, some girlfriends and wives, and they would sit in the grass by the fence with their men and quietly watch the mayhem under the basketball hoop. One couple asked Carl Lee if they could use his table for lunch. He shook his head, and they ate in the grass.

Gwen and the kids arrived before three. Deputy Hastings, her cousin, unlocked the gate and the children ran to meet their daddy. Gwen spread the food. Carl Lee was aware of the stares from the less fortunate, and he enjoyed the envy. Had he been white, or smaller and weaker, or perhaps charged with a lesser crime, he would have been asked to share his food. But he was Carl Lee Hailey, and no one stared too long. The game returned to its fury and violence, and the family ate in peace. Tonya always sat next to her daddy.

'They started an offerin' for us this mornin',' Gwen said after lunch.

'Who did?'

'The church. Reverend Agee said all the black churches in the county are gonna take up money ever Sunday for us and for the lawyer fees.'

'How much?'

'Don't know. He said they gonna pass the bucket ever Sunday until the trial.'

'That's mighty nice. What'd he say 'bout me?'

'Just talked about your case and all. Said how expensive it would be, and how we'd need help from the churches. Talked about Christian givin' and all that. Said you're a real hero to your people.'

What a pleasant surprise, thought Carl Lee. He expected some help from his church, but nothing financial. 'How many churches?'

'All the black ones in the county.'

'When do we get the money?'

'He didn't say.'

After he got his cut, thought Carl Lee. 'Boys, y'all take your sister and go play over there by the fence. Me and Momma needs to talk. Be careful now.'

Carl Lee, Jr., and Robert took their little sister by the hand and did exactly as ordered.

'What does the doctor say?' Carl Lee asked as he watched the children walk away.

'She's doin' good. Her jaw's healin' good. He might take the wire off in a month. She can't run and jump and play yet, but it won't be long. Still some soreness.'

'What about the, uh, the other?'

Gwen shook her head and covered her eyes. She began crying and wiping her eyes. She spoke and her voice cracked. 'She'll never have kids. He told me . . .' She stopped, wiped her face and tried to continue. She began sobbing loudly, and buried her face in a paper towel.

Carl Lee felt sick. He placed his forehead in his palms. He ground his teeth together as his eyes watered. 'What'd he say?'

Gwen raised her head and spoke haltingly, fighting back tears. 'He told me Tuesday there was too much damage . . .' She wiped her wet face with her fingers. 'But he wants to send her to a specialist in Memphis.'

'He's not sure?'

She shook her head. 'Ninety percent sure. But he thinks she should be examined by another doctor in Memphis. We're supposed to take her in a month.'

Gwen tore off another paper towel and wiped her face. She handed one to her husband, who quickly dabbed his eyes.

Next to the fence, Tonya sat listening to her brothers argue about which one would be a deputy and which one would be in jail. She watched her parents talk and shake their heads and cry. She knew something was wrong with her. She rubbed her eyes and started crying too.

'The nightmares are gettin' worse,' Gwen said, interrupting the silence. 'I have to sleep with her ever night. She dreams about men comin' to get her, men hidin' in the closets, chasin' her through the woods. She wakes up screamin' and sweatin'. The doctor says she needs to see a psychiatrist. Says it'll get worse before it gets better.'

'How much will it cost?'

'I don't know. I haven't called yet.'

'Better call. Where is this psychiatrist?'

'Memphis.'

'Figures.'

'How are the boys treatin' her?'

'They've been great. They treat her special. But the nightmares keep them scared. When she wakes up screamin' she wakes everybody. The boys run to her bed and try to help, but it scares them. Last night she wouldn't go back to sleep unless the boys slept on the floor next to her. We all laid there wide awake with the lights on.'

'The boys'll be all right.'

'They miss their daddy.'

Carl Lee managed a forced smile. 'It won't be much longer.'

'You really think so?'

'I don't know what to think anymore. But I don't plan to spend the rest of my life in jail. I hired Jake back.'

'When?'

'Yesterday. That Memphis lawyer never showed up, never even called. I fired him and hired Jake again.'

'But you said Jake is too young.'

'I was wrong. He is young, but he's good. Ask Lester.'

'It's your trial.'

Carl Lee walked slowly around the yard, never leaving the fence. He thought of the two boys, somewhere out there, dead and buried, their flesh rotting by now, their souls burning in hell. Before they died, they met his little girl, only briefly, and within two hours wrecked her little body and ruined her mind. So brutal was their attack that she could never have children; so violent the encounter that she now saw them hiding for her, waiting in closets. Could she ever forget about it, block it out, erase it from her mind so her life would be normal? Maybe a psychiatrist could do that. Would other children allow her to be normal?

She was just a little nigger, they probably thought. Somebody's little nigger kid. Illegitimate, of course, like all of them. Rape would be nothing new.

He remembered them in court. One proud, the other scared. He remembered them coming down the stairs as he awaited the execution. Then, the looks of horror as he stepped forward with the M-16. The sound of the gunfire, the cries for help, the screams as they fell backward together, one on top of the other, handcuffed, screaming and twisting, going nowhere. He remembered smiling, even laughing, as he watched them struggle with their heads half blown away, and when their bodies were still, he ran.

He smiled again. He was proud of it. The first gook he killed in Vietnam had bothered him more.

The letter to Walter Sullivan was to the point:

> Dear J. Walter:
> By now it's safe to assume Mr Marsharfsky has informed you that his employment by Carl Lee Hailey has been terminated. Your services as local counsel will, of course, no longer be needed. Have a nice day.
> Sincerely,
> Jake

A copy was sent to L. Winston Lotterhouse. The letter to Noose was just as short:

> Dear Judge Noose:
> Please be advised that I have been retained by Carl Lee Hailey. We are preparing for trial on July 22. Please show me as counsel of record.
> Sincerely,
> Jake

A copy was sent to Buckley.

Marsharfsky called at nine-thirty Monday. Jake watched the hold button blink for two minutes before he lifted the receiver. 'Hello.'

'How'd you do it?'

'Who is this?'

'Your secretary didn't tell you? This is Bo Marsharfsky, and I want to know how you did it.'

'Did what?'

'Hustled my case.'

Stay cool, thought Jake. He's an agitator. 'As I recall, it was hustled from me,' replied Jake.

'I never met him before he hired me.'

'You didn't have to. You sent your pimp, remember?'

'Are you accusing me of chasing cases?'

'Yes.'

Marsharfsky paused and Jake braced for the obscenities.

'You know something, Mr Brigance, you're right. I chase cases every day. I'm a pro at hustling cases. That's how I make so much money. If there's a big criminal case, I intend to get it. And I'll use whatever method I find necessary.'

'Funny, that wasn't mentioned in the paper.'

'And if I want the Hailey case, I'll get it.'

'Come on down.' Jake hung up and laughed for ten minutes. He lit a cheap cigar, and began working on his motion for a change of venue.

Two days later Lucien called and instructed Ethel to instruct Jake to come see him. It was important. He had a visitor Jake needed to meet.

The visitor was Dr W.T. Bass, a retired psychiatrist from Jackson. He had known Lucien for years, and they had collaborated on a couple of

318

insane criminals during their friendship. Both of the criminals were still in Parchman. His retirement had been one year before the disbarment and had been precipitated by the same thing that contributed heavily to the disbarment, to wit, a strong affection for Jack Daniel's. He visited Lucien occasionally in Clanton, and Lucien visited him more frequently in Jackson, and they enjoyed their visits because they enjoyed staying drunk together. They sat on the big porch and waited on Jake.

'Just say he was insane,' instructed Lucien.

'Was he?' asked the doctor.

'That's not important.'

'What is important?'

'It's important to give the jury an excuse to acquit the man. They won't care if he's crazy or not. But they'll need some reason to acquit him.'

'It would be nice to examine him.'

'You can. You can talk to him all you want. He's at the jail just waiting on someone to talk to.'

'I'll need to meet with him several times.'

'I know that.'

'What if I don't think he was insane at the time of the shooting?'

'Then you won't get to testify at trial, and you won't get your name and picture in the paper, and you won't be interviewed on TV.'

Lucien paused long enough to take a long drink. 'Just do as I say. Interview him, take a bunch of notes. Ask stupid questions. You know what to do. Then say he was crazy.'

'I'm not so sure about this. It hasn't worked too well in the past.'

'Look, you're a doctor, aren't you? Then act proud, vain, arrogant. Act like a doctor's supposed to act. Give your opinion and dare anyone to question it.'

'I don't know. It hasn't worked too well in the past.'

'Just do as I say.'

'I've done that before, and they're both at Parchman.'

'They were hopeless. Hailey's different.'

'Does he have a chance?'

'Slim.'

'I thought you said he was different.'

'He's a decent man with a good reason for killing.'

'Then why are his chances slim?'

'The law says his reason is not good enough.'

'That's par for the law.'

'Plus he's black, and this is a white county. I have no confidence in these bigots around here.'

'And if he were white?'

'If he were white and he killed two blacks who raped his daughter, the jury would give him the courthouse.'

Bass finished one glass and poured another. A fifth and a bucket of ice sat on the wicker table between the two.

'What about his lawyer?' he asked.

'He should be here in a minute.'

'He used to work for you?'

'Yeah, but I don't think you met him. He was in the firm about two years before I left. He's young, early thirties. Clean, aggressive, works hard.'

'And he used to work for you?'

'That's what I said. He's got trial experience for his age. This is not his first murder case, but, if I'm not mistaken, it's his first insanity case.'

'That's nice to hear. I don't want someone asking a lot of questions.'

'I like your confidence. Wait till you meet the D.A.'

'I just don't feel good about this. We tried it twice, and it didn't work.'

Lucien shook his head in bewilderment. 'You've got to be the humblest doctor I've known.'

'And the poorest.'

'You're supposed to be pompous and arrogant. You're the expert. Act like one. Who's gonna question your professional opinion in Clanton, Mississippi?'

'The State will have experts.'

'They will have one psychiatrist from Whitfield. He'll examine the defendant for a few hours, and then drive up for trial and testify that the defendant is the sanest man he's ever met. He's never seen a legally insane defendant. To him no one is insane. Everybody's blessed with perfect mental health. Whitfield is full of sane people, except when it applies for government money, then half the state's crazy. He'd get fired if he started saying defendants are legally insane. So that's who you're up against.'

'And the jury will automatically believe me?'

'You act as though you've never been through one of these before.'

'Twice, remember. One rapist, one murderer. Neither was insane, in spite of what I said. Both are now locked away where they belong.'

Lucien took a long drink and studied the light brown liquid and the floating ice cubes. 'You said you would help me. God knows you owe me the favor. How many divorces did I handle for you?'

'Three. And I got cleaned out every time.'

'You deserved it every time. It was either give in or go to trial and have your habits discussed in open court.'

'I remember.'

'How many clients, or patients, have I sent you over the years?'

'Not enough to pay my alimony.'

'Remember the malpractice case by the lady whose treatment consisted primarily of weekly sessions on your couch with the foldaway bed? Your malpractice carrier refused to defend, so you called your dear friend Lucien who settled it for peanuts and kept it out of court.'

'There were no witnesses.'

'Just the lady herself. And the court files showing where your wives had sued for divorce on the grounds of adultery.'

'They couldn't prove it.'

'They didn't get a chance. We didn't want them to try, remember?'

'All right, enough, enough. I said I would help. What about my credentials?'

'Are you a compulsive worrier?'

'No. I just get nervous when I think of court-rooms.'

'Your credentials are fine. You've been qualified before as an expert witness. Don't worry so much.'

'What about this?' He waved his drink at Lucien.

'You shouldn't drink so much,' he said piously.

The doctor dropped his drink and exploded in laughter. He rolled out of his chair and crawled to the edge of the porch, holding his stomach and shaking in laughter.

'You're drunk,' Lucien said as he left for another bottle.

When Jake arrived an hour later, Lucien was rocking slowly in his huge wicker rocker. The doctor was asleep in the swing at the far end of the porch. He was barefoot, and his toes had disappeared into the shrubbery that lined the porch. Jake walked up the steps and startled Lucien.

'Jake, my boy, how are you?' he slurred.

'Fine, Lucien. I see you're doing quite well.' He looked at the empty bottle and one not quite empty.

'I wanted you to meet that man,' he said, trying to sit up straight.

'Who is he?'

'He's our psychiatrist. Dr W.T. Bass, from Jackson. Good friend of mine. He'll help us with Hailey.'

'Is he good?'

'The best. We've worked together on several insanity cases.'

Jake took a few steps in the direction of the swing and stopped. The doctor was lying on his back with his shirt unbuttoned and his mouth wide open. He snored heavily, with an unusual guttural gurgling sound. A horsefly the size of a small sparrow buzzed around his nose and retreated to the top of the swing with each thunderous exhalation. A rancid vapor emanated with the snoring and hung like an invisible fog over the end of the porch.

'He's a doctor?' Jake asked as he sat next to Lucien.

'Psychiatry,' Lucien said proudly.

'Did he help you with those?' Jake nodded at the bottles.

'I helped him. He drinks like a fish, but he's always sober at trial.'

'That's comforting.'

'You'll like him. He's cheap. Owes me a favor. Won't cost a dime.'

'I like him already.'

Lucien's face was as red as his eyes. 'Wanna drink?'

'No. It's three-thirty in the afternoon.'

'Really! What day is it?'

'Wednesday, June 12. How long have y'all been drinking?'

''Bout thirty years.' Lucien laughed and rattled his ice cubes.

'I mean today.'

'We drank our breakfast. What difference does it make?'

'Does he work?'

'Naw, he's retired.'

'Was his retirement voluntary?'

'You mean, was he disbarred, so to speak?'

'That's right, so to speak.'

'No. He still has his license, and his credentials are impeccable.'

'He looks impeccable.'

'Booze got him a few years ago. Booze and alimony. I handled three of his divorces. He reached the point where all of his income went for alimony and child support, so he quit working.'

'How does he manage?'

'We, uh, I mean, he stashed some away. Hid it from his wives and their hungry lawyers. He's really quite comfortable.'

'He looks comfortable.'

'Plus he peddles a little dope, but only to a rich clientele. Not really dope, but narcotics which he can legally prescribe. It's not really illegal; just a little unethical.'

'What's he doing here?'

'He visits occasionally. He lives in Jackson but hates it. I called him Sunday after I talked to you. He wants to meet Hailey as soon as possible, tomorrow if he can.'

The doctor grunted and rolled to his side, causing the swing to move suddenly. It swung a few times, and he moved again, still snoring. He stretched his right leg, and his foot caught a thick branch in the shrubbery. The swing jerked sideways and threw the good doctor onto the porch. His head crashed onto the wooden floor while his right foot remained lodged through the end of the swing. He grimaced and coughed, then began snoring again. Jake instinctively started toward him, but stopped when it was apparent he was unharmed and still asleep.

'Leave him alone!' ordered Lucien between laughs.

Lucien slid an ice cube down the porch and just missed the doctor's head. The second cube landed perfectly on the tip of his nose. 'Perfect shot!' Lucien roared. 'Wake up, you drunk!'

Jake walked down the steps toward his car, listening to his former boss laugh and curse and throw ice cubes at Dr W.T. Bass, psychiatrist, witness for the defense.

Deputy DeWayne Looney left the hospital on crutches, and drove his wife and three children to the jail, where the sheriff, the other deputies, the reserves, and a few friends waited with a cake and small gifts. He would be a dispatcher now, and would retain his badge and uniform and full salary.

Chapter 21

The fellowship hall of the Springdale Church had been thoroughly cleaned and shined, and the folding tables and chairs dusted and placed in perfect rows around the room. It was the largest black church in the county and it was in Clanton, so the Reverend Agee deemed it necessary to meet there. The purpose of the press conference was to get vocal, to show support of the local boy who made good, and to announce the establishment of the Carl Lee Hailey Legal Defense Fund. The national director of the NAACP was present with a five-thousand-dollar check and a promise of serious money later. The executive director of the Memphis branch brought five thousand and grandly laid it on the table. They sat with Agee behind the two folding tables in the front of the room with every member of the council seated behind them and two hundred black church members in the crowded audience. Gwen sat next to Agee. A few reporters and cameras, much fewer than expected, grouped in the center of the room and filmed away.

Agee spoke first and was inspired by the cameras. He talked of the Haileys and their goodness and innocence, and of baptizing Tonya when she was only eight. He talked of a family wrecked by racism and hatred. There were sniffles in the audience. Then he got mean. He tore into the judicial system and its desire to prosecute a good and decent man who had done no wrong; a man, who, if white, would not be on trial; a man who was on trial only because he was black and that was what was so wrong with the prosecution and persecution of Carl Lee Hailey. He found his rhythm and the crowd joined in, and the press conference took on the fervor of a tent revival. He lasted for forty-five minutes.

He was a hard act to follow. But the national director did not hesitate. He delivered a thirty-minute oratorical condemnation of racism. He seized the moment and spouted national statistics on crime and arrests and convictions and inmate population and summed it all up by declaring that the criminal justice system was controlled by white people who unfairly persecuted black people. Then in a bewildering flurry of rationale he brought the national statistics to Ford County and pronounced the system unfit to deal with Carl Lee Hailey. The lights from the TV cameras produced a line of sweat above his eyebrows and he warmed to the task. He got angrier than Reverend Agee and pounded the podium and made the cluster of microphones jump and shake. He exhorted the blacks of Ford County and of Mississippi to give until it hurt. He promised demonstrations and marches. The trial would be a battle cry for black and oppressed folk everywhere.

He answered questions. How much money would be raised? At least fifty thousand, they hoped. It would be expensive to defend Carl Lee Hailey and fifty thousand may not be enough, but they would raise whatever it took. But time was running short. Where would the money go? Legal fees and litigation expenses. A battery of lawyers and doctors would be needed. Would NAACP lawyers be used? Of course. The legal staff in Washington was already at work on the case. The capital defense unit would handle all aspects of the trial. Carl Lee Hailey had become their top priority and all available resources would be devoted to his defense.

When he finished, Reverend Agee retook the podium and nodded at a piano player in the corner. The music started. They all stood, hand in hand, and sang a stirring rendition of 'We Shall Overcome.'

Jake read about the defense fund in Tuesday's paper. He had heard rumors of the special offering being administered by the council, but was told the money was for the support of the family. Fifty thousand for legal fees! He was angry, but interested. Would he be fired again? Suppose Carl Lee refused to hire the NAACP lawyers, what would happen to the money? The trial was five weeks away, plenty of time for the capital defense team to descend on Clanton. He had read about these guys; a team of six capital murder specialists who toured the South defending blacks accused of heinous and notorious crimes. 'The Death Squad' was their nickname. They were very bright, very talented, very educated lawyers dedicated to rescuing black murderers from the various gas chambers and electric chairs around the South. They handled nothing but capital murder cases and were very, very good at their work. The NAACP ran their interference, raising money, organizing local blacks, and generating publicity. Racism was their best, and sometimes only, defense and though they lost much more than they won, their record was not bad. The cases they handled were supposed to be lost, all of them. Their goal was to martyr the defendant before the trial and hopefully hang the jury.

Now they were coming to Clanton.

A week earlier Buckley had filed the proper motions to have Carl Lee examined by the State's doctors. Jake requested the doctors be required to conduct their examinations in Clanton, preferably in Jake's office. Noose declined, and ordered the sheriff to transport Carl Lee to the Mississippi State Mental Hospital at Whitfield. Jake requested that he be allowed to accompany his client and be present during the examinations. Again, Noose declined.

Early Wednesday morning, Jake and Ozzie sipped coffee in the sheriff's office and waited for Carl Lee to shower and change clothes. Whitfield was three hours away, and he was to check in at nine. Jake had final instructions for his client.

'How long will y'all be there?' Jake asked Ozzie.

'You're the lawyer. How long will it take?'

'Three or four days. You've been there before, haven't you?'

'Sure, we've had to transport plenty of crazy people. But nothin' like this. Where do they keep him?'

'They've got all kinds of cells.'

Deputy Hastings casually entered the office, sleepy-eyed and crunching on a stale doughnut. 'How many cars we takin'?'

'Two,' answered Ozzie. 'I'll drive mine and you drive yours. I'll take Pirtle and Carl Lee, you take Riley and Nesbit.'

'Guns?'

'Three shotguns in each car. Plenty of shells. Everybody wears a vest, includin' Carl Lee. Get the cars ready. I'd like to leave by five-thirty.'

Hastings mumbled something and disappeared.

'Are you expecting trouble?' Jake asked.

'We've had some phone calls. Two in particular mentioned the trip to Whitfield. Lot of highway between here and there.'

'How are you going?'

'Most folks take 22 to the interstate, wouldn't you say? It might be safer to take some smaller highways. We'll probably run 14 south to 89.'

'That would be unexpected.'

'Good. I'm glad you approve.'

'He's my client, you know.'

'For right now, anyway.'

Carl Lee quickly devoured the eggs and biscuits as Jake briefed him on what to expect during the stay at Whitfield.

'I know, Jake. You want me to act crazy, right?' Carl Lee said with a laugh. Ozzie thought it was funny too.

'This is serious, Carl Lee. Listen to me.'

'Why? You said yourself it won't matter what I say or do down there. They won't say I was insane when I shot them. Them doctors work for the State, right? The State's prosecutin' me, right? What difference does it make what I say or do? They've already made up their minds. Ain't that right, Ozzie?'

'I'm not gettin' involved. I work for the State.'

'You work for the County,' said Jake.

'Name, rank, and serial number. That's all they're gettin' outta me,' Carl Lee said as he emptied a small paper sack.

'Very funny,' said Jake.

'He's crackin' up, Jake,' Ozzie said.

Carl Lee stuck two straws up his nose and began tiptoeing around the office, staring at the ceiling and then grabbing at something above his head. He put it in the sack. He lunged at another one and put it in the sack. Hastings returned and stopped in the door. Carl Lee grinned at him with wild eyes, then grabbed at another one toward the ceiling.

'What the hell he's doin'?' Hastings asked.

'Catchin' butterflies,' Carl Lee said.

Jake grabbed his briefcase and headed for the door. 'I think you should leave him at Whitfield.' He slammed the door and left the jail.

Noose had scheduled the venue hearing for Monday, June 24, in Clanton. The hearing would be long and well publicized. Jake had requested the change of venue, and he had the burden of proving Carl Lee could not receive a fair and impartial trial in Ford County. He needed witnesses. Persons with credibility in the community who were willing to testify that a fair trial was not possible. Atcavage said he might do it as a favor, but the bank might not want him involved. Harry Rex had eagerly volunteered. Reverend Agee said he would be glad to testify, but that was before the NAACP announced its lawyers would be handling the case. Lucien had no credibility, and Jake did not seriously consider asking him.

Buckley, on the other hand, would line up a dozen credible witnesses – elected officials, lawyers, businessmen, maybe other sheriffs – all of whom would testify that they had vaguely heard of Carl Lee Hailey and he could most certainly receive a fair trial in Clanton.

Jake personally preferred the trial to be in Clanton, in his courthouse across the street from his office, in front of his people. Trials were pressure-filled, tedious, sleepless ordeals. It would be nice to have this one in a friendly arena, three minutes from his driveway. When the trial recessed, he could spend the free moments in his office doing research, preparing witnesses or relaxing. He could eat at the Coffee Shop or Claude's, or even run home for a quick lunch. His client could remain in the Ford County jail, near his family.

And, of course, his media exposure would be much greater. The reporters would gather in front of his office each morning of the trial and follow him as he walked slowly toward the courthouse. That thought was exciting.

Did it matter where they tried Carl Lee Hailey? Lucien was correct: the publicity had reached every resident of every county in Mississippi. So why change venue? His guilt or innocence had already been prejudged by every prospective juror in the state.

Sure it mattered. Some prospective jurors were white and some were black. Percentage-wise, there would be more white ones in Ford County than the surrounding counties. Jake loved black jurors, especially in criminal cases and especially when the criminal was black. They were not as anxious to convict. They were open minded. He preferred them in civil cases, too. They felt for the underdog against the big corporation or insurance company, and they were more liberal with other people's money. As a rule, he picked all the black jurors he could find, but they were scarce in Ford County.

It was imperative the case be tried in another county, a blacker county. One black could hang the jury. A majority could force, maybe, an acquittal. Two weeks in a motel and strange court-house was not appealing, but the small discom-forts were greatly outweighed by the need to have black faces in the jury box.

The venue question had been thoroughly researched by Lucien. As instructed, Jake arrived promptly, although reluctantly, at 8:00 A.M. Sallie served breakfast on the porch. Jake drank coffee and orange juice; Lucien, bourbon and water. For three hours they covered every aspect of a change of venue. Lucien had copies of every Supreme Court case for the past eighty years, and lectured like a professor. The pupil took notes, argued once or twice, but mainly listened.

Whitfield was located a few miles from Jackson in a rural part of Rankin County. Two guards waited by the front gate and argued with reporters. Carl Lee was scheduled to arrive at nine, that was all the guards knew. At eight-thirty two patrol cars with Ford County insignia rolled to a stop at the gate. The reporters and their cameramen ran to the driver of the first car. Ozzie's window was down.

'Where's Carl Lee Hailey?' a reporter shouted in a panic.

'He's in the other car,' Ozzie drawled, winking at Carl Lee in the back seat.

'He's in the second car!' someone shouted, and they ran to Hastings' car.

'Where's Hailey?' they demanded.

Pirtle, in the front seat, pointed to Hastings, the driver. 'That's him.'

'Are you Carl Lee Hailey?' a reporter screamed at Hastings.

'Yep.'

'Why are you driving?'

'What's with the uniform?'

'They made me a deputy,' answered Hastings with a straight face. The gate opened, and the two cars sped through.

Carl Lee was processed in the main building and led, along with Ozzie and the deputies, to another building where he was checked into his cell, or room, as it was called. The door was locked behind him. Ozzie and his men were excused and returned to Clanton.

After lunch, an assistant of some sort with a clipboard and white jacket arrived and began asking questions. Starting with birth, he asked Carl Lee about every significant event and person in his life. It lasted two hours. At 4:00 P.M., two security guards handcuffed Carl Lee and rode him in a golf cart to a modern brick building a half mile from his room. He was led to the office of Dr Wilbert Rodeheaver, head of staff. The guards waited in the hall by the door.

Chapter 22

It had been five weeks since the shootings of Billy Ray Cobb and Pete Willard. The trial was four weeks away. The three motels in Clanton were booked solid for the week of the trial and the week before. The Best Western was the largest and nicest, and had attracted the Memphis and Jackson press. The Clanton Court had the best bar and restaurant, and was booked by reporters from Atlanta, Washington, and New York. At the less than elegant East Side Motel the rates had curiously doubled for the month of July but it had nonetheless sold out.

The town had been friendly at first to these outsiders, most of whom were rude and spoke with different accents. But some of the descriptions of Clanton and its people had been less than flattering, and most of the locals now honored a secret code of silence. A noisy cafe would become instantly silent when a stranger walked in and took a seat. Merchants around the square offered little assistance to anyone they did not recognize. The employees in the courthouse had become deaf to questions asked a thousand times by nosy intruders. Even the Memphis and Jackson reporters had to struggle to extract anything new from the locals. The people were tired of being described as backward, redneck, and racist. They ignored the outsiders whom they could not trust and went about their business.

The bar at the Clanton Court became the watering hole for the reporters. It was the one place in town they could go to find a friendly face and good conversation. They sat in the booths under the big-screen TV and gossiped about the small town and the upcoming trial. They compared notes and stories and leads and rumors, and drank until they were drunk because there was nothing else to do in Clanton after dark.

The motels filled Sunday night, June 23, the night before the venue hearing. Early Monday morning they gathered in the restaurant at the Best Western to drink coffee and speculate. The hearing was the first major skirmish, and could likely be the only courtroom action until the trial. A rumor surfaced that Noose was ill and did not want to hear the case, and that he would ask the Supreme Court to appoint another judge. Just a rumor, with no source and nothing more definite, said a reporter from Jackson. At eight they packed their cameras and microphones and left for the square. One group set up outside the jail, another at the rear of the courthouse, but most headed for the courtroom. By eight-thirty it was filled.

From the balcony of his office, Jake watched the activity around the courthouse. His heart beat faster than normal, and his stomach tingled. He smiled. He was ready for Buckley, ready for the cameras.

Noose looked down past the end of his nose, over his reading glasses, and around the packed courtroom. Everyone was in place.

'The court has before it,' he began, 'the defendant's motion for a change of venue. The trial in this matter has been set for Monday, July 22. That's four weeks from today, according to my calendar. I have set a deadline for filing motions and disposing of same, and I believe those are the only two deadlines between now and trial.'

'That's correct, Your Honor,' thundered Buckley, half standing behind his table. Jake rolled his eyes and shook his head.

'Thank you, Mr Buckley,' Noose said dryly. 'The defendant has filed the proper notice that he intends to use an insanity defense. Has he been examined at Whitfield?'

'Yes sir, Your Honor, last week,' Jake answered.

'Will he employ his own psychiatrist?'

'Of course, Your Honor.'

'Has he been examined by his own?'

'Yes, sir.'

'Good. so that's out of the way. What other motions do you anticipate filing?'

'Your Honor, we expect to file a motion requesting the clerk to summons more than the usual number of prospective jurors—'

'The State will oppose that motion,' Buckley yelled as he jumped to his feet.

'Sit down, Mr Buckley!' Noose said sternly, ripping off his glasses and glaring at the D.A. 'Please don't yell at me again. Of course you will oppose it. You will oppose any motion filed by the defense. That's your job. Don't interrupt again. You'll have ample opportunity after we adjourn to perform for the media.'

Buckley slumped in his chair and hid his red face. Noose had never screamed at him before.

'Continue, Mr Brigance.'

Jake was startled by Ichabod's meanness. He looked tired and ill. Perhaps it was the pressure.

'We may have some written objections to anticipated evidence.'

'Motions *in limine*?'

'Yes, sir.'

'We'll hear those at trial. Anything else?'

'Not at this time.'

'Now, Mr Buckley, will the State file any motions?'

'I can't think of any,' Buckley answered meekly.

'Good. I want to make sure there are no surprises between now and trial. I will be here one week before trial to hear and decide any pretrial matters. I expect any motions to be filed promptly, so that we can tie up any loose ends well before the twenty-second.'

Noose flipped through his file and studied Jake's motion for a change of venue. Jake whispered to Carl Lee, whose presence was not required for the hearing, but he insisted. Gwen and the three boys sat in the first row behind their daddy. Tonya was not in the courtroom.

'Mr Brigance, your motion appears to be in order. How many witnesses?'

'Three, Your Honor.'

'Mr Buckley, how many will you call?'

'We have twenty-one,' Buckley said proudly.

'Twenty-one!' yelled the judge.

Buckley cowered and glanced at Musgrove. 'B-but, we probably won't need them all. In fact, I know we won't call all of them.'

'Pick your best five, Mr Buckley. I don't plan to be here all day.'

'Yes, Your Honor.'

'Mr Brigance, you've asked for a change of venue. It's your motion. You may proceed.'

Jake stood and walked slowly across the courtroom, behind Buckley, to the wooden podium in front of the jury box. 'May it please the court, Your Honor, Mr Hailey has requested that his trial be moved from Ford County. The reason is obvious: the publicity in this case will prevent a fair trial. The good people of this county have prejudged the guilt or innocence of Carl Lee Hailey. He is charged with killing two men, both of whom were born here and left families here. Their lives were not famous, but their deaths certainly have been. Mr Hailey was known by few outside his community until now. Now everyone in this county knows who he is, knows about his family and his daughter and what happened to

341

her, and knows most of the details of his alleged crimes. It will be impossible to find twelve people in Ford County who have not already prejudged this case. This trial should be held in another part of the state where the people are not so familiar with the facts.'

'Where would you suggest?' interrupted the judge.

'I wouldn't recommend a specific county, but it should be as far away as possible. Perhaps the Gulf Coast.'

'Why?'

'Obvious reasons, Your Honor. It's four hundred miles away, and I'm sure the people down there do not know as much as the people around here.'

'And you think the people in south Mississippi haven't heard about it?'

'I'm sure they have. But they are much further away.'

'But they have televisions and newspapers, don't they, Mr Brigance?'

'I'm sure they do.'

'Do you believe you could go to any county in this state and find twelve people who haven't heard the details of this case?'

Jake looked at his legal pad. He could hear the artists sketching on their pads behind him. He could see Buckley grinning out of the corner of his eye. 'It would be difficult,' he said quietly.

'Call your first witness.'

Harry Rex Vonner was sworn in and took his seat on the witness stand. The wooden swivel chair popped and creaked under the heavy load. He blew into the microphone and a loud hiss echoed around the courtroom. He smiled at Jake and nodded.

'Would you state your name?'

'Harry Rex Vonner.'

'And your address?'

'Eighty-four ninety-three Cedarbrush, Clanton, Mississippi.'

'How long have you lived in Clanton?'

'All my life. Forty-six years.'

'Your occupation?'

'I'm a lawyer. I've had my license for twenty-two years.'

'Have you ever met Carl Lee Hailey?'

'Once.'

'What do you know about him?'

'He supposedly shot two men, Billy Ray Cobb and Pete Willard, and he wounded a deputy, DeWayne Looney.'

'Did you know either of those boys?'

'Not personally. I know of Billy Ray Cobb.'

'How did you learn of the shootings?'

'Well, it happened on a Monday, I believe. I was in the courthouse, on the first floor, checking title on some land in the clerk's office, when I heard the gunshots. I ran out into the hall and bedlam had broken loose. I asked a deputy and he told me that the boys had been killed near the back door of the courthouse. I hung around here for a while, and pretty soon there was a rumor that the killer was the father of the little girl who got raped.'

'What was your initial reaction?'

'I was shocked, like most people. But I was shocked when I first heard of the rape too.'

'When did you learn that Mr Hailey had been arrested?'

'Later that night. It was all over the television.'

'What did you see on TV?'

'Well, I watched as much of it as I could. There were news reports from the local stations in Memphis and Tupelo. We've got the cable, you know, so I watched the news out of New York, Chicago, and Atlanta. Just about every channel had something about the shootings and the arrest. There was footage from the courthouse and jail. It was a big deal. Biggest thing that ever happened in Clanton, Mississippi.'

'How did you react when you learned that the girl's father had supposedly done the shooting?'

'It was no big surprise to me. I mean, we all sort of figured it was him. I admired him. I've got kids, and I sympathize with what he did. I still admire him.'

'How much do you know about the rape?'

Buckley leapt to his feet. 'Objection! The rape is irrelevant!'

Noose ripped off his glasses again and stared angrily at the D.A. Seconds passed and Buckley glanced at the table. He shifted his weight from one foot to the next, then sat down. Noose leaned forward and glared down from the bench.

'Mr Buckley, don't yell at me. If you do it again, so help me God, I will hold you in contempt. You may be correct, the rape may be irrelevant. But this is not the trial, is it? This is simply a hearing, isn't it? We don't have a jury in the box, do we? You're overruled and out of order. Now stay in your seat. I know it's hard with this sort of audience, but I instruct you to stay in your seat unless you have something truly worthy to say. At that point, you may stand and politely and quietly tell me what's on your mind.'

'Thank you, Your Honor,' Jake said as he smiled at Buckley. 'Now, Mr Vonner, as I was saying, how much do you know about the rape?'

'Just what I've heard.'

'And what's that?'

Buckley stood and bowed like a Japanese sumo wrestler. 'If Your Honor please,' he said softly and sweetly, 'I would like to object at this point, if it pleases the court. The witness may testify to only what he knows from first-hand knowledge, not from what he's heard from other people.'

Noose answered just as sweetly. 'Thank you, Mr Buckley. Your objection is noted, and you are overruled. Please continue, Mr Brigance.'

'Thank you, Your Honor.'

'What have you heard about the rape?'

'Cobb and Willard grabbed the little Hailey girl and took her out in the woods somewhere. They were drunk, they tied her to a tree, raped her repeatedly and tried to hang her. They even urinated on her.'

'They what?' asked Noose.

'They pissed on her, Judge.'

The courtroom buzzed at this revelation. Jake had never heard it, Buckley hadn't heard it, and evidently no one knew it but Harry Rex. Noose shook his head and lightly rapped his gavel.

Jake scribbled something on his legal pad and marveled at his friend's esoteric knowledge. 'Where did you learn about the rape?'

'All over town. It's common knowledge. The cops were giving the details the next morning at the Coffee Shop. Everybody knows it.'

'Is it common knowledge throughout the county?'

'Yes. I haven't talked to anybody in a month who did not know the details of the rape.'

'Tell us what you know about the shootings.'

'Well, like I said, it was a Monday afternoon. The boys were here in this courtroom for a bail hearing, I believe, and when they left the courtroom they were handcuffed and led by the deputies down the back stairs. When they got down the stairs, Mr Hailey jumped out of a closet with an M-16. They were killed and DeWayne Looney was shot. Part of his leg was amputated.'

'Exactly where did this take place?'

'Right below us here, at the rear entrance of the courthouse. Mr Hailey was hiding in a janitor's closet and just stepped out and opened fire.'

'Do you believe this to be true?'

'I know it's true.'

'Where did you learn all this?'

'Here and there. Around town. In the newspapers. Everybody knows about it.'

'Where have you heard it discussed?'

'Everywhere. In bars, in churches, at the bank, at the cleaners, at the Tea Shoppe, at the cafes around town, at the liquor store. Everywhere.'

'Have you talked to anyone who believes Mr Hailey did not kill Billy Ray Cobb and Pete Willard?'

'No. You won't find a single person in this county who believes he didn't do it.'

'Have most folks around here made up their minds about his guilt or innocence?'

'Every single one of them. There are no fence straddlers on this one. It's a hot topic, and everyone has an opinion.'

'In your opinion, could Mr Hailey receive a fair trial in Ford County?'

'No, sir. You couldn't find three people in this county of thirty thousand who have not already made up their minds, one way or the other. Mr Hailey has been judged already. There's just no way to find an impartial jury.'

'Thank you, Mr Vonner. No further questions, Your Honor.' Buckley patted his pompadour and ran his fingers over his ears to make sure every hair was in place. He walked purposefully to the podium.

'Mr Vonner,' he bellowed magnificently, 'have you already prejudged Carl Lee Hailey?'

'Damn right I have.'

'Your language, please,' said Noose.

'And what would your judgment be?'

'Mr Buckley, let me explain it this way. And I'll

347

do so very carefully and slowly so that even you will understand it. If I was the sheriff, I would not have arrested him. If I was on the grand jury, I would not have indicted him. If I was the judge, I would not try him. If I was the D.A., I would not prosecute him. If I was on the trial jury, I would vote to give him a key to the city, a plaque to hang on his wall, and I would send him home to his family. And, Mr Buckley, if my daugher is ever raped, I hope I have the guts to do what he did.'

'I see. You think people should carry guns and settle their disputes in shootouts?'

'I think children have a right not to be raped, and their parents have the right to protect them. I think little girls are special, and if mine was tied to a tree and gang raped by two dopeheads I'm sure it would make me crazy. I think good and decent fathers should have a constitutional right to execute any pervert who touches their children. And I think you're a lying coward when you claim you would not want to kill the man who raped your daughter.'

'Mr Vonner, please!' Noose said.

Buckley struggled, but kept his cool. 'You obviously feel very strongly about this case, don't you?'

'You're very perceptive.'

'And you want to see him acquitted, don't you?'

'I would pay money, if I had any.'

'And you think he stands a better chance of acquittal in another county, don't you?'

'I think he's entitled to a jury made up of people who don't know everything about the case before the trial starts.'

'You would acquit him, wouldn't you?'

'That's what I said.'

'And you've no doubt talked to other people who would acquit him?'

'I have talked to many.'

'Are there folks in Ford County who would vote to convict him?'

'Of course. Plenty of them. He's black, isn't he?'

'In all your discussions around the county, have you detected a clear majority one way or the other?'

'Not really.'

Buckley looked at his legal pad and made a note. 'Mr Vonner, is Jake Brigance a close friend of yours?'

Harry Rex smiled and rolled his eyes at Noose. 'I'm a lawyer, Mr Buckley, my friends are few and far between. But he is one of them. Yes, sir.'

'And he asked you to come testify?'

'No. I just happened to stumble through the courtroom a few moments ago and landed here in this chair. I had no idea you guys were having a hearing this morning.'

Buckley threw his legal pad on the table and sat down. Harry Rex was excused.

'Call your next witness,' Noose ordered.

'Reverend Ollie Agee,' Jake said.

The reverend was led from the witness room and seated in the witness stand. Jake had met him at his church the day before with a list of questions. He wanted to testify. They did not discuss the NAACP lawyers.

The reverend was an excellent witness. His deep, graveled voice needed no microphone as it carried around the courtroom. Yes, he knew the details of the rape and the shooting. They were members of his church. He had known them for years, they were family almost, and he had held their hands and suffered with them after the rape. Yes, he had talked to countless people since it happened and everyone had an opinion on guilt or innocence. He and twenty-two other black ministers were members of the council and they had all talked about the Hailey case. And, no, there were no unmade minds in Ford County. A fair trial was not possible in Ford County, in his opinion.

Buckley asked one question. 'Reverend Agee, have you talked to any black who would vote to convict Carl Lee Hailey?'

'No, suh, I have not.'

The reverend was excused. He took a seat in the courtroom between two of his brethren on the council.

'Call your next witness,' Noose said.

Jake smiled at the D.A., and announced, 'Sheriff Ozzie Walls.'

Buckley and Musgrove immediately locked heads and whispered. Ozzie was on their side, the side of law and order, the prosecution's side. It was not his job to help the defense. Proves you can't trust a nigger, thought Buckley. They take up for each other when they know they're guilty.

Jake led Ozzie through a discussion of the rape and the backgrounds of Cobb and Willard. It was boring and repetitious, and Buckley wanted to object. But he'd been embarrassed enough for one day. Jake sensed that Buckley would remain in his seat so he dwelt on the rape and the gory details. Finally, Noose had enough.

'Move on please, Mr Brigance.'

'Yes, Your Honor. Sheriff Walls, did you arrest Carl Lee Hailey?'

'I did.'

'Do you believe he killed Billy Ray Cobb and Pete Willard?'

'I do.'

'Have you met anybody in this county who believes he did not shoot them?'

'No, sir.'

'Is it widely believed in this county that Mr Hailey killed them?'

'Yes. Everbody believes it. At least everbody I've talked to.'

'Sheriff, do you circulate in this county?'

'Yes, sir. It's my job to know what's goin' on.'

'And you talk to a lot of people?'

'More than I would like.'

'Have you run across anyone who hasn't heard of Carl Lee Hailey?'

Ozzie paused and answered slowly. 'A person would have to be deaf, dumb, and blind not to know of Carl Lee Hailey.'

'Have you met anyone without an opinion on his guilt or innocence?'

'There's no such person in this county.'

'Can he get a fair trial here?'

'I don't know about that. I do know you can't find twelve people who don't know all about the rape and the shootin'.'

'No further questions,' Jake said to Noose.

'Is he your last witness?'

'Yes, sir.'

'Any cross-examination, Mr Buckley?'

Buckley remained in his seat and shook his head.

'Good,' said His Honor. 'Let's take a short recess. I would like to see the attorneys in chambers.'

The courtroom erupted in conversation as the attorneys followed Noose and Mr Pate through the door beside the bench. Noose closed the door to his chambers and removed his robe. Mr Pate brought him a cup of black coffee.

'Gentlemen, I am considering imposing a gag order from now until the trial is over. I am disturbed by the publicity, and I don't want this case tried by the press. Any comments?'

Buckley looked pale and shaken. He opened his mouth, but nothing happened.

'Good idea, Your Honor,' Jake said painfully. 'I had considered requesting such an order.'

'Yes, I'm sure you have. I've noticed how you run from publicity. What about you, Mr Buckley?'

'Uh, who would it apply to?'

'You, Mr Buckley. You, and Mr Brigance, would be ordered not to discuss any aspect of the case or the trial with the press. It would apply to everyone, at least everyone under the control of this court. The attorneys, the clerks, the court officials, the sheriff.'

'But why?' asked Buckley.

'I don't like the idea of the two of you trying this case through the media. I'm not blind. You've both fought for the spotlight, and I can only imagine what the trial will be like. A circus, that's what it will be. Not a trial, but a three-ring circus.' Noose walked to the window and mumbled something to himself. He paused for a moment, then continued mumbling. The attorneys looked at each other, then at the awkward frame standing in the window.

'I'm imposing a gag order, effective immediately, from now until the trial is over. Violation of the order will result in contempt of court proceedings. You are not to discuss any aspect of this case with any member of the press. Any questions?'

'No, sir,' Jake said quickly.

Buckley looked at Musgrove and shook his head.

'Now, back to this hearing. Mr Buckley, you said you have over twenty witnesses. How many do you really need?'

'Five or six.'

'That's much better. Who are they?'

'Floyd Loyd.'

'Who's he?'

'Supervisor, First District, Ford County.'

'What's his testimony?'

'He's lived here for fifty years, been in office ten years or so. In his opinion a fair trial is possible in this county.'

'I suppose he's never heard of this case?' Noose said sarcastically.

'I'm not sure.'

'Who else?'

'Nathan Baker. Justice of the Peace, Third District, Ford County.'

'Same testimony?'

'Well, basically, yes.'

'Who else?'

'Edgar Lee Baldwin, former supervisor, Ford County.'

'He was indicted a few years back, wasn't he?' Jake asked.

Buckley's face turned redder than Jake had ever seen it. His huge mouth dropped open and his eyes glazed over.

'He was not convicted,' shot Musgrove.

'I didn't say he was. I simply said he was indicted. FBI, wasn't it?'

'Enough, enough,' said Noose. 'What will Mr Baldwin tell us?'

'He's lived here all his life. He knows the people of Ford County, and thinks Mr Hailey can receive a fair trial here,' Musgrove answered. Buckley remained speechless as he stared at Jake.

'Who else?'

'Sheriff Harry Bryant, Tyler County.'

'Sheriff Bryant? What'll he say?'

Musgrove was talking for the State now. 'Your Honor, we have two theories we are submitting in opposition to the motion for a change of venue. First, we contend a fair trial is possible here in

Ford County. Second, if the court is of the opinion that a fair trial is not possible here, the State contends that the immense publicity has reached every prospective juror in this state. The same prejudices and opinions, for and against, which exist in this county exist in every county. Therefore, nothing will be gained by moving the trial. We have witnesses to support this second theory.'

'That's a novel concept, Mr Musgrove. I don't think I've heard it before.'

'Neither have I,' added Jake.

'Who else do you have?'

'Robert Kelly Williams, district attorney for the Ninth District.'

'Where's that?'

'Southwestern tip of the state.'

'He drove all the way up here to testify that everyone in his neck of the woods has already prejudged the case?'

'Yes, sir.'

'Who else?'

'Grady Liston, district attorney, Fourteenth District.'

'Same testimony?'

'Yes, sir.'

'Is that all?'

'Well, Your Honor, we have several more. But their testimony will pretty much follow the other witnesses'.'

'Good, then we can limit your proof to these six witnesses?'

'Yes, sir.'

'I will hear your proof. I will allow each of your five minutes to conclude your arguments, and I will rule on this motion within two weeks. Any questions?'

Chapter 23

It hurt to say no to the reporters. They followed Jake across Washington Street, where he excused himself, offered his no comments, and sought refuge in his office. Undaunted, a photographer from *Newsweek* pushed his way inside and asked if Jake would pose for a photograph. He wanted one of those important ones with a stern look and thick leather books in the background. Jake straightened his tie and showed the photographer into the conference room, where he posed in court-ordered silence. The photographer thanked him and left.

'May I have a few minutes of your time?' Ethel asked politely as her boss headed for the stairs.

'Certainly.'

'Why don't you sit down. We need to talk.'

She's finally quitting, Jake thought as he took a seat by the front window.

'What's on your mind?'

'Money.'

'You're the highest-paid legal secretary in town. You got a raise three months ago.'

'Not my money. Please listen. You don't have enough in the bank to pay this month's bills. June is almost gone, and we've grossed seventeen hundred dollars.'

Jake closed his eyes and rubbed his forehead.

'Look at these bills,' she said, waving a stack of invoices. 'Four thousand dollars worth. How am I supposed to pay these?'

'How much is in the bank?'

'Nineteen hundred dollars, as of Friday. Nothing came in this morning.'

'Nothing?'

'Not a dime.'

'What about the settlement on the Liford case? That's three thousand in fees.'

Ethel shook her head. 'Mr Brigance, that file has not been closed. Mr Liford has not signed the release. You were to take it by his house. Three weeks ago, remember?'

'No, I don't remember. What about Buck Britt's retainer? That's a thousand dollars.'

'His check bounced. The bank returned it, and it's been on your desk for two weeks.'

She paused and took a deep breath. 'You've stopped seeing clients. You don't return phone calls, and—'

'Don't lecture me, Ethel!'

'And you're a month behind on everything.'

'That's enough.'

'Ever since you took the Hailey case. That's all you think about. You're obsessed with it. It's going to break us.'

'Us! How many paychecks have you missed, Ethel? How many of those bills are past due? Huh?'

'Several.'

'But no more than usual, right?'

'Yes, but what about next month? The trial is four weeks away.'

'Shut up, Ethel. Just shut up. If you can't take the pressure, then quit. If you can't keep your mouth shut, then you're fired.'

'You'd like to fire me, wouldn't you?'

'I could care less.'

She was a tough, hard woman. Fourteen years with Lucien had toughened her skin and hardened her conscience, but she was a woman nonetheless, and at this moment her lip started to quiver, and her eyes watered. She dropped her head.

'I'm sorry,' she muttered. 'I'm just worried.'

'Worried about what?'

'Me and Bud.'

'What's wrong with Bud?'

'He's a very sick man.'

'I know that.'

'His blood pressure keeps acting up. Especially after the phone calls. He's had three strokes in five years, and he's due for another one. He's scared; we're both scared.'

'How many phone calls?'

'Several. They threaten to burn our house or blow it up. They always tell us they know where we live, and if Hailey is acquitted, then they'll burn it or stick dynamite under it while we are asleep. A couple have threatened to kill us. It's just not worth it.'

'Maybe you should quit.'

'And starve? Bud hasn't worked in ten years, you know that. Where else would I work?'

'Look, Ethel, I've had threats too. I don't take them seriously. I promised Carla I'd give up the case before I endangered my family, and you should be comforted by that. You and Bud should relax. The threats are not serious. There are a lot of nuts out there.'

'That's what worries me. People are crazy enough to do something.'

'Naw, you worry too much. I'll tell Ozzie to watch your house a bit closer.'

'Will you do that?'

'Sure. They've been watching mine. Take my word, Ethel, there's nothing to worry about. Probably just some young punks.'

She wiped her eyes. 'I'm sorry for crying, and I'm sorry for being so irritable lately.'

You've been irritable for forty years, Jake thought. 'That's okay.'

'What about these?' she asked, pointing to the invoices.

'I'll get the money. Don't worry about it.'

Willie Hastings finished the second shift at 10:00 P.M. and punched the clock next to Ozzie's office. He drove straight to the Hailey house. It was his night to sleep on the couch. Someone slept on

Gwen's couch every night; a brother, a cousin, or a friend. Wednesday was his night.

It was impossible to sleep with the lights on. Tonya refused to go near the bed unless every light in the house was on. Those men could be in the dark, waiting for her. She had seen them many times crawling along the floor toward her bed, and lurking in the closets. She had heard their voices outside her window, and she had seen their blood-shot eyes peering in, watching her as she got ready for bed. She heard noises in the attic, like the foot-steps of the bulky cowboy boots they had kicked her with. She knew they were up there, waiting for everyone to go to sleep so they could come down and take her back to the woods. Once a week her mother and oldest brother climbed the folding stairs and inspected the attic with a flash-light and a pistol.

Not a single room in the house could be dark when she went to bed. One night, as she lay wide awake next to her mother, a light in the hall burned out. She screamed violently until Gwen's brother drove to Clanton to an all-night quick shop for more bulbs.

She slept with her mother, who held her firmly for hours until the demons faded into the night and she drifted away. At first, Gwen had trouble with the lights, but after five weeks she napped periodically through the night. The small body next to her wiggled and jerked even while it slept.

Willie said good night to the boys and kissed Tonya. He showed her his gun and promised to stay awake on the couch. He walked through the house and checked the closets. When Tonya was satisfied, she lay next to her mother and stared at the ceiling. She cried softly.

Around midnight, Willie took off his boots and relaxed on the couch. He removed his holster and placed the gun on the floor. He was almost asleep when he heard the scream. It was the horrible, high-pitched cry of a child being tortured. He grabbed his gun and ran to the bedroom. Tonya was sitting on the bed, facing the wall, screaming and shaking. She had seen them in the window, waiting for her. Gwen hugged her. The three boys ran to the foot of the bed and watched helplessly. Carl Lee, Jr., went to the window and saw nothing. They had been through it many times in five weeks, and knew there was little they could do.

Gwen soothed her and laid her head gently on the pillow. 'It's okay, baby, Momma's here and Uncle Willie's here. Nobody's gonna get you. It's okay, baby.'

She wanted Uncle Willie to sit under the window with his gun and the boys to sleep on the floor around the bed. They took their positions. She moaned pitifully for a few moments, then grew quiet and still.

Willie sat on the floor by the window until they were all asleep. he carried the boys one at a time to their beds and tucked them in. He sat under her window and waited for the morning sun.

★　★　★

Jake and Atcavage met for lunch at Claude's on Friday. They ordered ribs and slaw. The place was packed as usual, and for the first time in four weeks there were no strange faces. The regulars talked and gossiped like old times. Claude was in fine form – ranting and scolding and cursing his loyal customers. Claude was one of those rare people who could curse a man and make him enjoy it.

Atcavage had watched the venue hearing, and would have testified had he been needed. The bank had discouraged his testifying, and Jake did not want to cause trouble. Bankers have an innate fear of courtrooms, and Jake admired his friend for overcoming this paranoia and attending the hearing. In doing so, he became the first banker in the history of Ford County to voluntarily appear in a courtroom without a subpoena while court was in session. Jake was proud of him.

Claude raced by and told them they had ten minutes, so shut up and eat. Jake finished a rib and mopped his face. 'Say, Stan, speaking of loans, I need to borrow five thousand for ninety days, unsecured.'

'Who said anything about loans?'

'You said something about banks.'

'I thought we were condemning Buckley. I was enjoying it.'

'You shouldn't criticize, Stan. It's an easy habit to acquire and an impossible one to break. It robs your soul of character.'

'I'm terribly sorry. How can you ever forgive me?'

'About the loan?'

'Okay. Why do you need it?'

'Why is that relevant?'

'What do you mean, "Why is that relevant?"'

'Look Stan, all you should worry about is whether or not I can repay the money in ninety days.'

'Okay. Can you repay the money in ninety days?'

'Good question. Of course I can.'

The banker smiled. 'Hailey's got you bogged down, huh?'

The lawyer smiled. 'Yeah,' he admitted. 'It's hard to concentrate on anything else. The trial is three weeks from Monday, and until then I won't concentrate on anything else.'

'How much will you make off this case?'

'Nine hundred minus ten thousand.'

'Nine hundred dollars!'

'Yeah, he couldn't borrow on his land, remember?'

'Cheap shot.'

'Of course, if you'd loan Carl Lee the money on his land, then I wouldn't have to borrow any.'

'I prefer to loan it to you.'

'Great. When can I get a check?'

'You sound desperate.'

'I know how long you guys take, with your loan committees and auditors and vice-presidents here and vice-presidents there, and maybe a vice-president will finally approve my loan in a month or so, if the manual says he can and if the home office is in the right mood. I know how you operate.'

Atcavage looked at his watch. 'Three o'clock soon enough?'

'I guess.'

'Unsecured?'

Jake wiped his mouth and leaned across the table. He spoke quietly. 'My house is a landmark with landmark mortgages, and you've got the lien on my car, remember? I'll give you the first mortgage on my daughter, but if you try to foreclose I'll kill you. Now what security do you have in mind?'

'Sorry I asked.'

'When can I get the check?'

'Three P.M.'

Claude appeared and refilled the tea glasses. 'You got five minutes,' he said loudly.

'Eight,' replied Jake.

'Listen Mr Big Shot,' Claude said with a grin. 'This ain't no courtroom, and your picture in the paper ain't worth two cents in here. I said five minutes.'

'Just as well. My ribs were tough anyway.'

'I notice you didn't leave any.'

'Might as well eat them, as much as they cost.'

'They cost more if you complain.'

'We're leaving,' Atcavage said as he stood and threw a dollar on the table.

Sunday afternoon the Haileys picnicked under the tree away from the violence under the basketball goal. The first heat wave of the summer had settled in, and the heavy, sticky humidity hung close to the ground and penetrated the shade. Gwen swatted flies as the children and their daddy ate warm fried chicken and sweated. The children ate hurriedly and ran to a new swing Ozzie had installed for the children of his inmates.

'What'd they do at Whitfield?' Gwen asked.

'Nothin' really. Asked a bunch of questions, made me do some tests. Bunch of crap.'

'How'd they treat you?'

'With handcuffs and padded walls.'

'No kiddin'. They put you in a room with padded walls?' Gwen was amused and managed a rare giggle.

'Sure did. They watched me like I was some animal. Said I was famous. My guards told me they was proud of me – one was white and one was black. Said that I did the right thing and they hoped I got off. They was nice to me.'

'What'd the doctors say?'

'They won't say nothin' till we get to trial, and then they'll say I'm fine.'

'How do you know what they'll say?'

'Jake told me. He ain't been wrong yet.'

'Has he found you a doctor?'

'Yeah, some crazy drunk he dug up somewhere. Says he's a psychiatrist. We've talked a couple of times in Ozzie's office.'

'What'd he say?'

'Not much. Jake said he'll say whatever we want him to say.'

'Must be a real good doctor.'

'He'd fit in good with those folks in Whitfield.'

'Where's he from?'

'Jackson, I think. He wasn't too sure of anything. He acted like I was gonna kill him too. I swear he was drunk both times we talked. He asked some questions that neither one of us understood. Took some notes like a real big shot. Said he thought he could help me. I asked Jake about him. Jake said not to worry, that he would be sober at the trial. But I think Jake's worried too.'

'Then why are we usin' him?'

''Cause he's free. Owes somebody some favors. A real shrink'd cost over a thousand dollars just to evaluate me, and then another thousand or so to come testify at trial. A cheap shrink. Needless to say, I can't pay it.'

Gwen lost her smile and looked away. 'We need some money around the house,' she said without looking at him.

'How much?'

'Coupla hundred for groceries and bills.'

'How much you got?'

'Less than fifty.'

'I'll see what I can do.'

She looked at him. 'What does that mean? What makes you think you can get money while you're in jail?'

Carl Lee raised his eyebrows and pointed at his wife. She was not to question him. He still wore the pants, even though he put them on in jail. He was the boss.

'I'm sorry,' she whispered.

Chapter 24

Reverend Agee peered through a crack in one of the huge stained glass windows of his church and watched with satisfaction as the clean Cadillacs and Lincolns arrived just before five Sunday afternoon. He had called a meeting of the council to assess the Hailey situation and plan strategy for the final three weeks before the trial, and to prepare for the arrival of the NAACP lawyers. The weekly collections had gone well – over seven thousand dollars had been gathered throughout the county and almost six thousand had been deposited by the reverend in a special account for the Carl Lee Hailey Legal Defense Fund. None had been given to the family. Agee was waiting for the NAACP to direct him in spending the money, most of which, he thought, should go to the defense fund. The sisters in the church could feed the family if they got hungry. The cash was needed elsewhere.

The council talked of ways to raise more money. It was not easy getting money from poor people, but the issue was hot and the time was right, and if they didn't raise it now it would not be raised. They agreed to meet the following day at the Springdale Church in Clanton. The NAACP people were expected in town by morning. No press; it was to be a work session.

Norman Reinfeld was a thirty-year-old genius in criminal law who held the record for finishing Harvard's law school at the age of twenty-one, and after graduation declined a most generous offer to join his father and grandfather's prestigious Wall Street law factory, opting instead to take a job with the NAACP and spend his time fighting furiously to keep Southern blacks off death row. He was very good at what he did although, through no fault of his own, he was not very successful at what he did. Most Southern blacks along with most Southern whites who faced the gas chamber deserved the gas chamber. But Reinfeld and his team of capital murder defense specialists won more than their share, and even in the ones they lost they usually managed to keep the convicts alive through a myriad of exhausting delays and appeals. Four of his former clients had either been gassed, electrocuted, or lethally injected, and that was four too many for Reinfeld. He had watched them all die, and with each execution he renewed his vow to break any law, violate any ethic, contempt any court, disrespect any judge, ignore any mandate, or do whatever it took to prevent a human from legally killing another human. He didn't worry much about the illegal killings of humans, such as those killings so artfully and cruelly achieved by his clients. It wasn't his business to think about those killings, so he didn't. Instead he vented his righteous and sanctimonious anger and zeal at the legal killings.

He seldom slept more than three hours a night. Sleep was difficult with thirty-one clients on death row. Plus seventeen clients awaiting trial. Plus eight egotistical attorneys to supervise. He was thirty and looked forty-five. He was old, abrasive, and ill-tempered. In the normal course of his business, he would have been much too busy to attend a gathering of local black ministers in Clanton, Mississippi. But this was not the normal case. This was Hailey. The vigilante. The father driven to revenge. The most famous criminal case in the country at the moment. This was Mississippi, where for years whites shot blacks for any reason or no reason and no one cared; where whites raped blacks and it was considered sport; where blacks were hanged for fighting back. And now a black father had killed two white men who raped his daughter, and faced the gas chamber for something that thirty years earlier would have gone unnoticed had he been white. This was the case, his case, and he would handle it personally.

On Monday he was introduced to the council by Reverend Agee, who opened the meeting with a lengthy and detailed review of the activities in Ford County. Reinfeld was brief. He and his team could not represent Mr Hailey because he had not been hired by Mr Hailey, so a meeting was imperative. Today, preferably. Tomorrow morning at the latest, because he had a flight out of Memphis at noon. He was needed in a murder trial somewhere in Georgia. Reverend Agee promised to arrange a meeting with the defendant as soon as possible. He was friends with the sheriff. Fine, said Reinfeld, just get it done.

'How much money have you raised?' Reinfeld asked.

'Fifteen thousand from you folks,' Agee answered.

'I know that. How much locally?'

'Six thousand,' Agee said proudly.

'Six thousand!' repeated Reinfeld. 'Is that all? I thought you people were organized. Where's all this great local support you were talking about? Six thousand! How much more can you raise? We've only got three weeks.'

The council members were silent. This Jew had a lot of nerve. The only white man in the group and he was on the attack.

'How much do we need?' asked Agee.

'That depends, Reverend, on how good a defense you want for Mr Hailey. I've only got eight other attorneys on my staff. Five are in trial at this very moment. We've got thirty-one capital murder convictions at various stages of appeal. We've got seventeen trials scheduled in ten states over the next five months. We get ten requests each week to represent defendants, eight of which we turn down because we simply don't have the staff or the money. For Mr Hailey, fifteen thousand has been contributed by two local chapters and the home office. Now you tell me that only six thousand has been raised locally. That's twenty-one thousand. For that amount you'll get the best defense we can afford. Two attorneys, at least one psychiatrist, but nothing fancy. Twenty-one thousand gets a good defense, but not what I had in mind.'

'What exactly did you have in mind?'

'A first-class defense. Three or four attorneys. A battery of psychiatrists. Half dozen investigators. A jury psychologist, just to name a few. This is not your run-of-the-mill murder case. I want to win. I was led to believe that you folks wanted to win.'

'How much?' asked Agee.

'Fifty thousand, minimum. A hundred thousand would be nice.'

'Look, Mr Reinfeld, you're in Mississippi. Our people are poor. They've given generously so far, but there's no way we can raise another thirty thousand here.'

Reinfeld adjusted his horn-rimmed glasses and scratched his graying beard. 'How much more can you raise?'

'Another five thousand, maybe.'

'That's not much money.'

'Not to you, but it is to the black folk of Ford County.'

Reinfeld studied the floor and continued stroking his beard. 'How much has the Memphis chapter given?'

'Five thousand,' answered someone from Memphis.

'Atlanta?'

'Five thousand.'

'How about the state chapter?'

'Which state?'

'Mississippi.'

'None.'

'None?'

'None.'

'Why not?'

'Ask him,' Agee said, pointing at Reverend Henry Hillman, the state director.

'Uh, we tryin' to raise some money now,' Hillman said weakly. 'But—'

'How much have you raised so far?' asked Agee.

'Well, uh, we got—'

'Nothin', right? You ain't raised nothin', have you, Hillman?' Agee said loudly.

'Come on, Hillman, tell us how much you raised,' chimed in Reverend Roosevelt, vice-chairman of the council.

Hillman was dumbfounded and speechless. He had been sitting quietly on the front pew minding his own business, half asleep. Suddenly he was under attack.

'The state chapter will contribute.'

'Sure you will, Hillman. You folks at state are constantly badgerin' us locals to contribute here and donate there for this cause and that cause, and we never see any of the money. You always cryin' about bein' so broke, and we're always sendin' money to state. But when we need help, state don't do a thing but show up here and talk.'

'That's not true.'

'Don't start lyin', Hillman.'

Reinfeld was embarrassed and immediately aware that a nerve had been touched. 'Gentlemen, gentlemen, let's move on,' he said diplomatically.

'Good idea,' Hillman said.

'When can we meet with Mr Hailey?' Reinfeld asked.

'I'll arrange a meetin' for in the mornin',' Agee said.

'Where can we meet?'

'I suggest we meet in Sheriff Walls' office in the jail. He's black, you know, the only black sheriff in Mississippi.'

'Yes, I've heard.'

'I think he'll let us meet in his office.'

'Good. Who is Mr Hailey's attorney?'

'Local boy. Jake Brigance.'

'Make sure he's invited. We'll ask him to help us on the case. It'll ease the pain.'

Ethel's obnoxious, high-pitched, bitchy voice broke the tranquility of the late afternoon and startled her boss. 'Mr Brigance, Sheriff Walls is on line two,' she said through the intercom.

'Okay.'

'Do you need me for anything else, sir?'

'No. See you in the morning.'

Jake punched line two. 'Hello, Ozzie. What's up?'

'Listen Jake, we've got a bunch of NAACP big shots in town.'

'What else is new?'

'No, this is different. They wanna meet with Carl Lee in the mornin'.'

'Why?'

'Some guy named Reinfeld.'

'I've heard of him. He heads up their capital murder team. Norman Reinfeld.'

'Yeah, that's him.'

'I've been waiting for this.'

'Well, he's here, and he wants to talk to Carl Lee.'

'Why are you involved?'

'Reverend Agee called me. He wants a favor, of course. He asked me to call you.'

'The answer is no. Emphatically no.'

Ozzie paused a few seconds. 'Jake, they want you to be present.'

'You mean I'm invited?'

'Yes. Agee said Reinfeld insisted on it. He wants you to be here.'

'Where?'

'In my office. Nine A.M.'

Jake breathed deeply and replied slowly. 'Okay, I'll be there. Where's Carl Lee?'

'In his cell.'

'Get him in your office. I'll be there in five minutes.'

'What for?'

'We need to have a prayer meeting.'

★   ★   ★

Reinfeld and Reverends Agee, Roosevelt, and Hillman sat in a perfect row of folding chairs and faced the sheriff, the defendant, and Jake, who puffed a cheap cigar in a determined effort to pollute the small office. He puffed mightily and stared nonchalantly at the floor, trying his best to show nothing but absolute contempt for Reinfeld and the reverends. Reinfeld was no pushover when it came to arrogance, and his disdain for this simple, small-time lawyer was not well hidden because he made no attempt to hide it. He was arrogant and insolent by nature. Jake had to work at it.

'Who called this meeting?' Jake asked impatiently, after a long, uncomfortable silence.

'Uh, well, I guess we did,' answered Agee as he searched Reinfeld for guidance.

'Well, get on with it. What do you want?'

'Take it easy now, Jake,' Ozzie said. 'Reverend Agee asked me to arrange the meeting so Carl Lee could meet Mr Reinfeld here.'

'Fine. They've met. Now what, Mr Reinfeld?'

'I'm here to offer my services, and the services of my staff and the entire NAACP to Mr Hailey,' said Reinfeld.

'What type of services?' asked Jake.

'Legal, of course.'

'Carl Lee, did you ask Mr Reinfeld to come here?' asked Jake.

'Nope.'

'Sounds like solicitation to me, Mr Reinfeld.'

'Skip the lecture, Mr Brigance. You know what I do, and you know why I'm here.'

'So you chase all your cases?'

'We don't chase anything. We're called in by local NAACP members and other civil rights activists. We handle only capital murder cases, and we're very good at what we do.'

'I suppose you're the only attorney competent to handle a case of this magnitude?'

'I've handled my share.'

'And lost your share.'

'Most of my cases are supposed to be lost.'

'I see. Is that your position on this case? Do you expect to lose it?'

Reinfeld picked at his beard and glared at Jake. 'I didn't come here to argue with you, Mr Brigance.'

'I know. You came here to offer your formidable legal skills to a defendant who's never heard of you and happens to be satisfied with his attorney. You came here to take my client. I know exactly why you're here.'

'I'm here because the NAACP invited me. Nothing more or less.'

'I see. Do you get all your cases from the NAACP?'

'I work for the NAACP, Mr Brigance. I'm in charge of its capital murder defense team. I go where the NAACP sends me.'

'How many clients do you have?'

'Several dozen. Why is that important?'

'Did they all have attorneys before you pushed yourself into their cases?'

'Some did, some didn't. We always try to work with the local attorney.'

Jake smiled. 'That's marvelous. You're offering me a chance to carry your briefcase and chauffeur you around Clanton. I might even get to fetch you a sandwich during the noon recess. What a thrill.'

Carl Lee sat frozen with arms crossed and his eyes fixed on a spot in the rug. The reverends watched him closely, waiting for him to say something to his lawyer, to tell him to shut up, that he was fired and the NAACP lawyers would handle the case. They watched and waited, but Carl Lee just sat calmly and listened.

'We have a lot to offer, Mr Hailey,' Reinfeld said. It was best to stay calm until the defendant decided who would represent him. A tantrum might ruin things.

'Such as?' Jake asked.

'Staff, resources, expertise, experienced trial lawyers who do nothing but capital defense. Plus we have a number of highly competent doctors we use in these cases. You name it, we have it.'

'How much money do you have to spend?'

'That's none of your business.'

'Is that so? Is it Mr Hailey's business? After all, it's his case. Perhaps Mr Hailey would like to know how much you have to spend in his defense. Would you, Mr Hailey?'

'Yep.'

'All right, Mr Reinfeld, how much do you have to spend?'

Reinfeld squirmed and looked hard at the reverends, who looked hard at Carl Lee.

'Approximately twenty thousand, so far,' Reinfeld admitted sheepishly.

Jake laughed and shook his head in disbelief. 'Twenty thousand! Y'all are really serious about this, aren't you? Twenty thousand! I thought you guys played in the big leagues. You raised a hundred and fifty thousand for the cop killer in Birmingham last year. And he was convicted, by the way. You spent a hundred thousand for the whore in Shreveport who killed her customer. And she, too, was convicted, I might add. And you think this case is worth only twenty thousand.'

'How much do you have to spend?' asked Reinfeld.

'If you can explain to me how that's any of your business, I'll be glad to discuss it with you.'

Reinfeld started to speak, then leaned forward and rubbed his temples. 'Why don't you talk to him, Reverend Agee.'

The reverends stared at Carl Lee. They wished they were alone with him, with no white folks around. They could talk to him like he was a nigger. They could explain things to him; tell him to fire this young white boy and get him some real lawyers. NAACP lawyers. Lawyers who knew how to fight for blacks. But they were not alone with him, and they couldn't curse him. They had to show respect for the white folks present. Agee spoke first.

'Look here, Carl Lee, we tryin' to help you. We brought in Mr Reinfeld here, and he's got all his lawyers and everbody at your disposal, to help you now. We ain't got nothin' against Jake here; he's a fine young lawyer. But he can work with Mr Reinfeld. We don't want you to fire Jake; we just want you to hire Mr Reinfeld too. They can all work together.'

'Forget that,' said Jake.

Agee paused and looked helplessly at Jake.

'Come on, Jake. We ain't got nothin' against you. It's a big chance for you. You can work with some real big lawyers. Get some real good experience. We—'

'Let me make it real clear, Reverend. If Carl Lee wants your lawyers, fine. But I'm not playing gofer for anyone. I'm either in or out. Nothing in between. My case or your case. The courtroom is not big enough for me, Reinfeld, and Rufus Buckley.'

Reinfeld rolled his eyes and looked at the ceiling, shaking his head slowly and grinning with an arrogant little smirk.

'You sayin' it's up to Carl Lee?' asked Reverend Agee.

'Of course it's up to him. He's hired me. He can fire me. He's already done it once. I'm not the one facing the gas chamber.'

'How 'bout it, Carl Lee?' asked Agee.

Carl Lee uncrossed his arms and stared at Agee. 'This twenty thousand, what's it for?'

'Really, it's more like thirty thousand,' answered Reinfeld. 'The local folks have pledged another ten thousand. The money will be used for your defense. None of it's attorney fees. We'll need two

380

or three investigators. Two, maybe three, psychiatric experts. We often use a jury psychologist to assist us in selecting the jury. Our defenses are very expensive.'

'Uh huh. How much money has been raised by local people?' asked Carl Lee.

'About six thousand,' answered Reinfeld.

'Who collected this money?'

Reinfeld looked at Agee. 'The churches,' answered the reverend.

'Who collected the money from the churches?' asked Carl Lee.

'We did,' answered Agee.

'You mean, you did,' said Carl Lee.

'Well, uh, right. I mean, each church gave the money to me, and I deposited it in a special bank account.'

'Yeah, and you deposited every nickel you received?'

'Of course I did.'

'Of course. Let me ask you this. How much of the money have you offered to my wife and kids?'

Agee looked a bit pale, or as pale as possible, and quickly searched the faces of the other reverends, who, at the moment, were preoccupied with a stink bug on the carpet. They offered no help. Each knew Agee had been taking his cut, and each knew the family had received nothing. Agee had profited more than the family. They knew it, and Carl Lee knew it.

'How much, Reverend?' repeated Carl Lee.

'Well, we thought the money—'

'How much, Reverend?'

'The money is gonna be spent on lawyer fees and stuff like that.'

'That ain't what you told your church, is it? You said it was for the support of the family. You almost cried when you talked about how my family might starve to death if the folks didn't donate all they could. Didn't you, Reverend?'

'The money's for you, Carl Lee. You and your family. Right now we think it could be better spent on your defense.'

'And what if I don't want your lawyers? What happens to the twenty thousand?'

Jake chuckled. 'Good question. What happens to the money if Mr Hailey doesn't hire you, Mr Reinfeld?'

'It's not my money,' answered Reinfeld.

'Reverend Agee?' asked Jake.

The reverend had had enough. He grew defiant and belligerent. He pointed at Carl Lee. 'Listen here, Carl Lee. We busted our butts to raise this money. Six thousand bucks from the poor people of this county, people who didn't have it to give. We worked hard for this money, and it was given by poor people, your people, people on food stamps and welfare and Medicaid, people who couldn't afford to donate a dime. But they gave for one reason, and only one reason: they believe in you and what you did, and they want you to walk outta that courtroom a free man. Don't say you don't want the money.'

'Don't preach to me,' Carl Lee replied softly. 'You say the poor folks of this county gave six thousand?'

'Right?'

'Where'd the rest of the money come from?'

'NAACP. Five thousand from Atlanta, five from Memphis, and five from national. And it's strictly for your defense fees.'

'If I use Mr Reinfeld here?'

'Right.'

'And if I don't use him, the fifteen thousand disappears?'

'Right.'

'What about the other six thousand?'

'Good question. We ain't discussed that yet. We thought you'd appreciate us for raisin' money and tryin' to help. We're offerin' the best lawyers and obviously you don't care.'

The room was silent for an eternity as the preachers, the lawyers, and the sheriff waited for some message from the defendant. Carl Lee chewed on his lower lip and stared at the floor. Jake lit another cigar. He had been fired before, and he could handle it again.

'You gotta know right now?' Carl Lee asked finally.

'No,' said Agee.

'Yes,' said Reinfeld. 'The trial is less than three weeks away, and we're two months behind already. My time is too valuable to wait on you, Mr Hailey. Either you hire me now or forget it. I've got a plane to catch.'

'Well, I'll tell you what you do, Mr Reinfeld. You go and catch your plane and don't ever worry 'bout comin' back to Clanton on my behalf. I'll take my chances with my friend Jake.'

Chapter 25

The Ford County Klavern was founded at midnight, Thursday, July 11, in a small pasture next to a dirt road deep in a forest somewhere in the northern part of the county. The six inductees stood nervously before the huge burning cross and repeated strange words offered by a wizard. A dragon and two dozen white-robed Klansmen watched and chanted when appropriate. A guard with a gun stood quietly down the road, occasionally watching the ceremony but primarily watching for uninvited guests. There were none.

Precisely at midnight the six fell to their knees and closed their eyes as the white hoods were ceremoniously placed onto their heads. They were Klansmen now, these six. Freddie Cobb, brother of the deceased, Jerry Maples, Clifton Cobb, Ed Wilburn, Morris Lancaster, and Terrell Grist. The grand dragon hovered above each one and chanted the sacred vows of klanhood. The flames from the cross scorched the faces of the new members as they knelt and quietly suffocated under the heavy robes and hoods. Sweat dripped from their red faces as they prayed fervently for the dragon to shut up with his nonsense and finish the ceremony. When the chanting stopped, the new members rose and quickly retreated from the cross. They were embraced by their new brothers, who grabbed their shoulders firmly and pounded primal incantations onto their sweaty collarbones. The heavy hoods were removed, and the Klansmen, both new members and old, walked proudly from the pasture and into the rustic cabin across the dirt road. The same guard sat on the front steps as the whiskey was poured around the table and plans were made for the trial of Carl Lee Hailey.

Deputy Pirtle pulled the graveyard shift, ten to six, and had stopped for coffee and pie at Gurdy's all-night diner on the highway north of town when his radio blared out the news that he was wanted at the jail. It was three minutes after midnight, Friday morning.

Pirtle left his pie and drove a mile south to the jail. 'What's up?' he asked the dispatcher.

'We got a call a few minutes ago, anonymous, from someone lookin' for the sheriff. I explained that he was not on duty, so they asked for whoever was on duty. That's you. They said it was very important, and they'd call back in fifteen minutes.'

Pirtle poured some coffee and relaxed in Ozzie's big chair. The phone rang. 'It's for you,' yelled the dispatcher.

'Hello,' answered Pirtle.

'Who's this?' asked the voice.

'Deputy Joe Pirtle. Who's this?'

'Where's the sheriff?'

'Asleep, I reckon.'

'Okay listen, and listen real good because this is important and I ain't callin' again. You know that Hailey nigger?'

'Yeah.'

'You know his lawyer, Brigance?'

'Yeah.'

'Then listen. Sometime between now and three A.M., they're gonna blow up his house.'

'Who?'

'Brigance.'

'No, I mean who's gonna blow up his house?'

'Don't worry about that, Deputy, just listen to me. This ain't no joke, and if you think it's a joke, just sit there and wait for his house to go up. It may happen any minute.'

The voice became silent but did not disappear. Pirtle listened. 'You still there?'

'Good night, Deputy.' The receiver clicked.

Pirtle jumped to his feet and ran to the dispatcher. 'Did you listen?'

'Of course I did.'

'Call Ozzie and tell him to get down here. I'll be at the Brigance house.'

Pirtle hid his patrol car in a driveway on Monroe Street and walked across the front lawns to Jake's house. He saw nothing. It was 12:55 A.M. He walked around the house with his flashlight and noticed nothing unusual. Every house on the street was dark and asleep. He unscrewed the light bulb on the front porch and took a seat in a wicker chair. He waited. The odd-looking foreign car was parked next to the Oldsmobile under the veranda. He would wait and ask Ozzie about notifying Jake.

Headlights appeared at the end of the street. Pirtle slumped lower in the chair, certain he could not be seen. A red pickup moved suspiciously toward the Brigance house but did not stop. He sat up and watched it disappear down the street.

Moments later he noticed two figures jogging from the direction of the square. He unbuttoned his holster and removed his service revolver. The first figure was much larger than the second, and seemed to run with more ease and grace. It was Ozzie. The other was Nesbit. Pirtle met the two in the driveway and they retreated into the darkness of the front porch. They whispered and watched the street.

'What exactly did he say?' asked Ozzie.

'Said someone's gonna blow up Jake's house between now and three A.M. Said it was no joke.'

'Is that all?'

'Yep. He wasn't real friendly.'

'How long you been here?'

'Twenty minutes.'

Ozzie turned to Nesbit. 'Give me your radio and go hide in the backyard. Stay quiet and keep your eyes open.'

Nesbit scurried to the rear of the house and

388

found a small opening between the shrubs along the back fence. Crawling on all fours, he disappeared into the shrubs. From his nest he could see the entire rear of the house.

'You gonna tell Jake?' asked Pirtle.

'Not yet. We might in a minute. If we knock on the door, they'll be turnin' on lights and we don't need that right now.'

'Yeah, but what if Jake hears us and comes through the door firin' away. He might think we're just a couple of niggers tryin' to break in.'

Ozzie watched the street and said nothing.

'Look, Ozzie, put yourself in his place. The cops have your house surrounded at one o'clock in the mornin' waitin' for somebody to throw a bomb. Now, would you wanna stay in bed asleep or would you wanna know about it?'

Ozzie studied the houses in the distance.

'Listen, Sheriff, we better wake them up. What if we don't stop whoever's plannin' this, and somebody inside the house gets hurt? We get blamed, right?'

Ozzie stood and punched the doorbell. 'Unscrew that light bulb,' he ordered, pointing at the porch ceiling.

'I already did.'

Ozzie punched the doorbell again. The wooden door swung open, and Jake walked to the storm door and stared at the sheriff. He was wearing a wrinkled nightshirt that fell just below his knees, and he held a loaded .38 in his right hand. He slowly opened the storm door.

'What is it, Ozzie?' he asked.

'Can I come in?'

'Yeah. What's going on?'

'Stay here on the porch,' Ozzie told Pirtle. 'I'll be just a minute.'

Ozzie closed the front door behind them and turned off the light in the foyer. They sat in the dark living room overlooking the porch and the front yard.

'Start talking,' Jake said.

''Bout a half hour ago we took an anonymous call from someone who said that someone planned to blow up your house between now and three A.M. We're takin' it serious.'

'Thanks.'

'I've got Pirtle on the front porch and Nesbit in the backyard. 'Bout ten minutes ago Pirtle saw a pickup drive by real interested like, but that's all we've seen.'

'Have you searched around the house?'

'Yeah, nothin'. They ain't been here yet. But somethin' tells me this is the real thing.'

'Why?'

'Just a hunch.'

Jake laid the .38 beside him on the couch and rubbed his temples. 'What's your suggestion?'

'Sit and wait. That's all we can do. You got a rifle?'

'I've got enough guns to invade Cuba.'

'Why don't you get it and get dressed. Take a position in one of those cute little windows upstairs. We'll hide outside and wait.'

390

'Have you got enough men?'

'Yeah, I figure there'll only be one or two of them.'

'Who's them?'

'Don't know. Could be the Klan, could be some freelancers. Who knows?'

Both men sat in deep thought and stared at the dark street. They could see the top of Pirtle's head as he slumped in the wicker chair just outside the window.

'Jake, you remember those three civil rights workers killed by the Klan back in '64? Found them buried in a levee down around Philadelphia.'

'Sure. I was a kid, but I remember.'

'Those boys would've never been found if someone hadn't told where they was. That someone was in the Klan. An informant. Seems like that always happened to the Klan. Somebody on the inside was always squealin'.'

'You think it's the Klan?'

'Sure looks like it. If it was just one or two freelancers, then who else would know about it? The bigger the group, the better the chance of someone tippin' us off.'

'That makes sense, but for some reason I'm not comforted by it.'

'Of course, it could be a joke.'

'Nobody's laughing.'

'You gonna tell your wife?'

'Yeah. I'd better go do that.'

'I would too. But don't be turnin' on lights. You might scare them off.'

'But I would like to scare them off.'

'And I'd like to catch them. If we don't catch them now, they'll try again, and next time they might forget to call us ahead of time.'

Carla dressed hurriedly in the dark. She was terrified. Jake laid Hanna on the couch in the den, where she mumbled something and went back to sleep. Carla held her head and watched Jake load a rifle.

'I'll be upstairs in the guest room. Don't turn on any lights. The cops have the place surrounded, so don't worry.'

'Don't worry! Are you crazy?'

'Try to go back to sleep.'

'Sleep! Jake, you've lost your mind.'

They didn't wait long. From his vantage point somewhere deep in the shrubs in front of the house, Ozzie saw him first: a lone figure walking casually down the street from the direction opposite the square. He had in his hand a small box or case of some sort. When he was two houses away, he left the street and cut through the front lawns of the neighbors. Ozzie pulled his revolver and nightstick and watched the man walk directly toward him. Jake had him in the scope of his deer rifle. Pirtle crawled like a snake across the porch and into the shrubs, ready to strike.

Suddenly, the figure darted across the front lawn next door and to the side of Jake's house. He carefully laid the small suitcase under Jake's bedroom window. As he turned to run, a huge black nightstick crashed across the side of his head, ripping his right ear in two places, each barely hanging to his head. He screamed and fell to the ground.

'I got him!' Ozzie yelled. Pirtle and Nesbit sprinted to the side of the house. Jake calmly walked down the stairs.

'I'll be back in a minute,' he told Carla.

Ozzie grabbed the suspect by the neck and sat him next to the house. He was conscious but dazed. The suitcase was inches away.

'What's your name?' Ozzie demanded.

He moaned and clutched his head and said nothing.

'I asked you a question,' Ozzie said as he hovered over his suspect. Pirtle and Nesbit stood nearby, guns drawn, too frightened to speak or move. Jake stared at the suitcase.

'I ain't sayin',' came the reply.

Ozzie raised the nightstick high over his head and drove it solidly against the man's right ankle. The crack of the bone was sickening.

He howled and grabbed his leg. Ozzie kicked him in the face. He fell backward and his head smashed into the side of the house. He rolled to his side and groaned in pain.

Jake knelt above the suitcase and put his ear next to it. He jumped and retreated. 'It's ticking,' he said weakly.

Ozzie bent over the suspect and laid the night-stick softly against his nose. 'I've got one more question before I break ever bone in your body. What's in the box?'

No answer.

Ozzie recoiled the nightstick and broke the other ankle. 'What's in the box!' he shouted.

'Dynamite!' came the anguished reply.

Pirtle dropped his gun. Nesbit's blood pressure shot through his cap and he leaned on the house. Jake turned white and his knees vibrated. He ran through the front door yelling at Carla. 'Get the car keys! Get the car keys!'

'What for?' she asked nervously.

'Just do as I say. Get the car keys and get in the car.'

He lifted Hanna and carried her through the kitchen, into the carport, and laid her in the back seat of Carla's Cutlass. He took Carla by the arm and helped her into the car. 'Leave, and don't come back for thirty minutes.'

'Jake, what's going on?' she demanded.

'I'll tell you later. There's no time now. Just leave. Go drive around for thirty minutes. Stay away from this street.'

'But why, Jake? What have you found?'

'Dynamite.'

She backed out of the driveway and disappeared.

When Jake returned to the side of the house, the suspect's left hand had been handcuffed to the gas meter next to the window. He was moaning, mumbling, cursing. Ozzie carefully lifted the suitcase by the handle and sat it neatly between the suspect's broken legs. Ozzie kicked both legs to spread them. He groaned louder. Ozzie, the deputies, and Jake backed away slowly and watched him. He began to cry.

'I don't know how to defuse it,' he said through clenched teeth.

'You'd better learn fast,' Jake said, his voice somewhat stronger.

The suspect closed his eyes and lowered his head. He bit his lip and breathed loudly and rapidly. Sweat dripped from his chin and eyebrows. His ear was shredded and hung like a falling leaf. 'Give me a flashlight.'

Pirtle handed him a flashlight.

'I need both hands,' he said.

'Try it with one,' Ozzie said.

He placed his fingers gently on the latch and closed his eyes.

'Let's get outta here,' Ozzie said. They ran around the corner of the house and into the carport, as far away as possible.

'Where's your family?' Ozzie asked.

'Gone. Recognize him?'

'Nope,' said Ozzie.

'I never seen him,' said Nesbit.

Pirtle shook his head.

Ozzie called the dispatcher, who called Deputy Riley, the self-trained explosives man for the county.

'What if he passes out and the bomb goes off?' Jake asked.

'You got insurance, don't you, Jake?' asked Nesbit.

'That's not funny.'

'We'll give him a few minutes, then Pirtle can go check on him,' said Ozzie.

'Why me?'

'Okay, Nesbit can go.'

'I think Jake should go,' said Nesbit. 'It's his house.'

'Very funny,' said Jake.

They waited and chatted nervously. Nesbit made another stupid remark about insurance. 'Quiet!' Jake said. 'I heard something.'

They froze. Seconds later the suspect yelled again. They ran back across the front yard, then slowly turned the corner. The empty suitcase had been tossed a few feet away. Next to the man was a neat pile of a dozen sticks of dynamite. Between his legs was a large, round-faced clock with wires bound together with silver electrical tape.

'Is it defused?' Ozzie asked anxiously.

'Yeah,' he replied between heavy, rapid breaths.

Ozzie knelt before him and removed the clock and the wires. He did not touch the dynamite. 'Where are your buddies?'

No response.

He removed his nightstick and moved closer to the man. 'I'm gonna start breakin' ribs one at a time. You better start talkin'. Now where are your buddies?'

'Kiss my ass.'

Ozzie stood and quickly looked around, not at Jake and the deputies, but at the house next door. Seeing nothing, he raised the nightstick. The suspect's left arm hung from the gas meter, and Ozzie planted the stick just below the left armpit. He squealed and jerked to the left. Jake almost felt sorry for him.

'Where are they?' Ozzie demanded.

No response.

Jake turned his head as the sheriff landed another blow to the ribs.

'Where are they?'

No response.

Ozzie raised the nightstick.

'Stop . . . please stop,' the suspect begged.

'Where are they?'

'Down that way. A couple of blocks.'

'How many?'

'One.'

'What vehicle?'

'Pickup. Red GMC.'

'Get the patrol cars,' Ozzie ordered.

Jake waited impatiently under the carport for his wife to return. At two-fifteen she drove slowly into the driveway and parked.

'Is Hanna asleep?' Jake asked as he opened the door.

'Yes.'

'Good. Leave her there. We'll be leaving in a few minutes.'

'Where are we going?'

'We'll discuss it inside.'

Jake poured the coffee and tried to act calm. Carla was scared and shaking and angry and making it difficult to act calm. He described the bomb and suspect and explained that Ozzie was searching for the accomplice.

'I want you and Hanna to go to Wilmington

and stay with your parents until after the trial,' he said.

She stared at the coffee and said nothing.

'I've already called your dad and explained everything. They're scared too, and they insist you stay with them until this thing is over.'

'And what if I don't want to go?'

'Please, Carla. How can you argue at a time like this?'

'What about you?'

'I'll be fine. Ozzie will give me a bodyguard and they'll watch the house around the clock. I'll sleep at the office some. I'll be safe, I promise.'

She was not convinced.

'Look, Carla, I've got a thousand things on my mind right now. I've got a client facing the gas chamber and his trial is ten days away. I can't lose it. I'll work night and day from now until the twenty-second, and once the trial starts you won't see me anyway. The last thing I need is to be worried about you and Hanna. Please go.'

'They were going to kill us, Jake. They tried to kill us.'

He couldn't deny it.

'You promised to withdraw if the danger became real.'

'It's out of the question. Noose would never allow me to withdraw at this late date.'

'I feel as though you've lied to me.'

'That's not fair. I think I underestimated this thing, and now it's too late.'

She walked to the bedroom and began packing.

'The plane leaves Memphis at six-thirty. Your father will meet you at the Raleigh airport at nine-thirty.'

'Yes, sir.'

Fifteen minutes later they left Clanton. Jake drove and Carla ignored him. At five, they ate breakfast in the Memphis airport. Hanna was sleepy but excited about seeing her grandparents. Carla said little. She had much to say, but as a rule, they didn't argue in front of Hanna. She ate quietly and sipped her coffee and watched her husband casually read the paper as if nothing had happened.

Jake kissed them goodbye and promised to call every day. The plane left on time. At seven-thirty he was in Ozzie's office.

'Who is he?' Jake asked the sheriff.

'We have no idea. No wallet, no identification, nothin'. And he ain't talkin'.'

'Does anybody recognize him?'

Ozzie thought for a second. 'Well, Jake, he's kinda hard to recognize right now. Got a lot of bandages on his face.'

Jake smiled. 'You play rough, don't you, big guy?'

'Only when I have to. I didn't hear you object.'

'No, I wanted to help. What about his friend?'

'We found him sleepin' in a red GMC 'bout a half a mile from your house. Terrell Grist. Local redneck. Lives out from Lake Village. I think he's a friend of the Cobb family.'

Jake repeated the name a few times. 'Never heard of him. Where is he?'

'Hospital. Same room with the other.'

'My God, Ozzie, did you break his legs too?'

'Jake, my friend, he resisted arrest. We had to subdue him. Then we had to interrogate him. He didn't want to cooperate.'

'What did he say?'

'Not much. Don't know nothin'. I'm convinced he doesn't know the guy with the dynamite.'

'You mean they brought in a professional?'

'Could be. Riley looked at the firecrackers and timin' device and said it was pretty good work. We'd have never found you, your wife, your daughter, probably never found your house. It was set for two A.M. Without the tip, you'd be dead, Jake. So would your family.'

Jake felt dizzy and sat on the couch. Reaction set in like a hard kick to the groin. A case of diarrhea almost manifested itself, and he was nauseated.

'You get your family off?'

'Yeah,' he said weakly.

'I'm gonna assign a deputy to you full-time. Got a preference?'

'Not really.'

'How 'bout Nesbit?'

'Fine. Thanks.'

'One other thing. I guess you want this kept quiet?'

'If possible. Who knows about it?'

'Just me and the deputies. I think we can keep it under wraps until after the trial, but I can't guarantee anything.'

'I understand. Try your best.'

'I will, Jake.'

'I know you will, Ozzie. I appreciate you.'

Jake drove to the office, made the coffee and lay on the couch in his office. He wanted a quick nap, but sleep was impossible. His eyes burned, but he could not close them. He stared at the ceiling fan.

'Mr Brigance,' Ethel called over the intercom.

No response.

'Mr Brigance!'

Somewhere in the deep recesses of his subconscious, Jake heard himself being paged. He bolted upright. 'Yes!' he yelled.

'Judge Noose is on the phone.'

'Okay, okay,' he mumbled as he staggered to his desk. He checked his watch. Nine A.M. He had slept for an hour.

'Good morning, Judge,' he said cheerfully, trying to sound alert and awake.

'Good morning, Jake. How are you?'

'Just fine, Judge. Busy getting ready for the big trial.'

'I thought so. Jake, what is your schedule today?'

What's today, he thought. He grabbed his appointment book. 'Nothing but office work.'

'Good. I would like to have lunch with you at my home. Say around eleven-thirty.'

'I would be delighted, Judge. What's the occasion?'

'I want to discuss the Hailey case.'

'Fine, Judge. I'll see you at eleven-thirty.'

★   ★   ★

The Nooses lived in a stately antebellum home off the town square in Chester. The home had been in the wife's family for over a century, and although it could stand some maintenance and repair, it was in decent condition. Jake had never been a guest in the house, and had never met Mrs Noose, although he had heard she was a snobby blue blood whose family at one time had money but lost it. She was as unattractive as Ichabod, and Jake wondered what the children looked like. She was properly polite when she met Jake at the door and attempted small talk as she led him to the patio, where His Honor was drinking iced tea and reviewing correspondence. A maid was preparing a small table nearby.

'Good to see you, Jake,' Ichabod said warmly. 'Thanks for coming over.'

'My pleasure, Judge. Beautiful place you have here.'

They discussed the Hailey trial over soup and chicken salad sandwiches. Ichabod was dreading the ordeal, although he didn't admit it. He seemed tired, as if the case was already a burden. He surprised Jake with an admission that he detested Buckley. Jake said he felt the same way.

'Jake, I'm perplexed over this venue ruling,' he said. 'I've studied your brief and Buckley's brief, and I've researched the law myself. It's a tough question. Last weekend I attended a judges' conference on the Gulf Coast, and I had a few drinks with Judge Denton on the Supreme Court. He and I were in law school together, and we were colleagues in the state senate. We're very close. He's from Dupree County in south Mississippi, and he says that everybody down there talks about the case. People on the street ask him how he's gonna rule if the case winds up on appeal. Everybody's got an opinion, and that's almost four hundred miles away. Now, if I agree to change venue, where do we go? We can't leave the state, and I'm convinced that everyone has not only heard about your client, but already prejudged him. Would you agree?'

'Well, there's been a lot of publicity,' Jake said carefully.

'Talk to me, Jake. We're not in court. That's why I invited you here. I want to pick your brain. I know there's been a lot of publicity. If we move it, where do we go?'

'How about the delta?'

Noose smiled. 'You'd like that, wouldn't you?'

'Of course. We could pick us a good jury over there. One that would truly understand the issues.'

'Yeah, and one that would be half black.'

'I hadn't thought about that.'

'Do you really believe those folks haven't already prejudged this defendant?'

'I suppose so.'

'So where do we go?'

'Did Judge Denton have a suggestion?'

'Not really. We discussed the court's traditional refusal to allow changes of venue except in the most heinous of cases. It's a difficult issue with a notorious crime that arouses passion both for and against the defendant. With television and all the press nowadays, these crimes are instant news, and everyone knows the details long before the trial. And this case tops them all. Even Denton admitted he'd never seen a case with this much publicity, and he admitted it would be impossible to find a fair and impartial jury anywhere in Mississippi. Suppose I leave it in Ford County and your man is convicted. Then you appeal claiming venue should have been changed. Denton indicated he would be sympathetic with my decision not to move it. He thinks a majority of the court would uphold my denial of the venue change. Of course, that's no guarantee, and we discussed it over several long drinks. Would you like a drink?'

'No thanks.'

'I just don't see any reason to move the trial from Clanton. If we did, we'd be fooling ourselves if we thought we could find twelve people who are undecided about Mr Hailey's guilt.'

'Sounds like you've already made up your mind, Judge.'

'I have. We're not changing venue. The trial will be held in Clanton. I'm not comfortable with it, but I see no reason to move the trial. Besides, I like Clanton. It's close to home and the air conditioning works in the courthouse.'

Noose reached for a file and found an envelope. 'Jake, this is an order, dated today, overruling the request to change venue. I've sent a copy to Buckley, and there's a copy for you. The original is in here, and I would appreciate you filing this with the clerk in Clanton.'

'I'll be glad to.'

'I just hope I'm doing the right thing. I've really struggled with this.'

'It's a tough job,' Jake offered, attempting sympathy.

Noose called the maid and ordered a gin and tonic. He insisted that Jake view his rose garden, and they spent an hour in the sprawling rear lawn admiring His Honor's flowers. Jake thought of Carla, and Hanna, and his home, and the dynamite, but gallantly remained interested in Ichabod's handiwork.

Friday afternoons often reminded Jake of law school, when, depending on the weather, he and his friends would either group in their favorite bar in Oxford and guzzle happy-hour beer and debate their new-found theories of law or curse the insolent, arrogant, terroristic law professors, or, if the weather was warm and sunny, pile the beer in Jake's well-used convertible Beetle and head for the beach at Sardis Lake, where the women from sorority row plastered their beautiful, bronze bodies with oil and sweated in the sun and coolly ignored the catcalls from the drunken law students and fraternity rats. He missed those innocent days. He hated law school – every law student with any sense hated law school – but he missed the friends and good times, especially the Fridays. He missed the pressureless lifestyle, although at times the pressure had seemed unbearable, especially during the first year when the professors were more abusive than normal. He missed being broke, because when he had nothing he owed nothing and most of his classmates were in the same boat. Now that he had an income he worried constantly about mortgages, the overhead, credit cards, and realizing the American dream of becoming affluent. Not wealthy, just affluent. He missed his Volkswagen because it had been his first new car, a gift at high school graduation, and it was paid for, unlike the Saab. He missed being single, occasionally, although he was happily married. And he missed beer, either from a pitcher, can, or bottle. It didn't matter. He had been a social drinker, only with friends, and he spent as much time as possible with his friends. He didn't drink every day in law school, and he seldom got drunk. But there had been several painful, memorable hangovers.

Then came Carla. He met her at the beginning of his last semester, and six months later they married. She was beautiful, and that's what got his attention. She was quiet, and a little snobby at first, like most of the wealthy sorority girls at Ole Miss. But he found her to be warm and personable and lacking in self-confidence. He had never understood how someone as beautiful as Carla could be insecure. She was a Dean's List scholar in liberal arts with no intention of ever doing more than teaching school for a few years. Her family had money, and her mother had never worked.

This appealed to Jake – the family money and the absence of a career ambition. He wanted a wife who would stay home and stay beautiful and have babies and not try to wear the pants. It was love at first sight.

But she frowned on drinking, any type of drinking. Her father drank heavily when she was a child, and there were painful memories. So Jake dried out his last semester in law school and lost fifteen pounds. He looked great, felt great, and he was madly in love. But he missed beer.

There was a country grocery a few miles out of Chester with a Coors sign in the window. Coors had been his favorite in law school, although at that time it was not for sale east of the river. It was a delicacy at Ole Miss, and the bootlegging of Coors had been profitable around the campus. Now that it was available everywhere most folks had returned to Budweiser.

It was Friday, and hot. Carla was nine hundred miles away. He had no desire to go to the office, and anything there could wait until tomorrow. Some nut just tried to kill his family and remove his landmark from the National Register of Historic Places. The biggest trial of his career was ten days away. He was not ready and the pressure was mounting. He had just lost his most critical pretrial motion. And he was thirsty. Jake stopped and bought a six-pack of Coors.

It took almost two hours to travel the sixty miles from Chester to Clanton. He enjoyed the diversion, the scenery, the beer. He stopped twice to relieve himself and once to get another six-pack. He felt great.

There was only one place to go in his condition. Not home, not the office, certainly not the courthouse to file Ichabod's villainous order. He parked the Saab behind the nasty little Porsche and glided up the sidewalk with cold beer in hand. As usual, Lucien was rocking slowly on the front porch, drinking and reading a treatise on the insanity defense. He closed the book and, noticing the beer, smiled at his former associate. Jake just grinned at him.

'What's the occasion, Jake?'

'Nothing, really. Just got thirsty.'

'I see. What about your wife?'

'She doesn't tell me what to do. I'm my own man. I'm the boss. If I want beer, I'll drink some beer, and she'll say nothing.' Jake took a long sip.

'She must be outta town.'

'North Carolina.'

'When did she leave?'

'Six this morning. Flew from Memphis with Hanna. She'll stay with her parents in Wilmington until the trial's over. They've got a fancy little beach house where they spend their summers.'

'She left this morning, and you're drunk by mid-afternoon.'

'I'm not drunk,' Jake answered. 'Yet.'

'How long you been drinkin'?'

'Coupla hours. I bought a six-pack when I left Noose's house around one-thirty. How long have you been drinking?'

'I normally drink my breakfast. Why were you at his house?'

'We discussed the trial over lunch. He refused to change venue.'

'He what?'

'You heard me. The trial will be in Clanton.'

Lucien took a drink and rattled his ice. 'Sallie!' he screamed.

'Did he give any reason?'

'Yeah. Said it would be impossible to find jurors anywhere who hadn't heard of the case.'

'I told you so. That's a good common sense reason not to move it, but it's a poor legal reason. Noose is wrong.'

Sallie returned with a fresh drink and took Jake's beer to the refrigerator. Lucien took a slug and smacked his lips. He wiped his mouth with his arm, and took another long drink.

'You know what that means, don't you?' he asked.

'Sure. An all-white jury.'

'That, plus a reversal on appeal if he's convicted.'

'Don't bet on it. Noose has already consulted with the Supreme Court. He thinks the Court will affirm him if challenged. He thinks he's on solid ground.'

'He's an idiot. I can show him twenty cases that say the trial should be moved. I think he's afraid to move it.'

'Why would Noose be afraid?'

'He's taking some heat.'

'From who?'

Lucien admired the golden liquid in his large glass and slowly stirred the ice cubes with a finger. He grinned and looked as though he knew something but wouldn't tell unless he was begged.

'From who?' Jake demanded, glaring at his friend with shiny, pink eyes.

'Buckley,' Lucien said smugly.

'Buckley,' Jake repeated. 'I don't understand.'

'I knew you wouldn't.'

'Do you mind explaining?'

'I guess I could. But you can't repeat it. It's very confidential. Came from good sources.'

'Who?'

'Can't tell.'

'Who are your sources?' Jake insisted.

'I said I can't tell. Won't tell. Okay?'

'How can Buckley put pressure on Noose?'

'If you'll listen, I'll tell you.'

'Buckley has no influence over Noose. Noose despises him. Told me so himself. Today. Over lunch.'

'I realize that.'

'Then how can you say Noose is feeling some heat from Buckley?'

'If you'll shut up, I'll tell you.'

Jake finished a beer and called for Sallie.

'You know what a cutthroat and political whore Buckley is.'

Jake nodded.

'You know how bad he wants to win this trial. If he wins, he thinks it will launch his campaign for attorney general.'

'Governor,' said Jake.

'Whatever. He's ambitious, okay?'

'Okay.'

'Well, he's been getting political chums throughout the district to call Noose and suggest that the trial be held in Ford County. Some have been real blunt with Noose. Like, move the trial, and we'll get you in the next election. Leave it in Clanton, and we'll help you get reelected.'

'I don't believe that.'

'Fine. But it's true.'

'How do you know?'

'Sources.'

'Who's called him?'

'One example. Remember that thug that used to be sheriff in Van Buren County? Motley? FBI got him, but he's out now. Still a very popular man in that county.'

'Yeah, I remember.'

'I know for a fact he went to Noose's house with a couple of sidekicks and suggested very strongly that Noose leave the trial here. Buckley put them up to it.'

'What did Noose say?'

'They all cussed each other real good. Motley told Noose he wouldn't get fifty votes in Van Buren County next election. They promised to stuff ballot boxes, harass the blacks, rig the absentee ballots, the usual election practices in Van Buren County. And Noose knows they'll do it.'

'Why should he worry about it?'

411

'Don't be stupid, Jake. He's an old man who can do nothing but be a judge. Can you imagine him trying to start a law practice? He makes sixty thousand a year and would starve if he got beat. Most judges are like that. He's got to keep that job. Buckley knows it, so he's talking to the local bigots and pumping them up and telling how this no-good nigger might be acquitted if the trial is moved and that they should put a little heat on the judge. That's why Noose is feeling some pressure.'

They drank for a few minutes in silence, both rocking quietly in the tall wooden rockers. The beer felt great.

'There's more,' Lucien said.

'To what?'

'To Noose.'

'What is it?'

'He's had some threats. Not political threats, but death threats. I hear he's scared to death. Got the police over there guarding his house. Carries a gun now.'

'I know the feeling,' Jake mumbled.

'Yeah, I heard.'

'Heard what?'

'About the dynamite. Who was he?'

Jake was flabbergasted. He stared blankly at Lucien, unable to speak.

'Don't ask. I got connections. Who was he?'

'No one knows.'

'Sounds like a pro.'

'Thanks.'

'You're welcome to stay here. I've got five bedrooms.'

The sun was gone by eight-fifteen when Ozzie parked his patrol car behind the Saab, which was still parked behind the Porsche. He walked to the foot of the steps leading up to the porch. Lucien saw him first.

'Hello, Sheriff,' he attempted to say, his tongue thick and ponderous.

'Evenin', Lucien. Where's Jake?'

Lucien nodded toward the end of the porch, where Jake lay sprawled on the swing.

'He's taking a nap,' Lucien explained helpfully.

Ozzie walked across the squeaking boards and stood above the comatose figure snoring peacefully. He punched him gently in the ribs. Jake opened his eyes, and struggled desperately to sit up.

'Carla called my office lookin' for you. She's worried sick. She's been callin' all afternoon and couldn't find you. Nobody's seen you. She thinks you're dead.'

Jake rubbed his eyes as the swing rocked gently. 'Tell her I'm not dead. Tell her you've seen me and talked to me and you are convinced beyond a shadow of a doubt that I am not dead. Tell her I'll call her tomorrow. Tell her, Ozzie, please tell her.'

'No way, buddy. You're a big boy, you call her and tell her.' Ozzie walked off the porch. He was not amused.

Jake struggled to his feet and staggered into the house. 'Where's the phone?' he yelled at Sallie. As he dialed, he could hear Lucien on the porch laughing uncontrollably.

Chapter 26

The last hangover had been in law school, six or seven years earlier; he couldn't remember. The date, that is. He couldn't remember the date, but the pounding head, dry mouth, short breath, and burning eyes brought back painful, vivid memories of long and unforgettable bouts with the tasty brown stuff.

He knew he was in trouble immediately, when his left eye opened. The eyelids on the right one were matted firmly together, and they would not open, unless manually opened with fingers, and he did not dare move. He lay there in the dark room on a couch, fully dressed, including shoes, listening to his head pound and watching the ceiling fan rotate slowly. He felt nauseated. His neck ached because there was no pillow. His feet throbbed because of the shoes. His stomach rolled and flipped and promised to erupt. Death would have been welcome.

Jake had problems with hangovers because he could not sleep them off. Once his eyes opened and his brain awoke and began spinning again, and the throbbing between his temples set in, he could not sleep. He had never understood this. His friends in law school could sleep for days with a hangover, but not Jake. He never managed more than a few hours after the last can or bottle was empty.

Why? That was always the question the next morning. Why did he do it? A cold beer was refreshing. Maybe two or three. But ten, fifteen, even twenty? He had lost count. After six, beer lost its taste, and from then on the drinking was just for the sake of drinking and getting drunk. Lucien had been very helpful. Before dark he had sent Sallie to the store for a whole case of Coors, which he gladly paid for, then encouraged Jake to drink. There were a few cans left. It was Lucien's fault.

Slowly he lifted his legs, one at a time, and placed his feet on the floor. He gently rubbed his temples, to no avail. He breathed deeply, but his heart pounded rapidly, pumping more blood to his brain and fueling the small jackhammers at work on the inside of his head. He had to have water. His tongue was dehydrated and puffed to the point where it was easier to leave his mouth open like a dog in heat. Why, oh why?

He stood, carefully, slowly, retardedly, and crept into the kitchen. The light above the stove was shielded and dim, but it penetrated the darkness and pierced his eyes. He rubbed his eyes and tried to clean them with his smelly fingers. He drank

416

the warm water slowly and allowed it to run from his mouth and drip on the floor. He didn't care. Sallie would clean it. The clock on the counter said it was two-thirty.

Gaining momentum, he walked awkwardly yet quietly through the living room, past the couch with no pillow, and out the door. The porch was littered with empty cans and bottles. Why?

He sat in the hot shower in his office for an hour, unable to move. It relieved some of the aches and soreness, but not the violence swirling around his brain. Once in law school, he had managed to crawl from his bed to the refrigerator for a beer. He drank it, and it helped; then he drank another, and felt much better. He remembered this now while sitting in the shower, and the thought of another beer made him vomit.

He lay on the conference table in his underwear and tried his best to die. He had plenty of life insurance. They would leave his house alone. The new lawyer could get a continuance.

Nine days to trial. Time was scarce, precious, and he had just wasted one day with a massive hangover. Then he thought of Carla, and his head pounded harder. He had tried to sound sober. Told her he and Lucien had spent the afternoon reviewing insanity cases, and he would have called earlier but the phones weren't working, at least Lucien's weren't. But his tongue was heavy and his speech slow, and she knew he was drunk. She was furious – a controlled fury.

417

Yes, her house was still standing. That was all she believed.

At six-thirty he called her again. She might be impressed if she knew he was at the office by dawn working diligently. She wasn't. With great pain and fortitude, he sounded cheerful, even hyper. She was not impressed.

'How do you feel?' she insisted.

'Great!' he answered with closed eyes.

'What time did you go to bed?'

What bed, thought Jake. 'Right after I called you.'

She said nothing.

'I got to the office at three o'clock this morning,' he said proudly.

'Three o'clock!'

'Yeah, I couldn't sleep.'

'But you didn't sleep any Thursday night.' A touch of concern edged through her icy words, and he felt better.

'I'll be okay. I may stay with Lucien some this week and next. It might be safer over there.'

'What about the bodyguard?'

'Yeah, Deputy Nesbit. He's parked outside asleep in his car.'

She hesitated and Jake could feel the phone lines thawing. 'I'm worried about you,' she said warmly.

'I'll be fine, dear. I'll call tomorrow. I've got work to do.'

He replaced the receiver, ran to the restroom and vomited again.

* * *

The knocking persisted at the front door. Jake ignored it for fifteen minutes, but whoever it was knew he was there and kept knocking.

He walked to the balcony. 'Who is it?' he yelled at the street.

The woman walked from the sidewalk under the balcony and leaned on a black BMW parked next to the Saab. Her hands were thrust deep into the pockets of faded, starched, well-fitting jeans. The noon sun burned brightly and blinded her as she looked up in his direction. It also illuminated her light, goldish red hair.

'Are you Jake Brigance?' she asked, shielding her eyes with a forearm.

'Yeah. Whatta you want?'

'I need to talk to you.'

'I'm very busy.'

'It's very important.'

'You're not a client, are you?' he asked, focusing his eyes on the slender figure and knowing she was indeed not a client.

'No. I just need five minutes of your time.'

Jake unlocked the door. She walked in casually as if she owned the place. She shook his hand firmly.

'I'm Ellen Roark.'

He pointed to a seat by the door. 'Nice to meet you. Sit down.'

Jake sat on the edge of Ethel's desk. 'One syllable or two?'

'I beg your pardon?'

She had a quick, cocky Northeast accent, but tempered with some time in the South.

'Is it Rork or Row Ark?'

'R-o-a-r-k. That's Rork in Boston, and Row Ark in Mississippi.'

'Mind if I call you Ellen?'

'Please do, with two syllables. Can I call you Jake?'

'Yes, please.'

'Good, I hadn't planned to call you Mister.'

'Boston, huh?'

'Yeah, I was born there. Went to Boston College. My dad is Sheldon Roark, a notorious criminal lawyer in Boston.'

'I guess I've missed him. What brings you to Mississippi?'

'I'm in law school at Ole Miss.'

'Ole Miss! How'd you wind up down here?'

'My mother's from Natchez. She was a sweet little sorority girl at Ole Miss, then moved to New York, where she met my father.'

'I married a sweet little sorority girl from Ole Miss.'

'They have a great selection.'

'Would you like coffee?'

'No thanks.'

'Well, now that we know each other, what brings you to Clanton?'

'Carl Lee Hailey.'

'I'm not surprised.'

'I'll finish law school in December, and I'm killing time in Oxford this summer. I'm taking criminal procedure under Guthrie, and I'm bored.'

'Crazy George Guthrie.'

420

'Yeah, he's still crazy.'

'He flunked me in constitutional law my first year.'

'Anyway, I'd like to help you with the trial.'

Jake smiled and took a seat in Ethel's heavy-duty, rotating secretarial chair. He studied her carefully. Her black cotton polo shirt was fashionably weathered and neatly pressed. The outlines and subtle shadows revealed a healthy bustline, no bra. The thick, wavy hair fell perfectly on her shoulders.

'What makes you think I need help?'

'I know you practice alone, and I know you don't have a law clerk.'

'How do you know all this?'

'*Newsweek*.'

'Ah, yes. A wonderful publication. It was a good picture, wasn't it?'

'You looked a bit stuffy, but it was okay. You look better in person.'

'What credentials do you bring with you?'

'Genius runs in my family. I finished *summa cum laude* at BC, and I'm second in my law class. Last summer I spent three months with the Southern Prisoners Defense League in Birmingham and played gofer in seven capital trials. I watched Elmer Wayne Doss die in the Florida electric chair and I watched Willie Ray Ash get lethally injected in Texas. In my spare time at Ole Miss I write briefs for the ACLU and I'm working on two death penalty appeals for a law firm in Spartanburg, South Carolina. I was raised in my father's law office, and I was proficient in legal research before I could drive. I've watched him defend murderers, rapists, embezzlers, extortionists, terrorists, assassins, child abusers, child fondlers, child killers, and children who killed their parents. I worked forty hours a week in his office when I was in high school and fifty when I was in college. He has eighteen lawyers in his firm, all very bright, very talented. It's a great training ground for criminal lawyers, and I've been there for fourteen years. I'm twenty-five years old, and when I grow up I want to be a radical criminal lawyer like my dad and spend a glorious career stamping out the death penalty.'

'Is that all?'

'My dad's filthy rich, and even though we're Irish Catholic I'm an only child. I've got more money than you do so I'll work for free. No charge. A free law clerk for three weeks. I'll do all the research, typing, answering the phone. I'll even carry your briefcase and make the coffee.'

'I was afraid you'd want to be a law partner.'

'No. I'm a woman, and I'm in the South. I know my place.'

'Why are you so interested in this case?'

'I want to be in the courtroom. I love criminal trials, big trials where there's a life on the line and pressure so thick you can see it in the air. Where the courtroom's packed and security is tight. Where half the people hate the defendant and his lawyers and the other half pray he gets off. I love it. And this is the trial of all trials. I'm not a Southerner and I find this place bewildering most of the time, but I have developed a perverse love for it. It'll never make sense to me, but it is fascinating. The racial implications are enormous. The trial of a black father for killing two white men who raped his daughter – my father said he would take the case for free.'

'Tell him to stay in Boston.'

'It's a trial lawyer's dream. I just want to be there. I'll stay out of the way, I promise. Just let me work in the background and watch the trial.'

'Judge Noose hates women lawyers.'

'So does every male lawyer in the South. Besides, I'm not a lawyer, I'm a law student.'

'I'll let you explain that to him.'

'So I've got the job.'

Jake stopped staring at her and breathed deeply. A minor wave of nausea vibrated through his stomach and lungs and took his breath. The jackhammers had returned with a fury and he needed to be near the restroom.

'Yes, you've got the job. I could use some free research. These cases are complicated, as I'm sure you are aware.'

She flashed a comely, confident smile. 'When do I start?'

'Now.'

Jake led her through a quick tour of the office, and assigned her to the war room upstairs. They laid the Hailey file on the conference table and she spent an hour copying it.

At two-thirty Jake awoke from a nap on his

couch. He walked downstairs to the conference room. She had removed half the books from the shelves and had them scattered the length of the table with page markers sticking up every fifty or so pages. She was busy taking notes.

'Not a bad library,' she said.

'Some of these books haven't been used in twenty years.'

'I noticed the dust.'

'Are you hungry?'

'Yes. I'm starving.'

'There's a little cafe around the corner where the specialty is grease and fried corn meal. My system needs a shot of grease.'

'Sounds delicious.'

They walked around the square to Claude's, where the crowd was thin for a Saturday afternoon. There were no other whites in the place. Claude was absent and the silence was deafening. Jake ordered a cheeseburger, onion rings, and three headache powders.

'Got a headache?' Ellen asked.

'Massive.'

'Stress?'

'Hangover.'

'Hangover? I thought you were a teetotaler.'

'And where'd you hear that?'

'*Newsweek*. The article said you were a clean-cut family man, workaholic, devout Presbyterian who drank nothing and smoked cheap cigars. Remember? How could you forget, right?'

'You believe everything you read?'

'No.'

'Good, because last night I got plastered, and I've puked all morning.'

The law clerk was amused. 'What do you drink?'

'I don't – remember. At least I didn't until last night. This is my first hangover since law school, and I hope it's my last. I'd forgotten how terrible these things are.'

'Why do lawyers drink so much?'

'They learn how in law school. Does your dad drink?'

'Are you kidding? We're Catholic. He's careful, though.'

'Do you drink?'

'Sure, all the time,' she said proudly.

'Then you'll make a great lawyer.'

Jake carefully mixed the three powders in a glass of ice water and slugged it down. He grimaced and wiped his mouth. She watched intently with an amused smile.

'What'd your wife say?'

'About what?'

'The hangover, from such a devout and religious family man.'

'She doesn't know about it. She left me early yesterday morning.'

'I'm sorry.'

'She went to stay with her parents until the trial is over. We've had anonymous phone calls and death threats for two months now, and early yesterday morning they planted dynamite outside our bedroom window. The cops found it in time and they caught the men, probably the Klan. Enough dynamite to level the house and kill all of us. That was a good excuse to get drunk.'

'I'm sorry to hear that.'

'The job you've just taken could be very dangerous. You should know that at this point.'

'I've been threatened before. Last summer in Dothan, Alabama, we defended two black teenagers who had sodomized and strangled an eighty-year-old woman. No lawyer in the state would take the case so they called the Defense League. We rode into town on black horses and the mere sight of us would cause lynch mobs to form instantly on street corners. I've never felt so hated in my life. We hid in a motel in another town and felt safe, until one night two men cornered me in the motel lounge and tried to abduct me.'

'What happened?'

'I carry a snub-nosed .38 in my purse and I convinced them I knew how to use it.'

'A snub-nosed .38?'

'My father gave it to me for my fifteenth birthday. I have a license.'

'He must be a hell of a guy.'

'He's been shot at several times. He takes very controversial cases, the kind you read about in the papers where the public is outraged and demanding that the defendant be hanged without a trial or a lawyer. Those are the cases he likes best. He has a full-time bodyguard.'

'Big deal. So do I. His name is Deputy Nesbit,

and he couldn't hit the side of a barn with a shotgun. He was assigned to me yesterday.'

The food arrived. She removed the onions and tomatoes from her Claudeburger, and offered him the french fries. She cut it in half and nibbled around the edges like a bird. Hot grease dripped to her plate. With each small bite, she carefully wiped her mouth.

Her face was gentle and pleasant with an easy smile that belied the ACLU, ERA, burn-the-bra, I-can-outcuss-you bitchiness Jake knew was lurking somewhere near the surface. There was not a trace of makeup anywhere on the face. None was needed. She was not beautiful, not cute, and evidently determined not to be so. She had the pale skin of a redhead, but it was healthy skin with seven or eight freckles splattered about the small, pointed nose. With each frequent smile, her lips spread wonderfully and folded her cheeks into neat, transient, hollow dimples. The smiles were confident, challenging, and mysterious. The metallic green eyes radiated a soft fury and were fixed and unblinking when she talked.

It was an intelligent face, attractive as hell.

Jake chewed on his burger and tried to nonchalantly ignore her eyes. The heavy food settled his stomach, and for the first time in ten hours he began to think he might live.

'Seriously, why'd you choose Ole Miss?' he asked.

'It's a good law school.'

'It's my school. But we don't normally attract

the brightest students from the Northeast. That's Ivy League country. We send our smartest kids up there.'

'My father hates every lawyer with an Ivy League degree. He was dirt poor and scratched his way through law school at night. He's endured the snubs from rich, well-educated, and incompetent lawyers all his life. Now he laughs at them. He told me I could go to law school anywhere in the country, but if I chose an Ivy League school he would not pay for it. Then there's my mother. I was raised on these enchanting stories of life in the Deep South, and I had to see for myself. Plus, the Southern states seemed determined to practice the death penalty, so I think I'll end up here.'

'Why are you so opposed to the death penalty?'

'And you're not?'

'No, I'm very much in favor of it.'

'That's incredible! Coming from a criminal defense lawyer.'

'I'd like to go back to public hangings on the courthouse lawn.'

'You're kidding, aren't you? I hope. Tell me you are.'

'I am not.'

She stopped chewing and smiling. The eyes glowed fiercely and watched him for a signal of weakness. 'You are serious.'

'I am very serious. The problem with the death penalty is that we don't use it enough.'

'Have you explained that to Mr Hailey?'

'Mr Hailey does not deserve the death penalty.

But the two men who raped his daughter certainly did.'

'I see. How do you determine who gets it and who doesn't?'

'That's very simple. You look at the crime and you look at the criminal. If it's a dope dealer who guns down an undercover narcotics officer, then he gets the gas. If it's a drifter who rapes a three-year-old girl, drowns her by holding her little head in a mudhole, then throws her body off a bridge, then you take his life and thank God he's gone. If it's an escaped convict who breaks into a farmhouse late at night and beats and tortures an elderly couple before burning them with their house, then you strap him in a chair, hook up a few wires, pray for his soul, and pull the switch. And if it's two dopeheads who gang-rape a ten-year-old girl and kick her with pointed-toe cowboy boots until her jaws break, then you happily, merrily, thankfully, gleefully lock them in a gas chamber and listen to them squeal. It's very simple.'

'It's barbaric.'

'Their crimes were barbaric. Death is too good for them, much too good.'

'And if Mr Hailey is convicted and sentenced to die?'

'If that happens, I'm sure I'll spend the next ten years cranking out appeals and fighting furiously to save his life. And if they ever strap him in the chair, I'm sure I'll be outside the prison with you and the Jesuits and a hundred other kindly souls marching and holding candles and singing hymns. And then I'll stand beside his grave behind his church with his widow and children and wish I'd never met him.'

'Have you ever witnessed an execution?'

'Not that I recall.'

'I've watched two. You'd change your mind if you saw one.'

'Good. I won't see one.'

'It's a horrible thing to watch.'

'Were the victims' families there?'

'Yes, in both instances.'

'Were they horrified? Were their minds changed? Of course not. Their nightmares were over.'

'I'm surprised at you.'

'And I'm bewildered by people like you. How can you be so zealous and dedicated in trying to save people who have begged for the death penalty and according to the law should get it?'

'Whose law? It's not the law in Massachusetts.'

'You don't say. What do you expect from the only state McGovern carried in 1972? You folks have always been tuned in with the rest of the country.'

The Claudeburgers were being ignored and their voices had grown too loud. Jake glanced around and caught a few stares. Ellen smiled again, and took one of his onion rings.

'What do you think of the ACLU?' she asked, crunching.

'I suppose you've got a membership card in your purse.'

'I do.'

'Then you're fired.'

'I joined when I was sixteen.'

'Why so late? You must've been the last one in your Girl Scout troop to join.'

'Do you have any respect for the Bill of Rights?'

'I adore the Bill of Rights. I despise the judges who interpret them. Eat.'

They finished the burgers in silence, watching each other carefully. Jake ordered coffee and two more headache powders.

'So how do we plan to win this case?' she asked.

'We?'

'I still have the job, don't I?'

'Yes. Just remember that I'm the boss and you're the clerk.'

'Sure, boss. What's your strategy?'

'How would you handle it?'

'Well, from what I gather, our client carefully planned the killings and shot them in cold blood, six days after the rape. It sounds exactly like he knew what he was doing.'

'He did.'

'So we have no defense and I think you should plead him guilty for a life sentence and avoid the gas chamber.'

'You're a real fighter.'

'Just kidding. Insanity is our only defense. And it sounds impossible to prove.'

'You're familiar with the M'Naghten Rule?' Jake asked.

'Yes. Do we have a psychiatrist?'

431

'Sort of. He'll say anything we want him to say; that is, if he's sober at trial. One of your more difficult tasks as my new law clerk will be to make sure he is sober at trial. It won't be easy, believe me.'

'I live for new challenges in the courtroom.'

'All right Row Ark, take a pen. Here's a napkin. Your boss is about to give you instructions.'

She began making notes on a paper napkin.

'I want a brief on the M'Naghten decisions rendered by the Mississippi Supreme Court in the past fifty years. There's probably a hundred. There's a big case from 1976, *State vs. Hill*, where the court was bitterly divided five to four, with the dissenters opting for a more liberal definition of insanity. Keep the brief short, less than twenty pages. Can you type?'

'Ninety words a minute.'

'I should've known. I'd like it by Wednesday.'

'You'll have it.'

'There are some evidentiary points I need researched. You saw those gruesome pictures of the two bodies. Noose normally allows the jury to see the blood and gore, but I'd like to keep them away from the jury. See if there's a way.'

'It won't be easy.'

'The rape is crucial to his defense. I want the jury to know details. This needs to be researched thoroughly. I've got two or three cases you can start from, and I think we can prove to Noose that the rape is very relevant.'

'Okay. What else?'

432

'I don't know. When my brain is alive again I'll think of more, but that will do it for now.'

'Do I report Monday morning?'

'Yes, but no sooner than nine. I like my quiet time.'

'What's the dress code?'

'You look fine.'

'Jeans and no socks?'

'I have one other employee, a secretary by the name of Ethel. She's sixty-four, top heavy, and thankfully she wears a bra. It wouldn't be a bad idea for you.'

'I'll think about it.'

'I don't need the distraction.'

Chapter 27

Monday, July 15. One week until trial. Over the weekend word spread quickly that the trial would be in Clanton, and the small town braced for the spectacle. The phones rang steadily at the three motels as the journalists and their crews confirmed reservations. The cafes buzzed with anticipation. A county maintenance crew swarmed around the courthouse after breakfast and began painting and polishing. Ozzie sent the yardboys from the jail with their mowers and weed-eaters. The old men under the Vietnam monument whittled cautiously and watched all this activity. The trusty who supervised the yard work asked them to spit their Red Man in the grass, not on the sidewalk. He was told to go to hell. The thick, dark Bermuda was given an extra layer of fertilizer, and a dozen lawn sprinklers were hissing and splashing by 9:00 A.M.

By 10:00 A.M. the temperature was ninety-two. The merchants in the small shops around the square opened their doors to the humidity and ran their ceiling fans. They called Memphis and

Jackson and Chicago for inventory to be sold at special prices next week.

Noose had called Jean Gillespie, the Circuit Court clerk, late Friday and informed her that the trial would be in her courtroom. He instructed her to summon one hundred and fifty prospective jurors. The defense had requested an enlarged panel from which to select the twelve, and Noose agreed. Jean and two deputy clerks spent Saturday combing the voter registration books randomly selecting potential jurors. Following Noose's specific instructions, they culled those over sixty-five. One thousand names were chosen, and each name along with its address was written on a small index card and thrown into a cardboard box. The two deputy clerks then took turns drawing cards at random from the box. One clerk was white, one black. Each would pull a card blindly from the box and arrange it neatly on a folding table with the other cards. When the count reached one hundred and fifty, the drawing ceased and a master list was typed. These were the jurors for State *vs.* Hailey. Each step of their selection had been carefully dictated by the Honorable Omar Noose, who knew exactly what he was doing. If there was an all-white jury, and a conviction, and a death sentence, every single elementary step of the jury selection procedure would be attacked on appeal. He had been through it before, and had been reversed. But not this time.

From the master list, the name and address of each juror was typed on a separate jury summons.

The stack of summonses was kept in Jean's office under lock until eight Monday morning when Sheriff Ozzie Walls arrived. He drank coffee with Jean and received his instructions.

'Judge Noose wants these served between four P.M. and midnight tonight,' she said.

'Okay.'

'The jurors are to report to the courtroom promptly by nine next Monday.'

'Okay.'

'The summons does not indicate the name or nature of the trial, and the jurors are not to be told anything.'

'I reckon they'll know.'

'Probably so, but Noose was very specific. Your men are to say nothing about the case when the summonses are served. The names of the jurors are very confidential, at least until Wednesday. Don't ask why – Noose's orders.'

Ozzie flipped through the stack. 'How many do we have here?'

'One fifty.'

'A hundred and fifty! Why so many?'

'It's a big case. Noose's orders.'

'It'll take ever man I've got to serve these papers.'

'I'm sorry.'

'Oh well. If that's what His Honor wants.'

Ozzie left, and within seconds Jake was standing at the counter flirting with the secretaries and smiling at Jean Gillespie. He followed her back to her office. He closed the door. She retreated behind her desk and pointed at him. He kept smiling.

'I know why you're here,' she said sternly, 'and you can't have it.'

'Give me the list, Jean.'

'Not until Wednesday. Noose's orders.'

'Wednesday? Why Wednesday?'

'I don't know. But Omar was very specific.'

'Give me the list, Jean.'

'Jake, I can't. Do you want me to get in trouble?'

'You won't get in trouble because no one will know it. You know how well I can keep a secret.' He was not smiling now. 'Jean, give me the damned list.'

'Jake, I just can't.'

'I need it, and I need it now. I can't wait until Wednesday. I've got work to do.'

'It wouldn't be fair to Buckley,' she said weakly.

'To hell with Buckley. Do you think he plays fair? He's a snake and you dislike him as much as I do.'

'Probably more.'

'Give me the list, Jean.'

'Look, Jake, we've always been close. I think more of you than any lawyer I know. When my son got in trouble I called you, right? I trust you and I want you to win this case. But I can't defy a judge's orders.'

'Who helped you get elected last time, me or Buckley?'

'Come on, Jake.'

'Who kept your son out of jail, me or Buckley?'

'Please.'

'Who tried to put your son in jail, me or Buckley?'

'That's not fair, Jake.'

'Who stood up for your husband when everybody, and I mean everybody, in the church wanted him gone when the books didn't balance?'

'It's not a question of loyalty, Jake. I love you and Carla and Hanna, but I just can't do it.'

Jake slammed the door and stormed out of the office. Jean sat at her desk and wiped tears from her cheeks.

At 10:00 A.M. Harry Rex barged into Jake's office and threw a copy of the jury list on his desk. 'Don't ask,' he said. Beside each name he had made notes, such as 'Don't know' or 'Former client – hates niggers' or 'Works at the shoe factory, might be sympathetic.'

Jake read each name slowly, trying to place it with a face or a reputation. There was nothing but names. No addresses, ages, occupations. Nothing but names. His fourth-grade schoolteacher from Karaway. One of his mother's friends from the Garden Club. A former client, shoplifting, he thought. A name from church. A regular at the Coffee Shop. A prominent farmer. Most of the names sounded white. There was a Willie Mae Jones, Leroy Washington, Roosevelt Tucker, Bessie Lou Bean, and a few other black names. But the list looked awfully pale. He recognized thirty names at most.

'Whatta you think?' asked Harry Rex.

'Hard to tell. Mostly white, but that's to be expected. Where'd you get this?'

'Don't ask. I made notes by twenty-six names. That's the best I can do. The rest I don't know.'

'You're a true friend, Harry Rex.'

'I'm a prince. Are you ready for trial?'

'Not yet. But I've found a secret weapon.'

'What?'

'You'll meet her later.'

'Her?'

'Yeah. You busy Wednesday night?'

'I don't think so. Why?'

'Good. Meet here at eight. Lucien will be here. Maybe one or two others. I want to take a couple of hours and talk about the jury. Who do we want? Let's get a profile of the model juror, and go from there. We'll cover each name and hopefully identify most of these people.'

'Sounds like fun. I'll be here. What's your model juror?'

'I'm not sure. I think the vigilante would appeal to rednecks. Guns, violence, protection of women. The rednecks would eat it up. But my man is black, and a bunch of rednecks would fry him. He killed two of their own.'

'I agree. I'd stay away from women. They would have no sympathy for the rapists, but they place a higher value on life. Taking an M-16 and blowing their heads off is something women just don't understand. You and I understand it because we're fathers. It appeals to us. The violence and blood doesn't bother us. We admire him. You've got to pick some admirers on that jury. Young fathers with some education.'

'That's interesting. Lucien said he would stick with women because they're more sympathetic.'

'I don't think so. I know some women who'd cut your throat if you crossed them.'

'Some of your clients?'

'Yeah, and one is on that list. Frances Burdeen. Pick her, and I'll tell her how to vote.'

'You serious?'

'Yep. She'll do anything I tell her.'

'Can you be in court Monday? I want you to watch the jury during the selection process, then help me decide on the twelve.'

'I wouldn't miss it.'

Jake heard voices downstairs and pressed his finger to his lips. He listened, then smiled and motioned for Harry Rex to follow him. They tiptoed to the top of the stairs and listened to the commotion around Ethel's desk.

'You most certainly do not work here,' Ethel insisted.

'I most certainly do. I was hired Saturday by Jake Brigance, who I believe is your boss.'

'Hired for what?' Ethel demanded.

'As a law clerk.'

'Well, he didn't discuss it with me.'

'He discussed it with me, and gave me the job.'

'How much is he paying you?'

'A hundred bucks an hour.'

'Oh my God! I'll have to speak with him first.'

'I've already spoken with him, Ethel.'

'It's Mrs Twitty to you.' Ethel studied her carefully from head to toe. Acid-washed jeans, penny loafers, no socks, an oversized white cotton button-down with, evidently, nothing on underneath. 'You're not dressed appropriately for this office. You're, you're indecent.'

Harry Rex raised his eyebrows and smiled at Jake. They watched the stairs and listened.

'My boss, who happens to be your boss, said I could dress like this.'

'But you forgot something, didn't you?'

'Jake said I could forget it. He told me you hadn't worn a bra in twenty years. He said most of the women in Clanton go braless, so I left mine at home.'

'He what?' Ethel screamed with arms crossed over her chest.

'Is he upstairs?' Ellen asked coolly.

'Yes, I'll call him.'

'Don't bother.'

Jake and Harry Rex retreated into the big office and waited for the law clerk. She entered carrying a large briefcase.

'Good morning, Row Ark,' Jake said. 'I want you to meet a good friend, Harry Rex Vonner.'

Harry Rex shook her hand and stared at her shirt. 'Nice to meet you. What was your first name?'

'Ellen.'

'Just call her Row Ark,' Jake said. 'She'll clerk here until Hailey's over.'

'That's nice,' said Harry Rex, still staring.

'Harry Rex is a local lawyer, Row Ark, and one of the many you cannot trust.'

'What'd you hire a female law clerk for, Jake?' he asked bluntly.

'Row Ark's a genius in criminal law, like most third-year law students. And she works very cheap.'

'You have something against females, sir?' Ellen asked.

'No ma'am. I love females. I've married four of them.'

'Harry Rex is the meanest divorce lawyer in Ford County,' Jake explained. 'In fact, he's the meanest lawyer, period. Come to think of it, he's the meanest man I know.'

'Thanks,' said Harry Rex. He had stopped staring at her.

She looked at his huge, dirty, scuffed, worn wingtips, his ribbed nylon socks that had drooped into thick wads around his ankles, his soiled and battered khaki pants, his frayed navy blazer, his brilliant pink wool tie that fell eight inches above his belt, and she said, 'I think he's cute.'

'I might make you wife number five,' Harry Rex said.

'The attraction is purely physical,' she said.

'Watch it,' Jake said. 'There's been no sex in this office since Lucien left.'

'A lot of things left with Lucien,' said Harry Rex.

'Who's Lucien?'

Jake and Harry Rex looked at each other. 'You'll meet him soon enough,' Jake explained.

442

'Your secretary is very sweet,' Ellen said.

'I knew y'all would hit it off. She's really a doll once you get to know her.'

'How long does that take?'

'I've known her for twenty years,' said Harry Rex, 'and I'm still waiting.'

'How's the research coming?' Jake asked.

'Slow. There are dozens of M'Naghten cases, and they are all very long. I'm about half through. I planned to work on it all day here; that is, if that pit bull downstairs doesn't attack me.'

'I'll take care of her,' Jake said.

Harry Rex headed for the door. 'Nice meetin' you, Row Ark. I'll see you around.'

'Thanks, Harry Rex,' said Jake. 'See you Wednesday night.'

The dirt and gravel parking lot of Tank's Tonk was full when Jake finally found it after dark. There had been no reason to visit Tank's before, and he was not thrilled about seeing the place now. It was well hidden off a dirt road, six miles out of Clanton. He parked far away from the small cinderblock building and toyed with the idea of leaving the engine running in case Tank was not there and a quick escape became necessary. But he quickly dismissed the stupid idea because he liked his car, and theft was not only likely but highly probable. He locked it, then double-checked it, almost certain that all or part of it would be missing when he returned.

The juke box blasted from the open windows,

and he thought he heard a bottle crash on the floor, or across a table or someone's head. He hesitated beside his car and decided to leave. No, it was important. He sucked in his stomach, held his breath, and opened the ragged wooden door.

Forty sets of black eyes immediately focused on this poor lost white boy with a coat and tie who was squinting and trying to focus inside the vast blackness of their tonk. He stood there awkwardly, desperately searching for a friend. There were none. Michael Jackson conveniently finished his song on the juke box, and for an eternity the tonk was silent. Jake stayed close to the door. He nodded and smiled and tried to act like one of the gang. There were no other smiles.

Suddenly, there was movement at the bar and Jake's knees began vibrating. 'Jake! Jake!' someone shouted. It was the sweetest two words he had ever heard. From behind the bar he saw his friend Tank removing his apron and heading for him. They shook hands warmly.

'What brings you here?'

'I need to talk to you for a minute. Can we step outside?'

'Sure. What's up?'

'Just business.'

Tank flipped on a light switch by the front door. 'Say, everbody, this here is Carl Lee Hailey's lawyer, Jake Brigance. A good friend of mine. Let's hear it for him.'

The small room exploded in applause and bravos. Several of the boys at the bar grabbed

Jake and shook his hand. Tank reached in a drawer under the bar and pulled out a handful of Jake's cards, which he passed out like candy. Jake was breathing again and the color returned to his face.

Outside, they leaned on the hood of Tank's yellow Cadillac. Lionel Richie echoed through the windows and the crowd returned to normal. Jake handed Tank a copy of the list.

'Look at each name. See how many of these folks you know. Ask around and find out what you can.'

Tank held the list near his eyes. The light from the Michelob sign in the window glowed over his shoulder. 'How many are black?'

'You tell me. That's one reason I want you to look at it. Circle the black ones. If you're not sure, find out. If you know any of the white folks, make a note.'

'I'll be glad to, Jake. This ain't illegal, is it?'

'Naw, but don't tell anybody. I need it back by Wednesday morning.'

'You're the boss.'

Tank got the last list, and Jake headed for the office. It was almost ten. Ethel had retyped the list from the initial one provided by Harry Rex, and a dozen copies had been hand-delivered to selected, trusted friends. Lucien, Stan Atcavage, Tank, Dell at the Coffee Shop, a lawyer in Karaway named Roland Isom, and a few others. Even Ozzie got a list.

* * *

Less than three miles from the tonk was a small, neat white-framed country house where Ethel and Bud Twitty had lived for almost forty years. It was a pleasant house with pleasant memories of raising children who were now scattered up North. The retarded son, the one who greatly resembled Lucien, lived in Miami for some reason. The house was quieter now. Bud hadn't worked in years, not since his first stroke in '75. Then a heart attack, followed by two more major strokes and several small ones. His days were numbered, and he had long since accepted the fact that he would most likely catch the big one and die on his front porch shelling butterbeans. That's what he hoped for, anyway.

Monday night he sat on the porch shelling butterbeans and listening to the Cardinals on the radio. Ethel was working in the kitchen. In the bottom of the eighth with the Cards at bat and two on, he heard a noise from the side of the house. He turned the volume down. Probably just a dog. Then another noise. He stood and walked to the end of the porch. Suddenly, a huge figure dressed in solid black with red, white, and black war paint smeared wickedly across his face jumped from the bushes, grabbed Bud and yanked him off the porch. Bud's anguished cry was not heard in the kitchen. Another warrior joined in and they dragged the old man to the foot of the steps leading up to the front porch. One maneuvered him into a half-nelson while the other pounded his soft belly and bloodied his face. Within seconds, he was unconscious.

Ethel heard noises and scurried through the front door. She was grabbed by a third member of the gang, who twisted her arm tightly behind her and wrapped a huge arm around her throat. She couldn't scream or talk or move, and was held there on the porch, terrified, watching below as the two thugs took turns with her husband. On the front sidewalk ten feet behind the violence stood three figures, each garbed in a full, flowing, white robe with red garnishment, each with a tall, white, pointed headdress from which fell a red and white mask that loosely covered each face. They emerged from the darkness and watched over the scene as though they were the three wise men attending the manger.

After a long, agonizing minute, the beating grew monotonous. 'Enough,' said the ruler in the middle. The three terrorists in black ran. Ethel rushed down the steps and slumped over her battered husband. The three in white disappeared.

Jake left the hospital after midnight with Bud still alive but everyone pessimistic. Along with the broken bones he had suffered another major heart attack. Ethel had made a scene and blamed it all on Jake.

'You said there was no danger!' she screamed. 'Tell that to my husband! It's all your fault!'

He had listened to her rant and rave, and the embarrassment turned to anger. He glanced around the small waiting room at the friends and relatives. All eyes were on him. Yes, they seemed to say, it was all his fault.

Chapter 28

Gwen called the office early Tuesday morning and the new secretary, Ellen Roark, answered the phone. She fumbled with the intercom until she broke it, then walked to the stairs and yelled: 'Jake, it's Mr Hailey's wife.'

He slammed a book shut and angrily picked up the receiver. 'Hello.'

'Jake, are you busy?'

'Very. What's on your mind?'

She started crying. 'Jake, we need money. We're broke, and the bills are past due. I haven't paid the house note in two months and the mortgage company is callin'. I don't know who else to turn to.'

'What about your family?'

'They're poor folks, Jake, you know that. They'll feed us and do what they can, but they can't make our house notes and pay the utilities.'

'Have you talked to Carl Lee?'

'Not about money. Not lately. There's not much

he can do except worry, and Lord knows he's got enough to worry about.'

'What about the churches?'

'Ain't seen a dime.'

'How much do you need?'

'At least five hundred, just to catch up. I don't know 'bout next month. I'll guess I'll worry then.'

Nine hundred minus five hundred left Jake with four hundred dollars for a capital murder defense. That had to be a record. Four hundred dollars! He had an idea.

'Can you be at my office at two this afternoon?'

'I'll have to bring the kids.'

'That's okay. Just be here.'

'I'll be there.'

He hung up and quickly searched the phone book for Reverend Ollie Agee. He found him at the church. Jake fed him a line about meeting to discuss the Hailey trial and covering Agee's testimony. Said the reverend would be an important witness. Agee said he would be there at two.

The Hailey clan arrived first, and Jake seated them around the conference table. The kids remembered the room from the press conference and were awed by the long table, thick swivel chairs, and impressive rows of books. When the reverend arrived he hugged Gwen and made a fuss over the kids, especially Tonya.

'I'll be very brief, Reverend,' started Jake. 'There are some things we need to discuss. For several weeks now, you and the other black ministers in this county have been raising money for the

Haileys. And you've done a real good job. Over six thousand, I believe. I don't know where the money is, and it's none of my business. You offered the money to the NAACP lawyers to represent Carl Lee, but as you and I know, those lawyers won't be involved in this case. I'm the lawyer, the only lawyer, and so far none of the money has been offered to me. I don't expect any of it. Evidently you don't care about what kind of defense he gets if you can't pick his lawyer. That's fine. I can live with that. What really bothers me, Reverend, is the fact that none, and I repeat none, of the money has been given to the Haileys. Right, Gwen?'

The empty look on her face had turned to one of amazement, then disbelief, then anger as she glared at the reverend.

'Six thousand dollars,' she repeated.

'Over six thousand, at last reported count,' said Jake. 'And the money is lying in some bank while Carl Lee sits in jail, Gwen's not working, the bills are past due, the only food comes from friends, and foreclosure is a few days away. Now, tell us, Reverend, what're your plans with the money?'

Agee smiled and said with an oily voice, 'That's none of your business.'

'But it's my business!' Gwen said loudly. 'You used my name and my family's name when you raised that money, didn't you, Reverend. I heard it myself. Told all the church folk that the love offerin', as you called it, was for my family. I figured you had done spent the money on lawyers' fee or somethin' like that. And now, today, I find out you've got it stuck in the bank. I guess you plan to keep it.'

Agee was unmoved. 'Now wait a minute, Gwen. We thought the money could best be spent on Carl Lee. He declined the money when he refused to hire the NAACP lawyers. So I asked Mr Reinfeld, the head lawyer, what to do with the money. He told me to save it because Carl Lee will need it for his appeal.'

Jake cocked his head sideways and clenched his teeth. He started to rebuke this ignorant fool, but realized Agee did not understand what he was saying. Jake bit his lip.

'I don't understand,' said Gwen.

'It's simple,' said the reverend with an accommodating smile. 'Mr Reinfeld said that Carl Lee would be convicted because he didn't hire him. So then we've got to appeal, right? And after Jake here loses the trial, you and Carl Lee will of course be lookin' for another lawyer who can save his life. That's when we'll need Reinfeld and that's when we'll need the money. So you see, it's all for Carl Lee.'

Jake shook his head and silently cursed. He cursed Reinfeld more than Agee.

Gwen's eyes flooded and she clenched her fists. 'I don't understand all that, and I don't want to understand it. All I know is that I'm tired of beggin' for food, tired of dependin' on others, and tired of worryin' about losin' my house.'

Agee looked at her sadly. 'I understand, Gwen, but—'

451

'And if you got six thousand dollars of our money in the bank, you're wrong not to give it to us. We've got enough sense to spend it right.'

Carl Lee, Jr., and Jarvis stood next to their mother and comforted her. They stared at Agee.

'But it's for Carl Lee,' the reverend said.

'Good,' Jake said. 'Have you asked Carl Lee how he wants his money spent?'

The dirty little grin left Agee's face and he squirmed in his chair. 'Carl Lee understands what we're doin',' he said without much conviction.

'Thank you. That's not what I asked. Listen to me carefully. Have you asked Carl Lee how he wants his money spent?'

'I think it's been discussed with him,' Agee lied.

'Let's see,' Jake said. He stood and walked to the door leading to the small office next to the conference room. The reverend watched nervously, almost in panic. Jake opened the door and nodded to someone. Carl Lee and Ozzie casually walked in. The kids yelled and ran to their father. Agee looked devastated.

After a few awkward minutes of hugs and kisses, Jake moved in for the kill. 'Now, Reverend, why don't you ask Carl Lee how he wants to spend his six thousand dollars.'

'It ain't exactly his,' said Agee.

'And it ain't exactly yours,' shot Ozzie.

Carl Lee removed Tonya from his knee and walked to the chair where Agee was sitting. He sat on the edge of the table, above the reverend, poised and ready to strike if necessary. 'Let me

452

make it real simple, preacher, so you won't have trouble understandin' it. You raised that money in my name, for the benefit of my family. You took it from the black folk of this county, and you took it with the promise that it'd go to help me and my family. You lied. You raised it so you could impress the NAACP, not to help my family. You lied in church, you lied in the newspapers, you lied everwhere.'

Agee looked around the room and noticed that everyone, including the kids, was staring at him and nodding slowly.

Carl Lee put his foot in Agee's chair and leaned closer. 'If you don't give us that money, I'll tell ever nigger I know that you're a lyin' crook. I'll call ever member of your church, and I'm one too, remember, and tell them we ain't got a dime from you, and when I get through you won't be able to raise two dollars on Sunday mornin'. You'll lose your fancy Cadillacs and your fancy suits. You may even lose your church, 'cause I'll ask everbody to leave.'

'You finished?' Agee asked. 'If you are, I just wanna say that I'm hurt. Hurt real bad that you and Gwen feel this way.'

'That's the way we feel, and I don't care how hurt you are.'

Ozzie stepped forward. 'I agree with them, Reverend Agee, you ain't done right, and you know it.'

'That hurts, Ozzie, comin' from you. It really hurts.'

'Lemme tell you what's gonna hurt a whole lot worse than that. Next Sunday me and Carl Lee will be in your church. I'll sneak him outta the jail early Sunday and we'll take a little drive. Just about the time you get ready to preach, we'll walk in the front door, down the aisle and up to the pulpit. If you get in my way, I'll put handcuffs on you. Carl Lee will do the preachin'. He'll tell all your people that the money they've given so generously has so far not left your pocket, that Gwen and the kids are about to lose their house 'cause you're tryin' to big-shot with the NAACP. He'll tell them that you lied to them. He may preach for an hour or so. And when he gets through, I'll say a few words. I'll tell them what a lyin', sleazy nigger you are. I'll tell them about the time you bought that stolen Lincoln in Memphis for a hundred dollars and almost got indicted. I'll tell them about the kickbacks from the funeral home. I'll tell them about the DUI charge in Jackson I got dismissed for you two years ago. And, Reverend, I'll tell—'

'Don't say it, Ozzie,' Agee begged.

'I'll tell them a dirty little secret that only you and me and a certain woman of ill repute know about.'

'When do y'all want the money?'

'How soon can you get it?' Carl Lee demanded.

'Awfully damned quick.'

Jake and Ozzie left the Haileys to themselves and went upstairs to the big office, where Ellen was

454

buried in law books. Jake introduced Ozzie to his law clerk, and the three sat around the big desk.

'How are my buddies?' Jake asked.

'The dynamite boys? They're recuperatin' nicely. We'll keep them in the hospital until the trial's over. We fixed a lock on the door, and I keep a deputy in the hall. They ain't goin' anywhere.'

'Who's the main man?'

'We still don't know. Fingerprint tests haven't come back yet. There may be no prints to match. He ain't talkin'.'

'The other is a local boy, isn't he?' asked Ellen.

'Yeah. Terrell Grist. He wants to sue because he got hurt during the arrest. Can you imagine?'

'I can't believe it's been kept quiet so far,' Jake said.

'Me neither. Of course, Grist and Mr X ain't talkin'. My men are quiet. That leaves you and your clerk here.'

'And Lucien, but I didn't tell him.'

'Figures.'

'When will you process them?'

'After the trial we'll move them to the jail and start the paperwork. It's up to us.'

'How's Bud?' Jake asked.

'I stopped by this mornin' to check on the other two, and I went downstairs to see Ethel. He's still critical. No changes.'

'Any suspects?'

'Gotta be the Klan. With the white robes and all. It all adds up. First there was the burnin' cross in your yard, then the dynamite, and now Bud. Plus all the death threats. I figure it's them. And we got an informant.'

'You what!'

'You heard me. Calls himself Mickey Mouse. He called me at home Sunday and told me that he saved your life. 'That nigger's lawyer' is what he called you. Said the Klan has officially arrived in Ford County. They've set up a klavern, whatever that is.'

'Who's in it?'

'He ain't much on details. He promised to call me only if someone is about to get hurt.'

'How nice. Can you trust him?'

'He saved your life.'

'Good point. Is he a member?'

'Didn't say. They've got a big march planned Thursday.'

'The Klan?'

'Yep. NAACP has a rally tomorrow in front of the courthouse. Then they're gonna march for a while. The Klan's supposed to show up for a peaceful march on Thursday.'

'How many?'

'The Mouse didn't say. Like I said, he ain't much on details.'

'The Klan, marching in Clanton. I can't believe it.'

'This is heavy stuff,' Ellen said.

'It'll get heavier,' Ozzie replied. 'I've asked the governor to keep the highway patrol on standby. It could be a rough week.'

'Can you believe Noose is willing to try this case in this town?' asked Jake.

'It's too big to move, Jake. It would draw marches, and protests, and Klansmen anywhere you tried it.'

'Maybe you're right. How about your jury list?'

'I'll have it tomorrow.'

After supper Tuesday Joe Frank Perryman sat on his front porch with the evening paper and a fresh chew of Red Man, and spat carefully, neatly through a small hand-carved hole in the porch. This was the evening ritual. Lela would finish the dishes and fix them a tall glass of iced tea, and they would sit on the porch until dark and talk about the crops, the grandchildren, the humidity. They lived out from Karaway on eighty acres of neatly trimmed and cultivated farmland that Joe Frank's father had stolen during the Depression. They were quiet, hardworking Christian folks.

After a few discharges through the hole, a pickup slowed out on the highway and turned into the Perrymans' long gravel driveway. It parked next to the front lawn, and a familiar face emerged. It was Will Tierce, former president of the Ford County Board of Supervisors. Will had served his district for twenty-four years, six consecutive terms, but had lost the last election in '83 by seven votes. The Perrymans had always supported Tierce because he took care of them with an occasional load of gravel or a culvert for the driveway.

'Evenin', Will,' said Joe Frank as the ex-supervisor walked across the lawn and up the steps.

'Evenin', Joe Frank.' They shook hands and relaxed on the porch.

'Gimme a chew,' Tierce said.

'Sure. What brings you around here?'

'Just passin' by. Thought about Lela's iced tea and got real thirsty. Hadn't seen you folks in a while.'

They sat and talked, chewed and spat, and drank iced tea until it was dark and time for the mosquitoes. The drought required most of their time and Joe Frank talked at length of the dry spell and how it was the worst in ten years. Hadn't had a drop of rain since the third week of June. And if it didn't let up, he could forget the cotton crop. The beans might make it, but he was worried about the cotton.

'Say, Joe Frank, I hear you got one of those jury summons for the trial next week.'

'Yeah, afraid so. Who told you?'

'I don't know. I just heard it around.'

'I didn't know it was public knowledge.'

'Well, I guess I must've heard it in Clanton today. I had business at the courthouse. That's where I heard it. It's that nigger's trial, you know.'

'That's what I figured.'

'How do you feel about that nigger shootin' them boys like he did?'

'I don't blame him,' inserted Lela.

'Yeah, but you can't take the law into your own hands,' explained Joe Frank to his wife. 'That's what the court system is for.'

458

'I'll tell you what bothers me,' said Tierce, 'is this insanity crap. They're gonna say the nigger was crazy and try to get him off by insanity. Like that nut who shot Reagan. It's a crooked way to get off. Plus it's a lie. That nigger planned to kill them boys, and just sat there and waited on them. It was cold-blooded murder.'

'What if it was your daughter, Will?' asked Lela.

'I'd let the courts handle it. When we catch a rapist around here, especially a nigger, we generally lock him up. Parchman's full of rapists who'll never get out. This ain't New York or California or some crazy place where criminals go free. We've got a good system, and old Judge Noose hands down tough sentences. You gotta let the courts handle it. Our system won't survive if we allow people, especially niggers, to take the law into their own hands. That's what really scares me. Suppose this nigger gets off, walks out of the courthouse a free man. Everybody in the country will know it, and the niggers will go crazy. Evertime somebody crosses a nigger, he'll just kill him, then say he was insane, and try to get off. That's what's dangerous about this trial.'

'You gotta keep the niggers under control,' agreed Joe Frank.

'You better believe it. And if Hailey gets off, none of us will be safe. Ever nigger in this county'll carry a gun and just look for trouble.'

'I hadn't really thought about that,' admitted Joe Frank.

'I hope you do the right thing, Joe Frank. I just

hope they put you in that jury box. We need some people with some sense.'

'Wonder why they picked me?'

'I heard they fixed up a hundred and fifty summonses. They're expectin' about a hundred to show up.'

'What're my chances of gettin' picked?'

'One in a hundred,' said Lela.

'I feel better then. I really ain't got time to serve, what with my farmin' and all.'

'We sure need you on that jury,' said Tierce.

The conversation drifted to local politics and the new supervisor and what a sorry job he was doing with the roads. Darkness meant bedtime for the Perrymans. Tierce said good night and drove home. He sat at his kitchen table with a cup of coffee and reviewed the jury list. His friend Rufus would be proud. Six names had been circled on Will's list, and he had talked to all six. He put an okay by each name. They would be good jurors, people Rufus could count on to keep law and order in Ford County. A couple had been noncommittal at first, but their good and trusted friend Will Tierce had explained justice to them and they were now ready to convict.

Rufus would be real proud. And he had promised that young Jason Tierce, a nephew, would never be tried on those dope charges.

Jake picked at the greasy pork chops and butterbeans, and watched Ellen across the table do the same thing. Lucien sat at the head of the table, ignored his food, fondled his drink, and flipped through the jury list offering comments on every name he recognized. He was drunker than normal. Most of the names he didn't recognize, but he commented on them anyway. Ellen was amused and winked repeatedly at her boss.

He dropped the list, and knocked his fork off the table.

'Sallie!' he yelled.

'Do you know how many ACLU members are in Ford County?' he asked Ellen.

'At least eighty percent of the population,' she said.

'One. Me. I was the first in history and evidently the last. These people are fools around here, Row Ark. They don't appreciate civil liberties. They're a bunch of right-wing knee-jerk conservative Republican fanatics, like our friend Jake here.'

'That's not true. I eat at Claude's at least once a week,' Jake said.

'So that makes you progressive?' asked Lucien.

'It makes me a radical.'

'I still think you're a Republican.'

'Look, Lucien, you can talk about my wife, or my mother, or my ancestors, but don't call me a Republican.'

'You look like a Republican,' said Ellen.

'Does he look like a Democrat?' Jake asked, pointing at Lucien.

'Of course. I knew he was a Democrat the moment I saw him.'

'Then I'm a Republican.'

461

'See! See!' yelled Lucien. He dropped his glass on the floor and it shattered.

'Sallie!'

'Row Ark, guess who was the third white man in Mississippi to join the NAACP?'

'Rufus Buckley,' said Jake.

'Me. Lucien Wilbanks. Joined in 1967. White people thought I was crazy.'

'Can you imagine,' Jake said.

'Of course, black folks, or Negroes as we called them back then, thought I was crazy too. Hell, everybody thought I was crazy back then.'

'Have they ever changed their minds?' Jake asked.

'Shut up, Republican. Row Ark, why don't you move to Clanton and we'll start us a law firm handling nothing but ACLU cases. Hell, bring your old man down from Boston and we'll make him a partner.'

'Why don't you just go to Boston?' Jake asked.

'Why don't you just go to hell?'

'What will we call it?' asked Ellen.

'The nut house,' said Jake.

'Wilbanks, Row and Ark. Attorneys at law.'

'None of whom have licenses,' said Jake.

Lucien's eyelids weighed several pounds each. His head nodded forward involuntarily. He slapped Sallie on the rear as she cleaned up his mess.

'That was a cheap shot, Jake,' he said seriously.

'Row Ark,' Jake said, imitating Lucien, 'guess who was the last lawyer permanently disbarred by the Mississippi Supreme Court?'

Ellen gracefully smiled at both men and said nothing.

'Row Ark,' Lucien said loudly, 'guess who will be the next lawyer in this county to be evicted from his office?' He roared with laughter, screaming and shaking. Jake winked at her.

When he settled down, he asked, 'What's this meeting tomorrow night?'

'I want to cover the jury list with you and a few others.'

'Who?'

'Harry Rex, Stan Atcavage, maybe one other.'

'Where?'

'Eight o'clock. My office. No alcohol.'

'It's my office, and I'll bring a case of whiskey if I want to. My grandfather built the building, remember?'

'How could I forget.'

'Row Ark, let's get drunk.'

'No thanks, Lucien. I've enjoyed dinner, and the conversation, but I need to get back to Oxford.'

They stood and left Lucien at the table. Jake declined the usual invitation to sit on the porch. Ellen left, and he went to his temporary room upstairs. He had promised Carla he would not sleep at home. He called her. She and Hanna were fine. Worried, but fine. He didn't mention Bud Twitty.

Chapter 29

A convoy of converted school buses, each with an original paint job of white and red or green and black or a hundred other combinations and the name of a church emblazoned along the sides under the windows, rolled slowly around the Clanton square after lunch Wednesday. There were thirty-one in all, each packed tightly with elderly black people who waved paper fans and handkerchiefs in a futile effort to overcome the stifling heat. After three trips around the courthouse, the lead bus stopped by the post office and thirty-one doors flew open. The buses emptied in a frenzy. The people were directed to a gazebo on the courthouse lawn, where Reverend Ollie Agee was shouting orders and handing out blue and white FREE CARL LEE placards.

The side streets leading into the square became congested as cars from all directions inched toward the courthouse and finally parked when they could move no closer. Hundreds of blacks left their vehicles in the streets and walked solemnly toward the square. They mingled around the gazebo and waited for their placards, then wandered through the oaks and magnolias looking for shade and greeting friends. More church buses arrived and were unable to circle the square because of the traffic. They unloaded next to the Coffee Shop.

For the first time that year the temperature hit a hundred and promised to go higher. The sky produced no clouds for protection, and there were no winds or breezes to weaken the burning rays or to blow away the humidity. A man's shirt would soak and stick to his back in fifteen minutes under a shade tree; five minutes without shade. Some of the weaker old folks found refuge inside the courthouse.

The crowd continued to grow. It was predominantly elderly, but there were many younger, militant, angry-looking blacks who had missed the great civil rights marches and demonstrations of the sixties and now realized that this might be a rare opportunity to shout and protest and sing 'We Shall Overcome,' and in general celebrate being black and oppressed in a white world. They meandered about waiting for someone to take charge. Finally, three students marched to the front steps of the courthouse, lifted their placards, and shouted, 'Free Carl Lee. Free Carl Lee.'

Instantly, the mob repeated the war cry:

'Free Carl Lee!'

'Free Carl Lee!'

'Free Carl Lee!'

They left the shade trees and courthouse and

moved closer together near the steps where a makeshift podium and PA system had been set up. They yelled in unison at no one or no place or nothing in particular, just howled the newly established battle cry in a perfect chorus:

'Free Carl Lee!'

'Free Carl Lee!'

The windows of the courthouse flew open as the clerks and secretaries gawked at the happening below. The roar could be heard for blocks and the small shops and offices around the square emptied. The owners and customers filled the sidewalks and watched in astonishment. The demonstrators noticed their spectators, and the attention fueled the chanting, which increased in tempo and volume. The vultures had loitered about waiting and watching, and the noise excited them. They descended upon the front lawn of the courthouse with cameras and microphones.

Ozzie and his men directed traffic until the highway and the streets were hopelessly gridlocked. They maintained a presence, although there was no hint they would be needed.

Agee and every full-time, part-time, retired, and prospective black preacher in three counties paraded through the dense mass of black screaming faces and made their way to the podium. The sight of the ministers pumped up the celebrants, and their unified chants reverberated around the square, down the side streets into the sleepy residential districts and out into the countryside. Thousands of blacks waved their placards and yelled their lungs out. Agee swayed with the crowd. He danced across the small podium. He slapped hands with the other ministers. He led the rhythmic noise like a choir director. He was a sight.

'Free Carl Lee!'

'Free Carl Lee!'

For fifteen minutes, Agee whipped the crowd into a frenzied, coalescent mob. Then, when with his finely trained ear he detected the first hint of fatigue, he walked to the microphones and asked for quiet. The panting, sweating faces yelled on but with less volume. The chants of freedom died quickly. Agee asked for room near the front so the press could congregate and do its job. He asked for stillness so they could go to the Lord in prayer. Reverend Roosevelt offered a marathon to the Lord, an eloquent, alliterative oratorical fiesta that brought tears to the eyes of many.

When he finally said 'Amen,' an enormous black woman with a sparkling red wig stepped to the microphones and opened her vast mouth. The opening stanza of 'We Shall Overcome' flowed forth in a deep, rich, mellow river of glorious a cappella. The ministers behind her immediately clasped hands and began to sway. Spontaneity swept the crowd and two thousand voices joined her in surprising harmony. The mournful, promising anthem rose above the small town.

When they finished, someone shouted 'Free Carl Lee!' and ignited another round of chanting. Agee quieted them again, and stepped to the microphones. He pulled an index card from his pocket, and began his sermon.

As expected, Lucien arrived late and half loaded. He brought a bottle and offered a drink to Jake, Atcavage, and Harry Rex, and each declined.

'It's a quarter till nine, Lucien,' Jake said. 'We've been waiting for almost an hour.'

'I'm being paid for this, am I?' he asked.

'No, but I asked you to be here at eight sharp.'

'And you also told me not to bring a bottle. And I informed you this was my building, built by my grandfather, leased to you as my tenant, for a very reasonable rent I might add, and I will come and go as I please, with or without a bottle.'

'Forget it. Did you—'

'What're those blacks doing across the street walking around the courthouse in the dark?'

'It's called a vigil,' explained Harry Rex. 'They've vowed to walk around the courthouse with candles, keeping a vigil until their man is free.'

'That could be an awfully long vigil. I mean, those poor people could be walking until they die. I mean, this could be a twelve-, fifteen-year vigil. They might set a record. They might have candle wax up to their asses. Evenin', Row Ark.'

Ellen sat at the rolltop desk under William Faulkner. She looked at a well-marked copy of the jury list. She nodded and smiled at Lucien.

'Row Ark,' Lucien said, 'I have all the respect in the world for you. I view you as an equal. I

468

believe in your right to equal pay for equal work. I believe in your right to choose whether to have a child or abort. I believe in all that crap. You are a woman and entitled to no special privileges because of your gender. You should be treated just like a man.' Lucien reached in his pocket and pulled out a clip of cash. 'And since you are a law clerk, genderless in my eyes, I think you should be the one to go buy a case of cold Coors.'

'No, Lucien,' Jake said.

'Shut up, Jake.'

Ellen stood and stared at Lucien. 'Sure, Lucien. But I'll pay for the beer.'

She left the office.

Jake shook his head and fumed at Lucien. 'This could be a long night.'

Harry Rex changed his mind and poured a shot of whiskey into his coffee cup.

'Please don't get drunk,' Jake begged. 'We've got work to do.'

'I work better when I'm drunk,' said Lucien.

'Me too,' said Harry Rex.

'This could be interesting,' said Atcavage.

Jake laid his feet on his desk and puffed on a cigar. 'Okay, the first thing I want to do is decide on a model juror.'

'Black,' said Lucien.

'Black as old Coaly's ass,' said Harry Rex.

'I agree,' said Jake. 'But we won't get a chance. Buckley will save his peremptory challenges for the blacks. We know that. We've got to concentrate on white people.'

'Women,' said Lucien. 'Always pick women for criminal trials. They have bigger hearts, bleeding hearts, and they're much more sympathetic. Always go for women.'

'Naw,' said Harry Rex. 'Not in this case. Women don't understand things like taking a gun and blowing people away. You need fathers, young fathers who would want to do the same thing Hailey did. Daddies with little girls.'

'Since when did you get to be such an expert on picking juries?' asked Lucien. 'I thought you were a sleazy divorce lawyer.'

'I am a sleazy divorce lawyer, but I know how to pick juries.'

'And listen to them through the wall.'

'Cheap shot.'

Jake raised his arms. 'Fellas, please. How about Victor Onzell? You know him, Stan?'

'Yeah, he banks with us. He's about forty, married, three or four kids. White. From somewhere up North. Runs the truck stop on the highway north of town. He's been here about five years.'

'I wouldn't take him,' Lucien said. 'If he's from up North, he doesn't think like we do. Probably in favor of gun control and all that crap. Yankees always scare me in criminal cases. I've always thought we should have a law in Mississippi that no certified yankee could sit on a jury down here regardless of how long he's lived here.'

'Thank you so much,' said Jake.

'I'd take him,' said Harry Rex.

'Why?'

'He's got kids, probably a daughter. If he's from the North he's probably not as prejudiced. Sounds good to me.'

'John Tate Aston.'

'He's dead,' said Lucien.

'What?'

'I said he's dead. Been dead for three years.'

'Why's he on the list?' asked Atcavage, the non-lawyer.

'They don't purge the voter registration list,' explained Harry Rex, between drinks. 'Some die and some move away, and it's impossible to keep the list up to date. They've issued a hundred and fifty summons, and you can expect a hundred to a hundred and twenty to show up. The rest have died or moved away.'

'Caroline Baxter. Ozzie says she's black,' Jake said flipping through his notes. 'Works at the carburetor plant in Karaway.'

'Take her,' said Lucien.

'I wish,' said Jake.

Ellen returned with the beer. She dropped it in Lucien's lap and tore a sixteen-ounce can out of a six-pack. She popped the top and returned to the rolltop desk. Jake declined, but Atcavage decided he was thirsty. Jake remained the non-drinker.

'Joe Kitt Shepherd.'

'Sounds like a redneck,' said Lucien.

'Why do you say that?' asked Harry Rex.

'The double first name,' Lucien explained.

'Most rednecks have double first names. Like Billy Ray, Johnny Ray, Bobby Lee, Harry Lee, Jesse Earl, Billy Wayne, Jerry Wayne, Eddie Mack. Even their women have double first names. Bobbie Sue, Betty Pearl, Mary Belle, Thelma Lou, Sally Faye.'

'What about Harry Rex?' asked Harry Rex.

'Never heard of a woman named Harry Rex.'

'I mean for a male redneck.'

'I guess it'll do.'

Jake interrupted. 'Dell Perry said he used to own a bait shop down by the lake. I take it no one knows him.'

'No, but I bet he's a redneck,' said Lucien. 'Because of his name. I'd scratch him.'

'Aren't you given their addresses, ages, occupations, basic information like that?' asked Atcavage.

'Not until the day of trial. On Monday each prospective juror fills out a questionnaire in the courtroom. But until then we have only the names.'

'What kind of juror are we looking for, Jake?' Ellen asked.

'Young to middle-aged men with families. I would prefer to have no one over fifty.'

'Why?' Lucien asked belligerently.

'Younger whites are more tolerant of blacks.'

'Like Cobb and Willard,' Lucien said.

'Most of the older folks will always dislike blacks, but the younger generation has accepted an integrated society. Less bigotry, as a rule, with youth.'

'I agree,' said Harry Rex, 'and I would stay away from women and rednecks.'

472

'That's my plan.'

'I think you're wrong,' said Lucien. 'Women are more sympathetic. Just look at Row Ark. She's sympathetic toward everyone. Right, Row Ark?'

'Right, Lucien.'

'She has sympathy for criminals, child pornographers, atheists, illegal immigrants, gays. Don't you, Row Ark?'

'Right, Lucien.'

'She and I hold the only two ACLU cards existing at this very moment in Ford County, Mississippi.'

'That's sick,' said Atcavage, the banker.

'Clyde Sisco,' Jake said loudly, trying to minimize controversy.

'He can be bought,' Lucien said smugly.

'What do you mean "He can be bought"?' Jake asked.

'Just what I said. He can be bought.'

'How do you know?' asked Harry Rex.

'Are you kidding? He's a Sisco. Biggest bunch of crooks in the eastern part of the county. They all live around the Mays community. They're professional thieves and insurance defrauders. They burn their houses every three years. You've never heard of them?' He was shouting at Harry Rex.

'No. How do you know he can be bought?'

'Because I bought him once. In a civil case, ten years ago. He was on the jury list, and I got word to him that I'd give him ten percent of the jury verdict. He's very persuasive.'

473

Jake dropped the jury lists and rubbed his eyes. He knew this was probably true, but didn't want to believe it.

'And?' asked Harry Rex.

'And he was selected for the jury, and I got the largest verdict in the history of Ford County. It's still the record.'

'Stubblefield?' Jake asked in disbelief.

'That's it, my boy. Stubblefield versus North Texas Pipeline. September 1974. Eight hundred thousand dollars. Appealed and affirmed by the Supreme Court.'

'Did you pay him?' asked Harry Rex.

Lucien finished a long drink and smacked his lips. 'Eighty thousand cash, in one-hundred-dollar bills,' he said proudly. 'He built a new house, then burned it down.'

'What was your cut?' asked Atcavage.

'Forty percent, minus eighty thousand.'

The room was silent as everybody but Lucien made the calculation.

'Wow,' Atcavage mumbled.

'You're kidding, aren't you, Lucien?' Jake asked half-heartedly.

'You know I'm serious, Jake. You know I lie compulsively, but never about things like this. I'm telling the truth, and I'm telling you this guy can be bought.'

'How much?' asked Harry Rex.

'Forget it!' said Jake.

'Five thousand cash, just guessing.'

'Forget it!'

There was a pause as each one looked at Jake to make sure he was not interested in Clyde Sisco, and when it was obvious he was not interested, they took a drink and waited for the next name. Around ten-thirty Jake had his first beer, and an hour later the case was gone and forty names remained. Lucien staggered to the balcony and watched the blacks carry their candles along the sidewalks next to the streets around the courthouse.

'Jake, why is this deputy sitting in his car in front of my office?' he asked.

'That's my bodyguard.'

'What's his name?'

'Nesbit.'

'Is he awake?'

'Probably not.'

Lucien leaned dangerously over the railing. 'Hey, Nesbit,' he yelled.

Nesbit opened the door of his patrol car. 'Yeah, what is it?'

'Jake here wants you to go to the store and get us some more beer. He's very thirsty. Here's a twenty. He'd like a case of Coors.'

'I can't buy it when I'm on duty,' Nesbit protested.

'Since when?' Lucien laughed at himself.

'I can't do it.'

'It's not for you, Nesbit. It's for Mr Brigance, and he really needs it. He's already called the sheriff, and it's okay.'

'Who called the sheriff?'

'Mr Brigance,' lied Lucien. 'Sheriff said he didn't care what you did as long as you didn't drink any.'

Nesbit shrugged and appeared satisfied. Lucien dropped a twenty from the balcony. Within minutes Nesbit was back with a case minus one which had been opened and was sitting on his radar gun. Lucien ordered Atcavage to fetch the beer from below and distribute the first six-pack.

An hour later the list was finished and the party was over. Nesbit loaded Harry Rex, Lucien, and Atcavage into his patrol car and took them home. Jake and his clerk sat on the balcony, sipping and watching the candles flicker and move slowly around the courthouse. Several cars were parked on the west side of the square, and a small group of blacks sat nearby in lawn chairs waiting to take their turns with the candles.

'We didn't do bad,' Jake said quietly, staring at the vigil. 'We made notes on all but twenty of the hundred and fifty.'

'What's next?'

'I'll try to find something on the other twenty, then we'll make an index card for each juror. We'll know them like family by Monday.'

Nesbit returned to the square and circled twice, watching the blacks. He parked between the Saab and the BMW.

'The M'Naghten brief is a masterpiece. Our psychiatrist, Dr Bass, will be here tomorrow, and I want you to review M'Naghten with him. You need to outline in detail the necessary questions to ask him at trial, and cover these with him. He worries me. I don't know him, and I'm relying on Lucien. Get his résumé and investigate his background. Make whatever phone calls are necessary. Check with the state medical association to make sure he has no history of disciplinary problems. He is very important to our case, and I don't want any surprises.'

'Okay, boss.'

Jake finished his last beer. 'Look, Row Ark, this is a very small town. My wife left five days ago, and I'm sure people will know it soon. You look suspicious. People love to talk, so be discreet. Stay in the office and do your research and tell anyone who asks that you're Ethel's replacement.'

'That's a big bra to fill.'

'You could do it if you wanted to.'

'I hope you know that I'm not nearly as sweet as I'm being forced to act.'

'I know that.'

They watched the blacks change shifts and a new crew take up the candles. Nesbit threw an empty beer can onto the sidewalk.

'You're not driving home are you?' Jake asked.

'It would not be a good idea. I'd register at least .20.'

'You can sleep on the couch in my office.'

'Thanks. I will.'

Jake said good night, locked the office, and spoke briefly to Nesbit. Then he placed himself carefully behind the wheel of the Saab. Nesbit followed him to his home on Adams. He parked under the carport, next to Carla's car, and Nesbit parked in the driveway. It was 1:00 A.M., Thursday, July 18.

Chapter 30

They arrived in groups of two and three and came from all over the state. They parked along the gravel road by the cabin deep in the woods. They entered the cabin dressed as normal working men, but once inside they slowly and meticulously changed into their neatly pressed and neatly folded robes and headdresses. They admired one another's uniforms and helped each other into the bulky outfits. Most of them knew each other, but a few introductions were necessary. They were forty in number; a good turnout.

Stump Sisson was pleased. He sipped whiskey and moved around the room like a head coach reassuring his team before the kickoff. He inspected the uniforms and made adjustments. He was proud of his men, and told them so. It was the biggest meeting of its kind in years, he said. He admired them and their sacrifices in being there. He knew they had jobs and families, but this was important. He talked about the glory days when they were feared in Mississippi and had clout. Those days must return, and it was up to this very group of dedicated men to take a stand for white people. The march could be dangerous, he explained. Niggers could march and demonstrate all day long and no one cared. But let white folks try and march and it was dangerous. The city had issued a permit, and the nigger sheriff promised order, but most Klan marches nowadays were disrupted by roving bands of young wild nigger punks. So be careful, and keep ranks. He, Stump, would do the talking.

They listened intently to Stump's pep talk, and when he finished they loaded into a dozen cars and followed him to town.

Few if any people in Clanton had ever seen the Klan march, and as 2:00 P.M. approached a great wave of excitement rippled around the square. The merchants and their customers found excuses to inspect the sidewalks. They milled about importantly and watched the side streets. The vultures were out in full force and had congregated near the gazebo on the front lawn. A group of young blacks gathered nearby under a massive oak. Ozzie smelled trouble. They assured him they had only come to watch and listen. He threatened them with jail if trouble started. He stationed his men at various points around the courthouse.

'Here they come!' someone yelled, and the spectators strained to get a glimpse of the marching Klansmen as they strutted importantly from a small street onto Washington Avenue, the north border of the square. They walked cautiously, but arrogantly, their faces hidden by the sinister red and white masks hanging from the royal head-dresses. The spectators gawked at the faceless figures as the procession moved slowly along Washington, then south along Caffey Street, then east along Jackson Street. Stump waddled proudly in front of his men. When he neared the front of the courthouse, he made a sharp left turn and led his troops down the long sidewalk in the center of the front lawn. They closed ranks in a loose semicircle around the podium on the courthouse steps.

The vultures had scrambled and fallen over themselves following the march, and when Stump stopped his men the podium was quickly adorned with a dozen microphones trailing wires in all directions to the cameras and recorders. Under the tree the group of blacks had grown larger, much larger, and some of them walked to within a few feet of the semicircle. The sidewalks emptied as the merchants and shopkeepers, their customers, and the other curious streamed across the streets onto the lawn to hear what the leader, the short fat one, was about to say. The deputies walked slowly through the crowd, paying particular attention to the group of blacks. Ozzie placed himself under the oak, in the midst of his people.

Jake watched intently from the window in Jean Gillespie's second floor office. The sight of the Klansmen, in full regalia, their cowardly faces hidden behind the ominous masks, gave him a sick feeling. The white hood, for decades a symbol of hatred and violence in the South, was back. Which one of those men had burned the cross in his yard? Were they all active in planning the bombing of his home? Which one would try something next? From the second floor, he could see the blacks inch closer.

'You niggers were not invited to this rally!' Stump screamed into the microphone, pointing at the blacks. 'This is a Klan meetin', not a meetin' for a buncha niggers!'

From the side streets and small alleys behind the rows of red brick buildings, a steady stream of blacks moved toward the courthouse. They joined the others, and in seconds Stump and his boys were outnumbered ten to one. Ozzie radioed for backup.

'My name's Stump Sisson,' he said as he removed his mask. 'And I'm proud to say I'm the Mississippi Imperial Wizard for the Invisible Empire of the Ku Klux Klan. I'm here to say that the law-abidin' white folks of Mississippi are sick and tired of niggers stealin', rapin', killin', and gettin' by with it. We demand justice, and we demand that this Hailey nigger be convicted and his black ass sent to the gas chamber!'

'Free Carl Lee!' screamed one of the blacks.

'Free Carl Lee!' they repeated in unison.

'Free Carl Lee!'

'Shut up, you wild niggers!' Stump shrieked back. 'Shut up, you animals!' His troops stood facing him, frozen, with their backs to the screaming crowd. Ozzie and six deputies moved between the groups.

'Free Carl Lee!'

'Free Carl Lee!'

Stump's naturally colorful face had turned an even deeper red. His teeth nearly touched the microphones. 'Shut up, you wild niggers! You had your rally yesterday and we didn't disturb you. We have a right to assemble in peace, just like you do! Now, shut up!'

The chanting intensified. 'Free Carl Lee! Free Carl Lee!'

'Where's the sheriff? He's supposed to keep law and order. Sheriff, do your job. Shut those niggers up so we can assemble in peace. Can't you do your job, Sheriff? Can't you control your own people? See, folks, that's what you get when you elect niggers to public office.'

The shouting continued and Stump stepped back from the microphones and watched the blacks. The photographers and TV crews spun in circles trying to record it all. No one noticed a small window on the third floor of the courthouse. It opened slowly, and from the darkness within a crude firebomb was thrown onto the podium below. It landed perfectly at Stump's feet and exploded, engulfing the wizard in flames.

The riot was on. Stump screamed and rolled wildly down the front steps. Three of his men shed their heavy robes and masks and attempted to cover him and smother the flames. The wooden podium and platform burned with the thick, unmistakable smell of gasoline. The blacks charged, wielding sticks and knives and hacking at anything with a white face or white robe. Under each white robe was a short black nightstick, and the Klansmen proved ready for the assault. Within seconds of the explosion, the front lawn of the Ford County Courthouse was a battlefield as men screamed and cursed and howled in pain through thick, heavy smoke. The air was filled with rocks and stones and nightsticks as the two groups brawled in hand-to-hand combat.

Bodies began falling on the lush, green grass. Ozzie fell first; the victim of a wicked smash to the base of his skull with a wrecking bar. Nesbit, Prather, Hastings, Pirtle, Tatum, and other deputies ran here and there attempting unsuccessfully to separate various combatants before they killed each other. Instead of running for cover, the vultures darted crazily through the midst of the smoke and violence valiantly trying to capture yet a better shot of the blood and gore. They were sitting ducks. One cameraman, his right eye buried deep in his camera, caught a jagged piece of brick with his left eye. He and his camera dropped quickly to the sidewalk, where, after a few seconds, another cameraman appeared and filmed his fallen comrade. A fearless, busy female reporter from a Memphis station charged into the melee with her microphone in hand and her cameraman at her heels. She dodged a brick, then maneuvered too close to a large Klansman who was just finishing off a couple of black teenagers, when, with a loud

484

piercing scream, he slapped her pretty head with his nightstick, kicked her as she fell, then brutally attacked her cameraman.

Fresh troops from the Clanton City Police arrived. In the center of the battle, Nesbit, Prather, and Hastings came together, stood with their backs to each other, and began firing their Smith & Wesson .357 magnum service revolvers into the air. The sound of the gunfire quelled the riot. The warriors froze and searched for the gunfire, then quickly separated and glared at each other. They retreated slowly to their own groups. The officers formed a dividing line between the blacks and the Klansmen, all of whom were thankful for the truce.

A dozen wounded bodies were unable to retreat. Ozzie sat dazed, rubbing his neck. The lady from Memphis was unconscious and bleeding profusely from the head. Several Klansmen, their white robes soiled and bloody, lay sprawled near the sidewalk. The fire continued to burn.

The sirens drew closer and finally the fire trucks and ambulances arrived and drove onto the battle-field. Firemen and medics attended the wounded. None were dead. Stump Sisson was taken away first. Ozzie was half dragged and half carried to a patrol car. More police arrived and broke up the crowd.

Jake, Harry Rex, and Ellen ate a lukewarm pizza and watched intently as the small television in the conference room broadcasted the day's events in Clanton, Mississippi. CBS ran the story halfway through the news. The reporter had apparently escaped the riot unscathed, and he narrated the video with a play by play of the march, the shouting, the firebomb, and the melee. 'As of late this afternoon,' he reported, 'the exact number of casualties is unknown. The most serious injuries are believed to be the extensive burns suffered by a Mr Sisson, who identified himself as an imperial wizard of the Ku Klux Klan. He is listed in serious condition at the Mid South Burn Hospital in Memphis.'

The video showed a closeup of Stump burning while all hell broke loose. He continued: 'The trial of Carl Lee Hailey is scheduled to start Monday here in Clanton. It is unknown at this time what effect, if any, today's riot will have on this trial. There is some speculation the trial will be postponed and/or moved to another county.'

'That's news to me,' said Jake.

'You haven't heard anything?' asked Harry Rex.

'Not a word. And I presume I would be notified before CBS.'

The reporter disappeared and Dan Rather said he would return in a moment.

'What does this mean?' asked Ellen.

'It means Noose is stupid for not changing venue.'

'Be glad he didn't,' said Harry Rex. 'It'll give you something to argue on appeal.'

'Thanks, Harry Rex. I appreciate your confidence in my ability as a trial lawyer.'

The phone rang. Harry Rex grabbed it and said

hello to Carla. He handed it to Jake. 'It's your wife. Can we listen?'

'No! Go get another pizza. Hello dear.'

'Jake, are you all right?'

'Of course I'm all right.'

'I just saw it on the news. It's awful. Where were you?'

'I was wearing one of those white robes.'

'Jake, please. This is not funny.'

'I was in Jean Gillespie's office on the second floor. We had wonderful seats. Saw the whole thing. It was very exciting.'

'Who are those people?'

'Same ones who burned the cross in our front yard and tried to blow up the house.'

'Where are they from?'

'Everywhere. Five are in the hospital and their addresses are scattered all over the state. One is a local boy. How's Hanna?'

'She's fine. She wants to come home. Will the trial be postponed?'

'I doubt it.'

'Are you safe?'

'Sure. I've got a full-time bodyguard and I carry a .38 in my briefcase. Don't worry.'

'But I'm worried, Jake. I need to be home with you.'

'No.'

'Hanna can stay here until it's over, but I want to come home.'

'No, Carla. I know you're safe out there. You won't be safe if you're here.'

'Then you're not safe either.'

'I'm as safe as I can get. But I'm not taking chances with you and Hanna. It's out of the question. That's final. How are your parents?'

'I didn't call to talk about my parents. I called because I'm scared and I want to be with you.'

'And I want to be with you, but not now. Please understand.'

She hesitated. 'Where are you staying?'

'At Lucien's most of the time. Occasionally at home, with my bodyguard in the driveway.'

'How's my house?'

'It's still there. Dirty, but still there.'

'I miss it.'

'Believe me, it misses you.'

'I love you, Jake, and I'm scared.'

'I love you, and I'm not scared. Just relax and take care of Hanna.'

'Goodbye.'

'Goodbye.'

Jake handed the receiver to Ellen. 'Where is she?'

'Wilmington, North Carolina. Her parents spend the summers there.'

Harry Rex had left for another pizza.

'You miss her, don't you?' asked Ellen.

'In more ways than you can imagine.'

'Oh, I can imagine.'

At midnight they were in the cabin drinking whiskey, cussing niggers, and comparing wounds. Several had returned from the hospital in Memphis where they had visited briefly with Stump Sisson. He told them to proceed as planned. Eleven had been released from the Ford County Hospital with various cuts and bruises, and the others admired their wounds as each took his turn describing to the last detail how he had gallantly battled multiple niggers before being wounded, usually from the rear or blind side. They were the heroes, the ones with the bandages. Then the others told their stories and the whiskey flowed. They heaped praise upon the largest one when he told of his attack on the pretty television reporter and her nigger cameraman.

After a couple of hours of drinking and story-telling the talk turned to the task at hand. A map of the county was produced, and one of the locals pinpointed the targets. There were twenty homes this night – twenty names taken from the list of prospective jurors someone had furnished.

Five teams of four each left the cabin in pickups and headed into the darkness to further their mischief. In each pickup were four wooden crosses, the smaller models, nine feet by four feet, each soaked with kerosene. They avoided Clanton and the small towns in the county and instead kept to the dark countryside. The targets were in isolated areas, away from traffic and neighbors, out in the country where things go unnoticed and people go to bed early and sleep soundly.

The plan of attack was simple: a truck would stop a few hundred feet down the road, out of sight, no headlights, and the driver remained with engine running while the other three carried the cross to the front yard, stuck it in the ground, and threw a torch on it. The pickup then met them in front of the house for a quiet getaway and joyride to the next target.

The plan worked simply and with no complications at nineteen of the twenty targets. But at Luther Pickett's residence a strange noise earlier in the night had aroused Luther, and he sat in the darkness of his front porch waiting for nothing in particular when he saw a strange pickup move suspiciously along the gravel road out beyond his pecan tree. He grabbed his shotgun and listened as the truck turned around and stopped down the road. He heard voices, and then saw three figures carrying a pole or something into his front yard, next to the gravel road. Luther crouched behind a shrub next to the porch, and aimed.

The driver took a slug of cold beer and watched to see the cross go up in flames. He heard a shotgun instead. His buddies abandoned the cross and the torch and the front yard, and jumped into a small ditch next to the road. Another shotgun blast. The driver could hear the screams and obscenities. They had to be rescued! He threw down his beer and stepped on the gas.

Old Luther fired again as he came off the porch, and again as the truck appeared and stopped by the shallow ditch. The three scrambled desperately from the mud, stumbling and sliding, cussing and yelling as they attacked the truck and furiously fought to jump into the bed.

'Hang on!' yelled the driver just as old Luther fired again, this time spraying the pickup. He watched with a smile as the truck sped away, spinning gravel and fishtailing from ditch to ditch. Just a bunch of drunk kids, he thought.

From a pay phone, a Kluxer held the list of twenty names and twenty phone numbers. He called them all, simply to ask them to take a look in their front yards.

Chapter 31

Friday morning Jake phoned the Noose home and was informed by Mrs Ichabod that His Honor was presiding over a civil trial in Polk County. Jake gave instructions to Ellen and left for Smithfield, an hour away. He nodded at His Honor as he entered the empty courtroom and sat on the front row. Except for the jurors, there were no other spectators. Noose was bored, the jurors were bored, the lawyers were bored, and after two minutes Jake was bored. After the witness finished Noose called for a short recess, and Jake went to his chambers.

'Hello, Jake. Why're you here?'

'You heard what happened yesterday.'

'I saw it on the news last night.'

'Have you heard what happened this morning?'

'No.'

'Evidently someone gave the Klan a list of the prospective jurors. Last night they burned crosses in the yards of twenty of the jurors.'

Noose was shocked. 'Our jurors!'

'Yes, sir.'

'Did they catch anybody?'

'Of course not. They were too busy putting out fires. Besides, you don't catch these people.'

'Twenty of our jurors,' Noose repeated.

'Yes, sir.'

Noose pawed at his mangled mass of brilliant gray hair and walked slowly around the small room, shaking his head and occasionally scratching his crotch.

'Sounds like intimidation to me,' he muttered.

What a mind, thought Jake. A real genius. 'I would say so.'

'So what am I supposed to do?' he asked with a touch of frustration.

'Change venue.'

'To where?'

'Southern part of the state.'

'I see. Perhaps Carey County. I believe it's sixty percent black. That would generate at least a hung jury, wouldn't it? Or maybe you would like Brower County. I think it's even blacker. You'd probably get an acquittal there, wouldn't you?'

'I don't care where you move it. It's not fair to try him in Ford County. Things were bad enough before the war yesterday. Now the white folks are really in a lynching mood, and my man's got the nearest available neck. The situation was terrible before the Klan started decorating the county with Christmas trees. Who knows what else they'll try before Monday. There's no way to pick a fair and impartial jury in Ford County.'

'You mean black jury?'

'No, sir! I mean a jury that hasn't prejudged this case. Carl Lee Hailey is entitled to twelve people who haven't already decided his guilt or innocence.'

Noose lumbered toward his chair and fell into it. He removed those glasses from that nose and picked at the end of it.

'We could excuse the twenty,' he wondered aloud.

'That won't help. The entire county knows about it or will know about it within a few hours. You know how fast word travels. The entire panel will feel threatened.'

'Then we could disqualify the entire panel and summon a new one.'

'Won't work,' Jake answered sharply, frustrated by Noose's stubbornness. 'All jurors must come from Ford County, and everybody in the county knows about it. And how do you keep the Klan from harassing the next panel? It won't work.'

'What makes you so confident the Klan won't follow the case if I move it to another county?' The sarcasm dripped from every word.

'I think they will follow it,' Jake admitted. 'But we don't know that for sure. What we do know is that the Klan is already in Ford County, that it's quite active now, and that it has already intimidated some potential jurors. That's the issue. The question is, what will you do about it?'

'Nothing,' Noose said bluntly.

'Sir?'

494

'Nothing. I will do nothing but dismiss the twenty. I will carefully interrogate the panel next Monday, when the trial starts in Clanton.'

Jake stared in disbelief. Noose had a reason, a motive, a fear, something he was not telling. Lucien was right – someone had gotten to him.

'May I ask why?'

'I don't think it matters where we try Carl Lee Hailey. I don't think it matters who we put in the jury box. I don't think it matters what color they are. Their minds are made up. All of them, wherever and whoever they are. They've already made up their minds, Jake, and it's your job to pick those who think your man is a hero.'

That's probably true, thought Jake, but he wouldn't admit it. He continued staring at the trees outside. 'Why are you afraid to move it?'

Ichabod's eyes narrowed, and he glared at Jake. 'Afraid? I'm not afraid of any ruling I make. Why are you afraid to try it in Ford County?'

'I thought I just explained it.'

'Mr Hailey will be tried in Ford County starting Monday. That's three days from today. And he will be tried there not because I'm afraid to move it, but because it wouldn't do any good to move it. I've considered all this very carefully, Mr Brigance, many times, and I feel comfortable with the trial in Clanton. It will not be moved. Anything further?'

'No, sir.'

'Good. See you Monday.'

★　　★　　★

Jake entered his office through the rear door. The front door had been locked for a week now, and there was always someone banging on it and yelling at it. Most of them were reporters, but many were friends just stopping by to gossip and find out what they could about the big trial. Clients were a thing of the past. The phone rang constantly. Jake never touched it and Ellen grabbed it if she was nearby.

He found her in the conference room up to her elbows in law books. The M'Naghten brief was a masterpiece. He had requested no more than twenty pages. She gave him seventy-five perfectly typed and plainly worded pages, and explained there was no way to cover the Mississippi version of M'Naghten in fewer words. Her research was painstaking and detailed. She had started with the original M'Naghten case in England in the 1800's and worked through a hundred and fifty years of insanity law in Mississippi. She discarded insignificant or confusing cases, and explained in wonderful simplicity the complicated, major cases. The brief concluded with a summary of current law, and applied it to the trial of Carl Lee Hailey.

In a smaller brief, only fourteen pages, she had reached the unmistakable conclusion that the jury would see the sickening pictures of Cobb and Willard with their brains splattered about the stairway. Mississippi admitted such inflammatory evidence, and she had found no way around it.

She had typed thirty-one pages of research on the defense of justifiable homicide, something Jake had considered briefly after the killings. She reached the same conclusion Jake had reached – it wouldn't work. She had found an old Mississippi case where a man had caught and killed an escaped convict who was armed. He had been acquitted, but the differences in that case and Carl Lee's case were enormous. Jake had not asked for the brief, and was irritated that so much energy had been spent on it. He said nothing, however, since she had produced everything he had asked for.

The most pleasant surprise had been her work with Dr W.T. Bass. She had met with him twice during the week, and they had covered M'Naghten in great detail. She prepared a twenty-five-page script of the questions to be asked by Jake and the answers to be given by Bass. It was a skillfully crafted dialogue, and he marveled at her reasoning. When he was her age, he was an average student more concerned with romance than research. She, on the other hand, as a third-year law student was writing briefs that read like treatises.

'How'd it go?' she asked.

'As expected. He did not budge. The trial will start here Monday with the same panel, minus the twenty who received their subtle warnings.'

'He's crazy.'

'What're you working on?'

'I'm finishing the brief to support our position that the details of the rape should be discussed before the jury. It looks good, at this point.'

'When will you finish it?'

'Is there some hurry?'

'By Sunday, if possible. I've got another chore, something a little different.'

She slid her legal pad away and listened.

'The State's psychiatrist will be Dr Wilbert Rodeheaver, head of staff at Whitfield. He's been there forever, and has testifed in hundreds of cases. I want you to dig a little and see how often his name appears in court decisions.'

'I've already run across his name.'

'Good. As you know, the only cases we read about from the Supreme Court are the ones where the defendant at trial was convicted and has appealed. The acquittals are not reported. I'm more interested in these.'

'Where are you coming from?'

'I have a hunch Rodeheaver is very reluctant to give an opinion that a defendant was legally insane. There's a chance he's never done it. Even in cases where the defendant was clearly crazy and did not know what he was doing. I'd like to ask Rodeheaver, on cross-examination, about some of the cases in which he's said there's nothing wrong with an obviously sick man, and the jury acquitted him.'

'Those cases will be very hard to find.'

'I know, but you can do it, Row Ark. I've watched you work for a week now, and I know you can do it.'

'I'm flattered, boss.'

'You may have to make phone calls to attorneys around the state who've crossed Rodeheaver before. It'll be hard, Row Ark, but get it done.'

'Yes, boss. I'm sure you wanted it yesterday.'

'Not really. I doubt if we'll get to Rodeheaver next week, so you have some time.'

'I don't know how to act. You mean it's not urgent?'

'No, but that rape brief is.'

'Yes, boss.'

'Have you had lunch?'

'I'm not hungry.'

'Good. Don't make any plans for dinner.'

'What does that mean?'

'It means I've got an idea.'

'Sort of like a date?'

'No, sort of like a business lunch with two professionals.'

Jake packed two briefcases and left. 'I'll be at Lucien's,' he told her, 'but don't call unless it's a dire emergency. Don't tell anyone where I am.'

'What are you working on?'

'The jury.'

Lucien had passed out drunk in the swing on the porch, and Sallie was not around. Jake helped himself to the spacious study upstairs. Lucien had more law books in his home than most lawyers had in their offices. He unpacked his mess in a chair, and on the desk he placed an alphabetical list of the jurors, a stack of three-by-five notecards, and several Magic Markers.

The first name was Acker, Barry Acker. The last name was written in large print across the top of a notecard with a blue Magic Marker. Blue for men, red for women, black for blacks, regardless of gender. Under Acker's name he made notes with a pencil. Age, about forty. Married to his second wife, three children, two daughters. Runs a small unprofitable hardware store on the highway in Clanton. Wife, secretary at a bank. Drives a pickup. Likes to hunt. Wears cowboy boots. Pretty nice guy. Atcavage had gone to the hardware store Thursday to get a look at Barry Acker. Said he looked okay, talked like he had some education. Jake wrote the number nine by the name Acker.

Jake was impressed with his research. Surely Buckley would not be as thorough.

The next name was Bill Andrews. What a name. There were six of them in the phonebook. Jake knew one, Harry Rex knew another one, and Ozzie knew a black one, but nobody knew which one got the summons. He put a question mark by the name.

Gerald Ault. Jake smiled when he wrote the name on the notecard. Ault had passed through his office a few years back when the bank foreclosed on his house in Clanton. His wife was stricken with kidney disease, and the medical bills broke them. He was an intellectual, educated at Princeton, where he met his wife. She was from Ford County, the only child of a once prominent family of fools who had invested all their money in railroads. He arrived in Ford County just in time for his in-laws to go under, and the easy life he had married dissolved into one of struggle. He taught school for a while, then ran the library, then worked as a clerk in the courthouse. He developed an aversion to hard work. Then his wife got sick, and they lost their modest house. He now worked in a convenience store.

Jake knew something about Gerald Ault that no one else knew. As a child in Pennsylvania, his family lived in a farmhouse near the highway. One night while they slept, the house caught fire. A passing motorist stopped, kicked in the front door and began rescuing the Aults. The fire spread quickly, and when Gerald and his brother awoke they were trapped in their upstairs bedroom. They ran to the window and screamed. Their parents and siblings yelled helplessly from the front lawn. Flames poured from every window in the house except for their bedroom. Suddenly, the rescuer soaked himself with water from the garden hose, dashed into the burning house, fought the flames and smoke as he raced upstairs, then bolted through the bedroom door. He kicked out the window, grabbed Gerald and his brother, and jumped to the ground. Miraculously, they were not hurt. They thanked him, through tears and embraces. They thanked this stranger, whose skin was black. He was the first Negro the children had ever seen.

Gerald Ault was one of the few white people in Ford County who truly loved black people. Jake put a ten by his name.

For six hours he went through the jury list, making note-cards, concentrating on each name, envisioning each juror in the box and in deliberation, talking to each one. He rated them. Every black got an automatic ten; the whites were not so easy. The men rated higher than the women; the young men higher than the old men; the educated slightly higher than the uneducated; the liberals, both of them, received the highest ratings.

He eliminated the twenty Noose planned to exclude. He knew something about one hundred and eleven of the prospective jurors. Surely Buckley could not know so much.

Ellen was typing on Ethel's machine when Jake returned from Lucien's. She turned it off, closed the law books she was typing from, and watched him.

'Where's dinner?' she asked with a wicked smile.

'We're taking a road trip.'

'All right! Where to?'

'Have you ever been to Robinsonville, Mississippi?'

'No, but I'm ready. What's there?'

'Nothing but cotton, soybeans, and a great little restaurant.'

'What's the dress code?'

Jake inspected her. She wore the usual – jeans, neatly starched and faded, no socks, a navy button-down that was four sizes too big but tucked in nicely above her slender hips.

'You look fine,' he said.

They turned off the copier and the lights and left Clanton in the Saab. Jake stopped at a liquor store in the black section of town and bought a six-pack of Coors and a tall, cold bottle of Chablis.

'You have to bring your own bottle to this place,' he explained as they left town. The sun was setting into the highway ahead, and Jake flipped down the sun visors. Ellen played bartender and opened two cans.

'How far is this place?' she asked.

'Hour and a half.'

'Hour and a half! I'm starving.'

'Then fill up on beer. Believe me it's worth it.'

'What's on the menu?'

'Barbecued, sauteed shrimp, frog legs, and char-broiled catfish.'

She sipped on the beer. 'We'll see.'

Jake stepped on the gas, and they raced across bridges over the countless tributaries of Lake Chatulla. They climbed steep hills covered with layers of dark green kudzu. They flew around corners and dodged pulpwood trucks making their last runs of the day. Jake opened the sunroof, lowered the windows and let the wind blow. Ellen leaned back in the seat and closed her eyes. Her thick, wavy hair swirled around her face.

'Look, Row Ark, this dinner is strictly business—'

'Sure, sure.'

'I mean it. I'm the employer, you're the employee, and this is a business meal. Nothing more or less. So don't get any lustful ideas in your ERA, sexually liberated brain.'

'Sounds like you're the one with the ideas.'

'Nope. I just know what you're thinking.'

'How do you know what I'm thinking? Why do

you assume you're so irresistible and that I'm planning a big seduction scene?'

'Just keep your hands to yourself. I'm a wonderfully happily married man with a gorgeous wife who'd kill if she thought I was fooling around.'

'Okay, let's pretend to be friends. Just two friends having dinner.'

'That doesn't work in the South. A male friend cannot have dinner with a female friend if the male friend has a wife. It just doesn't work down here.'

'Why not?'

'Because men don't have female friends. No way. I don't know of a single man in the entire South who is married and has a female friend. I think it goes back to the Civil War.'

'I think it goes back to the Dark Ages. Why are Southern women so jealous?'

'Because that's the way we've trained them. They learned from us. If my wife met a male friend for lunch or dinner, I'd tear his head off and file for divorce. She learned it from me.'

'That makes absolutely no sense.'

'Of course it doesn't.'

'Your wife has no male friends?'

'None that I know of. If you learn of any, let me know.'

'And you have no female friends?'

'Why would I want female friends? They can't talk about football, or duck hunting, or politics, or lawsuits, or anything that I want to talk about. They talk about kids, clothes, recipes, coupons, furniture, stuff I know nothing about. No, I don't have any female friends. Don't want any.'

'That's what I love about the South. The people are so tolerant.'

'Thank you.'

'Do you have any Jewish friends?'

'I don't know of any in Ford County. I had a real good friend in law school, Ira Tauber, from New Jersey. We were very close. I love Jews. Jesus was a Jew, you know. I've never understood anti-Semitism.'

'My God, you are a liberal. How about, uh, homosexuals?'

'I feel sorry for them. They don't know what they're missing. But that's their problem.'

'Could you have a homosexual friend?'

'I guess, as long as he didn't tell me.'

'Nope, you're a Republican.'

She took his empty can and threw it in the back seat. She opened two more. The sun was gone, and the heavy, humid air felt cool at ninety miles an hour.

'So we can't be friends?' she said.

'Nope.'

'Nor lovers.'

'Please. I'm trying to drive.'

'So what are we?'

'I'm the lawyer, you're the law clerk. I'm the employer, you're the employee. I'm the boss, you're the gofer.'

'You're the male, I'm the female.'

Jake admired her jeans and bulky shirt. 'There's not much doubt about that.'

Ellen shook her head and stared at the mountains of kudzu flying by. Jake smiled, drove faster, and sipped his beer. He negotiated a series of intersections on the rural, deserted highways and, suddenly, the hills disappeared and the land became flat.

'What's the name of the restaurant?' she asked.

'The Hollywood.'

'The what?'

'The Hollywood.'

'Why is it called that?'

'It was once located in a small town a few miles away by the name of Hollywood, Mississippi. It burned, and they moved it to Robinsonville. They still call it the Hollywood.'

'What's so great about it?'

'Great food, great music, great atmosphere, and it's a thousand miles from Clanton and no one will see me having dinner with a strange and beautiful woman.'

'I'm not a woman, I'm a gofer.'

'A strange and beautiful gofer.'

Ellen smiled to herself and ran her fingers through her hair. At another intersection, he turned left and headed west until they found a settlement near a railroad. A row of wooden buildings sat empty on one side of the road, and across the street, all by itself, was an old dry goods store with a dozen cars parked around it and music rolling softly out the windows. Jake grabbed the bottle of Chablis and escorted his law clerk up the steps, onto the front porch, and inside the building.

Next to the door was a small stage, where a beautiful old black lady, Merle, sat at her piano and sang 'Rainy Night in Georgia.' Three long rows of tables ran to the front and stopped next to the stage. The tables were half full, and a waitress in the back poured beer from a pitcher and motioned for them to come on in. She seated them in the rear, at a small table with a red-checkered tablecloth.

'Y'all want some fried dill pickles, honey?' she asked Jake.

'Yes! Two orders.'

Ellen frowned and looked at Jake. 'Fried dill pickles?'

'Yes, of course. They don't serve them in Boston?'

'Do you people fry everything?'

'Everything that's worth eating. If you don't like them, I'll eat them.'

A yell went up from the table across the aisle. Four couples toasted something or somebody, then broke into riotous laughing. The restaurant maintained a constant roar of yelling and talking.

'The good thing about the Hollywood,' Jake explained, 'is that you can make all the noise you want and stay as long as you want, and nobody cares. When you get a table here, it's yours for the night. They'll start singing and dancing in a minute.'

Jake ordered sauteed shrimp and charbroiled catfish for both of them. Ellen passed on the frog legs. The waitress hurried back with the Chablis

507

and two chilled glasses. They toasted Carl Lee Hailey and his insane mind.

'Whatta you think of Bass?' Jake asked.

'He's the perfect witness. He'll say anything we want him to say.'

'Does that bother you?'

'It would if he was a fact witness. But he's an expert, and he can get by with his opinions. Who will challenge him?'

'Is he believable?'

'When he's sober. We talked twice this week. On Tuesday he was lucid and helpful. On Wednesday, he was drunk and indifferent. I think he'll be as helpful as any psychiatrist we could find. He doesn't care what the truth is, and he'll tell us what we want to hear.'

'Does he think Carl Lee was legally insane?'

'No. Do you?'

'No. Row Ark, Carl Lee told me five days before the killings that he would do it. He showed me the exact place where he would ambush them, although at the time I didn't realize it. Our client knew exactly what he was doing.'

'Why didn't you stop him?'

'Because I didn't believe him. His daughter had just been raped and was fighting for her life.'

'Would you have stopped him if you could?'

'I did tell Ozzie. But at the time neither of us dreamed it could happen. No, I would not have stopped him if I knew for certain. I would have done the same thing.'

'How?'

'Exactly as he did it. It was very easy.'

Ellen approached a fried dill pickle with her fork and played with it suspiciously. She cut it in half, pierced it with the fork, and sniffed it carefully. She put it in her mouth and chewed slowly. She swallowed, then pushed her pile of pickles across the table toward Jake.

'Typical yankee,' he said. 'I don't understand you, Row Ark. You don't like fried dill pickles, you're attractive, very bright, you could go to work with any blue-chip law firm in the country for megabucks, yet you want to spend your career losing sleep over cutthroat murderers who are on death row and about to get their just rewards. What makes you tick, Row Ark?'

'You lose sleep over the same people. Now it's Carl Lee Hailey. Next year it'll be some other murderer who everybody hates but you'll lose sleep over him because he happens to be your client. One of these days, Brigance, you'll have a client on death row, and you'll learn how terrible it is. When they strap him in the chair and he looks at you for the last time, you'll be a changed man. You'll know how barbaric the system is, and you'll remember Row Ark.'

'Then I'll grow a beard and join the ACLU.'

'Probably, if they would accept you.'

The sauteed shrimp arrived in a small black skillet. It simmered in butter and garlic and barbeque sauce. Ellen dipped spoonfuls onto her plate and ate like a refugee. Merle lit into a stirring rendition of 'Dixie,' and the crowd sang and clapped along.

The waitress ran by and threw a platter of battered and crunchy frog legs on the table. Jake finished a glass of wine and grabbed a handful of the frog legs. Ellen tried to ignore them. When they were full of appetizers, the catfish was served. The grease popped and fizzed and they did not touch the china. It was charbroiled to a deep brown crisp with black squares from the grill burned on each side. They ate and drank slowly, watching each other and savoring the delicious entree.

At midnight, the bottle was empty and the lights were dimmed. They said good night to the waitress and to Merle. They walked carefully down the steps and to the car. Jake buckled his seat belt.

'I'm too drunk to drive,' he said.

'So am I. I saw a little motel not far down the road.'

'I saw it too, and there were no vacancies. Nice try, Row Ark. Get me drunk and try to take advantage of me.'

'I would if I could, mister.'

For a moment their eyes met. Ellen's face reflected the red light cast by the neon sign that flashed HOLLYWOOD atop the restaurant.

The moment grew longer and then the sign was turned off. The restaurant had closed.

Jake started the Saab, let it warm, and raced away into the darkness.

★　　★　　★

510

Mickey Mouse called Ozzie early Saturday morning at his home and promised more trouble from the Klan. The riot on Thursday had not been their fault, he explained, yet they were being blamed for it. They had marched in peace, and now their leader lay near death with seventy percent of his body covered with third-degree burns. There would be retaliation; it had been ordered from above. Reinforcements were on the way from other states, and there would be violence. No specifics now, but he would call later when he knew more.

Ozzie sat on the side of his bed, rubbed the swollen hump on the back of his neck and called the mayor. And he called Jake. An hour later they met in Ozzie's office.

'The situation is about to get outta hand,' Ozzie said, holding an ice pack to his neck and grimacing with every word. 'I've got it from a reliable informant that the Klan plans to retaliate for what happened Thursday. They're supposed to bring fresh troops from other states.'

'Do you believe it?' asked the mayor.

'I'm afraid not to believe it.'

'Same informant?' asked Jake.

'Yep.'

'Then I believe it.'

'Somebody said there was talk of movin' or postponin' the trial,' Ozzie said. 'Any chance of it?'

'No. I met with Judge Noose yesterday. It won't be moved and it'll start Monday.'

'Did you tell him about the burnin' crosses?'

'I told him everything.'

'Is he crazy?' asked the mayor.

'Yes, and stupid. But don't quote me on that.'

'Is he on solid legal ground?' asked Ozzie.

Jake shook his head. 'More like quicksand.'

'What have you got in mind?' asked the mayor.

Ozzie changed ice packs and carefully rubbed his neck. He spoke with pain. 'I have a strong desire to prevent another riot. Our hospital is not big enough to allow this crap to continue. We must do something. The blacks are angry and volatile, and it wouldn't take much to ignite them. Some blacks are just lookin' for a reason to start shootin', and those white robes are good targets. I've got a hunch the Klan may do somethin' really stupid, like try to kill somebody. They're gettin' more national exposure off this than they've had in ten years. The informant told me that after Thursday they've had calls from all over the country from volunteers wantin' to come down here and join the fun.'

He slowly rolled his head around his shoulders and changed ice packs again. 'I hate to say it, Mayor, but I think you should call the governor and ask for the National Guard. I know it's a drastic step, but I'd hate to get someone killed.'

'The National Guard!' the mayor repeated in disbelief.

'That's what I said.'

'Occupying Clanton?'

'Yep. Protectin' your people.'

'Patrolling the streets?'

'Yep. With guns and everthing.'

'Oh my, this is drastic. Aren't you overreacting a bit?'

'No. It's evident I don't have enough men to keep peace around here. We couldn't even stop a riot that happened right in front of us. The Klan's burnin' crosses all over the county, and we can't do anything about it. What will we do when the blacks decide to start some trouble? I don't have enough men, Mayor. I need some help.'

Jake thought it was a marvelous idea. How could a fair and impartial jury be chosen when the National Guard had the courthouse surrounded? He thought of the jurors arriving for court Monday and walking past the soldiers with guns and jeeps and maybe even a tank or two parked in front of the courthouse. How could they be fair and impartial? How could Noose insist on trying the case in Clanton? How could the Supreme Court refuse to reverse if, heaven forbid, there was a conviction? It was a great idea.

'Whatta you think, Jake?' asked the mayor, looking for help.

'I don't think you have a choice, Mayor. We can't stand another riot. It could hurt you politically.'

'I'm not worried about politics,' the mayor replied angrily, knowing Jake and Ozzie knew better. The mayor had been reelected last time by less than fifty votes and did not make a move without weighing the political fallout. Ozzie caught a grin from Jake as the mayor squirmed with the thought of having his quiet little town occupied by the army.

After dark Saturday, Ozzie and Hastings led Carl Lee out the rear door of the jail and into the sheriff's patrol car. They talked and laughed as Hastings drove in slow motion out into the country, past Bates Grocery and onto Craft Road. The Haileys' front yard was covered with cars when they arrived, so he parked in the road. Carl Lee walked through his front door like a free man and was immediately embraced by a mob of kinfolks, friends, and his children. They had not been told he was coming. He hugged them desperately, all four at the same time in one long bear hug as if there might be no more for a long time. The crowd watched in silence as this huge man knelt on the floor and buried his head among his weeping children. Most of those in the crowd wept too.

The kitchen was covered with food, and the guest of honor was seated in his usual chair at the head of the table with his wife and children seated around him. Reverend Agee returned thanks with a short prayer of hope and home-coming. A hundred friends waited on the family. Ozzie and Hastings filled their plates and retreated to the front porch, where they swatted mosquitoes and planned strategy for the trial. Ozzie was deeply concerned about Carl Lee's safety while they moved him from the jail to court and back each day. The defendant himself had proven clearly that such journeys are not always safe.

After supper the crowd spilled out into the front yard. The children played while the adults stayed on the porch, as close as possible to Carl Lee. He was their hero, the most famous man most of them would ever see, and they knew him personally. To his people he was on trial for one reason only. Sure he killed those boys, but that wasn't the issue. If he was white, he would receive civic awards for what he did. They would half-heartedly prosecute him, but with a white jury the trial would be a joke. Carl Lee was on trial because he was black. And if they convicted him, it would be because he was black. No other reason. They believed that. They listened carefully as he talked about the trial. He wanted their prayers and support, and wanted them all to be there and watch it and to protect his family.

They sat for hours in the sweltering humidity; Carl Lee and Gwen in the swing rocking slowly, surrounded by admirers all wanting to be near this great man. When they began to leave they all embraced him and promised to be there Monday. They wondered if they would see him again sitting on his front porch.

At midnight Ozzie said it was time to go. Carl

Lee hugged Gwen and the kids one last time, then took his seat in Ozzie's car.

Bud Twitty died during the night. The dispatcher called Nesbit, who told Jake. He made a note to send flowers.

Chapter 32

Sunday. One day before trial. Jake awoke at 5:00 A.M. with a knot in his stomach that he attributed to the trial, and a headache that he attributed to the trial and a late Saturday night session on Lucien's porch with his law clerk and former boss. Ellen had decided to sleep in a guest room at Lucien's, so Jake spent the night on his couch in the office.

He lay on the couch and heard voices from the street below. He staggered in the dark to the balcony, and stopped in amazement at the scene around the courthouse. D-Day! The war was on! Patton had arrived! The streets around the square were lined with transport trucks, jeeps, and soldiers busy running here and there in an effort to get organized and look military. Radios squawked, and potbellied commanders yelled to their men to hurry and get organized. A command post was set up near the gazebo on the front lawn. Three squads of soldiers hammered on stakes and pulled ropes and strung up three enormous canvas camouflage pavilions. Barricades were set up on the four corners of the square, and sentries took their positions. They smoked cigarettes and leaned on the street lights.

Nesbit sat on the trunk of his car and watched the fortifying of downtown Clanton. He chatted with a few of the guardsmen. Jake made coffee and took him a cup. He was awake now, safe and secure, and Nesbit could go home and rest until dark. Jake returned to the balcony and watched the activity until dawn. Once the troops were unloaded, the transport trucks were moved to the National Guard armory north of town, where the men would sleep. He estimated their number at two hundred. They piddled around the courthouse and walked in small groups around the square, looking in shops, waiting for daylight and the hope of some excitement.

Noose would be furious. How dare they call the National Guard without asking him. It was his trial. The mayor had mentioned this, and Jake had explained that it was the mayor's responsibility to keep Clanton safe, not the trial judge's. Ozzie concurred, and Noose was not called.

The sheriff and Moss Junior Tatum arrived and met with the colonel in the gazebo. They walked around the courthouse, inspecting troops and pavilions. Ozzie pointed in various directions and the colonel seemed to agree with whatever he wanted. Moss Junior unlocked the courthouse so the troops would have drinking water and toilet facilities. It was after nine before the first of the vultures stumbled onto the occupation of downtown Clanton. Within an hour they were running everywhere with cameras and microphones gathering important words from a sergeant or a corporal.

'What is your name, sir?'

'Sergeant Drumwright.'

'Where are you from?'

'Booneville.'

'Where's that?'

''Bout a hundred miles from here.'

'Why are you here?'

'Governor called us.'

'Why did he call you?'

'Keep things under control.'

'Are you expecting trouble?'

'No.'

'How long will you be here?'

'Don't know.'

'Will you be here until the trial's over?'

'Don't know.'

'Who knows?'

'The governor, I reckon.'

And so on.

Word of the invasion spread quickly through the quiet Sunday morning, and after church the townfolk streamed to the square to verify for themselves that the army had indeed captured the courthouse. The sentries removed the barricades and allowed the curious to drive around their square and gawk at the real live soldiers with their rifles and jeeps. Jake sat on the balcony, drinking coffee and memorizing the notecards of his jurors.

He called Carla and explained that the National Guard had been deployed, but he was still safe. In fact, he had never felt so safe. As he talked to her, he explained, there were hundreds of heavily armed army militiamen across Washington Street just waiting to protect him. Yes, he still had his bodyguard. Yes, the house was still standing. He doubted if the death of Bud Twitty had been reported yet, so he did not tell her. Maybe she would not hear of it. They were going fishing on her father's boat, and Hanna wanted her daddy to go. He said goodbye, and missed the two women in his life more than ever.

Ellen Roark unlocked the rear door of the office and placed a small grocery sack on the table in the kitchen. She pulled a file out of her briefcase and began looking for her boss. He was on the balcony, staring at notecards and watching the courthouse. 'Evenin', Row Ark.'

'Good evening, boss.' She handed him a brief an inch thick. 'It's the research you requested on the admissibility of the rape. It's a tough issue, and it got involved. I apologize for the size of it.'

It was as neat as her other briefs, complete with a table of contents, bibliography, and numbered pages. He flipped through it. 'Damn, Row Ark, I didn't ask for a textbook.'

'I know you're intimidated by scholarly work,

so I made a conscious effort to use words with fewer than three syllables.'

'My, aren't we frisky today. Could you summarize this in a dissertation of, say, thirty pages or so?'

'Look, it's a thorough study of the law by a gifted law student with a remarkable ability to think and write clearly. It's a work of genius, and it's yours, and it's absolutely free. So quit bitching.'

'Yes, ma'am. Does your head hurt?'

'Yes. It's been aching since I woke up this morning. I've typed on that brief for ten hours, and I need a drink. Do you have a blender?'

'A what?'

'Blender. It's a new invention we have up North. They're kitchen appliances.'

'There's one in the shelves next to the microwave.'

She disappeared. It was almost dark, and the traffic had thinned around the square as the Sunday drivers had grown bored with the sight of soldiers guarding their courthouse. After twelve hours of suffocating heat and foglike humidity in downtown Clanton, the troops were weary and homesick. They sat under trees and on folding canvas chairs, and cursed the governor. As it grew darker, they strung wires from inside the courthouse and hung floodlights around the pavilions. By the post office a carload of blacks arrived with lawn chairs and candles to start the nightly vigil. They began pacing the sidewalk along Jackson

Street under the suddenly aroused stares of two hundred heavily armed guardsmen. The lead walker was Miss Rosia Alfie Gatewood, a two-hundred-pound widow who had raised eleven children and sent nine to college. She was the first black known to have sipped cold water from the public fountain on the square and live to tell about it. She glared at the soldiers. They did not speak.

Ellen returned with two Boston College beer mugs filled with a pale green liquid. She sat them on the table and pulled up a chair.

'What's that?'

'Drink it. It'll help you relax.'

'I'll drink it. But I'd like to know what it is.'

'Margaritas.'

Jake studied the top of his mug. 'Where's the salt?'

'I don't like salt on mine.'

'Well, I don't either then. Why margaritas?'

'Why not?'

Jake closed his eyes and took a long drink. And then another. 'Row Ark, you are a talented woman.'

'Gofer.'

He took another long drink. 'I haven't had a margarita in eight years.'

'I'm very sorry.' Her twenty-ounce mug was half empty.

'What kind of rum?'

'I would call you a dumbass if you weren't my boss.'

'Thank you.'

'It's not rum. It's tequila, with lime juice and Cointreau. I thought every law student knew that.'

'How can you ever forgive me? I'm sure I knew it when I was a law student.'

She gazed around the square.

'This is incredible! It looks like a war zone.'

Jake drained his glass and licked his lips. Under the pavilions they played cards and laughed. Others sought refuge from the mosquitoes in the courthouse. The candles turned the corner and made a pass down Washington Street.

'Yes,' Jake said with a smile. 'It's beautiful, isn't it? Think of our fair and impartial jurors as they arrive in the morning and are confronted with that. I'll renew my motion for a change of venue. It'll be denied. I'll ask for a mistrial, and Noose will say no. And then I'll make sure the court reporter records the fact that this trial is being conducted in the middle of a three-ring circus.'

'Why are they here?'

'The sheriff and the mayor called the governor, and convinced him the National Guard was needed to preserve peace in Ford County. They told him our hospital is not large enough for this trial.'

'Where are they from?'

'Booneville and Columbus. I counted two hundred and twenty around lunch.'

'They've been here all day?'

'They woke me at five this morning. I've followed their movements all day. They were

pinned down a couple of times, but reinforce- ⟩
ments arrived. A few minutes ago they met the
enemy when Miss Gatewood and her friends
arrived with their candles. She stared them down,
so now they're playing cards.'

Ellen finished her drink and left for more. Jake
picked up the stack of notecards for the hundredth
time and flashed them on the table. Name, age,
occupation, family, race, education – he had read
and repeated the information since early morning.
Round Two arrived with haste, and she took the
cards.

'Correen Hagan,' she said, sipping.

He thought a second. 'Age, about fifty-five.
Secretary for an insurance agent. Divorced, two
grown children. Education, probably high
school, no more. Native of Florida, for what
that's worth.'

'Rating?'

'I think I gave her a six.'

'Very good. Millard Sills.'

'Owns a pecan orchard near Mays. About
seventy years old. His nephew was shot in the
head by two blacks during a robbery in Little Rock
several years ago. Hates blacks. He will not be on
the jury.'

'Rating?'

'Zero, I believe.'

'Clay Bailey.'

'Age, about thirty. Six kids. Devout Pentecostal.
Works at the furniture plant west of town.'

'You've given him a ten.'

'Yeah. I'm sure he's read that part in the Bible about an eye for an eye, etc. Plus, out of six kids, I'd think at least two would be daughters.'

'Do you have all of them memorized?'

He nodded and took a drink. 'I feel like I've known them for years.'

'How many will you recognize?'

'Very few. But I'll know more about them than Buckley.'

'I'm impressed.'

'What! What did you say! I have impressed you with my intellect!'

'Among other things.'

'I feel so honored. I've impressed a genius in criminal law. The daughter of Sheldon Roark, whoever he is. A real live *summa cum laude*. Wait'll I tell Harry Rex.'

'Where is that elephant? I miss him. I think he's cute.'

'Go call him. Ask him to join us for a patio party as we watch the troops prepare for the Third Battle of Bull Run.'

She headed for the phone on Jake's desk. 'What about Lucien?'

'No! I'm tired of Lucien.'

Harry Rex brought a fifth of tequila he found somewhere deep in his liquor cabinet. He and the law clerk argued violently over the proper ingredients of a good margarita. Jake voted with his clerk.

They sat on the balcony, calling names from

index cards, drinking the tangy concoction, yelling at the soldiers, and singing Jimmy Buffet songs. At midnight, Nesbit loaded Ellen in his patrol car and took her to Lucien's. Harry Rex walked home. Jake slept on the couch.

Chapter 33

Monday, July 22. Not long after the last margarita Jake bolted from the couch and stared at the clock on his desk. He had slept for three hours. A swarm of wild butterflies fought violently in his stomach. A nervous pain shot through his groin. He had no time for a hangover.

Nesbit slept like an infant behind the wheel. Jake roused him and jumped in the back seat. He waved at the sentries, who watched curiously from across the street. Nesbit drove two blocks to Adams, released his passenger, and waited in the driveway as instructed. He showered and shaved quickly. He chose a charcoal worsted wool suit, a white pinpoint button-down, and a very neutral, noncontroversial, expressionless burgundy silk tie with a few narrow navy stripes for good measure. The pleated pants hung perfectly from his trim waist. He looked great, much more stylish than the enemy.

Nesbit was asleep again when Jake released the dog and jumped in the back seat.

'Everything okay in there?' Nesbit asked, wiping the saliva from his chin.

'I didn't find any dynamite, if that's what you mean.'

Nesbit laughed at this, with the same irritating, laughing response he made to almost everything. They circled the square and Jake got out in front of his office. Thirty minutes after he left, he turned on the front lights and made the coffee.

He took four aspirin and drank a quart of grapefruit juice. His eyes burned and his head ached from abuse and fatigue, and the tiring part had not yet begun. On the conference table he spread out his file on Carl Lee Hailey. It had been organized and indexed by his law clerk, but he wanted to break it down and put it back together. If a document or case can't be found in thirty seconds, it's no good. He smiled at her talent for organization. She had files and sub-files on everything, all ten seconds away at a fingertip. In a one-inch, three-ring notebook she had a summary of Dr Bass's qualifications and the outline of his testimony. She had made notes on anticipated objections from Buckley, and provided case authority to fight his objections. Jake took great pride in his trial preparation, but it was humbling to learn from a third-year law student.

He repacked the file in his trial briefcase, the heavy black leather one with his initials in gold on the side. Nature called, and he sat on the toilet flipping through the index cards. He knew them all. He was ready.

A few minutes after five, Harry Rex knocked on the door. It was dark and he looked like a burglar.

'Whatta you doing up so early?' Jake asked.

'I couldn't sleep. I'm kinda nervous.' He thrust forward a loaded paper sack with grease spots. 'Dell sent these over. They're fresh and hot. Sausage biscuits, bacon and cheese biscuits, chicken and cheese biscuits, you name it. She's worried about you.'

'Thanks, Harry Rex, but I'm not hungry. My system is in revolt.'

'Nervous?'

'As a whore in church.'

'You look pretty haggard.'

'Thanks.'

'Nice suit though.'

'Carla picked it out.'

Harry Rex reached into the sack and produced a handful of biscuits wrapped in foil. He piled them on the conference table and fixed his coffee. Jake sat across from him and flipped through Ellen's brief on M'Naghten.

'She write that?' Harry Rex asked with both cheeks full and his jaws grinding rapidly.

'Yeah, it's a seventy-five-page summary of the insanity defense in Mississippi. It took her three days.'

'She seems very bright.'

'She's got the brains, and she writes fluidly. The intellect is there, but she has trouble applying what she knows to the real world.'

'Whatta you know about her?' Crumbs fell from his mouth and bounced on the table. He brushed them onto the floor with a sleeve.

'She's solid. Number two in her class at Ole Miss. I called Nelson Battles, Assistant Dean of the Law School, and she checked out fine. She has a good chance of finishing number one.'

'I finished ninety-third outta ninety-eight. I would've finished ninety-second but they caught me cheating on an exam. I started to protest, but I figured ninety-third was just as good. Hell, I figured, who cares in Clanton. These people were just glad I came back here to practice when I graduated instead of going to Wall Street or some place like that.'

Jake smiled at the story he had heard a hundred times.

Harry Rex unwrapped a chicken and cheese biscuit. 'You look nervous, buddy.'

'I'm okay. The first day is always the hardest. The preparation has been done. I'm ready. It's just a matter of waiting now.'

'What time does Row Ark make her entrance?'

'I don't know.'

'Lord, I wonder what she'll wear.'

'Or not wear. I just hope she's decent. You know what a prude Noose is.'

'You're not gonna let her sit at counsel table are you?'

'I don't think so. She'll stay in the background, sort of like you. She might offend some of the women jurors.'

'Yeah, keep her there, but outta sight.'

Harry Rex wiped his mouth with a huge paw. 'You sleeping with her?'

'No! I'm not crazy, Harry Rex.'

'You're crazy if you don't. That woman could be had.'

'Then have her. I've got enough on my mind.'

'She thinks I'm cute, don't she?'

'She says she does.'

'I think I'll give it a shot,' he said with a straight face, then he smiled, then he burst into laughter with crumbs spraying the bookshelves.

The phone rang. Jake shook his head, and Harry Rex picked up the receiver. 'He's not here, but I'll be glad to give him the message.' He winked at Jake. 'Yes sir, yes sir, uh huh, yes sir. It's a terrible thing, ain't it. Can you believe a man would do it? Yes sir, yes sir, I agree one hundred percent. Yes sir, and what's your name, sir? Sir?' Harry Rex smiled at the receiver and laid it down.

'What'd he want?'

'Said you was a shame to the white race for being that nigger's lawyer, and that he didn't see how any lawyer could represent a nigger such as Hailey. And that he hoped the Klan got ahold of you, and if they didn't he hoped the bar association looked into it and took away your license for helping niggers. Said he knew you were no 'count because you were trained by Lucien Wilbanks who lives with a nigger woman.'

'And you agreed with him!'

'Why not? He was really sincere, not hateful, and he feels better now that it's off his chest.'

The phone rang again. Harry Rex snatched the receiver. 'Jake Brigance, Attorney, Counselor, Consultant, Adviser, and Guru at Law.'

Jake left for the restroom. 'Jake, it's a reporter!' Harry Rex yelled.

'I'm on the potty.'

'He's got the runs!' Harry Rex told the reporter.

At six – seven in Wilmington – Jake called Carla. She was awake, reading the paper, drinking coffee. He told her about Bud Twitty, and Mickey Mouse, and the promise of more violence. No, he wasn't afraid of that. It did not bother him. He was afraid of the jury, of the twelve who would be chosen, and their reaction to him and his client. His only fear, at the moment, was of what the jury might do to his client. Everything else was irrelevant. For the first time, she did not mention coming home. He promised to call that night.

When he hung up, he heard a commotion downstairs. Ellen had arrived, and Harry Rex was talking loudly. She's wearing a see-through blouse with a miniskirt, thought Jake as he walked downstairs. She was not. Harry Rex was congratulating her on dressing like a Southern woman with all the accessories. She was wearing a gray glen plaid suit with a V-necked jacket and short slim skirt. The silk blouse was black, and apparently the necessary garment was underneath. Her hair was pulled back and braided in some fashion. Incredibly, traces of mascara, eyeliner, and lipstick were visible. In the words of Harry Rex, she looked as much like a lawyer as a woman could look.

'Thanks, Harry Rex,' she said. 'I wish I had your taste in clothes.'

'You look nice, Row Ark,' Jake said.

'So do you,' she said. She looked at Harry Rex, but said nothing.

'Please forgive us, Row Ark,' Harry Rex said. 'We're impressed because we had no idea you owned so many types of garments. We apologize for admiring you and we know how much this infuriates your little liberated heart. Yes, we're sexist pigs, but you chose to come to the South. And in the South we, as a rule, drool over well-dressed attractive females, liberated or not.'

'What's in the sack?' she said.

'Breakfast.'

She tore it open and unwrapped a sausage and biscuit. 'No bagels?' she asked.

'What's that?' asked Harry Rex.

'Forget it.'

Jake rubbed his hands together and tried to sound enthusiastic. 'Well, now that we've gathered here three hours before trial, what would y'all like to do?'

'Let's make some margaritas,' said Harry Rex.

'No!' said Jake.

'It'll take the edge off.'

'Not me,' said Ellen. 'This is business.'

Harry Rex unwrapped a biscuit, the last of the sack. 'What happens first today?'

'After the sun comes up, we start the trial. At

nine, Noose will say a few words to the jurors and we start the selection process.'

'How long will it take?' asked Ellen.

'Two or three days. In Mississippi, we have the right to interrogate each juror individually in chambers. That takes time.'

'Where do I sit and what do I do?'

'She certainly sounds experienced,' Harry Rex said to Jake. 'Does she know where the courthouse is?'

'You do not sit at counsel table,' said Jake. 'Just me and Carl Lee.'

She wiped her mouth. 'I see. Just you and the defendant sitting alone, surrounded by the forces of evil, facing death alone.'

'Something like that.'

'My father uses that tactic occasionally.'

'I'm glad you approve. You'll sit behind me, next to the railing. I'll ask Noose to allow you into chambers for the private discussions.'

'What about me?' asked Harry Rex.

'Noose doesn't like you, Harry Rex. He never has. He'd have a stroke if I asked if you could go in chambers. It'd be best if you pretended we'd never met.'

'Thanks.'

'But we do appreciate your assistance,' Ellen said.

'Up yours, Ellie Mae.'

'And you can still drink with us,' she said.

'And furnish the tequila.'

'There will be no more alcohol in this office,' Jake said.

'Until the noon recess,' said Harry Rex.

'I want you to stand behind the clerk's table, just loiter about like you always do, and take notes on the jury. Try to match them with the note-cards. There'll probably be a hundred and twenty.'

'Whatever you say.'

Daybreak brought the army out in force. The barricades were reinstalled, and on each corner of the square soldiers clustered around the orange and white barrels blocking the street. They were poised and anxious, watching every car intently, waiting for the enemy to attack, wanting some excitement. Things stirred a little when a few of the vultures in their compact wagons and minivans with fancy logos on the doors appeared at seven-thirty. The troops surrounded the vehicles and informed everyone there would be no parking around the courthouse during the trial. The vultures disappeared down the side streets, then moments later reappeared on foot with their bulky cameras and equipment. Some set up camp on the front steps of the courthouse, others by the back door, and another group in the rotunda outside the main door of the courtroom on the second floor.

Murphy, the janitor and only real eyewitness to the killings of Cobb and Willard, informed the press, as best he could, that the courtroom would be opened at eight, and not a minute before. A line formed and soon circled the rotunda.

The church buses parked somewhere off the square, and the marchers were led slowly down

Jackson Street by the ministers. They carried FREE CARL LEE signs and sang 'We Shall Overcome' in a perfect chorus. As they neared the square, the soldiers heard them and the radios began squawking. Ozzie and the colonel conferred quickly, and the soldiers relaxed. The marchers were led by Ozzie to a section of the front lawn where they milled about and waited under the watchful eyes of the Mississippi National Guard.

At eight, a metal detector was moved to the front doors of the courtroom, and a trio of heavily armed deputies began slowly searching and admitting the crowd of spectators that now filled the rotunda and trailed off into the halls. Inside the courtroom, Prather directed traffic, seating people on the long pews on one side of the aisle while reserving the other side for the jurors. The front pew was reserved for the family, and the second row was filled with courtroom artists who immediately began sketching the bench and the bar and the portraits of Confederate heroes.

The Klan felt obligated to make its presence known on opening day, especially to the prospective jurors as they arrived. Two dozen Kluxers in full parade dress walked quietly onto Washington Street. They were immediately stopped and surrounded by soldiers. The potbellied colonel swaggered across the street and for the first time in his life came face to face with a white-robed and white-hooded Ku Klux Klansman, who happened to be a foot taller. He then noticed the cameras, which had gravitated to this confrontation, and the bully in him vanished. His usual bark and growl was instantly replaced by a high-pitched, nervous, trembling stutter that was incomprehensible even to himself.

Ozzie arrived and saved him. 'Good mornin', fellas,' he said coolly as he stepped beside the faltering colonel. 'We've got you surrounded, and we've got you outnumbered. We also know we can't keep you from being here.'

'That's right,' said the leader.

'If you'll just follow me and do as I say, we won't have any trouble.'

They followed Ozzie and the colonel to a small area on the front lawn, where it was explained that this was their turf for the trial. Stay there and stay quiet, and the colonel would personally keep the troops off them. They agreed.

As expected, the sight of the white robes aroused the blacks who were some two hundred feet away. They began shouting: 'Free Carl Lee! Free Carl Lee! Free Carl Lee!'

The Klansmen shook their fists and shouted back:

'Fry Carl Lee!'

'Fry Carl Lee!'

'Fry Carl Lee!'

Two rows of troops lined the main sidewalk that divided the lawn and led to the front steps. Another row stood between the sidewalk and the Klansmen, and one between the sidewalk and the blacks.

As the jurors began arriving, they walked briskly through the rows of soldiers. They clutched their summonses and listened in disbelief as the two groups screamed at each other.

The Honorable Rufus Buckley arrived in Clanton and politely informed the guardsmen of who he was and what that meant, and he was allowed to park in his spot marked RESERVED FOR D.A. next to the courthouse. The reporters went wild. This must be important, someone had broken through the barricade. Buckley sat in his well-used Cadillac for a moment to allow the reporters to catch him. They surrounded him as he slammed the door. He smiled and smiled and made his way ever so slowly to the front door of the courthouse. The rapid fire of questions proved irresistible, and Buckley violated the gag order at least eight times, each time smiling and explaining that he could not answer the question he had just answered. Musgrove trailed behind carrying the great man's briefcase.

Jake paced nervously in his office. The door was locked. Ellen was downstairs working on another brief. Harry Rex was at the Coffee Shop eating another breakfast and gossiping. The notecards were scattered on his desk, and he was tired of them. He flipped through a brief, then walked to the French doors. The shouting echoed through the open windows. He returned to the desk and studied the outline of his opening comments to the prospective jurors. The first impression was critical.

He lay on the couch, closed his eyes, and

thought of a thousand things he'd rather be doing. For the most part, he enjoyed his work. But there were moments, frightening moments like this one, when he wished he'd become an insurance agent or a stockbroker. Or maybe even a tax lawyer. Surely those guys didn't regularly suffer from nausea and diarrhea at critical moments in their careers.

Lucien had taught him that fear was good; fear was an ally; that every lawyer was afraid when he stood before a new jury and presented his case. It was okay to be afraid – just don't show it. Jurors would not follow the lawyer with the quickest tongue or prettiest words. They would not follow the sharpest dresser. They would not follow a clown or court jester. They would not follow the lawyer who preached the loudest or fought the hardest. Lucien had convinced him that jurors followed the lawyer who told the truth, regardless of his looks, words, or superficial abilities. A lawyer had to be himself in the courtroom, and if he was afraid, so be it. The jurors were afraid too.

Make friends with fear, Lucien always said, because it will not go away, and it will destroy you if left uncontrolled.

The fear hit deep in his bowels, and he walked carefully downstairs to the rest room.

'How are you, boss?' Ellen asked when he checked on her.

'Ready, I guess. We'll leave in a minute.'

'There are some reporters waiting outside. I

told them you had withdrawn from the case and left town.'

'At this moment, I wish I had.'

'Have you heard of Wendall Solomon?'

'Not right off hand.'

'He's with the Southern Prisoner Defense Fund. I worked under him last summer. He's tried over a hundred capital cases all over the South. He gets so nervous before a trial he can neither eat nor sleep. His doctor gives him sedatives, but he's still so jumpy no one speaks to him on opening day. And that's after a hundred of these trials.'

'How does your father handle it?'

'He has a couple of martinis with a Valium. Then he lies on his desk with the door locked and the lights off until it's time for court. His nerves are ragged and he's ill-tempered. Of course, a lot of that is natural.'

'So you know the feeling?'

'I know it well.'

'Do I look nervous?'

'You look tired. But you'll do.'

Jake checked his watch. 'Let's go.'

The reporters on the sidewalk pounced on their prey. 'No comment' he insisted as he moved slowly across the street toward the courthouse. The barrage continued.

'Is it true you plan to ask for a mistrial?'

'I can't do that until the trial starts.'

'Is it true the Klan has threatened you?'

'No comment.'

'Is it true you sent your family out of town until after the trial?'

Jake hesitated and glanced at the reporter. 'No comment.'

'What do you think of the National Guard?'

'I'm proud of them.'

'Can your client get a fair trial in Ford County?'

Jake shook his head, then added, 'No comment.'

A deputy stood guard a few feet from where the bodies had come to rest. He pointed at Ellen. 'Who's she, Jake?'

'She's harmless. She's with me.'

They ran up the rear stairs. Carl Lee sat alone at the defense table, his back to the packed courtroom. Jean Gillespie was busy checking in jurors while deputies roamed the aisles looking for anything suspicious. Jake greeted his client warmly, taking special care to shake his hand, smile broadly at him, and put his hand on his shoulder. Ellen unpacked the briefcases and neatly arranged the files on the table.

Jake whispered to his client and looked around the courtroom. All eyes were on him. The Hailey clan sat handsomely in the front row. Jake smiled at them and nodded at Lester. Tonya and the boys were decked out in their Sunday clothes, and they sat between Lester and Gwen like perfect little statues. The jurors sat across the aisle, and they were carefully studying Hailey's lawyer. Jake thought this would be a good time for the jurors to see the family, so he walked through the swinging gate in the railing and went to speak to the Haileys. He patted Gwen on the shoulder, shook hands with Lester, pinched each of the boys, and, finally, hugged Tonya, the little Hailey girl, the one who had been raped by the two rednecks who got what they deserved. The jurors watched every move of this production, and paid special attention to the little girl.

'Noose wants us in chambers,' Musgrove whispered to Jake as he returned to the defense table.

Ichabod, Buckley, and the court reporter were chatting when Jake and Ellen entered chambers. Jake introduced his clerk to His Honor and Buckley and Musgrove, and to Norma Gallo, the court reporter. He explained that Ellen Roark was a third-year law student at Ole Miss who was clerking in his office, and requested that she be allowed to sit near counsel table and participate in the proceedings in chambers. Buckley had no objections. It was common practice, Noose explained, and he welcomed her.

'Preliminary matters, gentlemen?' Noose asked.

'None,' said the D.A.

'Several,' said Jake as he opened a file. 'I want this on the record.'

Norma Gallo started writing.

'First of all, I want to renew my motion for a change of venue—'

'We object,' interrupted Buckley.

'Shut up, Governor!' Jake yelled. 'I'm not through, and don't interrupt me again!'

Buckley and the others were startled by this loss of composure. It's all those margaritas, thought Ellen.

'I apologize, Mr Brigance,' Buckley said calmly. 'Please don't refer to me as governor.'

'Let me say something at this point,' Noose started. 'This trial will be a long and arduous ordeal. I can appreciate the pressure you're both under. I've been in your shoes many times myself, and I know what you're going through. You're both excellent lawyers, and I'm thankful that I have two fine lawyers for a trial of this magnitude. I can also detect a certain amount of ill will between you. That's certainly not uncommon, and I will not ask you to shake hands and be good friends. But I will insist that when you're in my courtroom or in these chambers that you refrain from interrupting each other, and that the shouting be held to a bare minimum. You will refer to each other as Mr Brigance, and Mr Buckley, and Mr Musgrove. Now do each of you understand what I'm saying?'

'Yes, sir.'

'Yes, sir.'

'Good. Then continue, Mr Brigance.'

'Thank you, Your Honor, I appreciate that. As I was saying, the defendant renews his motion for a change of venue. I want the record to reflect that as we sit here now in chambers, at nine-fifteen, July twenty-second, as we are about to select a jury, the Ford County Courthouse is surrounded by the Mississippi National Guard. On the front lawn a group of Ku Klux Klansmen, in white robes, is at this very moment yelling at a group of black demonstrators, who are, of course, yelling back. The two groups are separated by heavily armed National Guardsmen. As the jurors arrived for court this morning, they witnessed this circus on the courthouse lawn. It will be impossible to select a fair and impartial jury.'

Buckley watched with a cocky grin on his huge face, and when Jake finished he said, 'May I respond, Your Honor?'

'No,' Noose said bluntly. 'Motion is overruled. What else do you have?'

'The defense moves to strike this entire panel.'

'On what grounds?'

'On the grounds that there has been an overt effort by the Klan to intimidate this panel. We know of at least twenty cross burnings.'

'I intend to excuse those twenty, assuming they all showed up,' said Noose.

'Fine,' Jake replied sarcastically. 'What about the threats we don't know about? What about the jurors who've heard of the cross burnings?'

Noose wiped his eyes and said nothing. Buckley had a speech but didn't want to interrupt.

'I've got a list here,' Jake said, reaching into a file, 'of the twenty jurors who received visits. I've also got copies of the police reports, and an affidavit from Sheriff Walls in which he details the acts of intimidation. I am submitting these to the court in support of my motion to strike this panel. I want this made a part of the record so the Supreme Court can see it in black and white.'

'Expecting an appeal, Mr Brigance?' asked Mr Buckley.

Ellen had just met Rufus Buckley, and now, seconds later, she understood exactly why Jake and Harry Rex hated him.

'No, Governor, I'm not expecting an appeal. I'm trying to insure that my man gets a fair trial from a fair jury. You should understand that.'

'I'm not going to strike this panel. That would cost us a week,' Noose said.

'What's time when a man's life is at stake? We're talking about justice. The right to a fair trial, remember, a most basic constitutional right. It's a travesty not to strike this panel when you know for a fact that some of these people have been intimidated by a bunch of goons in white robes who want to see my client hanged.'

'Your motion is overruled,' Noose said flatly. 'What else do you have?'

'Nothing, really. I request that when you do excuse the twenty, you so do in such a way that the other jurors don't know the reason.'

'I can handle that, Mr Brigance.'

Mr Pate was sent to find Jean Gillespie. Noose handed her a list of the twenty names. She returned to the courtroom and read the list. They were not needed for jury duty, and were free to go. She returned to chambers.

'How many jurors do we have?' Noose asked her.

'Ninety-four.'

'That's enough. I'm sure we can find twelve who are fit to serve.'

'You couldn't find two,' Jake mumbled to Ellen,

loud enough for Noose to hear and Norma Gallo to record. His Honor excused them and they took their places in the courtroom.

Ninety-four names were written on small strips of paper that were placed in a short wooden cylinder. Jean Gillespie spun the cylinder, stopped it, and picked a name at random. She handed it to Noose, who sat above her and everyone else on his throne, or bench, as it was called. The courtroom watched in dead silence as he squinted down that nose and looked at the first name.

'Carlene Malone, juror number one,' he shrieked in his loudest voice. The front row had been cleared, and Mrs Malone took her seat next to the aisle. Each pew would seat ten, and there were ten pews, all to be filled with jurors. The ten pews on the other side of the aisle were packed with family, friends, spectators, but mainly reporters who scribbled down the name of Carlene Malone. Jake wrote her name too. She was white, fat, divorced, lower income. She was a two on the Brigance scale. Zero for one, he thought.

Jean spun again.

'Marcia Dickens, juror number two,' yelled Noose. White, fat, over sixty with a rather unforgiving look. Zero for two.

'Jo Beth Mills, number three.'

Jake sank a little in his seat. She was white, about fifty, and worked for minimum wage at a shirt factory in Karaway. Thanks to affirmative action, she had a black boss who was ignorant and abusive. She had a zero by her name on the Brigance notecard. Zero for three.

Jake stared desperately at Jean as she spun again. 'Reba Betts, number four.'

He sunk lower and began pinching his forehead. Zero for four. 'This is incredible,' he mumbled in the direction of Ellen. Harry Rex shook his head.

'Gerald Ault, number five.'

Jake smiled as his number-one juror took a seat next to Reba Betts. Buckley placed a nasty black mark by his name.

'Alex Summers, number six.'

Carl Lee managed a weak smile as the first black emerged from the rear and took a seat next to Gerald Ault. Buckley smiled too as he neatly circled the name of the first black.

The next four were white women, none of whom rated above three on the scale. Jake was worried as the first pew filled. By law he had twelve peremptory challenges, free strikes with no reason required. The luck of the draw would force him to use at least half of his peremptories on the first pew.

'Walter Godsey, number eleven,' announced Noose, his voice declining steadily in volume. Godsey was a middle-aged sharecropper with no compassion and no potential.

When Noose finished the second row, it contained seven white women, two black men, and Godsey. Jake sensed a disaster. Relief didn't come until the fourth row when Jean hit a hot streak and pulled the names of seven men, four of whom were black.

It took almost an hour to seat the entire panel. Noose recessed for fifteen minutes to allow Jean time to type a numerical list of names. Jake and Ellen used the break to review their notes and place the names with the faces. Harry Rex had sat at the counter behind the red docket books and feverishly taken notes while Noose called the names. He huddled with Jake and agreed things were not going well.

At eleven, Noose reassumed the bench, and the courtroom was silenced. Someone suggested he should use the mike, and he placed it within inches of his nose. He spoke loudly, and his fragile, obnoxious voice rattled violently around the courtroom as he asked a lengthy series of statutorily required questions. He introduced Carl Lee and asked if any juror was kin to him or knew him. They all knew of him, and Noose assumed that, but only two of the panel admitted knowing him prior to May. Noose introduced the lawyers, then explained briefly the nature of the charges. Not a single juror confessed to being ignorant of the Hailey case.

Noose rambled on and on, and mercifully finished at twelve-thirty. He recessed until two.

Dell delivered hot sandwiches and iced tea to the conference room. Jake hugged and thanked her, and told her to send him the bill. He ignored his food, and laid the notecards on the table in the order the jurors had been seated. Harry Rex attacked a roast beef and cheddar sandwich. 'We got a terrible draw,' he kept repeating with both cheeks stretched to the limit. 'We got a terrible draw.'

When the ninety-fourth card was in place, Jake stood back and studied them. Ellen stood beside him and nibbled on a french fry. She studied the cards.

'We got a terrible draw,' Harry Rex said, washing it all down with a pint of tea.

'Would you shut up,' Jake snapped.

'Of the first fifty, we have eight black men, three black women, and thirty white women. That leaves nine white men, and most are unattractive. Looks like a white female jury,' Ellen said.

'White females, white females,' Harry Rex said. 'The worst possible jurors in the world. White females!'

Ellen stared at him. 'I think fat white men are the worst jurors.'

'Don't get me wrong, Row Ark, I love white females. I've married four of them, remember. I just hate white female jurors.'

'I wouldn't vote to convict him.'

'Row Ark, you're an ACLU communist. You wouldn't vote to convict anybody of anything. In your little demented mind you think child pornographers and PLO terrorists are really swell people who've been abused by the system and should be given a break.'

'And in your rational, civilized, and compassionate mind, what do you think we should do with them?'

'Hang them by their toes, castrate them, and let them bleed to death, without a trial.'

'And the way you understand the law, that would be constitutional?'

'Maybe not, but it'd stop a lot of child pornography and terrorism. Jake, are you gonna eat this sandwich?'

'No.'

Harry Rex unwrapped a ham and cheese. 'Stay away from number one, Carlene Malone. She's one of those Malones from Lake Village. White trash and mean as hell.'

'I'd like to stay away from this entire panel,' Jake said, still staring at the table.

'We got a terrible draw.'

'Whatta you think, Row Ark?' Jake asked.

Harry Rex swallowed quickly. 'I think we oughtta plead him guilty and get the hell outta there. Run like a scalded dog.'

Ellen stared at the cards. 'It could be worse.'

Harry Rex forced a loud laugh. 'Worse! The only way it could be worse would be if the first thirty were sitting there wearing white robes with pointed hats and little masks.'

'Harry Rex, would you shut up,' Jake said.

'Just trying to help. Do you want your french fries?'

'No. Why don't you put all of them in your mouth and chew on them for a long time?'

'I think you're wrong about some of these women,' Ellen said. 'I'm inclined to agree with Lucien. Women, as a very general rule, will have

550

more sympathy. We're the ones who get raped, remember?'

'I have no response to that,' Harry Rex said.

'Thanks,' replied Jake. 'Which one of these girls is your former client who'll supposedly do anything for you if you'll simply wink at her?'

Ellen snickered. 'Must be number twenty-nine. She's five feet tall and weighs four hundred pounds.'

Harry Rex wiped his mouth with a sheet of paper. 'Very funny. Number seventy-four. She's too far back. Forget her.'

Noose rapped his gavel at two and the courtroom came to order.

'The State may examine the panel,' he said.

The magnificent district attorney rose slowly and walked importantly to the bar, where he stood and gazed pensively at the spectators and jurors. He realized the artists were sketching him, and he seemed to pose for just a moment. He smiled sincerely at the jurors, then introduced himself. He explained that he was the people's lawyer; his client, the State of Mississippi. He had served as their prosecutor for nine years now, and it was an honor for which he would always be grateful to the fine folks of Ford County. He pointed at them and told them that they, the very ones sitting there, were the folks who had elected him to represent them. He thanked them, and hoped he did not let them down.

Yes, he was nervous and frightened. He had

prosecuted thousands of criminals, but he was always scared with each trial. Yes! He was scared, and not ashamed to admit it. Scared because of the awesome responsibility the people had bestowed upon him as the man responsible for sending criminals to jail and protecting the people. Scared because he might fail to adequately represent his client, the people of this great state.

Jake had heard all this crap many times before. He had it memorized. Buckley the good guy, the state's lawyer, united with the people to seek justice, to save society. He was a smooth, gifted orator who one moment could chat softly with a jury, much like a grandfather giving advice to his grandchildren. The next moment he would launch into a tirade and deliver a sermon that any black preacher would envy. A split second later, in a fluid burst of eloquence, he could convince a jury that the stability of our society, yes, even the future of the human race, depended upon a guilty verdict. He was at his best in big trials, and this was his biggest. He spoke without notes, and held the courtroom captivated as he portrayed himself as the underdog, the friend and partner of the jury, who, together with him, would find the truth, and punish this man for his monstrous deed.

After ten minutes, Jake had enough. He stood with a frustrated look. 'Your Honor, I object to this. Mr Buckley is not selecting a jury. I'm not sure what he's doing, but he's not interrogating the panel.'

'Sustained!' Noose yelled into the mike. 'If you

don't have any questions for the panel, Mr Buckley, then please sit down.'

'I apologize, Your Honor,' Buckley said awkwardly, pretending to be hurt. Jake had drawn first blood.

Buckley picked up a legal pad and launched into a list of a thousand questions. He asked if anyone on the panel had ever served on a jury before. Several hands went up. Civil or criminal? Did you vote to acquit or convict? How long ago? Was the defendant black or white? Victim, black or white? Had anyone been the victim of a violent crime? Two hands. When? Where? Was the assailant caught? Convicted? Black or white? Jake, Harry Rex, and Ellen took pages of notes. Any member of your family been the victim of a violent crime? Several more hands. When? Where? What happened to the criminal? Any member of your family ever been charged with a crime? Indicted? Put on trial? Convicted? Any friends or family members employed in law enforcement? Who? Where?

For three nonstop hours Buckley probed and picked like a surgeon. He was masterful. The preparation was obvious. He asked questions that Jake had not considered. And he asked virtually every question Jake had written in his outline. He delicately pried details of personal feelings and opinions. And when the time was right, he would say something funny so everyone could laugh and relieve the tension. He held the courtroom in his palm, and when Noose stopped him at five o'clock he was in full stride. He would finish in the morning.

His Honor adjourned until nine the next morning. Jake talked to his client for a few moments while the crowd moved toward the rear. Ozzie stood nearby with the handcuffs. When Jake finished, Carl Lee knelt before his family on the front row and hugged them all. He would see them tomorrow, he said. Ozzie led him into the holding room and down the stairs, where a swarm of deputies waited to take him to jail.

Chapter 34

For Day Two the sun rose quickly in the east and in seconds burned the dew off the thick green Bermuda around the Ford County Courthouse. A sticky, invisible fog smoldered from the grass and clung to the heavy boots and bulky pants of the soldiers. The sun baked them as they nonchalantly paced the sidewalks of downtown Clanton. They loitered under shade trees and the canopies of small shops. By the time breakfast was served under the pavilions, the soldiers had stripped to their pale green undershirts and were drenched in sweat.

The black preachers and their followers went directly to their spot and set up camp. They unfolded lawn chairs under oak trees and placed coolers of ice water on card tables. Blue and white FREE CARL LEE placards were tacked on tomato stakes and stuck in the ground like neat fencerows. Agee had printed some new posters with an enlarged black and white photo of Carl Lee in the center and a red, white, and blue border. They were slick and professional.

The Klansmen went obediently to their section of the front lawn. They brought their own plac-ards – white backgrounds with bold red letters screaming FRY CARL LEE, FRY CARL LEE. They waved them at the blacks across the lawn, and the two groups started shouting. The soldiers formed neat lines along the sidewalk, and stood armed but casual as obscenities and chants flew over their heads. It was 8:00 A.M. of Day Two.

The reporters were giddy with all the news-worthiness. They rushed to the front lawn when the yelling started. Ozzie and the colonel walked around and around the courthouse, pointing here and there and yelling into their radios.

At nine, Ichabod said good morning to the standing-room-only crowd. Buckley stood slowly and with great animation informed His Honor that he had no further questions for the panel.

Lawyer Brigance rose from his seat with rubber knees and turbulence in his stomach. He walked to the railing and gazed into the anxious eyes of ninety-four prospective jurors.

The crowd listened intently to this young, cocky mouthpiece who had once boasted of never having lost a murder case. He appeared relaxed and confi-dent. His voice was loud, yet warm. His words were educated, yet colloquial. He introduced himself again, and his client, then his client's family, saving the little girl for last. He compli-mented the D.A. for such an exhaustive interro-gation yesterday afternoon, and confessed that most of his questions had already been asked. He glanced at his notes. His first question was a bomb-shell.

'Ladies and gentlemen, do any of you believe that the insanity defense should not be used under any circumstances?'

They squirmed a little, but no hands. He caught them off-guard, right off the bat. Insanity! Insanity! The seed had been planted.

'If we prove Carl Lee Hailey was legally insane when he shot Billy Ray Cobb and Pete Willard, is there a person on this panel who cannot find him not guilty?'

The question was hard to follow – intention-ally so. There were no hands. A few wanted to respond, but they were not certain of the appro-priate response.

Jake eyed them carefully, knowing most of them were confused, but also knowing that for this moment every member of the panel was thinking about his client being insane. That's where he would leave them.

'Thank you,' he said with all the charm he had ever mustered in his life. 'I have nothing further, Your Honor.'

Buckley looked confused. He stared at the judge, who was equally bewildered.

'Is that all?' Noose asked incredulously. 'Is that all, Mr Brigance?'

'Yes, sir, Your Honor, the panel looks fine to me,' Jake said with an air of trust, as opposed to Buckley, who had grilled them for three hours.

The panel was anything but acceptable to Jake, but there was no sense repeating the same questions Buckley had asked.

'Very well. Let me see the attorneys in chambers.'

Buckley, Musgrove, Jake, Ellen, and Mr Pate followed Ichabod through the door behind the bench and sat around the desk in chambers. Noose spoke: 'I assume, gentlemen, that you want each juror questioned individually on the death penalty.'

'Yes, sir,' said Jake.

'That's correct, Your Honor,' said Buckley.

'Very well. Mr Bailiff, would you bring in juror number one, Carlene Malone.'

Mr Pate left, walked to the courtroom and yelled for Carlene Malone. Moments later she followed him into chambers. She was terrified. The attorneys smiled but said nothing: Noose's instructions.

'Please have a seat,' Noose offered as he removed his robe. 'This will only take a minute, Mrs Malone. Do you have any strong feelings one way or the other about the death penalty?' asked Noose.

She shook her head nervously and stared at Ichabod. 'Uh, no, sir.'

'You realize that if you're selected for this jury and Mr Hailey is convicted, you will be called upon to sentence him to death?'

'Yes, sir.'

'If the State proves beyond a reasonable doubt that the killings were premeditated, and if you believe Mr Hailey was not legally insane at the time of the killings, could you consider imposing the death penalty?'

'Certainly. I think it should be used all the time. Might stop some of this meanness. I'm all for it.'

Jake continued smiling and nodding politely at juror number one. Buckley smiled too, and winked at Musgrove.

'Thank you, Mrs Malone. You may return to your seat in the courtroom,' Noose said.

'Bring in number two,' Noose ordered Mr Pate. Marcia Dickens, an elderly white woman with a hard frown, was led to chambers. Yes, sir, she said, she was very much in favor of the death penalty. Would have no problems voting for it. Jake sat there and smiled. Buckley winked again. Noose thanked her and called for number three.

Three and four were equally unforgiving, ready to kill if the proof was there. Then number five, Gerald Ault, Jake's secret weapon, was seated in chambers.

'Thank you Mr Ault, this will only take a minute,' Noose repeated. 'First of all, do you have strong feelings for or against the death penalty?'

'Oh, yes, sir.' Ault answered eagerly, his voice and face radiating compassion. 'I'm very much against it. It's cruel and unusual. I'm ashamed I live in a society which permits the legal killing of a human being.'

'I see. Could you, under any circumstances, if you were a juror, vote to impose the death penalty?'

'Oh, no, sir. Under no circumstances. Regardless of the crime. No, sir.'

Buckley cleared his throat and somberly announced, 'Your Honor, the State would challenge Mr Ault for cause and move to excuse him under the authority of State vs. Witherspoon.'

'Motion sustained. Mr Ault, you are excused from jury duty,' Noose said. 'You may leave the courtroom if you wish. If you choose to remain in the courtroom, I ask that you not sit with the other jurors.'

Ault was puzzled and looked helplessly at his friend Jake, who at the moment was staring at the floor with a tight mouth.

'May I ask why?' Gerald asked.

Noose removed his glasses and became the professor. 'Under the law, Mr Ault, the court is required to excuse any potential juror who admits he or she cannot consider, and the key word is consider, the death penalty. You see, whether you like it or not, the death penalty is a legal method of punishment in Mississippi and in most states. Therefore, it is unfair to select jurors who cannot follow the law.'

The curiosity of the crowd was piqued when Gerald Ault emerged from behind the bench, walked through the small gate in the railing, and left the courtroom. The bailiff fetched number six, Alex Summers, and led him to chambers. He returned moments later and took his seat on the first row. He lied about the death penalty. He opposed it as did most blacks, but he told Noose he had no objections to it. No problem. Later during a recess, he quietly met with other black jurors and explained how the questions in chambers should be answered.

The slow process continued until mid-afternoon, when the last juror left chambers. Eleven had been excused due to reservations about capital punishment. Noose recessed at three-thirty and gave the lawyers until four to review their notes.

In the library on the third floor, Jake and his team stared at the jury lists and notecards. It was time to decide. He had dreamed about names written in blue and red and black with numbers beside them. He had watched them in the courtroom for two full days now. He knew them. Ellen wanted women. Harry Rex wanted men.

Noose stared at his master list, with the jurors renumbered to reflect the dismissals for cause, and looked at his lawyers. 'Gentlemen, are you ready? Good. As you know this is a capital case, so each of you have twelve peremptory challenges. Mr Buckley, you are required to submit a list of twelve jurors to the defense. Please start with juror number one and refer to each juror only by number.'

'Yes sir. Your Honor, the State will accept jurors number one, two, three, four, use our first challenge on number five, accept numbers six, seven, eight, nine, use our second challenge on number ten, accept numbers eleven, twelve, thirteen, use our third challenge on number fourteen, and accept number fifteen. That's twelve, I believe.'

Jake and Ellen circled and made notes on their lists. Noose methodically recounted. 'Yes, that's twelve. Mr Brigance.'

Buckley submitted twelve white females. Two blacks and a white male had been stricken.

Jake studied his list and scratched names. 'The defense will strike jurors number one, two, three, accept four, six, and seven, strike eight, nine, eleven, twelve, accept thirteen, strike fifteen. I believe that's eight of our challenges.'

His Honor drew lines and check marks down his list, calculating slowly as he went. 'Both of you have accepted jurors number four, six, seven, and thirteen. Mr Buckley, it's back to you. Give us eight more jurors.'

'The State will accept sixteen, use our fourth challenge on seventeen, accept eighteen, nineteen, twenty, strike twenty-one, accept twenty-two, strike twenty-three, accept twenty-four, strike twenty-five and twenty-six, and accept twenty-seven and twenty-eight. That's twelve with four challenges remaining.'

Jake was flabbergasted. Buckley had again stricken all the blacks and all the men. He was reading Jake's mind.

'Mr Brigance, it's back to you.'

'May we have a moment to confer, Your Honor?'

'Five minutes,' Noose replied.

Jake and his clerk stepped next door to the coffee room, where Harry Rex was waiting. 'Look at this,' Jake said as he laid the list on a table and the three huddled around it. 'We're down to twenty-nine. I've got four challenges left and so does Buckley. He's struck every black and every male. It's an all-white female jury right now. The next two are white females, thirty-one is Clyde Sisco, and thirty-two is Barry Acker.'

'Then four of the next six are black,' Ellen said.

'Yeah, but Buckley won't take it that far. In fact, I'm surprised he's let us get this close to the fourth row.'

'I know you want Acker. What about Sisco?' asked Harry Rex.

'I'm afraid of him. Lucien said he's a crook who could be bought.'

'Great! Let's get him, then go buy him.'

'Very funny. How do you know Buckley hasn't already bought him?'

'I'd take him.'

Jake studied the list, counting and recounting. Ellen wanted to strike both men – Acker and Sisco.

They returned to chambers and sat down. The court reporter was ready. 'Your Honor, we will strike number twenty-two and number twenty-eight, with two challenges remaining.'

'Back to you, Mr Buckley. Twenty-nine and thirty.'

'The State will take them both. That's twelve with four challenges left.'

'Back to you, Mr Brigance.'

'We will strike twenty-nine and thirty.'

'And you're out of challenges, correct?' Noose asked.

'Correct.'

'Very well. Mr Buckley, thirty-one and thirty-two.'

'The State will take them both,' Buckley said

quickly, looking at the names of the blacks coming after Clyde Sisco.

'Good. That's twelve. Let's select two alternates. You will both have two challenges for the alternates. Mr Buckley, thirty-three and thirty-four.'

Juror thirty-three was a black male. Thirty-four was a white female Jake wanted. The next two were black males.

'We'll strike thirty-three, accept thirty-four and thirty-five.'

'The defense will accept both,' Jake said.

Mr Pate brought the courtroom to order as Noose and the lawyers took their places. His Honor called the names of the twelve and they slowly, nervously made their way to the jury box, where they were seated in order by Jean Gillespie. Ten women, two men, all white. The blacks in the courtroom mumbled and eyed each other in disbelief.

'Did you pick that jury?' Carl Lee whispered to Jake.

'I'll explain later,' Jake said.

The two alternates were called and seated next to the jury box.

'What's the black dude for?' Carl Lee whispered, nodding at the alternate.

'I'll explain later,' Jake said.

Noose cleared his throat and looked down at his new jury. 'Ladies and gentlemen, you have been carefully selected to serve as jurors in this case. You have been sworn to fairly try all issues presented before you and to follow the law as I instruct. Now, according to Mississippi law, you will be sequestered until this trial is over. This means you will be housed in a motel and will not be allowed to return home until it's over. I realize this is an extreme hardship, but it's one the law requires. In just a few moments we will recess until in the morning, and you will be given the chance to call home and order your clothes, toiletries, and whatever else you need. Each night you will stay in a motel at an undisclosed location outside of Clanton. Any questions?'

The twelve appeared dazed, bewildered by the thought of not going home for several days. They thought of families, kids, jobs, laundry. Why them? Out of all those people in the courtroom, why them?

With no response, Noose banged his gavel and the courtroom began to empty. Jean Gillespie escorted the first juror to the judge's chambers, where she called home and ordered clothes and a toothbrush.

'Where are we going?' she asked Jean.

'It's confidential,' Jean said.

'It's confidential,' she repeated over the phone to her husband.

By seven, the families had responded with a wild assortment of luggage and boxes. The chosen ones loaded a chartered Greyhound bus outside the rear door. Preceded by two patrol cars and an army jeep and followed by three state troopers, the bus circled the square and left Clanton.

★　★　★

Stump Sisson died Tuesday night at the burn hospital in Memphis. His short, fat body had been neglected over the years and proved itself deficient in resisting the complications bred by the serious burns. His death brought to four the number of fatalities related to the rape of Tonya Hailey. Cobb, Willard, Bud Twitty, and now Sisson.

Immediately, word of his death reached the cabin deep in the woods where the patriots met, ate, and drank each night after the trial. Revenge, they vowed, an eye for an eye and so on. There were new recruits from Ford County – five in all – making a total of eleven local boys. They were eager and hungry, and wanted some action.

The trial had been too quiet so far. It was time for excitement.

Jake paced in front of the couch and delivered his opening statement for the hundredth time. Ellen listened intently. She had listened, interrupted, objected, criticized, and argued for two hours. She was tired now. He had it perfect. The margaritas had calmed him and plated his tongue silver. The words flowed smoothly. He was gifted. Especially after a drink or two.

When he finished they sat on the balcony and watched the candles inch slowly in the darkness around the square. The laughter from the poker games under the pavilions echoed softly through the night. There was no moon.

Ellen left for the final round of drinks. She returned with her same beer mugs filled with ice and margaritas. She sat them on the table and stood behind her boss. She placed her hands on his shoulders and began rubbing the lower part of his neck with her thumbs. He relaxed and moved his head from side to side. She massaged his shoulders and upper back, and pressed her body against his.

'Ellen, it's ten-thirty, and I'm sleepy. Where are you staying tonight?'

'Where do you think I should stay?'

'I think you should stay at your apartment at Ole Miss.'

'I'm too drunk to drive.'

'Nesbit will drive you.'

'Where, may I ask, are you staying?'

'At the house my wife and I own on Adams Street.'

She stopped rubbing and grabbed her drink. Jake stood and leaned over the rail and yelled at Nesbit. 'Nesbit! Wake up! You're driving to Oxford!'

Chapter 35

Carla found the story on the second page of the front section. 'All White Jury Chosen for Hailey' read the headline. Jake had not called Tuesday night. She read the story and ignored her coffee.

The beach house sat by itself in a semisecluded area of the beach. The nearest neighbor was two hundred yards away. Her father owned the land in between and had no plans to sell it. He had built the house ten years earlier when he sold his company in Knoxville and retired wealthy. Carla was the only child, and now Hanna would be the only grandchild. The house – with four bedrooms and four bathrooms scattered over three levels – had room for a dozen grandchildren.

She finished the article and walked to the bay windows in the breakfast room overlooking the beach, and then the ocean. The brilliant orange mass of the sun had just cleared the horizon. She preferred the warmth of the bed until well after daybreak, but life with Jake had brought new adventure to the first seven hours of each day. Her body was conditioned to at least wake up at five-thirty. He once told her his goal was to go to work in the dark and return from work in the dark. He usually achieved this goal. He took great pride in working more hours each day than any lawyer in Ford County. He was different, but she loved him.

Forty-eight miles northeast of Clanton, the Milburn county seat of Temple lay peacefully beside the Tippah River. It had three thousand people and two motels. The Temple Inn was deserted, there being no moral reason to be there this time of year. At the end of one secluded wing, eight rooms were occupied and guarded by soldiers and a couple of state troopers. The ten women had paired off nicely, as had Barry Acker and Clyde Sisco. The black alternate, Ben Lester Newton, was awarded a room to himself, as was the other alternate, Francie Pitts. The televisions had been disconnected and no newspapers were allowed. Supper Tuesday night had been delivered to the rooms, and Wednesday's breakfast arrived promptly at seven-thirty while the Greyhound warmed and blew diesel fumes all over the parking lot. Thirty minutes later the fourteen loaded aboard and the entourage set out for Clanton.

They talked on the bus about their families and jobs. Two or three had known each other prior to Monday; most were strangers. They awkwardly avoided any mention of why they were all together and the task before them. Judge Noose had been very plain on this point; no discussions about the case. They wanted to talk about many things: the rape, the rapists, Carl Lee, Jake, Buckley, Noose, the Klan, lots of things. Everyone knew of the burning crosses, but they weren't discussed, at least they weren't discussed on the bus. There had been many discussions back in the motel rooms.

The Greyhound arrived at the courthouse five minutes before nine, and the jurors stared through dark windows to see how many blacks and how many Klansmen and how many others were being separated by the guardsmen. It eased past the barricades and parked at the rear of the courthouse, where the deputies were waiting to escort them upstairs as soon as possible. They went up the back stairs to the jury room, where coffee and doughnuts were waiting. The bailiff informed them it was nine, and His Honor was ready to start. He led them into the crowded courtroom and into the jury box, where they sat in their designated seats.

'All rise for the court,' Mr Pate yelled.

'Please be seated,' Noose said as he fell into the tall leather chair behind the bench. 'Good morning, ladies and gentlemen,' he said warmly to the jurors. 'I trust you're all feeling well this morning, and ready to go.'

They all nodded.

'Good. I'm going to ask you this question every morning: Did anybody attempt to contact you, talk to you, or influence you in any way last night?'

They all shook their heads.

'Good. Did you discuss this case among yourselves?'

They all lied and shook their heads.

'Good. If anyone attempts to contact you and discuss this case or influence you in any way, I expect you to notify me as soon as possible. Do you understand?'

They nodded.

'Now at this time we are ready to start the trial. The first order of business is to allow the attorneys to make opening statements. I want to caution you that nothing the attorneys say is testimony and is not to be taken as evidence. Mr Buckley, do you wish to make an opening statement?'

Buckley rose and buttoned his shiny polyester coat. 'Yes, Your Honor.'

'I thought so. You may proceed.'

Buckley lifted the small, wooden podium and moved it squarely in front of the jury box, where he stood behind it and breathed deeply and slowly flipped through some notes on a legal pad. He enjoyed the brief period of quietness with all eyes on him and all ears anxious for his words. He started by thanking the jurors for being there, for their sacrifices, for their citizenship (as if they had a choice, thought Jake). He was proud of them and honored to be associated with them in this most important case. Again, he was their lawyer. His client, the State of Mississippi. He expressed fear at this awesome responsibility that they, the people, had given to him, Rufus Buckley, a simple country lawyer from Smithfield. He rambled on about himself and his thoughts on the trial, and his hopes and prayers that he would do a good job for the people of this state.

He gave pretty much the same spiel in all of his opening statements, but this was a better performance. It was refined and polished garbage, and objectionable. Jake wanted to burn him, but from experience he knew Ichabod would not sustain an objection during an opening statement unless the offense was flagrant, and Buckley's rhetoric did not qualify – yet. All this fake sincerity and gushiness irritated Jake no end, primarily because the jury listened to it and, more often than not, fell for it. The prosecutor was always the good guy, seeking to right an injustice and punish a criminal for some heinous crime; to lock him away forever so he could sin no more. Buckley was master at convincing a jury, right off the mark, during the opening statement, that it was up to them, He and The Twelve Chosen Ones, to search diligently for the truth, together as a team, united against evil. It was the truth they were after, nothing but the truth. Find the truth and justice would win. Follow him, Rufus Buckley, the people's lawyer, and they would find the truth.

The rape was a terrible deed. He was a father, in fact had a daughter the same age of Tonya Hailey, and when he first heard of the rape he was sick at his stomach. He grieved for Carl Lee and his wife. Yes, he thought of his own little girls and had thoughts of retribution.

Jake smiled quickly at Ellen. This was interesting.

Buckley had chosen to confront the rape instead of keeping it from the jury. Jake was expecting a critical confrontation with him on the admissibility of any testimony regarding the rape. Ellen's research found the law to be clear that the lurid details were inadmissible, but it wasn't so clear as to whether it could be mentioned or referred to. Evidently Buckley felt it was better to acknowledge the rape than try to hide it. Good move, thought Jake, since all twelve and the rest of the world knew the details anyway.

Ellen smiled too. The rape of Tonya Hailey was about to be tried for the first time.

Buckley explained it would be natural for any parent to want revenge. He would too, he admitted. But, he continued with his voice growing heavier, there is a mighty distinction between wanting revenge and getting revenge.

He was warming up now as he paced deliberately back and forth, ignoring the podium, getting his rhythm. He launched himself into a twenty-minute discourse on the criminal justice system and how it was practiced in Mississippi, and how many rapists that he, Rufus Buckley, had personally sent to Parchman, for life, most of them. The system worked because Mississippians had enough good common sense to make it work, and it would collapse if people like Carl Lee Hailey were allowed to short-circuit the system and dispense justice according to their own terms. Imagine that. A lawless society where vigilantes roamed at will. No police, no jails, no courts, no trials, no juries. Every man for himself.

It was sort of ironic, he said, winding down for a moment. Carl Lee Hailey now sat before them asking for due process and a fair trial, yet he did not believe in such things. Ask the mothers of Billy Ray Cobb and Pete Willard. Ask them what kind of fair trials their sons received.

He paused to allow the jury and the courtroom to absorb and ponder that last thought. It sunk in heavy, and every person in the jury box looked at Carl Lee Hailey. They were not looks of compassion. Jake cleaned his fingernails with a small knife and looked thoroughly bored. Buckley pretended to review his notes at the podium, then checked his watch. He started again, this time in a most confident businesslike tone of voice. The State would prove that Carl Lee Hailey carefully planned the killings. He waited for almost an hour in a small room next to the stairs where he knew the boys would eventually be led as they were taken back to jail. He somehow managed to sneak an M-16 into the courthouse. Buckley walked to a small table by the court reporter and hoisted the M-16. 'This is the M-16!' he announced to the jury, waving it wildly about with one hand. He sat it on the podium and talked about how it was carefully selected by Carl Lee Hailey because he had used one before in close combat, and he knew how to kill with it. He had been trained with an M-16. It's an illegal weapon. You can't buy one down at the Western Auto. He had to go find it. He planned it.

The proof would be clear: premeditated, carefully planned, cold-blooded murder.

And then there was Deputy DeWayne Looney. A fourteen-year veteran of the Sheriff's Department. A family man – one of the finest law enforcement officers he had ever known. Gunned down in the line of duty by Carl Lee Hailey. His leg was partially amputated. What was his sin? Perhaps the defense would say it was accidental, that it shouldn't count. That's no defense in Mississippi.

There's no excuse, ladies and gentlemen, for any of this violence. The verdict must be guilty.

They each had an hour for their openings, and the lure of that much time proved irresistible for the D.A., whose remarks were becoming repetitive. He lost himself twice during his condemnation of the insanity ruse. The jurors began to look bored and searched for other points of interest around the courtroom. The artists quit sketching, the reporters quit writing, and Noose cleaned his glasses seven or eight times. It was a known fact that Noose cleaned the glasses to stay awake and fight boredom, and he usually cleaned them throughout the trial. Jake had seen him rub them with a handkerchief or tie or shirttail while witnesses broke down and cried and lawyers screamed and flailed their arms at each other. He didn't miss a word or objection or trick; he was just bored with it all, even a case of this magnitude. He never slept on the bench, although he was sorely tempted at times. Instead he removed his glasses, held them upward in the light, blew on them, rubbed them as though they were caked with grease, then remounted them just north of the wart. No more than five minutes later they would be dirty again. The longer Buckley droned on, the more they were cleaned.

Finally, after an hour and a half, Buckley shut up and the courtroom sighed.

'Ten-minute recess,' Noose announced, and lunged off the bench, through the door, past chambers to the men's room.

Jake had planned a brief opening, and after Buckley's marathon, he decided to make it even shorter. Most people don't like lawyers to begin with, especially long-winded, tall-talking, wordy lawyers who feel that every insignificant point must be repeated at least three times, and the major ones have to be hammered and drilled by constant repetition into whoever happened to be listening. Jurors especially dislike lawyers who waste time, for two very good reasons. First, they can't tell the lawyers to shut up. They're captives. Outside the courtroom a person can curse a lawyer and shut him up, but in the jury box they become trapped and forbidden to speak. Thus, they must resort to sleeping, snoring, glaring, squirming, checking their watches, or any one of a dozen signals which boring lawyers never recognize. Second, jurors don't like long trials. Cut the crap and get it over with. Give us the facts and we'll give you a verdict.

He explained this to his client during the recess.

'I agree. Keep it short,' said Carl Lee.

He did. Fourteen minutes worth of opening

statement, and the jury appreciated every word. He began by talking about daughters and how special they are. How they are different from little boys and need special protection. He told them of his own daughter and the special bond that exists between father and daughter, a bond that could not be explained and should not be tampered with. He admitted admiration for Mr Buckley and his alleged ability to be so forgiving and compassionate to any drunken pervert who might rape his daughter. He was a big man indeed. But in reality, could they, as jurors, as parents, be so tender and trusting and indulging if their daughter had been raped – by two drunk, stoned, brutal animals who tied her to a tree and—'

'Objection!' shouted Buckley.

'Sustained,' Noose shouted back.

He ignored the shouting and continued softly. He asked them to try to imagine, throughout the trial, how they would feel had it been their daughter. He asked them not to convict Carl Lee but to send him home to his family. He didn't mention insanity. They knew it was coming.

He finished shortly after he started, and left the jury with a marked contrast in the two styles.

'Is that all?' Noose asked in amazement.

Jake nodded as he sat by his client.

'Very well Mr Buckley, you may call your first witness.'

'The State calls Cora Cobb.'

The bailiff went to the witness room and fetched Mrs Cobb. He led her through the door by the jury box, into the courtroom where she was sworn by Jean Gillespie, and then he seated her in the witness chair.

'Speak into the microphone,' he instructed.

'You are Cora Cobb?' Buckley asked with full volume as he situated the podium near the railing.

'Yes, sir.'

'Where do you live?'

'Route 3, Lake Village, Ford County.'

'You are the mother of Billy Ray Cobb, deceased?'

'Yes, sir,' she said as her eyes watered. She was a rural woman whose husband had left when the boys were small. They had raised themselves while she worked two shifts at a cheap furniture factory between Karaway and Lake Village. She lost control over them at an early age. She was about fifty, tried to look forty with hair dye and makeup, but could easily pass for early sixties.

'How old was your son at the time of his death?'

'Twenty-three.'

'When did you last see him alive?'

'Just a few seconds before he was kilt.'

'Where did you see him?'

'Here in this courtroom.'

'Where was he killed?'

'Downstairs.'

'Did you hear the shots that killed your son?' She began to cry. 'Yes, sir.'

'Where did you last see him?'

'At the funeral home.'

'And what was his condition?'

'He was dead.'

'Nothing further,' Buckley announced.

'Cross-examination, Mr Brigance?'

She was a harmless witness, called to establish that the victim was indeed dead, and to evoke a little sympathy. Nothing could be gained by cross-examination, and normally she would have been left alone. But Jake saw an opportunity he couldn't pass. He saw a chance to set the tone for the trial, to wake Noose and Buckley and the jury; to just get everyone aroused. She was not really that pitiful; she was taking some. Buckley had probably instructed her to cry if possible.

'Just a few questions,' Jake said as he walked behind Buckley and Musgrove to the podium. The D.A. was immediately suspicious.

'Mrs Cobb, is it true that your son was convicted of selling marijuana?'

'Objection!' Buckley roared, springing to his feet. 'The criminal record of the victim is inadmissible!'

'Sustained!'

'Thank you, Your Honor,' Jake said properly, as if Noose had done him a favor.

She wiped her eyes and cried harder.

'You say your son was twenty-three when he died?'

'Yes.'

'In his twenty-three years, how many other children did he rape?'

'Objection! Objection!' yelled Buckley, waving his arms and looking desperately at Noose, who was yelling. 'Sustained! Sustained! You're out of order, Mr Brigance! You're out of order!'

Mrs Cobb burst into tears and bawled uncontrollably as the shouting erupted. She managed to keep the microphone in her face, and her wailing and carrying on resounded through the stunned courtroom.

'He should be admonished, Your Honor!' Buckley demanded, his face and eyes glowing with violent anger and his neck a deep purple.

'I'll withdraw the question,' Jake replied loudly as he returned to his seat.

'Cheap shot, Brigance,' Musgrove mumbled.

'Please admonish him,' Buckley begged, 'and instruct the jury to disregard.'

'Any redirect?' asked Noose.

'No,' answered Buckley as he dashed to the witness stand with a handkerchief to rescue Mrs Cobb, who had buried her head in her hands and was sobbing and shaking violently.

'You are excused, Mrs Cobb,' Noose said. 'Bailiff, please assist the witness.'

The bailiff lifted her by the arm, with Buckley's assistance, and led her down from the witness stand, in front of the jury box, through the railing, down the center aisle. She shrieked and whined every step of the way, and her noises increased as she neared the back door until she was roaring at full throttle when she made her exit.

Noose glared at Jake until she was gone and the courtroom was quiet again. Then he turned to the jury and said: 'Please disregard the last question by Mr Brigance.'

'What'd you do that for?' Carl Lee whispered to his lawyer.

'I'll explain later.'

'The State calls Earnestine Willard,' Buckley announced in a quieter tone and with much more hesitation.

Mrs Willard was brought from the witness room above the courtroom. She was sworn and seated.

'You are Earnestine Willard?' asked Buckley.

'Yes, sir,' she said in a fragile voice. Life had been rough on her too, but she had a certain dignity that made her more pitiful and believable than Mrs Cobb. The clothes were inexpensive, but clean and neatly pressed. The hair was minus the cheap black dye that Mrs Cobb relied on so heavily. The face was minus the layers of makeup. When she began crying, she cried to herself.

'And where do you live?'

'Out from Lake Village.'

'Pete Willard was your son?'

'Yes, sir.'

'When did you last see him alive?'

'Right here in this room, just before he was killed.'

'Did you hear the gunfire that killed him?'

'Yes, sir.'

'Where did you last see him?'

'At the funeral home.'

'And what was his condition?'

'He was dead,' she said, wiping tears with a Kleenex.

'I'm very sorry,' Buckley offered. 'No further questions,' he added, eyeing Jake carefully.

'Any cross-examination?' Noose asked, also eyeing Jake suspiciously.

'Just a couple,' Jake said.

'Mrs Willard, I'm Jake Brigance.' He stood behind the podium and looked at her without compassion.

She nodded.

'How old was your son when he died?'

'Twenty-seven.'

Buckley pushed his chair from the table and sat on its edge, ready to spring. Noose removed his glasses and leaned forward. Carl Lee lowered his head.

'During his twenty-seven years, how many other children did he rape?'

Buckley bolted upright. 'Objection! Objection! Objection!'

'Sustained! Sustained! Sustained!'

The yelling frightened Mrs Willard, and she cried louder.

'Admonish him, Judge! He must be admonished!'

'I'll withdraw the question,' Jake said on his way back to his seat.

Buckley pleaded with his hands. 'But that's not good enough, Judge! He must be admonished!'

'Let's go into chambers,' Noose ordered. He excused the witness and recessed until one.

★   ★   ★

Harry Rex was waiting on the balcony of Jake's office with sandwiches and a pitcher of margaritas. Jake declined and drank grapefruit juice. Ellen wanted just one, a small one she said to calm her nerves. For the third day, lunch had been prepared by Dell and personally delivered to Jake's office. Compliments of the Coffee Shop.

They ate and relaxed on the balcony and watched the carnival around the courthouse. What happened in chambers? Harry Rex demanded. Jake nibbled on a Reuben. He said he wanted to talk about something other than the trial.

'What happened in chambers, dammit?'

'Cardinals are three games out, did you know that, Row Ark?'

'I thought it was four.'

'What happened in chambers?'

'Do you really want to know?'

'Yes! Yes!'

'Okay. I've got to go use the rest room. I'll tell you when I get back.' Jake left.

'Row Ark, what happened in chambers?'

'Not much. Noose rode Jake pretty good, but no permanent damage. Buckley wanted blood, and Jake said he was sure some was forthcoming if Buckley's face got any redder. Buckley ranted and screamed and condemned Jake for intentionally inflaming the jury, as he called it. Jake just smiled at him and said he was sorry, Governor. Every time he would say governor, Buckley would scream at Noose, "He's calling me governor, Judge, do something." And Noose would say, "Please,

gentlemen, I expect you to act like professionals."
And Jake would say, "Thank you, Your Honor."
Then he would wait a few minutes and call him
governor again.'

'Why did he make those two old ladies cry?'

'It was a brilliant move, Harry Rex. He showed
the jury, Noose, Buckley, everybody, that it's his
courtroom and he's not afraid of a damned person
in it. He drew first blood. He's got Buckley so
jumpy right now he'll never relax. Noose respects
him because he's not intimidated by His Honor.
The jurors were shocked, but he woke them up
and told them in a not so subtle way that this is
war. A brilliant move.'

'Yeah, I thought so myself.'

'It didn't hurt us. Those women were asking
for sympathy, but Jake reminded the jury of what
their sweet little boys did before they died.'

'The scumbags.'

'If there's any resentment by the jury, they'll
forget by the time the last witness testifies.'

'Jake's pretty smooth, ain't he?'

'He's good. Very good. He's the best I've seen
for his age.'

'Wait till his closing argument. I've heard a couple.
He could get sympathy out of a drill sergeant.'

Jake returned and poured a small margarita.
Just a very small one, for his nerves. Harry Rex
drank like a sailor.

Ozzie was the first State witness after lunch.
Buckley produced large, multicolored plats of the

first and second floors of the courthouse, and together they traced the precise, last movements of Cobb and Willard.

Then Buckley produced a set of ten 16 x 24 color photographs of Cobb and Willard lying freshly dead on the stairs. They were gruesome. Jake had seen lots of pictures of dead bodies, and although none were particularly pleasant given their nature, some weren't so bad. In one of his cases, the victim had been shot in the heart with a .357 and simply fell over dead on his porch. He was a large, muscular old man, and the bullet never found its way out of the body. So there was no blood, just a small hole in his overalls, and then a small sealed hole in his chest. He looked as though he could have fallen asleep and slumped over, or passed out drunk on the porch, like Lucien. It was not a spectacular scene, and Buckley had not been proud of those photographs. They had not been enlarged. He had just handed the small Polaroids to the jury and looked disgusted because they were so clean.

But most murder pictures were grisly and sickening, with blood splashed on walls and ceilings, and parts of bodies blown free and scattered everywhere. Those were always enlarged by the D.A. and entered into evidence with great fanfare, then waved around the courtroom by Buckley as he and the witness described the scenes in the pictures. Finally, with the jurors fidgeting with curiosity, Buckley would politely ask the judge for permission to show the photographs to the jury, and the judge would always consent. Then Buckley and everybody else would watch their faces intently as they were shocked, horrified, and occasionally nauseated. Jake had actually seen two jurors vomit when handed photos of a badly slashed corpse.

Such pictures were highly prejudicial and highly inflammatory, and also highly admissible. 'Probative' was the word used by the Supreme Court. Such pictures could aid the jury, according to ninety years of decisions from the Court. It was well settled in Mississippi that murder pictures, regardless of their impact on the jury, were always admissible.

Jake had seen the Cobb and Willard photographs weeks earlier, and had filed the standard objection and received the standard denial.

These were mounted professionally on heavy posterboard, something the D.A. had not done before. He handed the first one into the jury box to Reba Betts. It was the one of Willard's head and brains taken at close range.

'My God!' she gasped, and shoved it to the next juror, who gawked in horror, and passed it on. They handed it to one another, then to the alternates. Buckley took it, and gave Reba another one. The ritual continued for thirty minutes until all the pictures were returned to the D.A.

Then he grabbed the M-16 and thrust it at Ozzie. 'Can you identify this?'

'Yes, it's the weapon found at the scene.'

'Who picked it up at the scene?'

'I did.'

'And what did you do with it?'

'Wrapped it in a plastic bag and placed it in the vault at the jail. Kept it locked up until I handed it to Mr Laird with the crime lab in Jackson.'

'Your Honor, the State would offer the weapon, Exhibit S-13, into evidence,' Buckley said, waving it wildly.

'No objections,' Jake said.

'We have nothing further of this witness,' Buckley announced.

'Cross-examination?'

Jake flipped through his notes as he walked slowly to the podium. He had just a few questions for his friend.

'Sheriff, did you arrest Billy Ray Cobb and Pete Willard?'

Buckley pushed his chair back and perched his ample frame on the edge, poised to leap and scream if necessary.

'Yes I did,' answered the sheriff.

'For what reason?'

'For the rape of Tonya Hailey,' he answered perfectly.

'And how old was she at the time she was raped by Cobb and Willard?'

'She was ten.'

'Is it true, Sheriff, that Pete Willard signed a written confession in—'

'Objection! Objection! Your Honor! That's inadmissible and Mr Brigance knows it.'

Ozzie nodded affirmatively during the objection.

'Sustained.'

Buckley was shaking. 'I ask that the question be stricken from the record and the jury be instructed to disregard it.'

'I'll withdraw the question,' Jake said to Buckley with a smile.

'Please disregard the last question from Mr Brigance,' Noose instructed the jury.

'No further questions,' said Jake.

'Any redirect examination, Mr Buckley?'

'No, sir.'

'Very well. Sheriff, you may step down.'

Buckley's next witness was a fingerprint man from Washington who spent an hour telling the jurors what they had known for weeks. His dramatic final conclusion unmistakably linked the prints on the M-16 to those of Carl Lee Hailey. Then came the ballistics expert from the state crime lab whose testimony was as boring and uninformative as his predecessor on the stand. Yes, without a doubt, the fragments recovered from the crime scene were fired from the M-16 lying there on the table. That was his final opinion, and with the charts and diagrams, it took Buckley an hour to get it to the jury. Prosecutorial overkill, as Jake called it; a debility suffered by all prosecutors.

The defense had no questions for either expert,

and at five-fifteen Noose said goodbye to the jurors with strict instructions against discussing the case. They nodded politely as they filed from the courtroom. Then he banged his gavel and adjourned until nine in the morning.

Chapter 36

The great civic duty of jury service had grown old rapidly. The second night in the Temple Inn had seen the telephones removed – judge's orders. Some old magazines donated by the Clanton library were circulated and quickly discarded, there being little interest among the group in *The New Yorker*, *The Smithsonian*, and *Architectural Digest*.

'Got any *Penthouse*s?' Clyde Sisco had whispered to the bailiff as he made the rounds. He said no, but he'd see what he could do.

Confined to their rooms with no television, newspapers, or phones, they did little but play cards and talk about the trial. A trip to the end of the hall for ice and a soft drink became a special occasion, something the roommates planned and rotated. The boredom descended heavily.

At each end of the hall two soldiers guarded the darkness and solitude, the stillness interrupted only by the systematic emergence of the jurors with change for the drink machine.

Sleep came early, and when the sentries knocked

on the doors at 6:00 A.M., all the jurors were awake, some even dressed. They devoured Thursday's breakfast of pancakes and sausage, and eagerly boarded the Greyhound at eight for the trip back home.

For the fourth straight day the rotunda was crowded by eight o'clock. The spectators had learned that all seats were taken by eight-thirty. Prather opened the door and the crowd filed slowly through the metal detector, past the careful eyes of the deputies and finally into the courtroom, where the blacks filled the left side and the whites the right. The front row was again reserved by Hastings for Gwen, Lester, the kids, and other relatives. Agee and other council members sat in the second row with the kinfolks who couldn't fit up front. Agee was in charge of alternating court-room duty and outside demonstration duty for the ministers. Personally, he preferred the courtroom duty, where he felt safer, but he did miss the cameras and reporters which were so abundant on the front lawn. To his right, across the aisle, sat the families and friends of the victims. They had behaved so far.

A few minutes before nine, Carl Lee was escorted from the small holding room. The hand-cuffs were removed by one of the many officers surrounding him. He flashed a big smile at his family and sat in his chair. The lawyers took their places and the courtroom grew quiet. The bailiff poked his head through the door beside the jury box, and, satisfied with whatever he saw, opened the door and released the jurors to their assigned seats. Mr Pate was watching all this from the door leading to chambers, and when all was perfect, he stepped forward and yelled: 'All rise for the Court!'

Ichabod, draped in his favorite wrinkled and faded black robe, loped to the bench and instructed everyone to have a seat. He greeted the jury and questioned them about what happened or didn't happen since yesterday's adjournment.

He looked at the lawyers. 'Where's Mr Musgrove?'

'He's running a bit late, Your Honor. We are ready to proceed,' Buckley announced.

'Call your next witness,' Noose ordered Buckley.

The pathologist from the state crime lab was located in the rotunda and entered the courtroom. Normally, he would have been much too busy for a simple trial and would have sent one of his underlings to explain to the jury precisely what killed Cobb and Willard. But this was the Hailey case, and he felt compelled to do the job himself. It was actually the simplest case he had seen in a while; the bodies were found as they were dying, the weapon was with the bodies, and there were enough holes in the boys to kill them a dozen times. Everybody in the world knew how those boys died. But the D.A. had insisted on the most thorough pathological workup, so the doctor took the stand Thursday morning laden with photos of the autopsies and multicolored anatomy charts.

Earlier in chambers, Jake had offered to stipulate to the causes of death, but Buckley would have no part of it. No sir, he wanted the jury to hear and know how they died.

'We will admit that they died by multiple wounds from bullets fired from the M-16,' Jake had stated precisely.

'No, sir. I have a right to prove it,' Buckley said stubbornly.

'But he's offering to stipulate to the causes of death,' Noose said incredulously.

'I have the right to prove it,' Buckley hung on.

So he proved it. In a classic case of prosecutorial overkill, Buckley proved it. For three hours the pathologist talked about how many bullets hit Cobb and how many hit Willard, and what each bullet did upon penetration, and the ghastly damage thereafter. The anatomy charts were placed on easels before the jury, and the expert took a plastic, numbered pellet that represented a bullet, and moved it ever so slowly through the body. Fourteen pellets for Cobb and eleven for Willard. Buckley would ask a question, elicit a response, then interrupt to belabor a point.

'Your Honor, we would be glad to stipulate as to the causes of death,' Jake announced with great frustration every thirty minutes.

'We won't,' Buckley replied tersely, and moved to the next pellet.

Jake fell into his chair, shook his head, and looked at the jurors, those who were awake.

The doctor finished at noon and Noose, tired

and numb with boredom, awarded a two-hour lunch break. The jurors were awakened by the bailiff and led to the jury room where they dined on barbeque specials on plastic plates, then struck up card games. They were forbidden to leave the courthouse.

In every small Southern town there's a kid who was born looking for the quick buck. He was the kid who at the age of five set up the first lemonade stand on his street and charged twenty-five cents a cup for four ounces of artificially flavored water. He knew it tasted awful, but he knew the adults thought he was adorable. He was the first kid on the street to purchase a lawn mower on credit at the Western Auto and knock on doors in February to line up yard work for the summer. He was the first kid to pay for his own bike, which he used for morning and afternoon paper routes. He sold Christmas cards to old ladies in August. He sold fruitcakes door to door in November. On Saturday mornings when his friends were watching cartoons, he was at the flea markets at the courthouse selling roasted peanuts and corn dogs. At the age of twelve he bought his first certificate of deposit. He had his own banker. At fifteen, he paid cash for his new pickup the same day he passed his driver's license exam. He bought a trailer to follow the truck and filled it with lawn equipment. He sold T-shirts at high school football games. He was a hustler; a millionaire to be.

In Clanton, his name was Hinky Myrick, age

sixteen. He waited nervously in the rotunda until Noose broke for lunch, then moved past the deputies and entered the courtroom. Seating was so precious that almost none of the spectators left for lunch. Some would stand, glare at their neighbors, point at their seats and make sure everybody knew it was theirs for the day, then leave for the rest room. But most of them sat in their highly treasured spaces on the pews, and suffered through lunch.

Hinky could smell opportunity. He could sense people in need. On Thursday, just as he had on Wednesday, he rolled a shopping cart down the aisle to the front of the courtroom. It was filled with a wide assortment of sandwiches and plate lunches in plastic containers. He began yelling toward the far end of the rows, then passing food down to his customers. He worked his way slowly toward the rear of the courtroom. He was a vicious scalper. A tuna salad on white bread went for two dollars; his cost, eighty cents. A plate lunch of cold chicken with a few peas went for three dollars; his cost, a buck twenty-five. A canned soft drink was one-fifty. But they gladly paid his prices and kept their seats. He sold out before he reached the fourth row from the front, and began taking orders from the rest of the courtroom. Hinky was the man of the hour.

With a fistful of orders, he raced from the courthouse, across the lawn, through the crowd of blacks, across Caffey Street and into Claude's. He ran to the kitchen, shoved a twenty-dollar bill at the cook and handed him the orders. He waited and watched his watch. The cook moved slowly. Hinky gave him another twenty.

The trial ushered a wave of prosperity Claude had never dreamed of. Breakfast and lunch in his small cafe became happenings as demand greatly exceeded the number of chairs and the hungry lined the sidewalk, waiting in the heat and haze for a table. After the lunch recess on Monday, he had dashed around Clanton buying every folding card table and matching chair set he could find. At lunch the aisles disappeared, forcing his wait-resses to maneuver nimbly among and between the rows of people, virtually all of whom were black.

The trial was the only topic of conversation. On Wednesday, the composition of the jury had been hotly condemned. By Thursday, the talk centered on the growing dislike for the prosecutor.

'I hear tell he wants to run for governor.'

'He Democrat or Republican?'

'Democrat.'

'He can't win without the black vote, not in this state.'

'Yeah, and he ain't likely to get much after this trial.'

'I hope he tries.'

'He acts more like a Republican.'

In pretrial Clanton, the noon hour began ten minutes before twelve when the young, tanned, pretty, coolly dressed secretaries from the banks, law offices, insurance agencies, and courthouse left their desks and took to the sidewalks. During lunch they ran errands around the square. They went to the post office. They did their banking. They shopped. Most of them bought their food at the Chinese Deli and ate on the park benches under the shade trees around the courthouse. They met friends and gossiped. At noon the gazebo in front of the courthouse attracted more beautiful women than the Miss Mississippi pageant. It was an unwritten rule in Clanton that an office girl on the square got a headstart on lunch and did not have to return until one. The men followed at twelve, and watched the girls.

But the trial changed things. The shade trees around the courthouse were in a combat zone. The cafes were full from eleven to one with soldiers and strangers who couldn't get seats in the court-room. The Chinese Deli was packed with foreigners. The office girls ran their errands and ate at their desks.

At the Tea Shoppe the bankers and other white collars discussed the trial more in terms of its publicity and how the town was being perceived. Of particular concern was the Klan. Not a single customer knew anyone connected with the Klan, and it had long been forgotten in north Mississippi. But the vultures loved the white robes, and as far as the outside world knew, Clanton, Mississippi, was the home of the Ku Klux Klan. They hated the Klan for being there. They cussed the press for keeping them there.

For lunch Thursday, the Coffee Shop offered

the daily special of country-fried pork chops, turnip greens, and either candied yams, creamed corn, or fried okra. Dell served the specials to a packed house that was evenly divided among locals, foreigners, and soldiers. The unwritten but firmly established rule of not speaking to anyone with a beard or funny accent was strictly enforced, and for a friendly people it was awkward not to smile and carry on with those from the outside. A tight-lipped arrogance had long since replaced the warm reception given to the visitors in the first few days after the shootings. Too many of the press hounds had betrayed their hosts and printed unkind, unflattering, and unfair words about the county and its people. It was amazing how they could arrive in packs from all over and within twenty-four hours become experts on a place they had never heard of and a people they had never met.

The locals had watched them as they scrambled like idiots around the square chasing the sheriff, the prosecutor, the defense lawyer, or anybody who might know anything. They watched them wait at the rear of the courthouse like hungry wolves to pounce on the defendant, who was invariably surrounded by cops, and who invariably ignored them as they yelled the same ridiculous questions at him. The locals watched with distaste as they kept their cameras on the Kluxers and the rowdier blacks, always searching for the most radical elements, and then making those elements appear to be the norm.

They watched them, and they hated them.

'What's that orange crap all over her face?' Tim Nunley asked, looking at a reporter sitting in a booth by the window. Jack Jones crunched on his okra and studied the orange face.

'I think it's something they use for the cameras. Makes her face look white on TV.'

'But it's already white.'

'I know, but it don't look white on TV unless it's painted orange.'

Nunley was not convinced. 'Then what do the niggers use on TV?' he asked.

No one could answer.

'Did you see her on TV last night?' asked Jack Jones.

'Nope. Where's she from?'

'Channel Four, Memphis. Last night she interviewed Cobb's mother, and of course she kept on pushing till the old woman broke down. All they showed on TV was the cryin'. It was sickenin'. Night before she had some Klansmen from Ohio talkin' about what we need here in Mississippi. She's the worst.'

The State finished its case against Carl Lee Thursday afternoon. After lunch Buckley put Murphy on the stand. It was gut-wrenching, nerve-wracking testimony as the poor little man stuttered uncontrollably for an hour.

'Calm down, Mr Murphy,' Buckley said a hundred times.

He would nod, and take a drink of water. He

nodded affirmatively and shook negatively as much as possible, but the court reporter had an awful time picking up the nods and shakes.

'I didn't get that,' she would say, her back to the witness stand. So he would try to answer and get hung, usually on a hard consonant like a 'P' or 'T.' He would blurt out something, then stutter and spit incoherently.

'I didn't get that,' she would say helplessly when he finished. Buckley would sigh. The jurors rocked furiously. Half the spectators chewed their fingernails.

'Could you repeat that?' Buckley would say with as much patience as he could find.

'I'm s-s-s-s-s-s-s-s-sorry,' he would say frequently. He was pitiful.

Through it all, it was determined that he had been drinking a Coke on the rear stairs, facing the stairs where the boys were killed. He had noticed a black man peeking out of a small closet some forty feet away. But he didn't think much about it. Then when the boys came down, the black man just stepped out and opened fire, screaming and laughing. When he stopped shooting, he threw down the gun and took off. Yes, that was him, sitting right there. The black one.

Noose rubbed holes in his glasses listening to Murphy. When Buckley sat down, His Honor looked desperately at Jake. 'Any cross-examination?' he asked painfully.

Jake stood with a legal pad. The court reporter

glared at him. Harry Rex hissed at him. Ellen closed her eyes. The jurors wrung their hands and watched him carefully.

'Don't do it,' Carl Lee whispered firmly.

'No, Your Honor, we have no questions.'

'Thank you, Mr Brigance,' Noose said, breathing again.

The next witness was Officer Rady, the investigator for the Sheriff's Department. He informed the jury that he found a Royal Crown Cola can in the closet next to the stairs, and the prints on the can matched those of Carl Lee Hailey.

'Was it empty or full?' Buckley asked dramatically.

'It was completely empty.'

Big deal, thought Jake, so he was thirsty. Oswald had a chicken dinner waiting on Kennedy. No, he had no questions for this witness.

'We have one final witness, Your Honor,' Buckley said with great finality at 4:00 P.M. 'Officer DeWayne Looney.'

Looney limped with a cane into the courtroom and to the witness stand. He removed his gun and handed it to Mr Pate.

Buckley watched him proudly. 'Would you state your name, please, sir?'

'DeWayne Looney.'

'And your address?'

'Fourteen sixty-eight Bennington Street, Clanton, Mississippi.'

'How old are you?'

'Thirty-nine.'

'Where are you employed?'

'Ford County Sheriff's Department.'

'And what do you do there?'

'I'm a dispatcher.'

'Where did you work on Monday, May 20?'

'I was a deputy.'

'Were you on duty?'

'Yes. I was assigned to transport two subjects from the jail to court and back.'

'Who were those two subjects?'

'Billy Ray Cobb and Pete Willard.'

'What time did you leave court with them?'

'Around one-thirty, I guess.'

'Who was on duty with you?'

'Marshall Prather. He and I were in charge of the two subjects. There were some other deputies in the courtroom helpin' us, and we had two or three men outside waitin' on us. But me and Marshall were in charge.'

'What happened when the hearing was over?'

'We immediately handcuffed Cobb and Willard and got them outta here. We took them to that little room over there and waited a second or two, and Prather walked on down the stairs.'

'Then what happened?'

'We started down the back stairs. Cobb first, then Willard, then me. Like I said, Prather had already gone on down. He was out the door.'

'Yes, sir. Then what happened?'

'When Cobb was near 'bout to the foot of the stairs, the shootin' started. I was on the landing, fixin' to go on down. I didn't see anybody at first for a second, then I seen Mr Hailey with the machine gun firin' away. Cobb was blown backward into Willard, and they both screamed and fell in a heap, tryin' to get back up where I was.'

'Yes, sir. Describe what you saw.'

'You could hear the bullets bouncin' off the walls and hittin' everywhere. It was the loudest gun I ever heard and seemed like he kept shootin' forever. The boys just twisted and thrashed about, screamin' and squealin'. They were handcuffed, you know.'

'Yes, sir. What happened to you?'

'Like I said, I never made it past the landing. I think one of the bullets ricocheted off the wall and caught me in the leg. I was tryin' to get back up the steps when I felt my leg burn.'

'And what happened to your leg?'

'They cut it off,' Looney answered matter-of-factly, as if an amputation happened monthly. 'Just below the knee.'

'Did you get a good look at the man with the gun?'

'Yes, sir.'

'Can you identify him for the jury?'

'Yes, sir. It's Mr Hailey, the man sittin' over there.'

That answer would have been a logical place to end Looney's testimony. He was brief, to the point, sympathetic and positive of the identification. The jury had listened to every word so far. But Buckley and Musgrove retrieved the large diagrams of the courthouse and arranged them before the jury so that Looney could limp around for a while. Under Buckley's direction, he retraced everybody's exact movements just before the killings.

Jake rubbed his forehead and pinched the bridge of his nose. Noose cleaned and recleaned his glasses. The jurors fidgeted.

'Any cross-examination, Mr Brigance?' Noose asked at last.

'Just a few questions,' Jake said as Musgrove cleared the debris from the courtroom.

'Officer Looney, who was Carl Lee looking at when he was shooting?'

'Them boys, as far as I could tell.'

'Did he ever look at you?'

'Well, now, I didn't spend a lotta time tryin' to make eye contact with him. In fact, I was movin' in the other direction.'

'So he didn't aim at you?'

'Oh, no, sir. He just aimed at those boys. Hit them too.'

'What did he do when he was shooting?'

'He just screamed and laughed like he was crazy. It was the weirdest thing I ever heard, like he was some kinda madman or something. And you know, what I'll always remember is that with all the noise, the gun firin', the bullets whistlin', the boys screamin' as they got hit, over all the noise I could hear him laughin' that crazy laugh.'

The answer was so perfect Jake had to fight off a smile. He and Looney had worked on it a hundred times, and it was a thing of beauty. Every word was perfect. Jake busily flipped through his legal pad and glanced at the jurors. They all stared at Looney, enthralled by his answer. Jake scribbled something, anything, nothing, just to kill a few more seconds before the most important questions of the trial.

'Now, Deputy Looney, Carl Lee Hailey shot you in the leg.'

'Yes, sir, he did.'

'Do you think it was intentional?'

'Oh, no, sir. It was an accident.'

'Do you want to see him punished for shooting you?'

'No, sir. I have no ill will toward the man. He did what I would've done.'

Buckley dropped his pen and slumped in his chair. He looked sadly at his star witness.

'What do you mean by that?'

'I mean I don't blame him for what he did. Those boys raped his little girl. I gotta little girl. Somebody rapes her and he's a dead dog. I'll blow him away, just like Carl Lee did. We oughtta give him a trophy.'

'Do you want the jury to convict Carl Lee?'

Buckley jumped and roared, 'Objection! Objection! Improper question!'

'No!' Looney yelled. 'I don't want him convicted. He's a hero. He—'

'Don't answer, Mr Looney!' Noose said loudly. 'Don't answer!'

'Objection! Objection!' Buckley continued, on his tiptoes.

'He's a hero! Turn him loose!' Looney yelled at Buckley.

'Order! Order!' Noose banged his gavel.

Buckley was silent. Looney was silent. Jake walked to his chair and said, 'I'll withdraw the question.'

'Please disregard,' Noose instructed the jury.

Looney smiled at the jury and limped from the courtroom.

'Call your next witness,' Noose said, removing his glasses.

Buckley rose slowly and with a great effort at drama, said, 'Your Honor, the State rests.'

'Good,' Noose replied, looking at Jake. 'I assume you have a motion or two, Mr Brigance.'

'Yes, Your Honor.'

'Very well, we'll take those up in chambers.'

Noose excused his jury with the same parting instructions and adjourned until nine Friday.

Chapter 37

Jake awoke in the darkness with a slight hangover, a headache due to fatigue and Coors, and the distant but unmistakable sound of his doorbell ringing continually as if held firmly in place by a large and determined thumb. He opened the front door in his nightshirt and tried to focus on the two figures standing on the porch. Ozzie and Nesbit, it was finally determined.

'Can I help you?' he asked as he opened the door. They followed him into the den.

'They're gonna kill you today,' Ozzie said.

Jake sat on the couch and massaged his temples. 'Maybe they'll succeed.'

'Jake, this is serious. They plan to kill you.'

'Who?'

'The Klan.'

'Mickey Mouse?'

'Yeah. He called yesterday and said something was up. He called back two hours ago and said you're the lucky man. Today is the big day. Time for some excitement. They bury Stump Sisson this

607

morning in Loydsville, and it's time for the eye-for-an-eye, tooth-for-a-tooth routine.'

'Why me? Why don't they kill Buckley or Noose or someone more deserving?'

'We didn't get a chance to talk about that.'

'What method of execution?' Jake asked, suddenly feeling awkward sitting there in his night-shirt.

'He didn't say.'

'Does he know?'

'He ain't much on details. He just said they'd try to do it sometime today.'

'So what am I supposed to do? Surrender?'

'What time you goin' to the office?'

'What time is it?'

'Almost five.'

'As soon as I can shower and dress.'

'We'll wait.'

At five-thirty, they rushed him into his office and locked the door. At eight, a platoon of soldiers gathered on the sidewalk under the balcony and waited for the target. Harry Rex and Ellen watched from the second floor of the courthouse. Jake squeezed between Ozzie and Nesbit, and the three of them crouched in the center tight formation. Off they went across Washington Street in the direction of the courthouse. The vultures sniffed something and surrounded the entourage.

The abandoned feed mill sat near the abandoned railroad tracks halfway down the tallest hill in Clanton, two blocks north and east of the square.

Beside it was a neglected asphalt and gravel street that ran downhill and intersected Cedar Street, after which it became much smoother and wider and continued downward until finally it terminated and merged into Quincy Street, the eastern boundary of the Clanton square.

From his position inside an abandoned silo, the marksman had a clear but distant view of the rear of the courthouse. He crouched in the darkness and aimed through a small opening, confident no one in the world could see him. The whiskey helped the confidence, and the aim, which he practiced a thousand times from seven-thirty until eight, when he noticed activity around the nigger's lawyer's office.

A comrade waited in a pickup hidden in a run-down warehouse next to the silo. The engine was running and the driver chain-smoked Lucky Strikes, waiting anxiously to hear the clapping sounds from the deer rifle.

As the armored mass stepped its way across Washington, the marksman panicked. Through the scope he could barely see the head of the nigger's lawyer as it bobbed and weaved awkwardly among the sea of green, which was surrounded and chased by a dozen reporters. Go ahead, the whiskey said, create some excitement. He timed the bobbing and weaving as best he could, and pulled the trigger as the target approached the rear door of the courthouse.

The rifle shot was clear and unmistakable.

Half the soldiers hit the ground rolling and the

other half grabbed Jake and threw him violently under the veranda. A guardsman screamed in anguish. The reporters and TV people crouched and stumbled to the ground, but valiantly kept the cameras rolling to record the carnage. The soldier clutched his throat and screamed again. Another shot. Then another.

'He's hit!' someone yelled. The soldiers scrambled on all fours across the driveway to the fallen one. Jake escaped through the doors to the safety of the courthouse. He fell onto the floor of the rear entrance and buried his head in his hands. Ozzie stood next to him, watching the soldiers through the door.

The gunman dropped from the silo, threw his gun behind the back seat, and disappeared with his comrade into the countryside. They had a funeral to attend in south Mississippi.

'He's hit in the throat!' someone screamed as his buddies waded around the reporters. They lifted him and dragged him to a jeep.

'Who got hit?' Jake asked without removing his palms from his eyes.

'One of the guardsmen,' Ozzie said. 'You okay?'

'I guess,' he answered as he clasped his hands behind his head and stared at the floor. 'Where's my briefcase?'

'It's out there on the driveway. We'll get it in a minute.' Ozzie removed his radio from his belt and barked orders to the dispatcher, something about all men to the courthouse.

When it was apparent the shooting was over,

Ozzie joined the mass of soldiers outside. Nesbit stood next to Jake. 'You okay?' he asked.

The colonel rounded the corner, yelling and swearing. 'What the hell happened?' he demanded. 'I heard some shots.'

'Mackenvale got hit.'

'Where is he?' the colonel said.

'Off to the hospital,' a sergeant replied, pointing at a jeep flying away in the distance.

'How bad is he?'

'Looked pretty bad. Got him in the throat.'

'Throat! Why did they move him?'

No one answered.

'Did anybody see anything?' the colonel demanded.

'Sounded like it came from up the hill,' Ozzie said looking up past Cedar Street. 'Why don't you send a jeep up there to look around.'

'Good idea.' The colonel addressed his eager men with a string of terse commands, punctuated liberally with obscenities. The soldiers scattered in all directions, guns drawn and ready for combat, in search of an assassin they could not identify, who was, in fact, in the next county when the foot patrol began exploring the abandoned feed mill.

Ozzie laid the briefcase on the floor next to Jake. 'Is Jake okay?' he whispered to Nesbit. Harry Rex and Ellen stood on the stairs where Cobb and Willard had fallen.

'I don't know. He ain't moved in ten minutes,' Nesbit said.

'Jake, are you all right?' the sheriff asked.

'Yes,' he said slowly without opening his eyes. The soldier had been on Jake's left shoulder. 'This is kinda silly, ain't it?' he had just said to Jake when a bullet ripped through his throat. He fell into Jake, grabbing at his neck, gurgling blood and screaming. Jake fell, and was tossed to safety.

'He's dead, isn't he?' Jake asked softly.

'We don't know yet,' replied Ozzie. 'He's at the hospital.'

'He's dead. I know he's dead. I heard his neck pop.'

Ozzie looked at Nesbit, then at Harry Rex. Four or five coin-sized drops of blood were splattered on Jake's light gray suit. He hadn't noticed them yet, but they were apparent to everyone else.

'Jake, you've got blood on your suit,' Ozzie finally said. 'Let's go back to your office so you can change clothes.'

'Why is that important?' Jake mumbled to the floor. They stared at each other.

Dell and the others from the Coffee Shop stood on the sidewalk and watched as they led Jake from the courthouse, across the street, and into his office, ignoring the absurdities thrown by the reporters. Harry Rex locked the front door, leaving the bodyguards on the sidewalk. Jake went upstairs and removed his coat.

'Row Ark, why don't you make some margaritas,' Harry Rex said. 'I'll go upstairs and stay with him.'

★　　★　　★

612

'Judge, we've had some excitement,' Ozzie explained as Noose unpacked his briefcase and removed his coat.

'What is it?' Buckley asked.

'They tried to kill Jake this mornin'.'

'What!'

'When?' asked Buckley.

''Bout an hour ago, somebody shot at Jake as he was comin' into the courthouse. It was a rifle at long range. We have no idea who did it. They missed Jake and hit a guardsman. He's in surgery now.'

'Where's Jake?' asked His Honor.

'Over in his office. He's pretty shook up.'

'I would be too,' Noose said sympathetically.

'He wanted you to call him when you got here.'

'Sure.' Ozzie dialed the number and handed the phone to the judge.

'It's Noose,' Harry Rex said, handing the phone to Jake.

'Hello.'

'Are you okay, Jake?'

'Not really. I won't be there today.'

Noose struggled for a response. 'Do what?'

'I said I won't be in court today. I'm not up to it.'

'Well, uh, Jake, where does that leave the rest of us?'

'I don't care, really,' Jake said, sipping on his second margarita.

'Beg your pardon?'

'I said I don't care, Judge. I don't care what you do, I won't be there.'

Noose shook his head and looked at the receiver. 'Are you hurt?' he asked with feeling.

'You ever been shot at, Judge?'

'No, Jake.'

'You ever seen a man get shot, hear him scream?'

'No, Jake.'

'You ever had somebody else's blood splashed on your suit?'

'No, Jake.'

'I won't be there.'

Noose paused and thought for a moment. 'Come on over, Jake, and let's talk about it.'

'No. I'm not leaving my office. It's dangerous out there.'

'Suppose we stand in recess until one. Will you feel better then?'

'I'll be drunk by then.'

'What!'

'I said I'll be drunk by then.'

Harry Rex covered his eyes. Ellen left for the kitchen.

'When do you think you might be sober?' Noose asked sternly. Ozzie and Buckley looked at each other.

'Monday.'

'What about tomorrow?'

'Tomorrow's Saturday.'

'Yes, I know, and I'd planned to hold court tomorrow. We've got a jury sequestered, remember?'

'Okay, I'll be ready in the morning.'

'That's good to hear. What do I tell the jury right now? They're sitting in the jury room waiting

614

on us. The courtroom is packed. Your client is sitting out there by himself waiting on you. What do I tell these people?'

'You'll think of something, Judge. I've got faith in you.' Jake hung up. Noose listened to the unbelievable until it was evident that he had in fact been hung up on. He handed the phone to Ozzie.

His Honor looked out the window and removed his glasses. 'He says he ain't comin' today.'

Uncharacteristically, Buckley remained silent.

Ozzie was defensive. 'It really got to him, Judge.'

'Has he been drinking?'

'Naw, not Jake,' Ozzie replied. 'He's just tore up over that boy gettin' shot like he did. He was right next to Jake, and caught the bullet that was aimed for him. It would upset anybody, Judge.'

'He wants us to remain in recess until tomorrow morning,' Noose said to Buckley, who shrugged and again said nothing.

As word spread, a regular carnival developed on the sidewalk outside Jake's office. The press set up camp and pawed at the front window in hopes of seeing someone or something newsworthy inside. Friends stopped by to check on Jake, but were informed by various of the reporters that he was locked away inside and would not come out. Yes, he was unhurt.

Dr Bass had been scheduled to testify Friday morning. He and Lucien entered the office through the rear door a few minutes after ten, and Harry Rex left for the liquor store.

With all the crying, the conversation with Carla had been difficult. He called after three drinks, and things did not go well. He talked to her father, told him he was safe, unhurt, and that half of the Mississippi National Guard had been assigned to protect him. Settle her down, he said, and he would call back later.

Lucien was furious. He had fought with Bass to keep him sober Thursday night so he could testify Friday. Now that he would testify Saturday, there was no way to keep him sober two days in a row. He thought of all the drinking they had missed Thursday, and was furious.

Harry Rex returned with a gallon of liquor. He and Ellen mixed drinks and argued over the ingredients. She rinsed the coffeepot, filled it with Bloody Mary mix and a disproportionate helping of Swedish vodka. Harry Rex added a lavish dose of Tabasco. He made the rounds in the conference room and refilled each cup with the delightful mixture.

Dr Bass gulped frantically and ordered more. Lucien and Harry Rex debated the likely identity of the gunman. Ellen silently watched Jake, who sat in the corner and stared at the bookshelves.

The phone rang. Harry Rex grabbed it and listened intently. He hung up and said, 'That was Ozzie. The soldier's outta surgery. Bullet's lodged in the spine. They think he'll be paralyzed.'

They all sipped in unison and said nothing. They made great efforts to ignore Jake as he rubbed his forehead with one hand and sloshed his drink with the other. The faint sound of someone knocking at the rear door interrupted the brief memorial.

'Go see who it is,' Lucien ordered Ellen, who left to see who was knocking.

'It's Lester Hailey,' she reported to the conference room.

'Let him in,' Jake mumbled, almost incoherently.

Lester was introduced to the party and offered a Bloody Mary. He declined and asked for something with whiskey in it.

'Good idea,' said Lucien. 'I'm tired of light stuff. Let's get some Jack Daniel's.'

'Sounds good to me,' added Bass as he gulped the remnants in his cup.

Jake managed a weak smile at Lester, then returned to the study of the bookshelves. Lucien threw a hundred-dollar bill on the table, and Harry Rex left for the liquor store.

When she awoke hours later, Ellen was on the couch in Jake's office. The room was dark and deserted, with an acrid, intoxicating smell to it. She moved cautiously. She found her boss peacefully snoring away in the war room, on the floor, partially under the war desk. There were no lights to extinguish, so she carefully walked down the stairs. The conference room was littered with empty liquor bottles, beer cans, plastic cups and chicken dinner boxes. It was 9:30 P.M. She had slept five hours.

She could stay at Lucien's, but needed to change clothes. Her friend Nesbit would drive her to Oxford, but she was sober. Plus, Jake needed all the protection he could get. She locked the front door and walked to her car.

Ellen almost made it to Oxford when she saw the blue lights behind her. As usual, she was driving seventy-five. She parked on the shoulder and walked to her taillights, where she searched her purse and waited on the trooper.

Two plainsclothesmen approached from the blue lights.

'You drunk, ma'am?' one of them asked, spewing tobacco juice.

'No, sir. I'm trying to find my license.'

She crouched before the taillights and fished for the license. Suddenly, she was knocked to the ground. A heavy quilt was thrown over her and both men held her down. A rope was wrapped around her chest and waist. She kicked and cursed, but could offer little resistance. The quilt covered her head and trapped her arms underneath. They pulled the rope tightly.

'Be still, bitch! Be still!'

One of them removed her keys from the ignition and opened the trunk. They threw her inside and slammed it shut. The blue lights were unplugged in the old Lincoln and it roared away, trailed by the BMW. They found a gravel road and followed it deep into the woods. It turned into a dirt road that led to a small pasture where a large cross was being burned by a handful of Kluxers.

The two assailants quickly donned their robes and masks and removed her from the trunk. She was thrown to the ground and the quilt removed. They bound and gagged her, and dragged her to a large pole a few feet from the cross where she was tied, her back to the Kluxers, her face to the pole.

She saw the white robes and pointed hats, and tried desperately to spit out the oily, cotton rag crammed in her mouth. She managed only to gag and cough.

The flaming cross illuminated the small pasture, discharging a glowing wave of heat that began to roast her as she wrestled with the pole and emitted strange, guttural noises.

A hooded figure left the others and approached her. She could hear him walking and breathing. 'You nigger-loving bitch,' he said in a crisp Midwestern voice. He grabbed the rear of her collar and ripped the white silk blouse until it hung in shreds around her neck and shoulders. Her hands were tied firmly around the pole. He removed a bowie knife from under the robe, and began cutting the remainder of the blouse from her body. 'You nigger-loving bitch. You nigger-loving bitch.'

Ellen cursed him, but her words were muffled groans.

He unzipped the navy linen skirt on the right side. She tried to kick, but the heavy rope around her ankles held her feet to the pole. He placed the tip of the knife at the bottom of the zipper, and cut downward through the hem. He grabbed around the waist and pulled it off like a magician. The Kluxers stepped forward.

He slapped her on the butt, and said, 'Nice, very nice.' He stepped back to admire his handiwork. She grunted and twisted but could not resist. The slip fell to mid-thigh. With great ceremony, he cut the straps, then sliced it neatly down the back. He yanked it off and threw it at the foot of the burning cross. He cut the bra straps and removed it. She jerked and the moans became louder. The silent semicircle inched forward and stopped ten feet away.

The fire was hot now. Her bare back and legs were covered with sweat. The light red hair was drenched around her neck and shoulders. He reached under his robe again and brought out a bullwhip. He popped it loudly near her, and she flinched. He marched backward, carefully measuring the distance to the pole.

He cocked the bullwhip and aimed at the bare back. The tallest one stepped forward with his back to her. He shook his head. Nothing was said, but the whip disappeared.

He walked to her and grabbed her head. With his knife, he cut her hair. He grabbed handfuls and hacked away until her scalp was gapped and ugly. It piled gently around her feet. She moaned and did not move.

They headed for their cars. A gallon of gasoline was splashed inside the BMW with Massachusetts tags and somebody threw a match.

When he was certain they were gone, Mickey Mouse slid from the bushes. He untied her and carried her to a small clearing away from the pasture. He gathered the remains of her clothing and tried to cover her. When her car finished burning beside the dirt road, he left her. He drove to Oxford, to a pay phone, and called the Lafayette County sheriff.

Chapter 38

Saturday court was unusual but not unheard of, especially in capital cases where the jury was locked up. The participants didn't mind because Saturday brought the end one day nearer.

The locals didn't mind either. It was their day off, and for most Ford Countians it was their only chance to watch the trial, or if they couldn't get a seat, at least hang around the square and see it all first-hand. Who knows, there may even be some more shooting.

By seven, the cafes downtown were at full capacity serving nonregulars. For every customer who was awarded a seat, two were turned away and left to loiter around the square and the court-house and wait for a seat in the courtroom. Most of them paused for a moment in front of the lawyer's office, hoping to catch a glimpse of the one they tried to kill. The braggarts told of being clients of this famous man.

Upward, a few feet, the target sat at his desk and sipped a bloody concoction left from yesterday's party. He smoked a Roi-Tan, ate headache powders, and rubbed the cobwebs from his brain. Forget about the soldier, he had told himself for the past three hours. Forget about the Klan, the threats, forget everything but the trial, and specifically Dr W.T. Bass. He uttered a short prayer, something about Bass being sober on the witness stand. The expert and Lucien had stayed through the afternoon, drinking and arguing, accusing each other of being a drunk and receiving a dishonorable discharge from their respective professions. Violence flared briefly at Ethel's desk when they were leaving. Nesbit intervened and escorted them to the patrol car for the ride home. The reporters burned with curiosity as the two blind drunks were led from Jake's office by the deputy and put in the car, where they continued to rage and cuss at each other, Lucien in the back seat, Bass in the front.

He reviewed Ellen's masterpiece on the insanity defense. Her outline of questions for Bass needed only minor changes. He studied his expert's résumé, and though unimpressive, it would suffice for Ford County. The nearest psychiatrist was eighty miles away.

Judge Noose glanced at the D.A. and looked sympathetically at Jake, who sat next to the door and watched the faded portrait of some dead judge hanging over Buckley's shoulder.

'How do you feel this morning, Jake?' Noose asked warmly.

'I'm fine.'

'How's the soldier?' asked Buckley.

'Paralyzed.'

Noose, Buckley, Musgrove, and Mr Pate looked at the same spot on the carpet and grimly shook their heads in a quiet moment of respect.

'Where's your law clerk?' Noose asked, looking at the clock on the wall.

Jake looked at his watch. 'I don't know. I expected her by now.'

'Are you ready?'

'Sure.'

'Is the courtroom ready, Mr Pate?'

'Yes, sir.'

'Very well. Let's proceed.'

Noose seated the courtroom, and for ten minutes offered a rambling apology to the jurors for yesterday's delay. They were the only fourteen in the county who did not know what happened Friday morning, and it might be prejudicial to tell them. Noose droned on about emergencies and how sometimes during trials things conspire to cause delays. When he finally finished, the jurors were completely bewildered and praying that somebody would call a witness.

'You may call your first witness,' Noose said in Jake's direction.

'Dr W.T. Bass,' Jake announced as he moved to the podium. Buckley and Musgrove exchanged winks and silly grins.

Bass was seated next to Lucien on the second row in the middle of the family. He stood noisily and made his way to the center aisle, stepping on feet and assaulting people with his heavy, leather, empty briefcase. Jake heard the commotion behind him and continued smiling at the jury.

'I do, I do,' Bass said rapidly at Jean Gillespie during his swearing in.

Mr Pate led him to the witness stand and delivered the standard orders to speak up and use the microphone. Though mortified and hung over, the expert looked remarkably arrogant and sober. He wore his most expensive dark gray hand-sewn wool suit, a perfectly starched white button-down, and a cute little red paisley bow tie that made him appear rather cerebral. He looked like an expert, in something. He also wore, over Jake's objections, a pair of light gray ostrich skin cowboy boots that he had paid over a thousand for and worn less than a dozen times. Lucien had insisted on the boots eleven years earlier in the first insanity case. Bass wore them, and the very sane defendant went to Parchman. He wore them in the second insanity trial, again at Lucien's behest; again, Parchman. Lucien referred to them as Bass's good luck charm.

Jake wanted no part of the damned boots. But the jury could relate to them, Lucien had argued. Not expensive ostrich skin, Jake countered. They're too dumb to know the difference, replied Lucien. Jake could not be swayed. The rednecks will trust someone with boots, Lucien had explained. Fine, said Jake, let him wear a pair of those camouflage squirrel-hunting boots with a little mud on the heels and soles, some boots they could really identify with. Those wouldn't complement his suit, Bass had inserted.

He crossed his legs, laying the right boot on his left knee, flaunting it. He grinned at it, then grinned at the jury. The ostrich would have been proud.

Jake looked from his notes on the podium and saw the boot, which was plainly visible above the rail of the witness stand. Bass was admiring it, the jurors pondering it. He choked and returned to his notes.

'State your name, please.'

'Dr W. T. Bass,' he replied, his attention suddenly diverted from the boot. He looked grimly, importantly at Jake.

'What is your address?'

'Nine-oh-eight West Canterbury, Jackson, Mississippi.'

'What is your profession?'

'I am a physician.'

'Are you licensed to practice in Mississippi?'

'Yes.'

'When were you licensed?'

'February 8, 1963.'

'Are you licensed to practice medicine in any other state?'

'Yes.'

'Where?'

'Texas.'

'When did you obtain that license?'

'November 3, 1962.'

'Where did you go to college?'

'I received my bachelor's degree from Millsaps College in 1956, and received my M.D., or Doctor of Medicine, from the University of Texas Health Science Center in Dallas, Texas, in 1960.'

'Is that an accredited medical school?'

'Yes.'

'By whom?'

'By the Council of Medical Education and Hospitals of the American Medical Association, the recognized accrediting agency of our profession, and by the educational authority of the State of Texas.'

Bass relaxed a bit, uncrossed and recrossed his legs, and displayed his left boot. He rocked gently and turned the comfortable swivel chair partially toward the jury.

'Where did you intern and for how long?'

'After graduation from medical school, I spent twelve months as an intern at the Rocky Mountain Medical Center in Denver.'

'What is your medical specialty?'

'Psychiatry.'

'Explain to us what that means.'

'Psychiatry is that branch of medicine concerned with the treatment of disorders of the mind. It usually, but not always, deals with mental malfunction, the organic basis of which is unknown.'

Jake breathed for the first time since Bass took the stand. His man was sounding good.

'Now, Doctor,' he said as he casually walked to within a foot of the jury box, 'describe to the jury the specialized training you received in the field of psychiatry.'

'My specialized training in psychiatry consisted of two years as a resident in psychiatry at the Texas State Mental Hospital, an approved training center. I engaged in clinical work with psychoneurotic and psychotic patients. I studied psychology, psychopathology, psychotherapy, and the physiological therapies. This training, supervised by competent psychiatric teachers, included instruction in the psychiatric aspects of general medicine, the behavior aspects of children, adolescents, and adults.'

It was doubtful if a single person in the courtroom comprehended any of what Bass had just said, but it came from the mouth of a man who suddenly appeared to be a genius, an expert, for he had to be a man of great wisdom and intelligence to pronounce those words. With the bow tie and vocabulary, and in spite of the boots, Bass was gaining credibility with each answer.

'Are you a diplomate of the American Board of Psychiatry?'

'Of course,' he answered confidently.

'In which branch are you certified?'

'I am certified in psychiatry.'

'And when were you certified?'

'April of 1967.'

'What does it take to become certified by the American Board of Psychiatry?'

'A candidate must pass oral and practical exams, as well as a written test at the direction of the Board.'

Jake glanced at his notes and noticed Musgrove winking at Buckley.

'Doctor, do you belong to any professional groups?'

'Yes.'

'Name them please.'

'I am a member of the American Medical Association, American Psychiatric Association, and the Mississippi Medical Association.'

'How long have you been engaged in the practice of psychiatry?'

'Twenty-two years.'

Jake walked three steps in the direction of the bench and eyed Noose, who was watching intently.

'Your Honor, the defense offers Dr Bass as an expert in the field of psychiatry.'

'Very well,' replied Noose. 'Do you wish to examine this witness, Mr Buckley?'

The D.A. stood with his legal pad. 'Yes, Your Honor, just a few questions.'

Surprised but not worried, Jake took his seat next to Carl Lee. Ellen was still not in the courtroom.

'Dr Bass, in your opinion, are you an expert in the field of psychiatry?' asked Buckley.

'Yes.'

'Have you ever taught psychiatry?'

'No.'

'Have you ever published any articles on psychiatry?'

'No.'

'Have you ever published any books on psychiatry?'

'No.'

'Now, I believe you testified that you are a member of the A.M.A., M.M.A., and the American Psychiatric Association?'

'Yes.'

'Have you ever served as an officer in any of these organizations?'

'No.'

'What hospital positions do you currently hold, as of today?'

'None.'

'Has your experience in psychiatry included any work under the auspices of the federal government or any state government?'

'No.'

The arrogance was beginning to fade from his face, and the confidence from his voice. He shot a glance at Jake, who was digging through a file.

'Dr Bass, are you now engaged in the practice of psychiatry full-time?'

The expert hesitated, and looked briefly at Lucien on the second row. 'I see patients on a regular basis.'

'How many patients and how regular?' Buckley retorted with an enormous air of confidence.

'I see from five to ten patients per week.'

'One or two a day?'

'Something like that.'

'And you consider that a full-time practice?'

'I'm as busy as I want to be.'

Buckley threw his legal pad on the table and looked at Noose. 'Your Honor, the State objects to this man testifying as an expert in the field of psychiatry. It's obvious he's not qualified.'

Jake was on his feet with his mouth open.

'Overruled, Mr Buckley. You may proceed, Mr Brigance.'

Jake gathered his legal pads and returned to the podium, well aware of the suspicion the D.A. had just artfully thrown over his star witness. Bass shifted boots.

'Now, Dr Bass, have you examined the defendant, Carl Lee Hailey?'

'Yes.'

'How many times?'

'Three.'

'When was your first examination?'

'June 10.'

'What was the purpose of this examination?'

'I examined him to determine his current mental condition as well as his condition on May 20, when he allegedly shot Mr Cobb and Mr Willard.'

'Where did this examination take place?'

'Ford County Jail.'

'Did you conduct this examination alone?'

'Yes. Just Mr Hailey and myself.'

'How long did the examination last?'

'Three hours.'

'Did you review his medical history?'

'In a roundabout way, you could say. We talked at great length about his past.'

'What did you learn?'

'Nothing remarkable, except for Vietnam.'

'What about Vietnam?'

Bass folded his hands over his slightly over-weight stomach and frowned intelligently at the defense attorney. 'Well, Mr Brigance, like many Vietnam vets I've worked with, Mr Hailey had some rather horrible experiences over there.'

War is hell, thought Carl Lee. He listened intently. Now, Vietnam was bad. He'd been shot. He'd lost friends. He'd killed people, many people. He'd killed children, Vietnamese children carrying guns and grenades. It was bad. He wished he'd never seen the place. He dreamed about it, had flashbacks and nightmares occasionally. But he didn't feel warped or insane because of it. He didn't feel warped or insane because of Cobb and Willard. In fact, he felt quite satisfied because they were dead. Just like those in Vietnam.

He had explained all this to Bass once at the jail, and Bass had seemed unimpressed by it. And they had talked only twice, and never more than an hour.

Carl Lee eyed the jury and listened suspiciously to the expert, who talked at length of Carl Lee's dreadful experiences in the war. Bass's vocabulary jumped several octaves as he explained to the laymen in nonlaymen terms the effects of Vietnam on Carl Lee. It sounded good. There had been nightmares over the years, dreams Carl Lee had never worried much about, but to hear Bass explain it, were extremely significant events.

'Did he talk freely of Vietnam?'

'Not really,' replied Bass, then explaining in great detail the tremendous task he confronted in dragging out the war from this complex, burdened,

632

probably unstable mind. Carl Lee didn't remember it that way. But he dutifully listened with a pained expression, wondering for the first time in his life if perhaps he could be a little off.

After an hour, the war had been refought and its effects flogged thoroughly. Jake decided to move on.

'Now, Dr Bass,' Jake said, scratching his head. 'Other than Vietnam, what other significant events did you note regarding his mental history?'

'None, except the rape of his daughter.'

'Did you discuss the rape with Carl Lee?'

'At great length, during each of the three examinations.'

'Explain to the jury what the rape did to Carl Lee Hailey.'

Bass stroked his chin and looked perplexed. 'Quite frankly, Mr Brigance, it would take a great deal of time to explain what the rape did to Mr Hailey.'

Jake thought a moment, and seemed to thoroughly analyze this last statement. 'Well, could you summarize it for the jury?'

Bass nodded gravely. 'I'll try.'

Lucien grew weary of listening to Bass, and began watching the jury in hopes of eyeing Clyde Sisco, who had also lost interest but appeared to be admiring the boots. Lucien watched intently from the corner of his eye, waiting for Sisco to gaze around the courtroom.

Finally, as Bass rambled on, Sisco left the testimony and looked at Carl Lee, then Buckley, then one of the reporters on the front row. Then his line of vision locked solidly into a wild-eyed, bearded old man who had once handed him eighty thousand cash for performing his civic duty and returning a just verdict. They focused unmistakably on each other, and both managed a slight grin. How much? was the look in Lucien's eyes. Sisco returned to the testimony, but seconds later he was staring at Lucien. How much? Lucien said, his lips actually moving but with no sound.

Sisco looked away and watched Bass, thinking of a fair price. He looked in Lucien's direction, scratched his beard, then suddenly, while staring at Bass, flashed five fingers across his face and coughed. He coughed again and studied the expert.

Five hundred or five thousand? Lucien asked himself. Knowing Sisco, it was five thousand, maybe fifty thousand. It made no difference; Lucien would pay it. He was worth a ton.

By ten-thirty, Noose had cleaned his glasses a hundred times and consumed a dozen cups of coffee. His bladder pressed forward toward the spillway. 'Time for the morning recess. We'll adjourn until eleven.' He rapped the gavel and disappeared.

'How'm I doing?' Bass asked nervously. He followed Jake and Lucien to the law library on the third floor.

'You're doing fine,' Jake said. 'Just keep those boots outta sight.'

'The boots are critical,' Lucien protested.

'I needa drink,' Bass said desperately.

'Forget it,' Jake said.

'So do I,' Lucien added. 'Let's run over to your office for a quick one.'

'Great idea!' Bass said.

'Forget it,' Jake repeated. 'You're sober and you're doing great.'

'We got thirty minutes,' Bass said as he and Lucien were leaving the library and heading for the stairs.

'No! Don't do it, Lucien!' Jake demanded.

'Just one,' Lucien replied, pointing a finger at Jake. 'Just one.'

'You've never had just one.'

'Come with us, Jake. It'll settle your nerves.'

'Just one,' Bass yelled as he disappeared down the steps.

At eleven, Bass sat himself in the witness chair and looked through glazed eyes at the jury. He smiled, and almost giggled. He was aware of the artists on the front row, so he looked as expert as possible. His nerves were indeed settled.

'Dr Bass, are you familiar with the criminal responsibility test relative to the M'Naghten Rule?' Jake asked.

'I certainly am!' Bass replied with a sudden air of superiority.

'Would you explain this rule to the jury?'

'Of course. The M'Naghten Rule is the standard for criminal responsibility in Mississippi, as in fifteen other states. It goes back to England, in the year

1843, when a man by the name of Daniel M'Naghten attempted to assassinate the prime minister, Sir Robert Peel. He mistakenly shot and killed the prime minister's secretary, Edward Drummond. During his trial the evidence plainly showed M'Naghten was suffering from what we would call paranoid schizophrenia. The jury returned a verdict of not guilty, by reason of insanity. From this the M'Naghten Rule was established. It is still followed in England and sixteen states.'

'What does the M'Naghten Rule mean?'

'The M'Naghten Rule is fairly simple. Every man is presumed to be sane, and to establish a defense on the ground of insanity, it must be clearly proven that when the defendant did what he did he was laboring under such a defect of reason, from a mental disease, that he did not know the nature and quality of the act he was doing, or if he did know what he was doing, he did not know it was wrong.'

'Could you simplify that?'

'Yes. If a defendant cannot distinguish right from wrong, he is legally insane.'

'Define insanity, please.'

'It has no significance, medically. It is strictly a legal standard for a person's mental state or condition.'

Jake breathed deeply and plowed forward. 'Now, Doctor, based upon your examination of the defendant, do you have an opinion as to the mental condition of Carl Lee Hailey on May 20 of this year, at the time of the shooting?'

'Yes, I do.'

'And what is that opinion?'

'It is my opinion,' Bass said slowly, 'that the defendant had a total break with reality when his daughter was raped. When he saw her immediately after the rape he didn't recognize her, and when someone told him she'd been gang-raped, and beaten, and almost hanged, something just snapped in Carl Lee's mind. That's a very elementary way of putting it, but that's what happened. Something snapped. He broke with reality.

'They had to be killed. He told me once that when he first saw them in court, he could not understand why the deputies were protecting them. He kept waiting for one of the cops to pull a gun and blow their heads off. A few days went by and nobody killed them, so he figured it was up to him. I mean, he felt as though someone in the system would execute the two for raping his little girl.

'What I'm saying, Mr Brigance, is that, mentally, he left us. He was in another world. He was suffering from delusions. He broke.'

Bass knew he was sounding good. He was talking to the jury now, not the lawyer.

'The day after the rape he spoke with his daughter in the hospital. She could barely talk, with the broken jaws and all, but she said she saw him in the woods running to save her, and she asked him why he disappeared. Now, can you imagine what that would do to a father? She later told him she begged for her daddy, and the two men laughed at her and told her she didn't have a daddy.'

Jake let those words sink in. He studied Ellen's outline and saw only two more questions.

'Now, Dr Bass, based upon your observations of Carl Lee Hailey, and your diagnosis of his mental condition at the time of the shooting, do you have an opinion, to a reasonable degree of medical certainty, as to whether Carl Lee Hailey was capable of knowing the difference between right and wrong when he shot these men?'

'I have.'

'And what is that opinion?'

'That due to his mental condition, he was totally incapable of distinguishing right from wrong.'

'Do you have an opinion, based upon the same factors, as to whether Carl Lee Hailey was able to understand and appreciate the nature and quality of his actions?'

'I do.'

'And what is that opinion?'

'In my opinion, as an expert in the field of psychiatry, Mr Hailey was totally incapable of understanding and appreciating the nature and quality of what he was doing.'

'Thank you, Doctor. I tender the witness.'

Jake gathered his legal pad and strolled confidently back to his seat. He glanced at Lucien, who was smiling and nodding. He glanced at the jury. They were watching Bass and thinking about his testimony. Wanda Womack, a young woman with a sympathetic glow about her, looked at Jake and smiled ever so slightly. It was the first positive signal he received from the jury since the trial started.

'So far so good,' Carl Lee whispered.

Jake smiled at his client. 'You're a real psycho, big man.'

'Any cross-examination?' Noose asked Buckley.

'Just a few questions,' Buckley said as he grabbed the podium.

Jake could not imagine Buckley arguing psychiatry with an expert, even if it was W.T. Bass.

But Buckley had no plans to argue psychiatry. 'Dr Bass, what is your full name?'

Jake froze. The question had an ominous hint to it; Buckley asked it with a great deal of suspicion.

'William Tyler Bass.'

'What do you go by?'

'W.T. Bass.'

'Have you ever been known as Tyler Bass?'

The expert hesitated. 'No,' he said meekly.

An immense feeling of anxiety hit Jake and felt like a hot spear tearing into his stomach. The question could only mean trouble.

'Are you positive?' Buckley asked with raised eyebrows and an enormous amount of distrust in his voice.

Bass shrugged. 'Maybe when I was younger.'

'I see. Now, I believe you testified that you studied medicine at the University of Texas Health Science Center?'

'That's correct.'

'And where is that?'

639

'Dallas.'

'And when were you a student there?'

'From 1956 to 1960.'

'And under what name were you registered?'

'William T. Bass.'

Jake was numb with fear. Buckley had something, a dark secret from the past known only to Bass and himself.

'Did you ever use the name Tyler Bass while you were a medical student?'

'No.'

'Are you positive?'

'I certainly am.'

'What is your social security number?'

'410-96-8585.'

Buckley made a check mark beside something on his legal pad.

'And what is your date of birth?' he asked carefully.

'September 14, 1934.'

'And what was your mother's name?'

'Jonnie Elizabeth Bass.'

'And her maiden name?'

'Skidmore.'

Another check mark. Bass looked nervously at Jake.

'And your place of birth?'

'Carbondale, Illinois.'

Another check mark.

An objection to the relevance of these questions was in order and sustainable, but Jake's knees were like Jell-O and his bowels were suddenly fluid. He feared he would embarrass himself if he stood and tried to speak.

Buckley studied his check marks and waited a few seconds. Every ear in the courtroom waited for the next question, knowing it would be brutal. Bass watched the D.A. like a prisoner watching the firing squad, hoping and praying the guns would somehow misfire.

Finally, Buckley smiled at the expert. 'Dr Bass, have you ever been convicted of a felony?'

The question echoed throughout the silence and landed from all directions on the trembling shoulders of Tyler Bass. Even a cursory look at his face revealed the answer.

Carl Lee squinted and looked at his lawyer.

'Of course not!' Bass answered loudly, desperately.

Buckley just nodded and walked slowly to the table, where Musgrove, with much ceremony, handed him some important-looking papers.

'Are you certain?' Buckley thundered.

'Of course I'm certain,' Bass protested as he eyed the important-looking papers.

Jake knew he needed to rise and say something or do something to stop the carnage that was seconds away, but his mind was paralyzed.

'You're certain?' Buckley asked.

'Yes,' Bass answered through clenched teeth.

'You've never been convicted of a felony?'

'Of course not.'

'Are you as certain of that as you are of the rest of your testimony before this jury?'

That was the trap, the killer, the deadliest question of all; one Jake had used many times, and when he heard it, he knew Bass was finished. And so was Carl Lee.

'Of course,' Bass answered with feigned arrogance.

Buckley moved in for the kill. 'You're telling this jury that on October 17, 1956, in Dallas, Texas, you were not convicted of a felony under the name of Tyler Bass?'

Buckley asked the question while looking at the jury and reading from the important-looking documents.

'That's a lie,' Bass said quietly, and unconvincingly.

'Are you sure it's a lie?' Buckley asked.

'A bald-faced lie.'

'Do you know a lie from the truth, Dr Bass?'

'Damn right I do.'

Noose placed his glasses on his nose and leaned forward. The jurors quit rocking. The reporters quit scribbling. The deputies along the back wall stood still and listened.

Buckley picked out one of the important-looking documents and studied it. 'You're telling this jury that on October 17, 1956, you were not convicted of statutory rape?'

Jake knew it was important, in the midst of any great courtroom crisis, even this one, to maintain a straight, poker face. It was important for the jurors, who missed nothing, to see the defendant's lawyer with a positive look about him. Jake had practiced this positive, everything's-wonderful, I'm-in-control look through many trials and many surprises, but with the 'statutory rape' the positive and confident and certain look was immediately replaced by a sickly, pale, pained expression that was being scrutinized by at least half of those in the jury box.

The other half scowled at the witness on the stand.

'Were you convicted of statutory rape, Doctor?' Buckley asked again after a lengthy silence.

No answer.

Noose uncoiled and leaned downward in the direction of the witness. 'Please answer the question, Dr Bass.'

Bass ignored His Honor and stared at the D.A., then said, 'You've got the wrong man.'

Buckley snorted and walked to Musgrove, who was holding some more important-looking papers. He opened a large white envelope and removed something that resembled an 8 x 10 photograph.

'Well, Dr Bass, I've got some photographs of you taken by the Dallas Police Department on September 11, 1956. Would you like to see them?'

No answer.

Buckley held them out to the witness. 'Would you like to see these, Dr Bass? Perhaps they could refresh your memory.'

Bass slowly shook his head, then lowered it and stared blankly at his boots.

'Your Honor, the State would introduce into evidence these copies, certified under the Acts of

Congress, of the Final Judgment and Sentencing Order in the case styled State of Texas versus Tyler Bass, said records being obtained by the State from the proper officials in Dallas, Texas, and showing that on October 17, 1956, a one Tyler Bass pled guilty to the charge of statutory rape, a felony under the laws of the State of Texas. We can prove that Tyler Bass and this witness, Dr W.T. Bass, are one and the same.'

Musgrove politely handed Jake a copy of everything Buckley was waving.

'Any objections to this introduction into evidence?' Noose asked in Jake's direction.

A speech was needed. A brilliant, emotional explanation that would touch the hearts of the jurors and make them weep with pity for Bass and his patient. But the rules of procedure did not permit one at this point. Of course the evidence was admissible. Unable to stand, Jake waved in the negative. No objections.

'We have no further questions,' Buckley announced.

'Any redirect, Mr Brigance?' Noose asked.

In the split second available, Jake could not think of a single thing he could ask Bass to improve the situation. The jury had heard enough from the defense expert.

'No,' Jake said quietly.

'Very well, Dr Bass, you are excused.'

Bass made a quick exit through the small gate in the railing, down the center aisle, and out of the courtroom. Jake watched his departure intently, conveying as much hatred as possible. It was important for the jury to see how shocked the defendant and his lawyer were. The jury had to believe a convicted felon was not knowingly put on the stand.

When the door closed and Bass was gone, Jake scanned the courtroom in hopes of finding an encouraging face. There were none. Lucien stroked his beard and stared at the floor. Lester sat with his arms folded and a disgusted look on his face. Gwen was crying.

'Call your next witness,' Noose said.

Jake continued searching. In the third row, between Reverend Ollie Agee and Reverend Luther Roosevelt, sat Norman Reinfeld. When his eyes met Jake's, he frowned and shook his head as if to say 'I told you so.' On the other side of the courtroom, most of the whites looked relaxed and a few even grinned at Jake.

'Mr Brigance, you may call your next witness.'

Against his better judgment, Jake attempted to stand. His knees buckled and he leaned forward with his palms flat against the table. 'Your Honor,' he said in a high-pitched, shrill, defeated voice, 'could we recess till one?'

'But Mr Brigance, it's only eleven-thirty.'

A lie seemed appropriate. 'Yes, Your Honor, but our next witness is not here, and will not arrive until one.'

'Very well. We'll stand in recess until one. I need to see the attorneys in chambers.'

Next to chambers was a coffee room where the

lawyers loitered and gossiped by the hour, and next to it was a small rest room. Jake closed and locked the rest room door and removed his coat, throwing it to the floor. He knelt beside the toilet, waited momentarily, then vomited.

Ozzie stood before the judge and attempted small talk while Musgrove and the D.A. smiled at each other. They waited on Jake. Finally, he entered chambers and apologized.

'Jake, I have some bad news,' Ozzie said.

'Let me sit down.'

'I got a call an hour ago from the sheriff of Lafayette County. Your law clerk, Ellen Roark, is in the hospital.'

'What happened?'

'The Klan got her last night. Somewhere between here and Oxford. They tied her to a tree and beat her.'

'How is she?' Jake asked.

'Stable but serious.'

'What happened?' Buckley asked.

'We ain't sure. They stopped her car somehow and took her out in the woods. Cut her clothes off her and cut her hair. She's got a concussion and cuts on the head, so they figure she was beat.'

Jake needed to vomit again. He couldn't speak. He massaged his temples and thought how nice it would be to tie Bass to a tree and beat him.

Noose studied the defense attorney with compassion. 'Mr Brigance, are you okay?'

No response.

'Let's recess until two. I think we could all use the break,' Noose said.

Jake walked slowly up the front steps with an empty Coors bottle and for a moment gave serious thought to smashing it against Lucien's head. He realized the injury would not be felt.

Lucien rattled his ice cubes and stared off in the distance, in the direction of the square, which had long been deserted except for the soldiers and the regular crowd of teenagers flocking to the theater for the Saturday night double feature.

They said nothing. Lucien stared away. Jake glared at him with the empty bottle. Bass was hundreds of miles away.

After a minute or so, Jake asked, 'Where's Bass?'

'Gone.'

'Gone where?'

'Gone home.'

'Where's his home?'

'Why do you wanna know?'

'I'd like to see his home. I'd like to see him in his home. I'd like to beat him to death with a baseball bat in his home.'

Lucien rattled some more. 'I don't blame you.'

'Did you know?'

'Know what?'

'About the conviction?'

'Hell no. No one knew. The record was expunged.'

'I don't understand.'

'Bass told me the record of the conviction in

Texas was expunged three years after it was entered.'

Jake placed the beer bottle on the porch beside his chair. He grabbed a dirty glass, blew into it, then filled it with ice cubes and Jack Daniel's.

'Do you mind explaining, Lucien?'

'According to Bass, the girl was seventeen, and the daughter of a prominent judge in Dallas. They fell in heat, and the judge caught them screwing on the couch. He pressed charges, and Bass didn't have a chance. He pled guilty to the statutory rape. But the girl was in love. They kept seeing each other and she comes up pregnant. Bass married her, and gives the judge a perfect baby boy for his first grandchild. The old man has a change of heart, and the record is expunged.'

Lucien drank and watched the lights from the square.

'What happened to the girl?'

'According to Bass, a week before he finished medical school, his wife, who's pregnant again, and the little boy were killed in a train wreck in Fort Worth. That's when he started drinking, and quit living.'

'And he's never told you this before?'

'Don't interrogate me. I told you I knew nothing about it. I put him on the witness stand twice myself, remember. If I had known it, he would never have testified.'

'Why didn't he ever tell you?'

'I guess because he thought the record was erased. I don't know. Technically, he's right. There is no record after the expungement. But he was convicted.'

Jake took a long, bitter drink of whiskey. It was nasty.

They sat in silence for ten minutes. It was dark and the crickets were in full chorus. Sallie walked to the screen door and asked Jake if he wanted supper. He said no thanks.

'What happened this afternoon?' Lucien asked.

'Carl Lee testified, and we adjourned at four. Buckley didn't have his psychiatrist ready. He'll testify Monday.'

'How'd he do?'

'Fair. He followed Bass, and you could feel the hatred from the jurors. He was stiff and sounded rehearsed. I don't think he scored too many points.'

'What'd Buckley do?'

'Went wild. Screamed at Carl Lee for an hour. Carl Lee kept getting smart with him, and they sniped back and forth. I think they both got hurt. On redirect, I propped him up some and he came across pitiful and sympathetic. Almost cried at the end.'

'That's nice.'

'Yeah, real nice. But they'll convict him, won't they?'

'I would imagine.'

'After we adjourned, he tried to fire me. Said I'd lost his case and he wanted a new lawyer.'

Lucien walked to the edge of the porch and unzipped his pants. He leaned on a column and sprayed the shrubs. He was barefoot and looked like a flood victim. Sallie brought him a fresh drink.

'How's Row Ark?' he asked.

'Stable, they say. I called her room and a nurse said she couldn't talk. I'll go over tomorrow.'

'I hope she's okay. She's a fine girl.'

'She's a radical bitch, but a very smart one. I feel like it's my fault, Lucien.'

'It's not your fault. It's a crazy world, Jake. Full of crazy people. Right now I think half of them are in Ford County.'

'Two weeks ago, they planted dynamite outside my bedroom window. They beat to death my secretary's husband. Yesterday they shot at me and hit a guardsman. Now they grab my law clerk, tie her to a pole, rip her clothes off, cut her hair, and she's in the hospital with a concussion. I wonder what's next.'

'I think you should surrender.'

'I would. I would march down to the courthouse right now and surrender my briefcase, lay down my arms, give up. But to whom? The enemy is invisible.'

'You can't quit, Jake. Your client needs you.'

'To hell with my client. He tried to fire me today.'

'He needs you. This thing ain't over till it's over.'

Nesbit's head hung halfway out the window and the saliva dripped down the left side of his chin, down the door, forming a small puddle over the 'O' in the Ford of the Sheriff's Department insignia on the side of the car. An empty beer can moistened his crotch. After two weeks of bodyguard duty he had grown accustomed to sleeping with the mosquitoes in his patrol car while protecting the nigger's lawyer.

Moments after Saturday turned into Sunday, the radio violated his rest. He grabbed the mike while wiping his chin on his left sleeve.

'S.O. 8,' he responded.

'What's your 10–20?'

'Same place it was two hours ago.'

'The Wilbanks house?'

'10–4.'

'Is Brigance still there?'

'10–4.'

'Get him and take him to his house on Adams. It's an emergency.'

Nesbit walked past the empty bottles on the porch, through the unlocked door, where he found Jake sprawled on the couch in the front room.

'Get up, Jake! You gotta go home! It's an emergency!'

Jake jumped to his feet and followed Nesbit. They stopped on the front steps and looked past the dome of the courthouse. In the distance a boiling funnel of black smoke rose above an orange glow and drifted peacefully toward the half moon.

Adams Street was blocked with an assortment of volunteer vehicles, mostly pickups. Each had a variety of red and yellow emergency lights, at least a thousand in all. They spun and flashed and streaked through the darkness in a silent chorus, illuminating the street.

The fire engines were parked haphazardly in front of the house. The firemen and volunteers worked frantically laying lines and getting organized, responding occasionally to the commands of the chief. Ozzie, Prather, and Hastings stood near an engine. Some guardsmen lingered benignly near a jeep.

The fire was brilliant. Flames roared from every window across the front of the house, upstairs and down. The carport was completely engulfed. Carla's Cutlass burned inside and out – the four tires emitting a darker glow of their own. Curiously, another, smaller car, not the Saab, burned next to the Cutlass.

The thundering, crackling noise of the fire, plus the rumbling of the fire engines, plus the loud voices, attracted neighbors from several blocks. They crowded together in the lawns across the street and watched.

Jake and Nesbit ran down the street. The chief spotted them and came running.

'Jake! Is anybody in the house?'

'No!'

'Good. I didn't think so.'

'Just a dog.'

'A dog!'

Jake nodded and watched the house.

'I'm sorry,' said the chief.

They gathered at Ozzie's car in front of Mrs Pickle's house. Jake answered questions.

'That's not your Volkswagen under there, is it, Jake?'

Jake stared in stunned silence at Carla's landmark. He shook his head.

'I didn't think so. Looks like that's where it started.'

'I don't understand,' said Jake.

'If it ain't your car, then somebody parked it there, right? Notice how the floor of the carport is burnin'? Concrete don't normally burn. It's gasoline. Somebody loaded the VW with gasoline, parked it and ran away. Probably had some kinda device which set the thing off.'

Prather and two volunteers agreed.

'How long's it been burning?' Jake asked.

'We got here ten minutes ago,' the chief said, 'and it was well involved. I'd say thirty minutes. It's a good fire. Somebody knew what they's doin'.'

'I don't suppose we could get anything out of there, could we?' Jake asked in general, knowing the answer.

'No way, Jake. It's too involved. My men couldn't go in there if people were trapped. It's a good fire.'

'Why do you say that?'

'Well, look at it. It's burnin' evenly through the house. You can see flames in every window. Downstairs and up. That's very unusual. In just a minute, it'll burn through the roof.'

Two squads inched forward with the lines, shooting water in the direction of the windows by the front porch. A smaller line was aimed at a window upstairs. After watching for a minute or two as the water disappeared into the flames with no noticeable effect, the chief spat and said, 'It'll burn to the ground.' With that he disappeared around an engine and began shouting.

Jake looked at Nesbit. 'Will you do me a favor?'

'Sure, Jake.'

'Drive over to Harry Rex's and bring him back. I'd hate for him to miss this.'

'Sure.'

For two hours Jake, Ozzie, Harry Rex, and Nesbit sat on the patrol car and watched the fire fulfill the chief's prediction. From time to time a neighbor would stop by and extend sympathies and ask about the family. Mrs Pickle, the sweet old woman next door, cried loudly when informed by Jake that Max had been consumed.

By three, the deputies and other curious had disappeared, and by four the quaint little Victorian had been reduced to smoldering rubble. The last of the firemen smothered any sign of smoke from the ruins. Only the chimney and burnt frames of two cars stood above the remains as the heavy rubber boots kicked and plowed through the waste looking for sparks or hidden flames that might somehow leap from the dead and burn the rest of the wreckage.

They rolled up the last of the lines as the sun began to appear. Jake thanked them when they left. He and Harry Rex walked through the backyard and surveyed the damage.

'Oh well,' Harry Rex said. 'It's just a house.'

654

'Would you call Carla and tell her that?'

'No. I think you should.'

'I think I'll wait.'

Harry Rex looked at his watch. 'It's about breakfast time, isn't it?'

'It's Sunday morning, Harry Rex. Nothing's open.'

'Ah, Jake, you're an amateur, and I'm a professional. I can find hot food at any time of any day.'

'The truck stop?'

'The truck stop!'

'Okay. And when we finish we'll go to Oxford to check on Row Ark.'

'Great. I can't wait to see her with a butch haircut.'

Sallie grabbed the phone and threw it at Lucien, who fumbled with it until it was arranged properly next to his head.

'Yeah, who is it?' he asked, squinting through the window into the darkness.

'Is this Lucien Wilbanks?'

'Yeah, who's this?'

'Do you know Clyde Sisco?'

'Yeah.'

'It's fifty thousand.'

'Call me back in the morning.'

Chapter 39

Sheldon Roark sat in the window with his feet on the back of a chair, reading the Memphis Sunday paper's version of the Hailey trial. On the bottom of the front page was a picture of his daughter and the story about her encounter with the Klan. She rested comfortably in the bed a few feet away. The left side of her head was shaved and covered with a thick bandage. The left ear was sewn with twenty-eight stitches. The severe concussion had been downgraded to a mild concussion, and the doctors had promised she could leave by Wednesday.

She had not been raped or whipped. When the doctors called him in Boston they were short on details. He had flown for seven hours not knowing what they had done to her, but expecting the worst. Late Saturday night, the doctors ran more X rays and told him to relax. The scars would fade and the hair would grow back. She had been frightened and roughed up, but it could have been much worse.

656

He heard a commotion in the hall. Someone was arguing with a nurse. He laid the paper on her bed and opened the door.

A nurse had caught Jake and Harry Rex sneaking down the hall. She explained that visiting hours started at 2:00 P.M., and that happened to be six hours away; that only family members were allowed; and that she would call security if they didn't leave. Harry Rex explained that he didn't give a damn about visiting hours or any other silly rules of the hospital; that it was his fiancée and that he would see her one last time before she died; and that if the nurse didn't shut up he would sue her for harassment because he was a lawyer and hadn't sued anybody in a week and was getting anxious.

'What's going on here?' Sheldon said.

Jake looked at the small man with the red hair and green eyes, and said, 'You must be Sheldon Roark.'

'I am.'

'I'm Jake Brigance. The one—'

'Yes, I've been reading about you. It's okay, nurse, they're with me.'

'Yeah,' Harry Rex said. 'It's okay. We're with him. Now would you please leave us alone before I garnishee your check.'

She vowed to call security, and stormed down the hall.

'I'm Harry Rex Vonner,' he said, shaking hands with Sheldon Roark.

'Step inside,' he said. They followed him into

the small room and stared at Ellen. She was still asleep.

'How bad is she?' Jake asked.

'Mild concussion. Twenty-eight stitches in her ear, and eleven in her head. She'll be fine. Doctor said she might leave by Wednesday. She was awake last night and we talked for a long time.'

'Her hair looks awful,' Harry Rex observed.

'They yanked it and cut it with a dull knife, she said. They also cut her clothes off, and at one time threatened to bullwhip her. The head injuries are self-inflicted. She thought they would either kill her or rape her, or both. So she banged her brains out against the pole she was tied to. Must have scared them.'

'You mean they didn't beat her?'

'No. They didn't hurt her. Just scared the hell out of her.'

'What did she see?'

'Not much. Burning cross, white robes, about a dozen men. Sheriff said it was a pasture eleven miles east of here. Owned by some paper company.'

'Who found her?' Harry Rex asked.

'The sheriff received an anonymous phone call from a fella by the name of Mickey Mouse.'

'Ah yes. My old friend.'

Ellen moaned softly and stretched.

'Let's step outside,' Sheldon said.

'Does this place have a cafeteria?' Harry Rex asked. 'I get hungry when I get near a hospital.'

'Sure. Let's have coffee.'

The cafeteria on the first floor was empty. Jake and Mr Roark drank black coffee. Harry Rex started with three sweet rolls and a pint of milk.

'According to the paper, things aren't going too well,' Sheldon said.

'The paper is very kind,' Harry Rex said with a mouthful. 'Jake here is gettin' his ass kicked all over the courtroom. And life ain't so great outside the courtroom, either. When they're not shooting at him, or kidnapping his law clerk, they're burning his house.'

'They burned your house!'

Jake nodded. 'Last night. It's still smoldering.'

'I thought I detected the smell of smoke.'

'We watched it burn to the ground. It took four hours.'

'I'm sorry to hear that. They've threatened me with that before, but the worst I've had was slashed tires. I've never been shot at either.'

'I've been shot at a couple of times.'

'Do y'all have the Klan in Boston?' asked Harry Rex.

'Not that I know of.'

'It's a shame. Those folks add a real dimension to your law practice.'

'Sounds like it. We saw the television reports of the riot around the courthouse last week. I've watched it pretty close since Ellen became involved. It's a famous case. Even up there. I wish I had it.'

'It's all yours,' said Jake. 'I think my client is looking for a new lawyer.'

'How many shrinks will the State call?'

'Just one. He'll testify in the morning, and we'll have closing arguments. The jury should get it by late tomorrow afternoon.'

'I hate that Ellen will miss it. She called me every day and talked about the case.'

'Where did Jake go wrong?' Harry Rex asked.

'Don't talk with your mouth full,' Jake said.

'I think Jake has done a good job. It's a lousy set of facts to begin with. Hailey committed the murders, planned them carefully, and is relying on a rather weak plea of insanity. Juries in Boston would not be too sympathetic.'

'Nor in Ford County,' added Harry Rex.

'I hope you have a soul-stirring final summation up your sleeve,' Sheldon said.

'He doesn't have any sleeves,' said Harry Rex. 'They've all been burned. Along with his pants and underwear.'

'Why don't you come over tomorrow and watch?' Jake asked. 'I'll introduce you to the judge and ask that you have privileges of chambers.'

'He wouldn't do that for me,' Harry Rex said.

'I can understand why,' Sheldon said with a smile. 'I might just do that. I had planned to stay until Tuesday anyway. Is it safe over there?'

'Not really.'

Woody Mackenvale's wife sat on a plastic bench in the hall next to his room and cried quietly while trying to be brave for her two small sons seated next to her. Each boy squeezed a well-used wad

660

of Kleenexes, occasionally wiping their cheeks and blowing their noses. Jake knelt before her and listened intently as she described what the doctors had said. The bullet had lodged in the spine – the paralysis was severe and permanent. He was a foreman at a plant in Booneville. Good job. Good life. She didn't work, at least until now. They would make it somehow, but she wasn't sure how. He coached his sons' Little League team. He was very active.

She cried louder and the boys wiped their cheeks.

'He saved my life,' Jake said to her, and looked at the boys.

She closed her eyes and nodded. 'He was doing his job. We'll make it.'

Jake took a Kleenex from the box on the bench and wiped his eyes. A group of relatives stood nearby and watched. Harry Rex paced nervously at the end of the hall.

Jake hugged her and patted the boys on the head. He gave her his phone number – office – and told her to call if he could do anything. He promised to visit Woody when the trial was over.

The beer stores opened at noon on Sunday, as if the church folks needed it then and would stop on the way home from the Lord's house to pick up a couple of six-packs, then on to Grandmother's for Sunday dinner and an afternoon of hell-raising. Oddly, they would close again at six in the afternoon, as if the same folks should then be denied beer as they returned to church for the Sunday night services. On the other six days beer was sold from six in the morning until midnight. But on Sunday, the selling was curtailed in honor of the Almighty.

Jake bought a six-pack at Bates Grocery and directed his chauffeur toward the lake. Harry Rex's antique Bronco carried three inches of dried mud across the doors and fenders. The tires were imperceptible. The windshield was cracked and dangerous, with thousands of splattered insects caked around the edges. The inspection sticker was four years old and unseen from the outside. Dozens of empty beer cans and broken bottles littered the floorboard. The air conditioner had not worked in six years. Jake had suggested use of the Saab. Harry Rex had cursed him for his stupidity. The red Saab was an easy target for snipers. No one would suspect the Bronco.

They drove slowly in the general direction of the lake, to no place in particular. Willie Nelson wailed from the cassette. Harry Rex tapped the steering wheel and sang along. His normal speaking voice was coarse and unrefined. With song, it was heinous. Jake sipped his beer and searched for daylight through the windshield.

The heat wave was about to be broken. Dark clouds loomed to the southwest, and when they passed Huey's Lounge the rains fell and showered the parched earth. It cleansed and removed the dust from the kudzu that lined the roadbeds and hung like Spanish moss from the trees. It cooled the scorched pavement and created a sticky fog that rose three feet above the highway. The red baked gullies absorbed the water, and when full began to carry tiny streams downward to the larger field drains and road ditches. The rains drenched the cotton and soybeans, and pounded the crop rows until small puddles formed between the stalks.

Remarkably, the windshield wipers worked. They slapped back and forth furiously and removed the mud and insect collection. The storm grew. Harry Rex increased the volume of the stereo.

The blacks with their cane poles and straw hats camped under the bridges and waited for the storm to blow over. Below them, the still creeks came to life. Muddy water from the fields and gullies rushed downward and stirred the small streams and brooks. The water rose and moved forward. The blacks ate bologna and crackers and told fishing stories.

Harry Rex was hungry. He stopped at Treadway's Grocery near the lake, and bought more beer, two catfish dinners, and a large bag of Cajun-spiced red-hot barbecue pork skins. He threw them at Jake.

They crossed the dam in a blinding downpour. Harry Rex parked next to a small pavilion over a picnic area. They sat on the concrete table and watched the rain batter Lake Chatulla. Jake drank beer while Harry Rex ate the catfish dinners.

'When you gonna tell Carla?' he asked, slurping beer.

The tin roof roared above. 'About what?'

'The house.'

'I'm not gonna tell her. I think I can have it rebuilt before she gets back.'

'You mean by the end of the week?'

'Yeah.'

'You're cracking up, Jake. You're drinking too much, and you're losing your mind.'

'I deserve it. I've earned it. I'm two weeks away from bankruptcy. I'm about to lose the biggest case of my career, for which I have been paid nine hundred dollars. My beautiful home that everyone took pictures of and the old ladies from the Garden Club tried to get written up in *Southern Living* has been reduced to rubble. My wife has left me, and when she hears about the house, she'll divorce me. No question about that. So I'll lose my wife. And once my daughter learns that her damned dog died in the fire, she'll hate me forever. There's a contract on my head. I've got Klan goons looking for me. Snipers shooting at me. There's a soldier lying up in the hospital with my bullet in his spine. He'll be a vegetable, and I'll think about him every hour of every day for the rest of my life. My secretary's husband was killed because of me. My last employee is in the hospital with a punk haircut and a concussion because she worked for me. The jury thinks I'm a lying crook because of my expert witness. My client wants to fire me. When he's convicted, everybody will blame me. He'll hire another lawyer for the appeal, one of those ACLU types, and they'll sue me claiming ineffective trial counsel. And they'll be right. So I'll get my ass sued for malpractice. I'll have no wife, no daughter, no house, no practice, no clients, no money, nothing.'

'You need psychiatric help, Jake. I think you should make an appointment with Dr Bass. Here, have a beer.'

'I guess I'll move in with Lucien and sit on the porch all day.'

'Can I have your office?'

'Do you think she'll divorce me?'

'Probably so. I've had four divorces, and they'll file for damned near anything.'

'Not Carla. I worship the ground she walks on, and she knows it.'

'She'll be sleeping on the ground when she gets back to Clanton.'

'Naw, we'll get a nice, cozy little double-wide trailer. It'll do us fine until the bankruptcy is over. Then we'll find another old house and start over.'

'You'll probably find you another wife and start over. Why would she leave a swanky cottage on the beach and return to a house trailer in Clanton?'

'Because I'll be in the house trailer.'

'That's not good enough, Jake. You'll be a drunk, bankrupt, disbarred lawyer, living in a house trailer. You will be publicly disgraced. All of your friends, except me and Lucien, will forget about you. She'll never come back. It's over, Jake. As your friend and divorce lawyer, I advise you to file first. Do it now, tomorrow, so she'll never know what hit her.'

'Why would I sue her for divorce?'

'Because she's gonna sue you. We'll file first and allege that she deserted you in your hour of need.'

'Is that grounds for divorce?'

'No. But we'll also claim that you're crazy, temporary insanity. Just let me handle it. The M'Naghten Rule. I'm the sleazy divorce lawyer, remember.'

'How could I forget?'

Jake poured hot beer from his neglected bottle, and opened another. The rain slackened and the clouds lightened. A cool wind blew up from the lake.

'They'll convict him, won't they, Harry Rex?' he asked, staring at the lake in the distance.

He quit chomping and wiped his mouth. He laid the paper plate on the table, and took a long drink of beer. The wind blew light drops of water onto his face. He wiped it with a sleeve.

'Yeah, Jake. Your man is about to be sent away. I can see it in their eyes. The insanity crap just didn't work. They didn't want to believe Bass to begin with, and after Buckley yanked his pants down, it was all over. Carl Lee didn't help himself any. He seemed rehearsed and too sincere. Like he was begging for sympathy. He was a lousy witness. I watched the jury while he testified. I saw no support for him. They'll convict, Jake. And quickly.'

'Thanks for being so blunt.'

'I'm your friend, and I think you should start preparing for a conviction and a long appeal.'

'You know, Harry Rex, I wish I'd never heard of Carl Lee Hailey.'

'I think it's too late, Jake.'

Sallie answered the door and told Jake she was sorry about the house. Lucien was upstairs in his study, working and sober. He pointed to a chair and instructed Jake to sit down. Legal pads littered his desk.

'I've spent all afternoon working on a closing argument,' he said, waving at the mess before him. 'Your only hope of saving Hailey is with a spell-binding performance on final summation. I mean, we're talking about the greatest closing argument in the history of jurisprudence. That's what it'll take.'

'And I assume you've created such a master-piece.'

'As a matter of fact, I have. It's much better than anything you could come up with. And I assumed – correctly – that you would spend your Sunday afternoon mourning the loss of your home and drowning your sorrows with Coors. I knew you would have nothing prepared. So I've done it for you.'

'I wish I could stay as sober as you, Lucien.'

'I was a better lawyer drunk than you are sober.'

'At least I'm a lawyer.'

Lucien tossed a legal pad at Jake. 'There it is. A compilation of my greatest closing arguments. Lucien Wilbanks at his best, all rolled into one for you and your client. I suggest you memorize it and use it word for word. It's that good. Don't try to modify it, or improvise. You'll just screw it up.'

'I'll think about it. I've done this before, remember?'

'You'd never know it.'

'Dammit, Lucien! Get off my back!'

'Take it easy, Jake. Let's have a drink. Sallie! Sallie!'

Jake threw the masterpiece on the couch and walked to the window overlooking the backyard. Sallie ran up the stairs. Lucien ordered whiskey and beer.

'Were you up all night?' Lucien asked.

'No. I slept from eleven to twelve.'

'You look terrible. You need a good night's rest.'

'I feel terrible, and sleep will not help. Nothing will help, except the end of this trial. I don't understand, Lucien. I don't understand how everything has gone so wrong. Surely to God we're entitled to a little good luck. The case should not even be tried in Clanton. We were dealt the worst possible jury – a jury that's been tampered with. But I can't prove it. Our star witness was completely destroyed. The defendant made a lousy witness. And the jury does not trust me. I don't know what else could go wrong.'

'You can still win the case, Jake. It'll take a miracle, but those things happen sometimes. I've snatched victory from the jaws of defeat many times with an effective closing argument. Zero in on one or two jurors. Play to them. Talk to them. Remember, it just takes one to hang the jury.'

'Should I make them cry?'

'If you can. It's not that easy. But I believe in tears in the jury box. It's very effective.'

Sallie brought the drinks, and they followed her downstairs to the porch. After dark, she fed them sandwiches and fried potatoes. At ten, Jake excused himself and went to his room. He called Carla and talked for an hour. There was no mention of the house. His stomach cramped when he heard her voice and realized that one day very soon he would be forced to tell her that the house, her house, no longer existed. He hung up and prayed she didn't read about it in the newspaper.

Chapter 40

Clanton returned to normal Monday morning as the barricades were put in place around the square and the ranks of the soldiers swelled to preserve the public peace. They loitered about in loose formation, watching as the Kluxers returned to their appointed ground on one side, and the black protestors on the other. The day of rest brought renewed energy to both groups, and by eight-thirty they were in full chorus. The collapse of Dr Bass had been big news, and the Kluxers smelled victory. Plus they had scored a direct hit on Adams Street. They appeared to be louder than normal.

At nine, Noose summoned the attorneys to chambers. 'Just wanted to make sure you were all alive and well.' He grinned at Jake.

'Why don't you kiss my ass, Judge?' Jake said under his breath, but loud enough to be heard. The prosecutors froze. Mr Pate cleared his throat.

Noose cocked his head sideways as if hard of hearing. 'What did you say, Mr Brigance?'

'I said, "Why don't we get started, Judge?"'

'Yes, that's what I thought you said. How's your clerk, Ms Roark?'

'She'll be fine.'

'Was it the Klan?'

'Yes, Judge. The same Klan that tried to kill me. Same Klan that lit up the county with crosses and who knows what else for our jury panel. Same Klan that's probably intimidated most of those jurors sitting out there. Yes, sir, it's the same Klan.'

Noose ripped off his glasses. 'Can you substantiate that?'

'You mean, do I have written, signed, notarized confessions from the Klansmen? No, sir. They're most uncooperative.'

'If you can't prove it, Mr Brigance, then leave it alone.'

'Yes, Your Honor.'

Jake left chambers and slammed the door. Seconds later Mr Pate called the place to order and everyone rose. Noose welcomed his jury back and promised the ordeal was almost over. No one smiled at him. It had been a lonely weekend at the Temple Inn.

'Does the State have any rebuttal?' he asked Buckley.

'One witness, Your Honor.'

Dr Rodeheaver was fetched from the witness room. He carefully situated himself in the witness chair and nodded warmly at the jury. He looked like a psychiatrist. Dark suit, no boots.

Buckley assumed the podium and smiled at the jury. 'You are Dr Wilbert Rodeheaver?' he

671

thundered, looking at the jury as if to say, 'Now you'll meet a real psychiatrist.'

'Yes, sir.'

Buckley asked questions, a million questions, about his educational and professional background. Rodeheaver was confident, relaxed, prepared, and accustomed to the witness chair. He talked at great length about his broad educational training, his vast experience as a practicing physician, and more recently, the enormous magnitude of his job as head of staff at the state mental hospital. Buckley asked him if he had written any articles in his field. He said yes, and for thirty minutes they discussed the writings of this very learned man. He had received research grants from the federal government and from various states. He was a member of all the organizations Bass belonged to, and a few more. He had been certified by every association remotely touching the study of the human mind. He was polished, and sober.

Buckley tendered him as an expert, and Jake had no questions.

Buckley continued. 'Dr Rodeheaver, when did you first examine Carl Lee Hailey?'

The expert checked his notes. 'June 19.'

'Where did the examination take place?'

'In my office at Whitfield.'

'How long did you examine him?'

'Couple of hours.'

'What was the purpose of this examination?'

'To try and determine his mental condition at

that time and also at the time he killed Mr Cobb and Mr Willard.'

'Did you obtain his medical history?'

'Most of the information was taken by an associate at the hospital. I reviewed it with Mr Hailey.'

'What did the history reveal?'

'Nothing remarkable. He talked a lot about Vietnam, but nothing remarkable.'

'Did he talk freely about Vietnam?'

'Oh yes. He wanted to talk about it. It was almost like he had been told to discuss it as much as possible.'

'What else did you discuss at the first examination?'

'We covered a wide variety of topics. His childhood, family, education, various jobs, just about everything.'

'Did he discuss the rape of his daughter?'

'Yes, in great detail. It was painful for him to talk about it, the same as it would have been for me had it been my daughter.'

'Did he discuss with you the events leading up to the shootings of Cobb and Willard?'

'Yes, we talked about that for quite a while. I tried to ascertain the degree of knowledge and understanding he had about those events.'

'What did he tell you?'

'Initially, not much. But with time, he opened up and explained how he inspected the courthouse three days before the shooting and picked a good place to attack.'

'What about the shootings?'

673

'He never told me much about the actual killings. Said he didn't remember much, but I suspect otherwise.'

Jake sprang to his feet. 'Objection! The witness can only testify as to what he actually knows. He cannot speculate.'

'Sustained. Please continue, Mr Buckley.'

'What else did you observe concerning his mood, attitude, and manner of speech?'

Rodeheaver crossed his legs and rocked gently. He lowered his eyebrows in deep thought. 'Initially, he was distrustful of me and had difficulty looking me in the eye. He gave short answers to my questions. He was very resentful of the fact that he was guarded and sometimes handcuffed while at our facility. He questioned the padded walls. But after a while, he opened up and talked freely about most everything. He flatly refused to answer a few questions, but other than that I would say he was fairly cooperative.'

'When and where did you examine him again?'

'The next day, same place.'

'What was his mood and attitude?'

'About the same as the day before. Cool at first, but he opened up eventually. He discussed basically the same topics as the day before.'

'How long did this examination last?'

'Approximately four hours.'

Buckley reviewed something on a legal pad, then whispered to Musgrove. 'Now, Dr Rodeheaver, as a result of your examinations of Mr Hailey on June 19 and 20, were you able to arrive at a medical diagnosis of the defendant's psychiatric condition on those dates?'

'Yes, sir.'

'And what is that diagnosis?'

'On June 19 and 20, Mr Hailey appeared to be of sound mind. Perfectly normal, I would say.'

'Thank you. Based on your examinations, were you able to arrive at a diagnosis of Mr Hailey's mental condition on the day he shot Billy Ray Cobb and Pete Willard?'

'Yes.'

'And what is that diagnosis?'

'At that time his mental condition was sound, no defects of any nature.'

'Upon what factors do you base this?'

Rodeheaver turned to the jury and became a professor. 'You must look at the level of premeditation involved in this crime. Motive is an element of premeditation. He certainly had a motive for doing what he did, and his mental condition at that time did not prevent him from entertaining the requisite premeditation. Frankly, Mr Hailey carefully planned what he did.'

'Doctor, you are familiar with the M'Naghten Rule as a test for criminal responsibility?'

'Certainly.'

'And you are aware that another psychiatrist, a Dr W.T. Bass, has told this jury that Mr Hailey was incapable of knowing the difference between right and wrong, and, further, that he was unable to understand and appreciate the nature and quality of his actions.'

'Yes, I am aware of that.'

'Do you agree with that testimony?'

'No. I find it preposterous, and I am personally offended by it. Mr Hailey himself has testified he planned the murders. He's admitted, in effect, that his mental condition at the time did not prevent him from possessing the ability to plan. That's called premeditation in every legal and medical book. I've never heard of someone planning a murder, admitting he planned it, then claiming he did not know what he was doing. It's absurd.'

At that moment, Jake felt it was absurd too, and as it echoed around the courtroom it sounded mighty absurd. Rodeheaver sounded good and infinitely credible. Jake thought of Bass and cursed to himself.

Lucien sat with the blacks and agreed with every word of Rodeheaver's testimony. When compared to Bass, the State's doctor was terribly believable. Lucien ignored the jury box. From time to time he would cut his eyes without moving his head and catch Clyde Sisco blatantly and openly staring directly at him. But Lucien would not allow their eyes to meet. The messenger had not called Monday morning as instructed. An affirmative nod or wink from Lucien would consummate the deal, with payment to be arranged later, after the verdict. Sisco knew the rules, and he watched for an answer. There was none. Lucien wanted to discuss it with Jake.

'Now, Doctor, based upon these factors and

your diagnosis of his mental condition as of May 20, do you have an opinion, to a reasonable degree of medical certainty, as to whether Mr Hailey was capable of knowing the difference between right and wrong when he shot Billy Ray Cobb, Pete Willard, and Deputy DeWayne Looney?'

'I have.'

'And what is that opinion?'

'His mental condition was sound, and he was very capable of distinguishing right from wrong.'

'And do you have an opinion, based upon the same factors, as to whether Mr Hailey was able to understand and appreciate the nature and quality of his actions?'

'I have.'

'And what is that opinion?'

'That he fully appreciated what he was doing.'

Buckley snatched his legal pad and bowed politely. 'Thank you, Doctor. I have no further questions.'

'Any cross-examination, Mr Brigance?' Noose asked.

'Just a few questions.'

'I thought so. Let's take a fifteen-minute recess.'

Jake ignored Carl Lee, and moved quickly out of the courtroom, up the stairs, and into the law library on the third floor. Harry Rex was waiting, and smiling.

'Relax, Jake. I've called every newspaper in North Carolina, and there's no story about the house. There's nothing about Row Ark. The Raleigh morning paper ran a story about the trial, but it was in real general terms. Nothing else. Carla doesn't know about it, Jake. As far as she knows, her pretty little landmark is still standing. Isn't that great?'

'Wonderful. Just wonderful. Thanks, Harry Rex.'

'Don't mention it. Look, Jake, I sorta hate to bring this up.'

'I can't wait.'

'You know I hate Buckley. Hate him worse than you do. But me and Musgrove get along okay. I can talk to Musgrove. I was thinking last night that it might be a good idea to approach them – me through Musgrove – and explore the possibilities of a plea bargain.'

'No!'

'Listen, Jake. What harm will it do? None! If you can plead him guilty to murder with no gas chamber, then you know you have saved his life.'

'No!'

'Look, Jake. Your man is about forty-eight hours away from a death penalty conviction. If you don't believe that, then you're blind, Jake. My blind friend.'

'Why should Buckley cut a deal? He's got us on the ropes.'

'Maybe he won't. But let me at least find out.'

'No, Harry Rex. Forget it.'

Rodeheaver returned to his seat after the recess, and Jake looked at him from behind the podium. In his brief legal career, he had never won an argument, in court or out, with an expert witness. And the way his luck was running, he decided not to argue with this one.

'Dr Rodeheaver, psychiatry is the study of the human mind, is it not?'

'It is.'

'And it is an inexact science at best, is it not?'

'That is correct.'

'You might examine a person and reach a diagnosis, and the next psychiatrist might reach a completely different diagnosis?'

'That's possible, yes.'

'In fact, you could have ten psychiatrists examine a mental patient, and arrive at ten different opinions about what's wrong with the patient.'

'That's unlikely.'

'But it could happen, couldn't it, Doctor?'

'Yes, it could. Just like legal opinions, I guess.'

'But we're not dealing with legal opinions in this case, are we, Doctor?'

'No.'

'The truth is, Doctor, in many cases psychiatry cannot tell us what is wrong with a person's mind?'

'That is true.'

'And psychiatrists disagree all the time, don't they, Doctor?'

'Of course.'

'Now, who do you work for, Doctor?'

'The State of Mississippi.'

'And for how long?'

'Eleven years.'

'And who is prosecuting Mr Hailey?'

'The State of Mississippi.'

'During your eleven-year career with the State, how many times have you testified in trials where the insanity defense was used?'

Rodeheaver thought for a moment. 'I think this is my forty-third trial.'

Jake checked something in a file and eyed the doctor with a nasty little smile. 'Are you sure it's not your forty-sixth?'

'It could be, yes. I'm not certain.'

The courtroom became still. Buckley and Musgrove hovered over their legal pads, but watched their witness carefully.

'Forty-six times you've testified for the State in insanity trials?'

'If you say so.'

'And forty-six times you've testified that the defendant was not legally insane. Correct, Doctor?'

'I'm not sure.'

'Well, let me make it simple. You've testified forty-six times, and forty-six times it has been your opinion the defendant was not legally insane. Correct?'

Rodeheaver squirmed just a little, and a hint of discomfort broke around his eyes. 'I'm not sure.'

'You've never seen a legally insane criminal defendant, have you, Doctor?'

'Of course I have.'

'Good. Would you then, please, sir, tell us the name of the defendant and where he was tried?'

Buckley rose and buttoned his coat. 'Your Honor, the State objects to these questions. Dr

Rodeheaver cannot be required to remember the names and places of the trials he has testified in.'

'Overruled. Sit down. Answer the question, Doctor.'

Rodeheaver breathed deeply and studied the ceiling. Jake glanced at the jurors. They were awake and waiting on an answer.

'I can't remember,' he finally said.

Jake lifted a thick stack of papers and waved it at the witness. 'Could it be, Doctor, that the reason you can't remember is that in eleven years, forty-six trials, you have never testified in favor of the defendant?'

'I honestly can't remember.'

'Can you honestly name us one trial in which you found the defendant to be legally insane?'

'I'm sure there are some.'

'Yes or no, Doctor. One trial?'

The expert looked briefly at the D.A. 'No. My memory fails me. I cannot at this time.'

Jake walked slowly to the defense table and picked up a thick file.

'Dr Rodeheaver, do you recall testifying in the trial of a man by the name of Danny Booker in McMurphy County in December of 1975? A rather gruesome double homicide?'

'Yes, I recall that trial.'

'And you testified to the effect that he was not legally insane, did you not?'

'That is correct.'

'Do you recall how many psychiatrists testified in his behalf?'

'Not exactly. There were several.'

'Do the names Noel McClacky, M.D.; O.G. McGuire, M.D.; and Lou Watson, M.D., ring a bell?'

'Yes.'

'They're all psychiatrists, aren't they?'

'Yes.'

'They're all qualified, aren't they?'

'Yes.'

'And they all examined Mr Booker and testified at trial that in their opinions the poor man was legally insane?'

'That's correct.'

'And you testified he was not legally insane?'

'That's correct.'

'How many other doctors supported your position?'

'None, that I recall.'

'So it was three against one?'

'Yes, but I'm still convinced I was right.'

'I see. What did the jury do, Doctor?'

'He, uh, was found not guilty by reason of insanity.'

'Thank you. Now, Dr Rodeheaver, you're the head doctor at Whitfield, aren't you?'

'Yes, so to speak.'

'Are you directly or indirectly responsible for the treatment of every patient at Whitfield?'

'I'm directly responsible, Mr Brigance. I may not personally see every patient, but their doctors are under my supervision.'

'Thank you. Doctor, where is Danny Booker today?'

Rodeheaver shot a desperate look at Buckley, and immediately covered it with a warm, relaxed grin for the jury. He hesitated for a few seconds, then hesitated one second too long.

'He's at Whitfield, isn't he?' Jake asked in a tone of voice that informed everyone that the answer was yes.

'I believe so,' Rodeheaver said.

'So, he's directly under your care, then, Doctor?'

'I suppose.'

'And what is his diagnosis, Doctor?'

'I really don't know. I have a lot of patients and—'

'Paranoid schizophrenic?'

'It's possible, yes.'

Jake walked backward and sat on the railing. He turned up the volume. 'Now, Doctor, I want to make this clear for the jury. In 1975 you testified that Danny Booker was legally sane and understood exactly what he was doing when he committed his crime, and the jury disagreed with you and found him not guilty, and since that time he has been a patient in your hospital, under your supervision, and treated by you as a paranoid schizophrenic. Is that correct?'

The smirk on Rodeheaver's face informed the jury that it was indeed correct.

Jake picked up another piece of paper and seemed to review it. 'Do you recall testifying in the trial of a man by the name of Adam Couch in Dupree County in May of 1977?'

'I remember that case.'

'It was a rape case, wasn't it?'

'Yes.'

'And you testified on behalf of the State against Mr Couch?'

'That's correct.'

'And you told the jury that he was not legally insane?'

'That was my testimony.'

'Do you recall how many doctors testified on his behalf and told the jury he was a very sick man, that he was legally insane?'

'There were several.'

'Have you ever heard of the following doctors: Felix Perry, Gene Shumate, and Hobny Wicker?'

'Yes.'

'Are they all qualified psychiatrists?'

'They are.'

'And they all testified on behalf of Mr Couch, didn't they?'

'Yes.'

'And they all said he was legally insane, didn't they?'

'They did.'

'And you were the only doctor in the trial who said he was not legally insane?'

'As I recall, yes.'

'And what did the jury do, Doctor?'

'He was found not guilty.'

'By reason of insanity?'

'Yes.'

'And where is Mr Couch today, Doctor?'

'I think he's at Whitfield.'

'And how long has he been there?'

'Since the trial, I believe.'

'I see. Do you normally admit patients and keep them for several years if they are of perfectly sound mind?'

Rodeheaver shifted his weight and began a slow burn. He looked at his lawyer, the people's lawyer, as if to say he was tired of this, do something to stop it.

Jake picked up more papers. 'Doctor, do you recall the trial of a man by the name of Buddy Wooddall in Cleburne County, May of 1979?'

'Yes, I certainly do.'

'Murder, wasn't it?'

'Yes.'

'And you testified as an expert in the field of psychiatry and told the jury that Mr Wooddall was not insane?'

'I did.'

'Do you recall how many psychiatrists testified on his behalf and told the jury the poor man was legally insane?'

'I believe there were five, Mr Brigance.'

'That's correct, Doctor. Five against one. Do you recall what the jury did?'

The anger and frustration was building in the witness stand. The wise old grandfather/professor with all the right answers was becoming rattled. 'Yes, I recall. He was found not guilty by reason of insanity.'

'How do you explain that, Dr Rodeheaver? Five against one, and the jury finds against you?'

'You just can't trust juries,' he blurted, then caught himself. He fidgeted and grinned awkwardly at the jurors.

Jake stared at him with a wicked smile, then looked at the jury in disbelief. He folded his arms and allowed the last words to sink in. He waited, staring and grinning at the witness.

'You may proceed, Mr Brigance,' Noose finally said.

Moving slowly and with great animation, Jake gathered his files and notes while staring at Rodeheaver. 'I think we've heard enough from this witness, Your Honor.'

'Any redirect, Mr Buckley?'

'No, sir. The State rests.'

Noose addressed the jury. 'Ladies and gentlemen, this trial is almost over. There will be no more witnesses. I will now meet with the attorneys to cover some technical areas, then they will be allowed to make their final arguments to you. That will begin at two o'clock and take a couple of hours. You will finally get the case around four, and I will allow you to deliberate until six. If you do not reach a verdict today, you will be taken back to your rooms until tomorrow. It is now almost eleven, and we'll recess until two. I need to see the attorneys in chambers.'

Carl Lee leaned over and spoke to his lawyer for the first time since Saturday's adjournment. 'You tore him up pretty good, Jake.'

'Wait till you hear the closing argument.'

★　　★　　★

Jake avoided Harry Rex, and drove to Karaway. His childhood home was an old country house in downtown, surrounded by ancient oaks and maples and elms that kept it cool in spite of the summer heat. In the back, past the trees, was a long open field which ran for an eighth of a mile and disappeared over a small hill. A chickenwire backstop stood over the weeds in one corner. Here, Jake had taken his first steps, rode his first bike, thrown his first football and baseball. Under an oak beside the field, he had buried three dogs, a raccoon, a rabbit, and some ducks. A tire from a '54 Buick swung not far from the small cemetery.

The house had been locked and deserted for two months. A neighborhood kid cut the grass and tended the lawn. Jake checked the house once a week. His parents were somewhere in Canada in a camper – the summer ritual. He wished he were with them.

He unlocked the door and walked upstairs to his room. It would never change. The walls were covered with team pictures, trophies, baseball caps, posters of Pete Rose, Archie Manning, and Hank Aaron. A row of baseball gloves hung above the closet door. A cap and gown picture sat on the dresser. His mother still cleaned it weekly. She once told him she often went to his room and expected to find him doing homework or sorting baseball cards. She would flip through his scrapbooks, and get all teary eyed.

He thought of Hanna's room, with the stuffed

animals and Mother Goose wallpaper. A thick knot formed in his throat.

He looked out the window, past the trees, and saw himself swinging in the tire near the three white crosses where he buried his dogs. He remembered each funeral, and his father's promises to get another dog. He thought of Hanna and her dog, and his eyes watered.

The bed was much smaller now. He removed his shoes and lay down. A football helmet hung from the ceiling. Eighth grade, Karaway Mustangs. He scored seven touchdowns in five games. It was all on film downstairs under the bookshelves. The butterflies floated wildly through his stomach.

He carefully placed his notes – his notes, not Lucien's – on the dresser. He studied himself in the mirror.

He addressed the jury. He began by facing his biggest problem, Dr W.T. Bass. He apologized. A lawyer walks into a courtroom, faces a strange jury, and has nothing to offer but his credibility. And if he does anything to hurt his credibility, he has hurt his cause, his client. He asked them to believe that he would never put a convicted felon on the stand as an expert witness in any trial. He did not know of the conviction, he raised his hand and swore to this. The world is full of psychiatrists, and he could easily have found another if he had known Bass had a problem, but he simply did not know. And he was sorry.

But what about Bass's testimony? Thirty years

ago he had sex with a girl under eighteen in Texas. Does that mean he is lying now in this trial? Does that mean you cannot trust his professional opinion? Please be fair to Bass the psychiatrist, forget Bass the person. Please be fair to his patient, Carl Lee Hailey. He knew nothing of the doctor's past.

There was something about Bass they might like to know. Something that was not mentioned by Mr Buckley when he was ripping the doctor to pieces. The girl he had sex with was seventeen. She later became his wife, bore him a son, and was pregnant when she and the boy were killed in a train—

'Objection!' Buckley shouted. 'Objection, Your Honor. That evidence is not in the record!'

'Sustained. Mr Brigance, you are not to refer to facts not in evidence. The jury will disregard the last statements by Mr Brigance.'

Jake ignored Noose and Buckley and stared painfully at the jury.

When the shouting died, he continued. What about Rodeheaver? He wondered if the State's doctor had ever engaged in sex with a girl under eighteen. Seemed silly to think about such things, didn't it? Bass and Rodeheaver in their younger days – it seemed so unimportant now in this court-room almost thirty years later.

The State's doctor is a man with an obvious bias. A highly trained specialist who treats thousands for all sorts of mental illnesses, yet when crimes are involved he cannot recognize insanity. His testimony should be carefully weighed.

They watched him, listened to every word. He was not a courtroom preacher, like his opponent. He was quiet, sincere. He looked tired, almost hurt.

Lucien was sober, and he sat with folded arms and watched the jurors, all except Sisco. It was not his closing, but it was good. It was coming from the heart.

Jake apologized for his inexperience. He had not been in many trials, not nearly as many as Mr Buckley. And if he seemed a little green, or if he made mistakes, please don't hold it against Carl Lee. It wasn't his fault. He was just a rookie trying his best against a seasoned adversary who tried murder cases every month. He made a mistake with Bass, and he made other mistakes, and he asked the jury to forgive him.

He had a daughter, the only one he would ever have. She was four, almost five, and his world revolved around her. She was special; she was a little girl, and it was up to him to protect her. There was a bond there, something he could not explain. He talked about little girls.

Carl Lee had a daughter. Her name was Tonya. He pointed to her on the front row next to her mother and brothers. She's a beautiful little girl, ten years old. And she can never have children. She can never have a daughter because—'

'Objection,' Buckley said without shouting.

'Sustained,' Noose said.

Jake ignored the commotion. He talked about rape for a while, and explained how rape is much worse than murder. With murder, the victim is gone, and not forced to deal with what happened to her. The family must deal with it, but not the victim. But rape is much worse. The victim has a lifetime of coping, of trying to understand, of asking questions, and, the worst part, of knowing the rapist is still alive and may someday escape or be released. Every hour of every day, the victim thinks of the rape and asks herself a thousand questions. She relives it, step by step, minute by minute, and it hurts just as bad.

Perhaps the most horrible crime of all is the violent rape of a child. A woman who is raped has a pretty good idea why it happened. Some animal was filled with hatred, anger and violence. But a child? A ten-year-old child? Suppose you're a parent. Imagine yourself trying to explain to your child why she was raped. Imagine yourself trying to explain why she cannot bear children.

'Objection.'

'Sustained. Please disregard that last statement, ladies and gentlemen.'

Jake never missed a beat. Suppose, he said, your ten-year-old daughter is raped, and you're a Vietnam vet, very familiar with an M-16, and you get your hands on one while your daughter is lying in the hospital fighting for her life. Suppose the rapist is caught, and six days later you manage to maneuver to within five feet of him as he leaves court. And you've got the M-16.

What do you do?

Mr Buckley has told you what he would do. He

would mourn for his daughter, turn the other cheek, and hope the judicial system worked. He would hope the rapist would receive justice, be sent to Parchman, and hopefully never paroled. That's what he would do, and they should admire him for being such a kind, compassionate, and forgiving soul. But what would a reasonable father do?

What would Jake do? If he had the M-16? Blow the bastard's head off!

It was simple. It was justice.

Jake paused for a drink of water, then shifted gears. The pained and humble look was replaced with an air of indignation. Let's talk about Cobb and Willard. They started this mess. It was their lives the State was attempting to justify. Who would miss them except their mothers? Child rapists. Drug pushers. Would society miss such productive citizens? Wasn't Ford County safer without them? Were not the other children in the county better off now that two rapists and pushers had been removed? All parents should feel safer. Carl Lee deserves a medal, or at least a round of applause. He was a hero. That's what Looney said. Give the man a trophy. Send him home to his family.

He talked about Looney. He had a daughter. He also had one leg, thanks to Carl Lee Hailey. If anyone had a right to be bitter, to want blood, it was DeWayne Looney. And he said Carl Lee should be sent home to his family.

He urged them to forgive as Looney had forgiven. He asked them to follow Looney's wishes.

He became much quieter, and said he was almost through. He wanted to leave them with one thought. Picture this if they could. When she was lying there, beaten, bloodied, legs spread and tied to trees, she looked into the woods around her. Semiconscious and hallucinating, she saw someone running toward her. It was her daddy, running desperately to save her. In her dreams she saw him when she needed him the most. She cried out for him, and he disappeared. He was taken away.

She needs him now, as much as she needed him then. Please don't take him away. She waits on the front row for her daddy.

Let him go home to his family.

The courtroom was silent as Jake sat next to his client. He glanced at the jury, and saw Wanda Womack brush away a tear with her finger. For the first time in two days he felt a flicker of hope.

At four, Noose bid farewell to his jury. He told them to elect a foreman, get organized, and get busy. He told them they could deliberate until six, maybe seven, and if no verdict was reached he would recess until nine Tuesday morning. They stood and filed slowly from the courtroom. Once out of sight, Noose recessed until six and instructed the attorneys to remain close to the courtroom or leave a number with the clerk.

The spectators held their seats and chatted quietly. Carl Lee was allowed to sit on the front row with his family. Buckley and Musgrove waited in chambers with Noose. Harry Rex, Lucien, and Jake left for the office and a liquid supper. No one expected a quick verdict.

The bailiff locked them in the jury room and instructed the two alternates to take a seat in the narrow hallway. Inside, Barry Acker was elected foreman by acclamation. He laid the jury instructions and exhibits on a small table in a corner. They sat anxiously around two folding tables placed end to end.

'I suggest we take an informal vote,' he said. 'Just to see where we are. Any objections to that?'

There were none. He had a list of twelve names.

'Vote guilty, not guilty, or undecided. Or you can pass for now.'

'Reba Betts.'

'Undecided.'

'Bernice Toole.'

'Guilty.'

'Carol Corman.'

'Guilty.'

'Donna Lou Peck.'

'Undecided.'

'Sue Williams.'

'Pass.'

'Jo Ann Gates.'

'Guilty.'

'Rita Mae Plunk.'

'Guilty.'

'Frances McGowan.'

'Guilty.'

'Wanda Womack.'

'Undecided.'

'Eula Dell Yates.'

'Undecided, for now. I wanna talk about it.'

'We will. Clyde Sisco.'

'Undecided.'

'That's eleven. I'm Barry Acker, and I vote not guilty.'

He tallied for a few seconds and said, 'That's five guilties, five undecideds, one pass, and one not guilty. Looks like we've got our work cut out for us.'

They worked through the exhibits, photographs, fingerprints, and ballistics reports. At six, they informed the judge they had not reached a verdict. They were hungry and wanted to go. He recessed until Tuesday morning.

Chapter 41

They sat for hours on the porch, saying little, watching as darkness surrounded the town below and ushered in the mosquitoes. The heat wave had returned. The soggy air clung to their skin and moistened their shirts. The sounds of a hot summer night echoed softly across the front lawn. Sallie had offered to cook. Lucien declined and ordered whiskey. Jake had no appetite for food, but the Coors filled his system and satisfied any hunger pangs stirring within. When things were good and dark, Nesbit emerged from his car, walked across the porch, through the front screen door, and into the house. A moment later he slammed the door, walked past them with a cold beer, and disappeared down the driveway in the direction of his car. He never said a word.

Sallie stuck her head through the door and made one last offer of food. Both declined.

'Jake, I got a call this afternoon. Clyde Sisco wants twenty-five thousand to hang the jury, fifty thousand for an acquittal.'

Jake began shaking his head.

'Before you say no, listen to me. He knows he can't guarantee an acquittal, but he can guarantee a hung jury. It just takes one. That's twenty-five thousand. I know it's a lot of money, but you know I've got it. I'll pay it and you can repay me over the years. Whenever, I don't care. If you never repay it, I don't care. I've got a bankful of C.D.'s. You know money means nothing to me. If I were you I'd do it in a minute.'

'You're crazy, Lucien.'

'Sure I'm crazy. You haven't been acting so good yourself. Trial work'll drive you crazy. Just take a look at what this trial has done to you. No sleep, no food, no routine, no house. Plenty of booze, though.'

'But I've still got ethics.'

'And I have none. No ethics, no morals, no conscience. But I won, bubba. I won more than anybody has ever won around here, and you know it.'

'It's corrupt, Lucien.'

'And I guess you think Buckley's not corrupt. He would lie, cheat, bribe, and steal to win this case. He's not worried about fancy ethics, rules, and opinions. He's not concerned about morality. He's concerned with one thing and only one thing – winning! And you've got a golden chance to beat him at his own game. I'd do it, Jake.'

'Forget it, Lucien. Please, just forget it.'

An hour passed with no words. The lights of the town below slowly disappeared. Nesbit's snoring was audible in the darkness. Sallie brought one last drink and said good night.

'This is the hardest part,' Lucien said. 'Waiting on twelve average, everyday people to make sense of all this.'

'It's a crazy system, isn't it?'

'Yes, it is. But it usually works. Juries are right ninety percent of the time.'

'I just don't feel lucky. I'm waiting on the miracle.'

'Jake, my boy, the miracle happens tomorrow.'

'Tomorrow?'

'Yes. Early tomorrow morning.'

'Would you care to elaborate?'

'By noon tomorrow, Jake, there will be ten thousand angry blacks swarming like ants around the Ford County Courthouse. Maybe more.'

'Ten thousand! Why?'

'To scream and shout and chant "Free Carl Lee, Free Carl Lee." To raise hell, to scare everybody, to intimidate the jury. To just disrupt the hell out of everything. There'll be so many blacks, white folks will run for cover. The governor will send in more troops.'

'And how do you know all this?'

'Because I planned it, Jake.'

'You?'

'Listen, Jake, when I was in my prime I knew every black preacher in fifteen counties. I've been in their churches. Prayed with them, marched with them, sang with them. They sent me clients, and I sent them money. I was the only white radical

698

NAACP lawyer in north Mississippi. I filed more race discrimination lawsuits than any ten firms in Washington. These were my people. I've just made a few phone calls. They'll start arriving in the morning, and by noon you won't be able to stir niggers with a stick in downtown Clanton.'

'Where will they come from?'

'Everywhere. You know how blacks love to march and protest. This will be great for them. They're looking forward to it.'

'You're crazy, Lucien. My crazy friend.'

'I win, bubba.'

In Room 163, Barry Acker and Clyde Sisco finished their last game of gin rummy and made preparations for bed. Acker gathered some coins and announced he wanted a soft drink. Sisco said he was not thirsty.

Acker tiptoed past a guardsman asleep in the hall. The machine informed him it was out of order, so he quietly opened the exit door and walked up the stairs to the second floor, where he found another machine next to an ice maker. He inserted his coins. The machine responded with a diet Coke. He bent over to pick it up.

Out of the darkness two figures charged. They knocked him to the floor, kicked him and pinned him in a dark corner beside the ice maker, next to a door with a chain and padlock. The large one grabbed Acker's collar and threw him against the cinder block wall. The smaller one stood by the Coke machine and watched the dark hall.

'You're Barry Acker!' said the large one through clenched teeth.

'Yeah! Let go of me!' Acker attempted to shake free, but his assailant lifted him by the throat and held him to the wall with one hand. He used the other hand to unsheathe a shiny hunting knife, which he placed next to Acker's nose. The wiggling stopped.

'Listen to me,' he demanded in a loud whisper, 'and listen good. We know you're married and you live at 1161 Forrest Drive. We know you got three kids, and we know where they play and go to school. Your wife works at the bank.'

Acker went limp.

'If that nigger walks free, you'll be sorry. Your family will be sorry. It may take years, but you'll be awfully sorry.'

He dropped him to the floor and grabbed his hair. 'You breathe one word of this to anyone, and you'll lose a kid. Understand?'

They vanished. Acker breathed deeply, almost gasping for breath. He rubbed his throat and the back of his head. He sat in the darkness, too scared to move.

Chapter 42

At hundreds of small black churches across north Mississippi, the faithful gathered before dawn and loaded picnic baskets, coolers, lawn chairs, and water jugs into converted school buses and church vans. They greeted friends and chatted nervously about the trial. For weeks they had read and talked about Carl Lee Hailey; now, they were about to go help. Many were old and retired, but there were entire families with children and playpens. When the buses were full, they piled into cars and followed their preachers. They sang and prayed. The preachers met other preachers in small towns and county seats, and they set out in force down the dark highways. When daylight materialized, the highways and roads leading to Ford County were filled with caravans of pilgrims.

They jammed the side streets for blocks around the square. They parked where they stopped and unloaded.

The fat colonel had just finished breakfast and stood in the gazebo watching intently. Buses and cars, many with horns honking, were coming from all directions to the square. The barricades held firm. He barked commands and the soldiers jumped into high gear. More excitement. At seven-thirty, he called Ozzie and told him of the invasion. Ozzie arrived immediately and found Agee, who assured him it was a peaceful march. Sort of like a sit-in. How many were coming? Ozzie asked. Thousands, said Agee. Thousands.

They set up camp under the stately oaks, and milled around the lawn inspecting things. They arranged tables and chairs and playpens. They were indeed peaceful, until a group began the familiar cry of 'Free Carl Lee!' They cleared their throats and joined in. It was not yet eight o'clock.

A black radio station in Memphis flooded the airwaves early Tuesday with a call for help. Black bodies were needed to march and demonstrate in Clanton, Mississippi, an hour away. Hundreds of cars met at a mall and headed south. Every civil rights activist and black politician in the city made the trip.

Agee was a man possessed. He used a bullhorn to shout orders here and there. He herded new arrivals into their places. He organized the black preachers. He assured Ozzie and the colonel everything was okay.

Everything was okay until a handful of Klansmen made their routine appearance. The sight of the white robes was new to many of the blacks, and they reacted loudly. They inched forward, screaming and jeering. The troops surrounded the robes and protected them. The Kluxers were stunned and scared, and did not yell back.

By eight-thirty, the streets of Clanton were gridlocked. Deserted cars, vans, and buses were scattered haphazardly through parking lots and along the quiet residential streets. A steady stream of blacks walked toward the square from all directions. Traffic did not move. Driveways were blocked. Merchants parked blocks away from their shops. The mayor stood in the center of the gazebo, wringing his hands and begging Ozzie to do something. Around him thousands of blacks swarmed and yelled in perfect unison. Ozzie asked the mayor if he wanted him to start arresting everybody on the courthouse lawn.

Noose parked at a service station a half mile south of the jail, and walked with a group of blacks to the courthouse. They watched him curiously, but said nothing. No one would suspect he was a person of authority. Buckley and Musgrove parked in a driveway on Adams Street. They cursed and walked toward the square. They noticed the pile of rubble that had been Jake's house but said nothing. They were too busy cursing. With state troopers leading the way, the Greyhound from Temple reached the square at twenty minutes after nine. Through the dark windows, the fourteen passengers stared in disbelief at the carnival around the courthouse.

Mr Pate called the packed courtroom to order, and Noose welcomed his jury. He apologized for the trouble outside, but there was nothing he could do. If there were no problems to report, they could continue deliberations.

'Very well, you may retire to the jury room and get to work. We will meet again just before lunch.'

The jurors filed out and went to the jury room. The Hailey children sat with their father at the defense table. The spectators, now predominantly black, remained seated and struck up conversations. Jake returned to his office.

Foreman Acker sat at the end of the long, dusty table and thought of the hundreds, perhaps thousands, of Ford Countians who had served in this room and sat around this table and argued about justice over the past century. Any pride he may have felt for serving on the jury of the most famous case was greatly overshadowed by what happened last night. He wondered how many of his predecessors had been threatened with death. Probably a few, he decided.

The others fixed their coffee and slowly found seats around the tables. The room brought back fond memories for Clyde Sisco. Prior jury duty had proved lucrative for him, and he relished the thought of another handsome payoff for another just and true verdict. His messenger had not contacted him.

'How would y'all like to proceed?' the foreman asked.

Rita Mae Plunk had an especially hard and unforgiving look about her. She was a rough woman with a house trailer, no husband, and two outlaws for sons, both of whom had expressed hatred for Carl Lee Hailey. She had a few things she wanted to get off her large chest.

'I got a few things I wanna say,' she informed Acker.

'Fine. Why don't we start with you, Miss Plunk, and go around the table.'

'I voted guilty yesterday in the first vote, and I'll vote guilty next time. I don't see how anybody could vote not guilty, and I want just one of you to explain to me how you could vote in favor of this nigger!'

'Don't say that word again!' yelled Wanda Womack.

'I'll say "nigger" if I wanna say "nigger," and there ain't a damned thing you can do,' replied Rita Mae.

'Please don't use that word,' said Frances McGowan.

'I find it personally offensive,' said Wanda Womack.

'Nigger, Nigger, Nigger, Nigger, Nigger, Nigger,' Rita Mae yelled across the table.

'Come on,' said Clyde Sisco.

'Oh boy,' said the foreman. 'Look, Miss Plunk, let's be honest, okay. Most of us use that word, from time to time. I'm sure some of us use it more than others. But it's offensive to many people, and I think it'd be a good idea not to use it during our deliberations. We've got enough to worry about as it is. Can we all agree not to use that word?'

Everyone nodded but Rita Mae.

Sue Williams decided to answer. She was well dressed, attractive, about forty. She worked for the county welfare department. 'I didn't vote yesterday. I passed. But I tend to sympathize with Mr Hailey. I have a daughter, and if she was raped, it would greatly affect my mental stability. I can understand how a parent might crack in that situation, and I think it's unfair for us to judge Mr Hailey as if he was supposed to act completely rational.'

'You think he was legally insane?' asked Reba Betts, an undecided.

'I'm not sure. But I know he wasn't stable. He couldn't have been.'

'So you believe that nut of a doctor who testified for him?' asked Rita Mae.

'Yes. He was as believable as the State's doctor.'

'I liked his boots,' said Clyde Sisco. No one laughed.

'But he's a convict,' said Rita Mae. 'He lied and tried to cover it up. You can't believe a word he said.'

'He had sex with a girl under eighteen,' Clyde said. 'If that's a crime, then a bunch of us should've been indicted.'

Again, no one appreciated the attempt at humor. Clyde decided to stay quiet for a while.

'He later married the girl,' said Donna Lou Peck, an undecided.

They went around the table, one at a time, expressing opinions and answering questions. The N word was carefully avoided by those wanting a conviction. The battle lines became clearer. Most of the undecideds leaned toward guilty, it seemed. The careful planning by Carl Lee, knowing the exact movements of the boys, the M-16 – it all seemed so premeditated. If he had caught them in the act and killed them on the spot, he would not be held accountable. But to plan it so carefully for six days did not indicate an insane mind.

Wanda Womack, Sue Williams, and Clyde Sisco leaned toward acquittal – the rest toward conviction. Barry Acker was noticeably noncommittal.

Agee unfurled a long blue and white FREE CARL LEE banner. The ministers gathered fifteen abreast behind it, and waited for the parade to form behind them. They stood in the center of Jackson Street, in front of the courthouse, while Agee screamed instructions to the masses. Thousands of blacks packed tightly behind them, and off they went. They inched down Jackson, and turned left on Caffey, up the west side of the square. Agee led the marchers in their now familiar battle cry of 'Free Carl Lee! Free Carl Lee!' They screamed it in an endless, repetitive, numbing chorus. As the crowd moved around the square, it grew in number and volume.

Smelling trouble, the merchants locked up and headed for home and safety. They checked their policies to see if they were insured for riot damage. The green soldiers were lost in a sea of black. The colonel, sweating and nervous, ordered his troops to circle the courthouse and stand firm. While

Agee and the marchers were turning onto Washington Street, Ozzie met with the handful of Kluxers. In a sincere and diplomatic way, he convinced them things could get out of hand, and he could no longer guarantee their safety. He acknowledged their right to assemble, said they had made their point, and asked them to get away from the square before there was trouble. They huddled quickly, and disappeared.

When the banner passed under the jury room, all twelve gaped from the window. The incessant chanting rattled the glass panes. The bullhorn sounded like a loudspeaker hanging from the ceiling. The jurors stared in disbelief at the mob, the black mob which filled the street and trailed around the corner onto Caffey. A varied assortment of homemade signs bobbed above the masses and demanded that the man be freed.

'I didn't know there were this many niggers in Ford County,' Rita Mae Plunk said. At that moment, the other eleven held the same thought.

Buckley was furious. He and Musgrove watched from a third-floor window in the library. The roar below had disrupted their quiet conversation.

'I didn't know there were this many niggers in Ford County,' Musgrove said.

'There ain't. Somebody shipped these niggers in here. I wonder who put them up to it.'

'Probably Brigance.'

'Yeah, probably so. It's mighty convenient that they start all this hell-raising when the jury is deliberating. There must be five thousand niggers down there.'

'At least.'

Noose and Mr Pate watched and listened from a second-floor window in chambers. His Honor was not happy. He worried about his jury. 'I don't see how they can concentrate on much with all this going on.'

'Pretty good timing, ain't it, Judge?' Mr Pate said.

'It certainly is.'

'I didn't know we had that many blacks in the whole county.'

It took twenty minutes for Mr Pate and Jean Gillespie to find the attorneys and bring the court-room to order. When it was quiet, the jurors filed into their seats. There were no smiles.

Noose cleared his throat. 'Ladies and gentlemen, it is time for lunch. I don't suppose you have anything to report.'

Barry Acker shook his head.

'That's what I figured. Let's break for lunch, until one-thirty. I realize you cannot leave the courthouse, but I want you to eat for a while without working on the case. I apologize for the disturbance outside, but, frankly, I can't do anything about it. We'll be in recess until one-thirty.'

In chambers, Buckley went wild. 'This is crazy, Judge! There's no way the jury can concentrate on this case with all that noise out there. This is a deliberate effort to intimidate the jury.'

'I don't like it,' Noose said.

'It was planned, Judge! It's intentional!' Buckley yelled.

'It looks bad,' Noose added.

'I'm almost ready for a mistrial!'

'I won't grant one. What do you say, Jake?'

Jake grinned for a moment, and said, 'Free Carl Lee.'

'Very funny,' Buckley growled. 'You probably planned all this.'

'No. If you will recall, Mr Buckley, I tried to prevent it. I have repeatedly asked for a change of venue. I have repeatedly said the trial should not be held in this courthouse. You wanted it here, Mr Buckley, and you kept it here, Judge Noose. You both now look foolish complaining.'

Jake was impressed with his arrogance. Buckley growled and stared out the window. 'Look at them. Wild niggers. Must be ten thousand out there.'

During lunch the ten thousand grew to fifteen thousand. Cars from a hundred miles away – some with Tennessee plates – parked on the shoulders of the highways outside the city limits. The people hiked for two and three miles under a blistering sun to join the festivities around the courthouse. Agee broke for lunch, and the square quieted.

The blacks were peaceful. They opened their coolers and picnic baskets, and shared with each other. They congregated in the shade, but there were not enough trees to go around. They filled the courthouse in search of cold water and rest rooms. They walked the sidewalks and gazed in the windows of the closed shops and stores. Fearing trouble from the horde, the Coffee Shop and the Tea Shoppe closed during lunch. Outside of Claude's, they lined the sidewalk for a block and a half.

Jake, Harry Rex, and Lucien relaxed on the balcony and enjoyed the circus below. A pitcher of fresh, slushy margaritas sat on the table and slowly disappeared. At times they participated in the rally, yelling 'Free Carl Lee' or humming along with 'We Shall Overcome.' No one knew the words but Lucien. He had learned them during the glorious civil rights days of the sixties, and still claimed to be the only white in Ford County who knew all the words to every stanza. He had even joined a black church back then, he explained between drinks, after his church voted to exclude black members. He dropped out after a three-hour sermon ruptured a disc. He had decided white people were not cut out for that kind of worship. He still contributed, however.

Occasionally, a crew of TV people would stray near Jake's office and serve up a question. Jake would pretend not to hear, then finally yell 'Free Carl Lee.'

Precisely at one-thirty, Agee found his bullhorn, unfurled his banner, lined up the ministers and gathered his marchers. He started with the hymn, sung directly into the bullhorn, and the parade crawled down Jackson, then onto Caffey, and around and around the square. Each lap attracted more people and made more noise.

The jury room was silent for fifteen minutes after Reba Betts was converted from an undecided to a not guilty. If a man raped her, she just might blow his head off if she got the chance. It was now five to five with two undecideds, and a compromise looked hopeless. The foreman continued to straddle the fence. Poor old Eula Dell Yates had cried one way, then cried the other, and everyone knew she would eventually go with the majority. She had burst into tears at the window, and was led to her seat by Clyde Sisco. She wanted to go home. Said she felt like a prisoner.

The shouting and marching had taken its toll. When the bullhorn passed nearby, the anxiety level in the small room reached a frenzied peak. Acker would ask for quiet, and they would wait impatiently until the racket faded to the front of the courthouse. It never disappeared completely. Carol Corman was the first to inquire about their safety. For the first time in a week, the quiet motel was awfully attractive.

Three hours of nonstop chanting had unraveled whatever nerves were left. The foreman suggested they talk about their families and wait until Noose sent for them at five.

Bernice Toole, a soft guilty, suggested something they had all thought about but no one had mentioned. 'Why don't we just tell the judge we are hopelessly deadlocked?'

'He'd declare a mistrial, wouldn't he?' asked Jo Ann Gates.

'Yes,' answered the foreman. 'And he would be retried in a few months. Why don't we call it a day, and try again tomorrow?'

They agreed. They were not ready to quit. Eula Dell cried softly.

At four, Carl Lee and the kids walked to one of the tall windows lining each side of the courtroom. He noticed a small knob. He turned it, and the windows swung open to a tiny platform hanging over the west lawn. He nodded at a deputy, and stepped outside. He held Tonya and watched the crowd.

They saw him. They yelled his name and rushed to the building under him. Agee led the marchers off the street and across the lawn. A wave of black humanity gathered under the small porch and pressed forward for a closer look at their champion.

'Free Carl Lee!'

'Free Carl Lee!'

'Free Carl Lee!'

He waved at his fans below him. He kissed his daughter and hugged his sons. He waved and told the kids to wave.

Jake and his small band of hombres used the diversion to stagger across the street to the courthouse. Jean Gillespie had called. Noose wanted to see the lawyers in chambers. He was disturbed. Buckley was raging.

'I demand a mistrial! I demand a mistrial!' he yelled at Noose the second Jake walked in.

'You move for a mistrial, Governor. You don't demand,' Jake said through glassy eyes.

'You go to hell, Brigance! You planned all this. You plotted this insurrection. Those are your niggers out there.'

'Where's the court reporter?' Jake asked. 'I want this on the record.'

'Gentlemen, gentlemen,' Noose said. 'Let's be professionals.'

'Judge, the State moves for a mistrial,' Buckley said, somewhat professionally.

'Overruled.'

'All right, then. The State moves to allow the jury to deliberate at someplace other than the courthouse.'

'Now that's an interesting idea,' Noose said.

'I see no reason why they can't deliberate at the motel. It's quiet and few people know where it is,' Buckley said confidently.

'Jake?' Noose said.

'Nope, it won't work. There is no statutory provision giving you the authority to allow deliberations outside the courthouse.' Jake reached in his pocket and found several folded papers. He threw them on the desk. 'State versus Dubose, 1963 case from Linwood County. The air conditioning in the Linwood County Courthouse quit during a heat wave. The circuit judge allowed the jury to deliberate in a local library. The defense objected. Jury convicted. On appeal, the Supreme Court ruled the judge's decision was improper and an abuse of discretion. The court went on to hold that the jury deliberations must take place in the jury room in the courthouse where the defendant is being tried. You can't move them.'

Noose studied the case and handed it to Musgrove.

'Get the courtroom ready,' he said to Mr Pate.

With the exception of the reporters, the courtroom was solid black. The jurors looked haggard and strained.

'I take it you do not have a verdict,' Noose said.

'No, sir,' replied the foreman.

'Let me ask you this. Without indicating any numerical division, have you reached a point where you can go no further?'

'We've talked about that, Your Honor. And we'd like to leave, get a good night's rest, and try again tomorrow. We're not ready to quit.'

'That's good to hear. I apologize for the distractions, but, again, there's nothing I can do. I'm sorry. You'll just have to do your best. Anything further?'

'No, sir.'

'Very well. We'll stand adjourned until nine A.M. tomorrow.'

Carl Lee pulled Jake's shoulder. 'What does all this mean?'

'It means they're deadlocked. It could be six to six, or eleven to one against you, or eleven to one for acquittal. So don't get excited.'

Barry Acker cornered the bailiff and handed him a folded sheet of paper. It read:

Luann:
Pack the kids and go to your mother's. Don't tell anyone. Stay there until this thing is over. Just do as I say. Things are dangerous.
Barry

'Can you get this to my wife today? Our number is 881–0774.'
'Sure,' said the bailiff.

Tim Nunley, mechanic down at the Chevrolet place, former client of Jake Brigance, and Coffee Shop regular, sat on a couch in the cabin deep in the woods and drank a beer. He listened to his Klan brothers as they got drunk and cursed niggers. Occasionally, he cursed them too. He had noticed whispering for the past two nights now, and felt something was up. He listened carefully.

He stood to get another beer. Suddenly, they jumped him. Three of his comrades pinned him against the wall and pounded him with fists and feet. He was beaten badly, then gagged, bound, and dragged outside, across the gravel road, and into the field where he had been inducted as a member. A cross was lit as he was tied to a pole and stripped. A bullwhip lashed him until his shoulders, back, and legs were solid crimson.

Two dozen of his ex-brethren watched in mute horror as the pole and limp body were soaked with kerosene. The leader, the one with the bull-whip, stood next to him for an eternity. He pronounced the death sentence, then threw a match.

Mickey Mouse had been silenced.

They packed their robes and belongings, and left for home. Most would never return to Ford County.

Chapter 43

Wednesday. For the first time in weeks Jake slept more than eight hours. He had fallen asleep on the couch in his office, and he awoke at five to the sounds of the military preparing for the worst. He was rested, but the nervous throbbing returned with the thought that this day would probably be the big day. He showered and shaved downstairs, and ripped open a new pack of Fruit of the Loom he had purchased at the drug store. He dressed himself in Stan Atcavage's finest navy all-season suit, which was an inch too short and a bit loose, but not a bad fit under the circumstances. He thought of the rubble on Adams Street, then Carla, and the knot in his stomach began to churn. He ran for the newspapers.

On the front pages of the Memphis, Jackson, and Tupelo papers were identical photos of Carl Lee standing on the small porch over the mob, holding his daughter and waving to his people. There was nothing about Jake's house. He was relieved, and suddenly hungry.

Dell hugged him like a lost child. She removed her apron and sat next to him in a corner booth. As the regulars arrived and saw him, they stopped by and patted him on the back. It was good to see him again. They had missed him, and they were for him. He looked gaunt, she said, so he ordered most of the menu.

'Say, Jake, are all those blacks gonna be back today?' asked Bert West.

'Probably,' he said as he stabbed a chunk of pancakes.

'I heard they's plannin' to bring more folks this mornin',' said Andy Rennick. 'Ever nigger radio station in north Mississippi is tellin' folks to come to Clanton.'

Great, thought Jake. He added Tabasco to his scrambled eggs.

'Can the jury hear all that yellin'?' asked Bert.

'Sure they can,' Jake answered. 'That's why they're doing it. They're not deaf.'

'That's gotta scare them.'

Jake certainly hoped so.

'How's the family?' Dell asked quietly.

'Fine, I guess. I talked to Carla every night.'

'She scared?'

'Terrified.'

'What have they done to you lately?'

'Nothing since Sunday morning.'

'Does Carla know?'

Jake chewed and shook his head.

'I didn't think so. You poor thing.'

'I'll be okay. What's the talk in here?'

719

'We closed at lunch yesterday. There were so many blacks outside, and we were afraid of a riot. We'll watch it close this morning, and we may close again. Jake, what if there's a conviction?'

'It could get hairy.'

He stayed for an hour and answered their questions. Strangers arrived, and Jake excused himself.

There was nothing to do but wait. He sat on the balcony, drank coffee, smoked a cigar, and watched the guardsmen. He thought of the clients he once had; of a quiet little Southern law office with a secretary and clients waiting to see him. Of docket calls and interviews at the jail. Of normal things, like a family, a home, and church on Sunday mornings. He was not meant for the big time.

The first church bus arrived at seven-thirty and was halted by the soldiers. The doors flew open and an endless stream of blacks with lawn chairs and food baskets headed for the front lawn. For an hour Jake blew smoke into the heavy air and watched with great satisfaction as the square filled beyond capacity with noisy yet peaceful protestors. The reverends were out in full force, directing their people and assuring Ozzie and the colonel they were nonviolent folk. Ozzie was convinced. The colonel was nervous. By nine, the streets were crammed with demonstrators. Someone spotted the Greyhound. 'Here they come!' Agee screamed into the loudspeaker. The mob pushed to the corner of Jackson and Quincy, where the soldiers, troopers, and deputies formed a mobile barricade around the bus and walked it through the crowd to the rear of the courthouse.

Eula Dell Yates cried openly. Clyde Sisco sat next to the window and held her hand. The others stared in fear as the bus inched around the square. A heavily armed passageway was cleared from the bus to the courthouse, and Ozzie came aboard. The situation was under control, he assured them over the roar. Just follow him and walk as fast as possible.

The bailiff locked the door as they gathered around the coffeepot. Eula Dell sat by herself in the corner crying softly and flinching as each 'Free Carl Lee!' boomed from below.

'I don't care what we do,' she said. 'I really don't care, but I just can't take any more of this. I haven't seen my family in eight days, and now this madness. I didn't sleep any last night.' She cried louder. 'I think I'm close to a nervous breakdown. Let's just get outta here.'

Clyde handed her a Kleenex and rubbed her shoulder.

Jo Ann Gates was a soft guilty who was ready to crack. 'I didn't sleep either last night. I can't take another day like yesterday. I wanna go home to my kids.'

Barry Acker stood by the window and thought of the riot that would follow a guilty verdict. There wouldn't be a building left downtown, including the courthouse. He doubted if anybody would protect the jurors in the aftermath of a wrong verdict. They probably wouldn't make it back to the bus. Thankfully, his wife and kids had fled to safety in Arkansas.

'I feel like a hostage,' said Bernice Toole, a firm guilty. 'That mob would storm the courthouse in a split second if we convict him. I feel intimidated.'

Clyde handed her a box of Kleenexes.

'I don't care what we do,' Eula Dell whined in desperation. 'Let's just get outta here. I honestly don't care if we convict him or cut him loose, let's just do something. My nerves can't take it.'

Wanda Womack stood at the end of the table and nervously cleared her throat. She asked for attention. 'I have a proposal,' she said slowly, 'that just might settle this thing.'

The crying stopped, and Barry Acker returned to his seat. She had their complete attention.

'I thought of something last night when I couldn't sleep, and I want you to consider it. It may be painful. It may cause you to search your heart and take a long look at your soul. But I'll ask you to do it anyway. And if each of you will be honest with yourself, I think we can wrap this up before noon.'

The only sounds came from the street below.

'Right now we are evenly divided, give or take a vote. We could tell Judge Noose that we are hopelessly deadlocked. He would declare a mistrial, and we would go home. Then in a few months this entire spectacle would be repeated. Mr Hailey would be tried again in this same courtroom, with the same judge, but with a different jury, a jury drawn from this county, a jury of our friends, husbands, wives, and parents. The same kind of people who are now in this room. That jury will be confronted with the same issues before us now, and those people will not be any smarter than we are.

'The time to decide this case is now. It would be morally wrong to shirk our responsibilities and pass the buck to the next jury. Can we all agree on that?'

They silently agreed.

'Good. This is what I want you to do. I want you to pretend with me for a moment. I want you to use your imaginations. I want you to close your eyes and listen to nothing but my voice.'

They obediently closed their eyes. Anything was worth a try.

Jake lay on the couch in his office and listened to Lucien tell stories about his prestigious father and grandfather, and their prestigious law firm, and all the people they screwed out of money and land.

'My inheritance was built by my promiscuous ancestors!' he yelled. 'They screwed everybody they could!'

Harry Rex laughed uncontrollably. Jake had heard the stories before, but they were always funny, and different.

'What about Ethel's retarded son?' Jake asked.

'Don't talk that way about my brother,' Lucien protested. 'He's the brightest one in the family.

Sure he's my brother. Dad hired her when she was seventeen, and believe it or not, she looked good back then. Ethel Twitty was the hottest thing in Ford County. My dad couldn't keep his hands off her. Sickening to think about now, but it's true.'

'It's disgusting,' Jake said.

'She had a houseful of kids, and two of them looked just like me, especially the dunce. It was very embarrassing back then.'

'What about your mother?' asked Harry Rex.

'She was one of those dignified old Southern ladies whose main concern was who had blue blood and who didn't. There's not much blue blood around here, so she spent most of her time in Memphis trying to impress and be accepted by the cotton families. I spent a good part of my childhood at the Peabody Hotel all starched out with a little red bow tie, trying to act polished around the rich kids from Memphis. I hated it, and I didn't care much for my mother either. She knew about Ethel, but she accepted it. She told the old man to be discreet and not embarrass the family. He was discreet, and I wound up with a retarded half-brother.'

'When did she die?'

'Six months before my father was killed in the plane crash.'

'How'd she die?' asked Harry Rex.

'Gonorrhea. Caught it from the yard boy.'

'Lucien! Seriously?'

'Cancer. Carried it for three years, but she was dignified to the very end.'

'Where'd you go wrong?' Jake asked.

'I think it started in the first grade. My uncle owned the big plantation south of town, and he owned several black families. This was in the Depression, right? I spent most of my childhood there because my father was too busy right here in this office and my mother was too busy with her hot-tea-drinkers clubs. All of my playmates were black. I'd been raised by black servants. My best friend was Willie Ray Wilbanks. No kidding. My great-grandfather purchased his great-grandfather. And when the slaves were freed, most of them just kept the family name. What were they supposed to do? That's why you've got so many black Wilbankses around here. We owned all the slaves in Ford County, and most of them became Wilbankses.'

'You're probably kin to some,' Jake said.

'Given the proclivities of my forefathers, I'm probably kin to all of them.'

The phone rang. They froze and stared at it. Jake sat up and held his breath. Harry Rex picked up the receiver, then hung up. 'Wrong number,' he said.

They studied each other, then smiled.

'Anyway, back to the first grade,' Jake said.

'Okay. When it came time to start school, Willie Ray and the rest of my little buddies got on the bus headed for the black school. I jumped on the bus too, and the driver very carefully took my hand and made me get off. I cried and screamed, and my uncle took me home and told my mother,

725

'Lucien got on the nigger school bus.' She was horrified, and beat my little ass. The old man beat me too, but years later admitted it was funny. So I went to the white school where I was always the little rich kid. Everybody hated the little rich kid, especially in a poor town like Clanton. Not that I was lovable to begin with, but everyone got a kick out of hating me just because we had money. That's why I've never thought much of money. That's where the nonconformity started. In the first grade. I decided not to be like my mother because she frowned all the time and looked down on the world. And my old man was always too busy to enjoy himself. I said piss on it. I'm gonna have some fun.'

Jake stretched and closed his eyes.

'Nervous?' Lucien asked.

'I just want it to be over.'

The phone rang again, and Lucien grabbed it. He listened, then hung up.

'What is it?' Harry Rex demanded.

Jake sat up and glared at Lucien. The moment had arrived.

'Jean Gillespie. The jury is ready.'

'Oh my God,' Jake said as he rubbed his temples.

'Listen to me, Jake,' Lucien lectured. 'Millions of people will see what is about to happen. Keep your cool. Be careful what you say.'

'What about me?' Harry Rex moaned. 'I need to go vomit.'

'That's strange advice coming from you, Lucien,' Jake said as he buttoned Stan's coat.

726

'I've learned a lot. Show your class. If you win, watch what you say to the press. Be sure and thank the jury. If you lose—'

'If you lose,' Harry Rex said, 'run like hell, because those niggers will storm the courthouse.'

'I feel weak,' Jake admitted.

Agee took the platform on the front steps and announced the jury was ready. He asked for quiet, and instantly the mob grew still. They moved toward the front columns. Agee asked them to fall to their knees and pray. They knelt obediently and prayed earnestly. Every man, woman, and child on the front lawn bowed before God and begged him to let their man go.

The soldiers stood bunched together and also prayed for an acquittal.

Ozzie and Moss Junior seated the courtroom and lined deputies and reserves around the walls and down the aisle. Jake entered from the holding room and stared at Carl Lee at the defense table. He glanced at the spectators. Many were praying. Many were biting their fingers. Gwen was wiping tears. Lester looked fearfully at Jake. The children were confused and scared.

Noose assumed the bench and an electrified silence engulfed the courtroom. There was no sound from the outside. Twenty thousand blacks knelt on the ground like Muslims. Perfect stillness inside the courtroom and out.

'I have been advised that the jury has reached a verdict, is that correct, Mr Bailiff? Very well. We will soon seat the jury, but before we do so I have some instructions. I will not tolerate any outbursts or displays of emotion. I will direct the sheriff to remove any person who creates a disturbance. If need be, I will clear the courtroom. Mr Bailiff, will you seat the jury.'

The door opened, and it seemed like an hour before Eula Dell Yates appeared first with tears in her eyes. Jake dropped his head. Carl Lee stared gamely at the portrait of Robert E. Lee above Noose. They awkwardly filled the jury box. They seemed jittery, tense, scared. Most had been crying. Jake felt sick. Barry Acker held a piece of paper that attracted the attention of everyone.

'Ladies and gentlemen, have you reached a verdict?'

'Yes, sir, we have,' answered the foreman in a high-pitched, nervous voice.

'Hand it to the clerk, please.'

Jean Gillespie took it and handed it to His Honor, who studied it forever. 'It is technically in order,' he finally said.

Eula Dell was flooding, and her sniffles were the only sounds in the courtroom. Jo Ann Gates and Bernice Toole padded their eyes with handkerchiefs. The crying could mean only one thing. Jake had vowed to ignore the jury before the verdict was read, but it was impossible. In his first criminal trial, the jurors had smiled as they took their seats. At that moment, Jake had become confident of an acquittal. Seconds later he learned that the smiles were because a criminal was about to be removed from the streets. Since that trial, he had vowed never to look at the jurors. But he always did. It would be nice to see a wink or a thumbs up, but that never happened.

Noose looked at Carl Lee. 'Will the defendant please rise.'

Jake knew there were probably more terrifying requests known to the English tongue, but to a criminal lawyer that request at that particular moment had horrible implications. His client stood awkwardly, pitifully. Jake closed his eyes and held his breath. His hands shook and his stomach ached.

Noose handed the verdict back to Jean Gillespie. 'Please read it, Madam Clerk.'

She unfolded it and faced the defendant. 'As to each count of the indictment, we the jury find the defendant not guilty by reason of insanity.'

Carl Lee turned and bolted for the railing. Tonya and the boys sprang from the front pew and grabbed him. The courtroom exploded in pandemonium. Gwen screamed and burst into tears. She buried her head in Lester's arms. The reverends stood, looked upward, and shouted 'Hallelujah!' and 'Praise Jesus!' and 'Lord! Lord! Lord!'

Noose's admonition meant nothing. He rapped the gavel half-heartedly and said, 'Order, order, order in the courtroom.' He was inaudible in the midst of the roar, and seemed content to allow a little celebration.

Jake was numb, lifeless, paralyzed. His only

movement was a weak smile in the direction of the jury box. His eyes watered and his lip quivered, and he decided not to make a spectacle of himself. He nodded at Jean Gillespie, who was crying, and just sat at the defense table nodding and trying to smile, unable to do anything else. From the corner of his eye he could see Musgrove and Buckley removing files, legal pads, and important-looking papers, and throwing it all into their briefcases. Be gracious, he told himself.

A teenager darted between two deputies, through the door, and ran through the rotunda screaming 'Not guilty! Not guilty!' He ran to a small balcony over the front steps and screamed to the masses below '*Not guilty! Not guilty!*' Bedlam erupted.

'Order, order in the court,' Noose was saying when the delayed reaction from the outside came thundering through the windows.

'Order, order in the courtroom.' He tolerated the excitement for another minute, then asked the sheriff to restore order. Ozzie raised his hands and spoke. The clapping, hugging and praising died quickly. Carl Lee released his children and returned to the defense table. He sat close to his attorney and put his arm around him, grinning and crying at the same time.

Noose smiled at the defendant. 'Mr Hailey, you have been tried by a jury of your peers and found not guilty. I do not recall any expert testimony that you are now dangerous or in need of further psychiatric treatment. You are a free man.'

His Honor looked at the attorneys. 'If there is nothing further, this court will stand adjourned until August 15.'

Carl Lee was smothered by his family and friends. They hugged him, hugged each other, hugged Jake. They wept unashamedly and praised the Lord. They told Jake they loved him.

The reporters pressed against the railing and began firing questions at Jake. He held up his hands, and said he would have no comment. But there would be a full-blown press conference in his office at 2:00 P.M.

Buckley and Musgrove left through a side door. The jurors were locked in the jury room to await the last bus ride to the motel. Barry Acker asked to speak to the sheriff. Ozzie met him in the hallway, listened intently, and promised to escort him home and provide protection around the clock.

The reporters assaulted Carl Lee. 'I just wanna go home,' he said over and over. 'I just wanna go home.'

The celebration kicked into high gear on the front lawn. There was singing, dancing, crying, back-slapping, hugging, thanks-giving, congratulating, outright laughing, cheering, chanting, high fives, low fives, and soul brother shakes. The heavens were praised in one glorious, tumultuous, irreverent jubilee. They packed closer together in front of the courthouse and waited impatiently for their hero to emerge and bask in his much deserved adulation.

Their patience grew thin. After thirty minutes of screaming 'We Want Carl Lee! We Want Carl Lee!' their man appeared at the door. An ear-splitting, earth-shaking roar greeted him. He inched forward through the mass with his lawyer and family, and stopped on the top step under the pillars where the plywood platform held a thousand microphones. The whooping and yelling of twenty thousand voices was deafening. He hugged his lawyer, and they waved to the sea of screaming faces.

The shouting from the army of reporters was completely inaudible. Occasionally, Jake would stop waving and yell something about a press conference in his office at two.

Carl Lee hugged his wife and children, and they waved. The crowd roared its approval. Jake slid away and into the courthouse, where he found Lucien and Harry Rex waiting in a corner, away from the mad rush of spectators. 'Let's get out of here,' Jake yelled. They pushed through the mob, down the hall and out the rear door. Jake spotted a swarm of reporters on the sidewalk outside his office.

'Where are you parked?' he asked Lucien. He pointed to a side street, and they disappeared behind the Coffee Shop.

Sallie fried pork chops and green tomatoes, and served them on the porch. Lucien produced a bottle of expensive champagne, and swore he had saved it just for the occasion. Harry Rex ate with his fingers, gnawing on the bones as if he hadn't seen food in a month. Jake played with his food and worked on the ice-cold champagne. After two glasses, he smiled into the distance. He savored the moment.

'You look silly as hell,' Harry Rex said with a mouthful of pork.

'Shut up, Harry Rex,' Lucien said. 'Let him enjoy his finest hour.'

'He's enjoying it. Look at that smirk.'

'What should I tell the press?' Jake asked.

'Tell them you need some clients,' Harry Rex said.

'Clients will be no problem,' Lucien said. 'They'll line the sidewalks waiting for appointments.'

'Why didn't you talk to the reporters in the courthouse? They had their cameras running and everything. I started to say something for them,' Harry Rex said.

'I'm sure it would've been a gem,' Lucien said.

'I've got them at my fingertips,' Jake said. 'They're not going anywhere. We could sell tickets to the press conference and make a fortune.'

'Can I sit and watch, please, Jake, please,' Harry Rex said.

Chapter 44

They argued over whether they should take the antique Bronco or the nasty little Porsche. Jake said he was not driving. Harry Rex cursed the loudest, and they loaded into the Bronco. Lucien found a spot in the rear seat. Jake rode shotgun and gave instructions. They hit the back streets, and missed most of the traffic from the square. The highway was crowded, and Jake directed his driver through a myriad of gravel roads. They found blacktop, and Harry Rex raced away in the direction of the lake.

'I have one question, Lucien,' Jake said.

'What?'

'And I want a straight answer.'

'What?'

'Did you cut a deal with Sisco?'

'No, my boy, you won it on your own.'

'Do you swear?'

'I swear to God. On a stack of Bibles.'

Jake wanted to believe him, so he dropped it. They rode in silence, in the sweltering heat, and listened as Harry Rex sang along with the stereo. Suddenly, Jake pointed and yelled. Harry Rex slammed on the brakes, made a wild left turn, and sped down another gravel road.

'Where are we going?' Lucien demanded.

'Just hang on,' Jake said as he looked at a row of houses approaching on the right. He pointed to the second one, and Harry Rex pulled into the driveway and parked under a shade tree. Jake got out, looked around the front yard, and walked onto the porch. He knocked on the screen door.

A man appeared. A stranger. 'Yeah, whatta you want?'

'I'm Jake Brigance, and—'

The door flew open, and the man rushed onto the porch and grabbed Jake's hand. 'Nice to meet you, Jake. I'm Mack Loyd Crowell. I was on the grand jury that almost didn't indict. You done a real good job. I'm proud of you.'

Jake shook his hand and repeated his name. Then he remembered. Mack Loyd Crowell, the man who told Buckley to shut up and sit down in the grand jury. 'Yeah, Mack Loyd, now I remember. Thanks.'

Jake looked awkwardly through the door.

'You lookin' for Wanda?' Crowell asked.

'Well, yes. I was just passing by, and remembered her address from the jury research.'

'You've come to the right place. She lives here, and I do too most of the time. We ain't married or nothing, but we go together. She's layin' down takin' a nap. She's pretty wore out.'

'Don't wake her,' Jake said.

'She told me what happened. She won it for you.'

'How? What happened?'

'She made them all close their eyes and listen to her. She told them to pretend that the little girl had blond hair and blue eyes, that the two rapists were black, that they tied her right foot to a tree and her left foot to a fence post, that they raped her repeatedly and cussed her because she was white. She told them to picture the little girl layin' there beggin' for her daddy while they kicked her in the mouth and knocked out her teeth, broke both jaws, broke her nose. She said to imagine two drunk blacks pouring beer on her and pissing in her face, and laughing like idiots. And then she told them to imagine that the little girl belonged to them – their daughter. She told them to be honest with themselves and to write on a piece of paper whether or not they would kill those black bastards if they got the chance. And they voted, by secret ballot. All twelve said they would do the killing. The foreman counted the votes. Twelve to zero. Wanda said she'd sit in that jury room until Christmas before she'd vote to convict, and if they were honest with themselves, then they ought to feel the same way. Ten of them agreed with her, and one lady held out. They all started cryin' and cussin' her so bad, she finally caved in. It was rough in there, Jake.'

Jake listened to every word without breathing. He heard a noise. Wanda Womack walked to the screen door. She smiled at him and began crying. He stared at her through the screen, but could not talk. He bit his lip and nodded. 'Thanks,' he managed weakly. She wiped her eyes and nodded.

On Craft Road, a hundred cars lined both shoulders east and west of the Hailey driveway. The long front yard was packed with vehicles, children playing, and parents sitting under shade trees and on car hoods. Harry Rex parked in a ditch by the mailbox. A crowd rushed to greet Carl Lee's lawyer. Lester grabbed him and said, 'You done it again, you done it again.'

They shook hands and slapped backs across the yard and up to the porch. Agee hugged him and praised God. Carl Lee left the swing and walked down the steps, followed by his family and admirers. They gathered around Jake as the two great men came face to face. They clutched hands and smiled at each other, both searching for words. They embraced. The crowd clapped and shouted.

'Thank you, Jake,' Carl Lee said softly.

The lawyer and client sat in the swing and answered questions about the trial. Lucien and Harry Rex joined Lester and some of his friends under a shade tree for a little drink. Tonya ran and jumped around the yard with a hundred other kids.

At two-thirty, Jake sat at his desk and talked to Carla. Harry Rex and Lucien drank the last of the margaritas, and quickly got drunk. Jake drank coffee and told his wife he would leave Memphis in three hours and be in North Carolina by ten. Yes, he was fine, he said. Everything was okay, and everything was over. There were dozens of reporters packed into his conference room, so be sure and watch the evening news. He would meet with them briefly, then drive to Memphis. He said he loved her, missed her body, and would be there soon. He hung up.

Tomorrow, he'd call Ellen.

'Why are you leaving today?' Lucien demanded.

'You're stupid, Jake, just stupid. You've got a thousand reporters in the palm of your hand, and you're leaving town. Stupid, just stupid,' Harry Rex shouted.

Jake stood. 'How do I look, fellas?'

'Like a dumbass if you leave town,' Harry Rex said.

'Hang around for a couple of days,' Lucien pleaded. 'This is an opportunity you'll never have again. Please, Jake.'

'Relax, fellas. I'm going to meet with them now, let them take my picture, answer a few of their stupid questions, then I'm leaving town.'

'You're crazy, Jake,' Harry Rex said.

'I agree,' said Lucien.

Jake checked the mirror, adjusted Stan's tie, and smiled at his friends. 'I appreciate you guys. I really do. I got paid nine hundred dollars for this trial, and I plan to share it with y'all.'

They poured the last of the margaritas, gulped it down, and followed Jake Brigance down the stairs to face the reporters.

The Client

John Grisham

A US State Senator is dead, and 11-year-old Mark Sway is the only one who knows where the body is hidden.

The FBI want him to tell them where it is at whatever cost to Mark and his family.

The killer wants him silenced forever.

Reggie Love has been practising law for less than five years. Only she can save Mark from these twin threats. Together they must take on the might of the State and the wiles of a cold-blooded killer.

'Hard to put down'
Daily Telegraph

'Take it from me, this man Grisham spins a damned good yarn and is going to be around for a long, long time'
Time Out

'It's gripping enough to be best read in daylight'
Sunday Express

arrow books

The Partner

John Grisham

They kidnapped him in a small town in Brazil. He had changed his name and his appearance, but they were sure they had their man.

Four years before, he had been called Patrick S. Lanigan. He had died in a car crash in February 1992. His gravestone lay in a cemetery in Biloxi, Mississippi. He had been a partner at an up-and-coming law firm, had a pretty wife, a new daughter, and a bright future. Six weeks after his death, $90 million had disappeared from the law firm. It was then that his partners knew he was still alive.

'All the ingredients of suspense, drama and meticulous attention to detail that have made Grisham's novels bestsellers . . . A terrific read'
Sunday Mirror

'A narrative triumph and a stylish joy, this novel has me gasping for more of the new, satirical Grisham'
Daily Telegraph

'Excellent'
Times

arrow books

ALSO AVAILABLE IN ARROW

The Runaway Jury

John Grisham

In Biloxi, Mississippi, a landmark trial with hundreds of millions of dollars at stake begins routinely, then swerves mysteriously off course. The jury is behaving strangely, and at least one juror is convinced he's being watched. Soon they have to be sequestered. Then a tip from an anonymous young woman suggests she is able to predict the juror's increasingly odd behaviour.

Is the jury somehow being manipulated, or even controlled? And, more importantly, why?

'A marvellous read' *Sunday Telegraph*

'This book is a joy. One of those books you regret having to finish' *Daily Express*

'Grisham creates a terrific level of suspense. I could not put it down' . *Mail on Sunday*

'Riveting . . . Grisham is a superb, instinctive storyteller' *The Times*

arrow books